THE MAKING

of

MARTIN SPARROW

Peter Cochrane is a widely published historian and writer based in Sydney. He is best known for his book *Colonial Ambition: Foundations of Australian Democracy*, which won the inaugural Prime Minister's Prize for Australian History and the *Age* Book of the Year in 2007. His first venture into fiction was the novella *Governor Bligh and the Short Man*. He is a Fellow of the Australian Academy of the Humanities.

Also by Peter Cochrane

Peter Cochrane

The Making

of

Martin Sparrow

VIKING
an imprint of
PENGUIN BOOKS

VIKING

UK | USA | Canada | Ireland | Australia
India | New Zealand | South Africa | China

Penguin Books is part of the Penguin Random House group of companies
whose addresses can be found at global.penguinrandomhouse.com.

Penguin
Random House
Australia

First published by Penguin Random House Australia Pty Ltd, 2018

1 3 5 7 9 10 8 6 4 2

Cover design by Alex Ross © Penguin Random House Australia Pty Ltd
Cover photographs: landscape © Ben Pearse Photography; figure by H. Armstrong Roberts/
ClassicStock/Getty Images; jug by EJ-J/Getty Images; texture by Shutterstock.
Typeset in Adobe Garamond by Midland Typesetters, Australia
Printed and bound in Australia by Griffin Press, an accredited ISO AS/NZS 14001
Environmental Management Systems printer.

 A catalogue record for this
book is available from the
National Library of Australia

ISBN: 978 0 67007 406 8

penguin.com.au

MIX
Paper from
responsible sources
FSC® C009448

Colonies are built on dreams, but some dreams threaten ruin.

DRAMATIS PERSONAE

The Constables
Alister Mackie, Chief Constable
Thaddeus Cuff
Dan Sprodd

The Bottoms & Environs
Martin Sparrow, expiree, farmer
Joe Franks, ex-soldier, farmer
Freddie Giddes, farmer
Harper Sneezby, ex-soldier, distiller
Thyne Kunkle, ex-soldier, farmer
Rupert Chaseling, assigned convict
Agnes Archambault, widow, farmer

The Bawdy House
Betty Pepper, madam
Biddie Happ, strumpet
Thelma Rowntree, strumpet

The Magistrates
Warrington Abbott, Reverend and
    magistrate
Thomas Woody, doctor and magistrate

Jason 'Jug' Woody, the doctor's son

The Corps
Henry Kettle, Captain
Reuben Peskett, Sergeant
Alvin Redenbach, Private

The Gaol
Hat Thistlewaite, gaoler and
    executioner

The Convivial Hive
Sam Rattle, tapster
Fish, drudge
Atilio, cook

Peachey's Tap
Seamus Peachey, tavernkeeper
Winifred Peachey, his wife
Alfie Shivers, assigned convict

The Felons on the Shovel
Mortimer Craggs
Shug McCafferty

The Sealers
Gudgeon Ketilsson
Crispin Parsonage
Nimrod Parsonage
Jonas Wick
Beatrice Faa

The Rovers
Griffin Pinney, game hunter
George Catley, botanist
Guthrie, river skipper, trader
Dudley Boggitt, wagoner

The First People
Old Wolgan
Caleb
Napoleon
Moowut'tin
Nabbinum

Part 1

The Quest for Renewal

Sparrow woke on wet sand somewhere downriver with a terrible stink in his nostrils, the smell of death and decay, rot and ruin all about. At first he did not stir, there in the pre-dawn, pale light to the east beyond the river, the tide on the turn, ebbing now, the flow yet a faint murmur in his ears.

Confusion held him still, as did the formidable lassitude in his bones and the damp cold on his skin. The sound of his breathing confirmed the likelihood that he was alive. He raised his head and looked about, sucked up a wad of gritty phlegm and spat onto the sand. He wondered if perhaps his deliverance was the work of a kindly fate, a chance to make good his miserable existence. Hard to know.

The sand was strewn with muck and wreckage. The hen coop was there, his hens dead, in company with tangles of lumber and thatch, fence posts and scoured saplings, a big, raggedy cut of wagon canvas and a lidless coffin, the muddied panelling infested with yellow mould that glowed bright in the soft dawn light.

He sat up and brushed himself off, noticed a long cut on the inside of his forearm, but it wasn't bad. If it was bad, deep, he might have bled to death while he lay there in the dark, half drowned. But it wasn't and he didn't. That was lucky.

He studied the coffin; reckoned sooner or later he'd have to take a look, in all probability stare rotting death in the face. A crow alighted on the rim, shuffled one way then the other, then hopped in, keen to join its companions. Sparrow saw a flurry of black wings as the disputatious gathering settled to its work.

There was a blood-soaked tear in his britches and a hungry leech on his thigh, like a small, fat velvet purse. He flicked the greedy little sucker onto the ground, took a twig and pierced it, watching his own blood spill out and colour the sand to russet.

In the shallows he scooped up a fragment of the *Sydney Gazette*, but the newspaper dissolved in his fingers as he tried to unfold the sodden sheet.

Sparrow surveyed the farms beyond the river, the flooded fields; wildfowl feeding on the flattened corn, flood-wrack washing seawards on the flow. He dropped to his knees and laved water onto the little puncture wound on his thigh and the cut on his arm. Quite why he did that he did not know for he was otherwise layered in muck all over.

Memories washed about inside his head dispelling some of the confusion – the lightning storm, the torrents of rain, the hen coop caught in the violent flow; wheat stacks coursing the river; the unremitting fury of the waters, crops awash, the bottoms gone; the exodus of reptiles; the dismal cries from distant quarters, the sound of muskets dangerously charged.

He got up and turned about, scanned the lowlands to the west, the mountains far off, full of mystery and foreboding, and full of promise too.

The sound: the ebbing tide, the pecking crows.

Sparrow stepped quietly from the water. Stood. Listened some more. He crossed the sand, took hold of the wagon sheet, heavy with wet, and edged towards the coffin until he could see the beaks spearing into that shrunken face riddled with wounds, a fledgling on the old man's chest, pecking at his coffin suit. He did not hesitate, for their pleasure had filled him with an unfamiliar wrath and rendered him vengeful. He hurled the wagon sheet across the coffin. The captive birds panicked and leapt into the cloth and flapped and squawked and leapt again, like hearts beating in some hideous thing.

Sparrow took hold of a heavy stick and began to beat the cloth with all his might. A wing appeared askew the panelling and he smashed at it and heard the creature scream. And he kept on just so, until the canvas lay sunken in the coffin and the birds were all but still, dead or dying, their frames faintly visible. He leant on the stick, sucking for breath, awaiting further movement in the coffin, watching as blood seeped into the cloth. The birds made a few pitiful sounds, now and then a ripple or a shudder or the flap of a wing.

Sparrow stood over the coffin until the cloth stopped moving. He looked west to the mountains. Tiredness took hold. 'Maybe it's true, maybe I don't got the mettle,' he said.

He crossed the sand, stood over his coop, dropped to his knees. His hens in death, his good, sweet, giving birds, were naught but a lumpy pile of dirty feathers and claws.

He reached into the coop and gently palmed his birds apart, settling his hand upon a muddied wing; recalled the signs: the lightning storm in that inky blackness over the mountains, the discolouration of the flow and the rapid rise of the river.

But the waters had receded, briefly – a most deceptive interval that filled Sparrow with a false notion of security and he had not then seized his opportunity. He had not got in his crop, not one ear of corn; nor had he got his scarce possessions off the floor of his hut, nor moved the coop to higher ground, thus condemning the hens to a most frightful expiration, such an end as filled Sparrow with dread for reasons he did not care to contemplate. For all that, he was truly sorry.

More than once Mortimer Craggs had told him to stop being sorry. 'Sorry for this, sorry for that,' said Mort. 'You got to stop being sorry, Marty, you gotta stop forthwith and seize the dream, for therein lies our path to an unfettered liberty, y'foller me?'

Sparrow did not quite follow, but he'd said yes anyway for he did not want further badgering from Mort, who was a fierce badgerer and a most indiscriminately violent man once roused. Mort might well whack a man; or he might take a filleting knife and slit his nose. You never did know what Mort might do.

Sparrow felt the sun on his back at last. Once more he looked west across the water-logged lowlands to the foothills and thence the mountains. He recalled his last conversation with Mort Craggs, before Mort took off with Shug McCafferty, before they bolted for freedom.

'I just ain't ready to go,' he'd said. He was uncertain as to why Mort had invited him to join the bolt, for they were not friends, just acquaintances, a lethal acquaintance dating back to the years of his youth in the village of Blackley on the river Irk.

'I think you don't got the mettle, Martin,' said Mort, fingering the ridge of proud flesh on his cropped ear.

'I have things to say to Biddie first,' said Sparrow.

'Forget the whore, there's women on the other side, there's a big river, there's a village, women aplenty, copper-coloured beauties, the diligence of their affections something to behold.'

'How do you know that?'

'Can't say, not till you commit to the venture, swear a binding oath.'

'I cannot swear an oath, binding or otherwise, not yet.'

The very idea of copper-coloured women on the other side of the mountains puzzled Sparrow, deeply. He was somewhat lost for a perspective on this startling infomation. 'Like the Otahetians?' he said.

'No, nothin' like them and I can say no more Marty, not another word.'

And that was the last conversation he'd had with Mort Craggs.

———

Sparrow had to wonder if perhaps his yearning for Biddie Happ was a foolish dream. If it was not a foolish dream before the flood it most likely was now. His thirty-acre patch was swamped, his corn crib gone, his corn crop flat in the mud, the wildfowl, the borers and the mould most likely hard at work this very day. His hut might well be gone too, lost to the flood. His hens were dead, he was deep in hock, mostly to Alister Mackie, and would have to beg for seed for another crop and that meant more hock, regardless of the weather to come. In short, it was now most unlikely that Biddie would see any chance of elevating her prospects by joining with him, Martin Sparrow, former felon, time-expired convict, failed farmer on the flood-prone bottoms of the Hawkesbury River. Fool of a man.

He sat on the sand, bowed his head and ran his fingers down his forehead, over the faint indentations that continued onto his eyelids and cheeks, the all but faded scars that folk took to be the remnants of small pox.

He tried to sort his pictorial thoughts. That wasn't easy with Biddie presenting herself in one instant and the copper-coloured beauties in the next. 'I should have gone with Mort,' he said aloud. He thought about the birthmark on Biddie's face, the mark she tried to hide with that lovely sweep of hair, pinned just so. He wondered if copper-coloured women ever got birthmarks. As to that, he just didn't know. The mysteries, numberless.

2

Alister Mackie sipped his *Hai Seng* tea, treading the porch boards by the tavern door, treading to waken his bones as the pale grey light of dawn brought the distant mountains into view and the mass of huddled humanity on the village square came to life, the refugees from the flood stirring from makeshift tents on rickety frames, tattered paniers lumpy with tools and keepsakes, waifs bedded in carts and barrows, piglets trussed and tumbled in the mud, game dogs on tethers and crated fowls crooning their disquiet.

He held the mug in his two hands, sniffed at the steam coming off the brew, searching the scene: the double guard on the stone granary and the commissariat store; soldiers by the barracks door in various measures of infantry undress; washerwomen in and out of the washhouse; the butcher, busy on his scaffold, a hundred pounds of pork on the hook; the little church, the smithy, the stone gaol. The village they called Prominence.

The drudge called Fish joined Mackie on the porch. He wiped his hands on his apron. 'You want I take the mug?' he said.

Mackie handed him the mug.

'They're hammered, like castaways, every last one of them,' said Fish.

'They are, yes.'

'I seen floods, but I never seen a flood like this one.'

'Nor I.'

'Here and there the tops of trees, otherwise an ocean.'

'Yes.'

Mackie stepped off the porch. He weaved his way through the bivouac to the commissariat store on the far side of the square and from there he followed the ridgeline past the granary to the top of the switchback path, where he paused by the doctor's cabin to scrutinise the work of the floodwaters below. The government garden, gone, an acre of greens torn from the slope as if scythed away by some pale rider's mighty blade; the cottages on the terrace, squat and sodden, the weatherboard swollen and warped. Felons in the shallows, gathering up the ruins of the wharf, the guards perched on their haunches.

Mackie joined his constables, Thaddeus Cuff and Dan Sprodd, at the foot of the switchback path and together they stepped from spongy duckboards into the shallows and clambered aboard the government sloop. Packing away the mooring lines, they drifted into the current and settled at their ease. A light westerly, a port tack, the wind and the tide obliging.

Cuff patted the planking beneath the rowlock, looking up into the big gaff rig as the sail took the wind. 'This tub reminds me of Betty Pepper,' he said. 'Deceptive quickness in stout disguise, charms you'd never guess first off.'

He glanced back at the cottages on the terrace and there she was, Bet, watching them go; her porch strewn with soaked possessions, the high-water mark like a dirty wainscot on the cottage wall. The young strumpet Biddie Happ was there too, squaring a muddied rug on a makeshift line. Cuff raised his hat and Bet responded with a curt swish of her hand and took a broom and set to sweeping the mud off her porch. Biddie patted at the swathe of red hair that covered the birthmark on her face.

'They'll miss me,' said Cuff, 'they cannot help themselves.' He grabbed the wicker handles on a gallon glass demijohn, upended it, took a swig, then another, and then he passed the receptacle to Dan Sprodd.

Sprodd took a swig and passed it back to Cuff who took another swig, knowing it would aggravate the chief constable.

'Hardly underway, you set a fine example, Thaddeus,' said Mackie.

'Thank you!' said Cuff.

'You should ration that.' Mackie wagged a finger at him.

'I don't go with the shoulds, the shoulds are a tyranny. I see no joy in rationing bang-head, or anything else for that matter,' said Cuff.

'Americans take their liberties very seriously,' said Sprodd, as if Mackie was sorely in need of the information.

'Indeed, we do!' said Cuff.

'As do I,' said Mackie.

'I'll tell you now, spirits put clout and vigour in a man. You'll get honest toil from a pint of bang-head, miracles of effort from a quart.'

'That or the fatal dysenteries!'

Cuff quite liked the sound of the chief's lowland brogue but it was too early to argue with any persistence. Sleepiness, briefly, had the better of his contrarian temperament. 'Hear that Dan?' he said, 'We are not to be trusted with the drink; *we*, the meritorious constabulary.'

The sloop was midstream, the westerly freshening as they turned onto York Reach, the wind off the port bow, the air thick and damp and pungent with the miasma from the ooze. Wreckage and refuse and ribbons of bark were thick on the flow as they close-hauled in company with slender saplings and tangles of river grass and all manner of dead and rootless shrubbery.

They sailed past patchworks of ruined fields, some abandoned, some warming to reclamation with weary figures labouring in the waste, pyres piled high, flesh and wreckage awaiting the flame; and here the remnants of a cottage – footings, a wall, a mere chimney – and there the lean of great trees bowed by the torrent, their bark and leaves coated in muck, and others upturned, their roots skyward, piles of misshapen desolation.

The sloop coursed around a thickly forested promontory where, at their peak, the floodwaters had hurtled a miscellany of chattels and trappings into the trees, the strangest things now lodged in the canopy – a butter barrel, a window panel, a Dutch clock, a fishnet and shreds of rigging, and a big teakettle cradled in a clutch of driftwood like a nesting heron.

On a small beachhead they saw a gig on its side with a wheel dislodged, the shaft snapped and shreds of harness in the underbrush, the horse gone forever.

'That gig's beggin' for salvage,' said Dan Sprodd. He took off his hat, scratched at his scalp, pulled at wisps of thin grey hair.

'You could set up a regular thieves' market right there,' said Cuff.

Sprodd took on a hurt look. 'No theft in salvage,' he said.

'It's theft if you don't declare it,' said Mackie.

'I would declare it, I'd put a note in the *Gazette*, but I'd want a salvage fee.'

Cuff was contemplating the devastation they'd seen thus far. 'This river's an avenue for a carnival of ghouls.'

'No time for a carnival just now,' said Sprodd.

Cuff worked his earlobe between thumb and forefinger and cast a glance upward as if searching for assistance from the Lord above. It was his view that a prolonged exchange with Dan Sprodd could make a man jump off a cliff. He reckoned it was about eight years since he first met Sprodd. All that time he'd found the man moderately exasperating, Sprodd's top paddock being not much turned and sparsely seeded. He was the only man Cuff had ever known to miss the point every time. But that was not the half of Sprodd. The man hardly said a bad word about anyone, ever. He was unfailingly generous in spirit and deed and steady too, dependably steady. And he could fish like no other man. If Sprodd put in a line, you could wager a good feed was on the way, you could bet your fob watch on that.

'I wouldn't mind that harness neither, that'll scrub up,' he said.

'Well Dan, I'm sure it'll be there when next you happen this way, the traffic being somewhat reticent at the present time, so don't agitate your kidneys.'

Cuff took another mouthful from the demijohn, wiped his chin and licked his fingers and turned his attention to the chief constable. 'I'm happy to put aside the clout, but if anyone needs a shot of vigour it's you. You're so tired you look like a weathered corpse. Look at me, twice your age, a regular imbiber and nothin' but vigour and beauty to show for it.'

'Vigour for talk and rut and not much else,' said Mackie.

He had the palest of pale green eyes, one of which bore a black spot, a flaw upon the iris. Cuff had often wondered about that black spot. It seemed to draw his own eye whenever he was caught in the grip of Mackie's scrutinising gaze.

Once past Cattai Creek they stopped regularly so Mackie might better survey the damage and make his appraisal of the plight of the small farms – the losses of grain on the stem and grain in store, livestock losses, the standing maize that might be salvaged, the surviving wheat seed and other seed, and the acreage committed to planting in April, weather permitting.

Mackie was in no mood for blather but the settlers, some of them at least, were charged with the wild energy of miraculous survival and they were full of blather. They were like pots on the boil, spilling over with talk of the calamity, the strangest of tales – of hours spent clinging to rooftops, of wheat stacks and barley mows carried off, stock and forest creatures helpless on the torrent, pigs and dogs and prodigious quantities of poultry clinging to driftwood, the bottoms gone, swamped, the country transformed, a vast archipelago, naught but a scattering of runty atolls and the air thick and damp and the sky so black and the lightning, *oh the lightning*, the bolts and the javelins and the harpoons of blue fire, darts like serpents' tongues and forks like banshee talons, their work rending the earth with the smell of sulphur and fissured saplings, young and pale and tinged with green, like prawn flesh rotting. Of all this and more they were compelled to speak and the grain assessor was compelled to listen until they settled, and made some bush tea, and set themselves upon logs or refuse of some description and readied to answer his questions as to their losses of wheat, maize and barley, seed in hand and prospects for planting.

The breeze was light. On the fading tide the sloop moved slowly, in company with the flood-wrack on the flow. They tacked again, this time across the oxbow on Sickle Reach, and they came in sight of Martin Sparrow cross-legged on the furthest edge of a small beach on the west bank, his obedient shadow squat upon the sandy slope. They saw him get to his feet and jump about like he was bitten. They saw him wave and shout, lest they sail on by, deaf and blind to his predicament.

Cuff was first to step ashore. 'You're on the wrong side of the river Mr Sparrow,' he said.

'I near got drowned,' said Sparrow, watching Mackie step from the boat.

'But you didn't, and now you're saved,' said Cuff.

Sparrow shuddered. 'I got carried off, me and the hens, and the hens are dead, drowned, that's all I know.'

Cuff studied the coop and then the coffin. 'I trust you didn't wash down in that,' he said.

'That was here when I woke up.'

Mackie went straight to the coffin, followed by Sprodd. He lifted the drape, studied the carnage beneath. 'Is this your work?' he said to Sparrow.

'I had to stop them crows.'

'You get your corn in?'

'No, sir.'

'Your corn is in the mud then?'

'You know that.'

'I do, I saw your patch, the crop flattened, the grain rotting in muck. I saw your neighbours busy at work, but I did not see you.'

'That river was a chute.'

'You had ample warning, ample time to get your crop in.'

'I did yes, I see that now.'

'And why are you not rescuing what corn you can. Why are you thus?'

'I am on the wrong side of the river, I cannot get back.' Sparrow's voice had lifted an octave or two, edging to shrill.

'You might have walked south, got yourself to Monty Bushell's patch.'

'I can hardly lift my legs.'

'When is that not the case, save your regular pilgrimage to Bet Pepper's establishment?'

Sparrow chuckled. 'I don't exactly worship there.'

'I think you do, I think that's half your trouble, duchessed by flounce and rouge,' said Mackie.

Sparrow was flummoxed. Biddie Happ was not one for flounce nor rouge, but that was hardly the point. Here he was, marooned, considerably wasted, a victim of nature's wrath, the devil conducting the elements, and Alister Mackie was warning him off whores. 'You take me across I'll wing my way back I swear. I'll salvage what I can.'

'Do you have any intention of planting wheat for the store, as required by our arrangement?'

'Weather permitting, I'll get a crop in within the month but, um . . . I got no seed.'

'Yet again cap in hand, to me.'

'Yes sir, seed wheat for two acres, one for me, one to cover a parcel o' debt, that's all I need . . . and maize enough to see me through to the harvest, just for bread. Only bread.'

Mackie crossed the sand and stepped up the bank, the better to survey the lowlands and the mountains beyond. Herons scuttled off and wildfowl burst into the air, the downdraught stirring the surface on freshly formed ponds, a silvery light on the ripples. He turned to Sparrow. 'Have you seen your friend the bolter, Mort Craggs?'

Sparrow was shocked to think Mackie might consider him in any way a party to Mort's escape.

'I have not seen him and he is not my friend,' said Sparrow.

'And you know nothing of the plot?' said Mackie.

'No,' he said, intent upon a still tongue.

Cuff patted Sparrow on the shoulder. 'Let's just get him across, Alister, and he can hurry on home.'

'I'll salvage what I can, I promise.'

'There!' said Cuff.

'You see me when we get back,' said Mackie.

'I will, yes, thank you sir.'

They made ready to depart but Sparrow detained them. He retrieved a hen from the coop, the hen he called Geraldine, his favourite. He cradled the bird in his arms. 'I want to bury them,' he said.

Mackie turned away. Cuff made every effort not to laugh and he succeeded in this endeavour for he was no mocker, not of lesser mortals, the likes of Sparrow. He got the sand shovel from the sloop and handed it to Sparrow and Sparrow looked about, unsure what to do with Geraldine.

'Give me the bird,' said Cuff, and he gathered Geraldine from the crook of Sparrow's arm and Sparrow went up the bank and set to digging a little grave. Sprodd brought the other hens and dropped them close by.

'They never failed me,' said Sparrow. He was on his knees, digging.

Cuff thought the former felon a most pathetic sight. He went down on his haunches so he could talk to Sparrow quietly, eye to eye. 'A wise man does not burn his bridges till he knows he can part the waters,' he said.

'What?'

'Martin, Mr Mackie is a hard man, but he's a friend to any man sober who would persevere. You must *endeavour to persevere,* y'understand?'

'Yes.'

'Make a show, Marty, look to your grain, that's all he wants, grain's all that matters in this little world of ours. Grain is money, it's credit at the store, grain is your ticket to a little comfort in this world, to your . . . *renewal.*'

Sparrow knew Cuff was right. Grain, wheat, that was money – tradeable at the commissariat store for foodstuffs, hardware, timber, clothing, candied ginger, whatever came off the transports in the way of government provisions.

Cuff spoke softly into Sparrow's ear. 'You meet your obligations Marty or he'll foreclose on you. Believe me, Alister will have your patch.'

'I know,' said Sparrow. He patted down the dirt with the head of the shovel.

Mackie had lost all patience. 'Enough, time to go, now!'

'Why?' said Cuff.

'You kill time you injure eternity, that's why.'

'You could learn something from eternity, Alister. It's just *there*, unhurried, an example to us all.'

'It's notice to get moving is what it is.'

'If it weren't forever it wouldn't trouble me at all,' said Sprodd.

They loaded into the sloop and crossed the broad turn in the river, running with the wind, the westerly full in the sail.

Sparrow stepped into the shallows. He thanked them and hurried off, south, wondering how he might ford the bloated fresh water creeks and his own creek, the Cattai, and how he might begin to reclaim his patch. How he might set about his *renewal.* The very thought put lead in his legs.

3

The boatmen took to the deep once again, the tide briefly in abeyance, the westerly obliging for the run to the Branch, raptors wheeling in the sky, the river yet a carpet of driftwood and leaves.

Mackie was not inclined to stop at the game hunter's camp at Pig Creek for there was no life there, just a dead ox and otherwise nothing, no sign of Griffin Pinney's hut, nor his old tent, nothing to suggest a campsite until Sprodd said 'Oh Lord' and pointed to the limp, blue, lacerated body of a woman wedged in the fork of an old grey gum, the rooting half out of the ground.

They beached the boat near the Pig Creek outflow.

The tree was bent so low they could almost reach up and touch her.

They stood there, trying to make sense of the fatal predicament above them.

'Poor soul,' said Cuff. He looked away, studied the scene upriver.

'That's Griffin Pinney's concubine up there,' said Sprodd.

'I know who she is and it's a damn shame.' Her face was mostly obscured by her long hair, but they all knew it was Thelma Rowntree, formerly one of Betty Pepper's girls. 'She was better off servicin' the corps than take up with Griffin Pinney, I know that much,' said Cuff.

'Where's he got to?' said Sprodd.

'Who the hell would know, that villain.'

'He might be drowned dead too.'

'You don't need to say dead when you say drowned, Dan, drowned means dead.'

'I know that,' said Sprodd.

Cuff was pondering this most unlikely coupling, the fearsome game hunter and the nice-looking strumpet. 'Pinney's a wily customer,' he said. 'Filled her head with that nonsense about the far side of the wilderness, place of milk and honey.'

'You don't know it's nonsense.'

'You been there?'

'No, but you ain't neither.'

'Dan, there's nowhere like that. Look at the Frogs, *liberty liberty liberty*, and what have they got?'

'Napoleon Bonaparte?'

'The scourge of the *con-ti-nent*, I rest my case.'

'But this ain't France.' Sprodd looked about, certain he was right.

'No, it ain't France. It's the river where we got nature bless'd and fecund, dirt so rich you can sing up a crop with a song if you want to . . . I call that Arcadia.'

'What's Arcadia?'

Mackie stepped away, unbuttoned, took a piss on the sand. He stared into the timber further up the creek, listening to the chatter as Cuff talked on.

'Dan, that nonsense about a settlement on the other side of the mountains, that comes out of Peachey's Tap. Feckless felons and Irishmen pickled in bang-head. Seamus Peachey and friends don't know paradise when they're livin' in it.'

'Where'd they get the idea then?'

'Some mischievous Frenchman I'd reckon. You put a Frenchy in with Irish you get a compound of wild dreams and silliness with a strong tendency to bloody outcomes.'

'But Peachey's from Birmingham.'

'He's half full of Irish blood and he's Irish in his head. He is not a trustworthy entity, that is my point.'

Sprodd was in agreement with Cuff as regards Peachey's blood, but he could not dismiss the idea that white men might be living a life entirely free of bondage on the far side of the mountains. 'I heard there's a village on the other side, and a big river.'

'We ought get poor Thelma out of that tree,' said Cuff.

They took her down and laid her on the sand and drew back the mouse-coloured hair from her face. Mercifully, her eyes were closed, but they were closed so tight her entire face was contorted, once bonny, now wrinkled up like old rind. They all agreed no one could have foretold the full extent of the rise in the river. 'The foreseeable, that's what never happens,' said Cuff.

Mackie came and stood over the woman. 'A busy quim no more,' he said, without sadness or pity.

Cuff followed Mackie in some things, notably the enforcement of select law and a seasoned distrust of the military, but on the subject of women he was set at sharp variance. He looked at Thelma, bruised and cut, spotted with silt and sediment and smeared in grey muck; looked upon her once lovely face, where hard living had carved grooves way too soon. He knew Mackie to be a man who stood off from women, as if they were diseased or foul-breathed or some lesser species from the animal world, or perhaps merely a peril to the vigour of his enterprise. 'Only the wretched have no compassion,' he said.

Mackie stared. 'I state a fact.'

'Fact or no fact, now is not the time to sit in judgement.'

'She had airs, told me she was a hostess,' said Sprodd.

'That ain't a crime, we all got airs. The crime is to pretend we don't.'

'You been with her?'

'Ev'body's been with her, except a certain chief constable I happen to know.' Cuff wanted Mackie to hear that. He looked at the poor young woman's fingers, the knuckles chafed and torn. Now, it seemed, his time with Thelma was time well spent. They had always been happy in the course of their leisurely communion. Thelma said she liked to be with him, said she felt safe with him, said she liked to hear him talk, said most of the traffic was not interested in talk. That was no surprise to Cuff for he knew he was a good talker. He also knew most of the traffic was the soldiers and most of the soldiers were poor talkers. The memory of Thelma made Cuff a little bit angry, made him want to chastise Mackie before the present company. 'Alister, if you got no charity in your heart, you got nothin'.'

But Mackie was not about to be admonished. 'We may all lift ourselves up and others with us, but charity is for the deserving.'

Cuff threw his hands in the air. 'I rest my case.'

4

It was late in the afternoon when Sparrow got home, wet and tired. His corn crop lay flattened in the mud, the wildfowl feeding at their leisure. His hut was ripe with the smell of rot and mould and the dirt floor turned to mush when he walked upon it. Some of the roof shingles were gone too, the dismal interior patterned in square-cut shafts of blue-grey light.

He went outside and slumped onto a stump stool on his porch. Where to begin? The question overwhelmed him. He studied the cut on his forearm, felt himself sinking into a slough of despond. He could hear the wildfowl at work, that soft cooing sound they make when they're happy. He wished he had a pistol to blast them with a fan of slugs and make of them a stew. What with the crows in the coffin, and his hens, now buried, he concluded he was having an unusually bird-filled day.

His thoughts turned to Biddie Happ. Biddie never failed to excite the most tender and amorous sensations in his breast, and the most vigorous throbbing in his pizzle. All he wanted was a word, a sign, any sign she favoured him, that would be enough – a mere scrap of hope – enough to fortify his agricultural resolve and spark him into the work of restoration, an almighty fit of renewal. But until that time, until she gave him a sign, he could hardly lift a finger such was his sorrow. He therefore resolved that the best way to get started on his patch was to go see Biddie and hope for a pleasant interlude.

His little plan filled him with cheer but then he began to worry again. He worried his clothes were rags and he stank of sweat and grime. He worried he was ugly, pock-faced and poor. He worried an interlude with Biddie would come to nothing. He reckoned it was most unlikely Biddie would give him a sign such as he required to restore his sense of purpose in the world, for she would surely know he was no improver. She would know he was deep in hock and his patch was ruined. In all likelihood, she would not be gulled by his talk of renewal.

It occurred to Sparrow that he should have bolted with Mort Craggs when he had the chance. Mort most certainly had the mettle and they were at least acquaintances, back in Blackley, on the river Irk.

Sparrow came from a long line of eel catchers who had caught fat eels on the Irk as far back as the fourteenth century, perhaps even earlier than that, for eeling and the name Sparrow were mentioned together in the Domesday Book, apparently. That being his heritage, it followed that at the tender age of eight, nimble fingered, Sparrow was weaving or repairing the wicker traps his father set daily on the river, and by the time he was ten he was selling live eels from a bucket.

Carting a turbulent knot of live eels in a bucket of river water was arduous work for a skinny boy, skinny as a wading bird, so Sparrow quickly fell into the habit of calling first at a tavern called The Dirty Sack, where a notorious woman called Misty Knapp would usually take half the catch, thus half the weight, thus easing Sparrow's burden and, also, on one occasion, providing Sparrow with an entertainment that awakened him, like a fire in his blood, to the charms of the female form. Misty would happily dance naked for small sums of money and for the general enhancement of the Sack and its proprietor, Mortimer Craggs.

It happened that Mort and Misty were engaged in a secondary trade, namely the fleecing of heavily sedated wayfarers of small coin and select adornments such as rings and pendants, the latter conveyed to an infamous receiving house on the outskirts of Manchester by means of a most clever concealment – the oily mud and murk at the bottom of a bucket of eels.

At the trial, 24th of July 1795, Mort was named as the instigator and architect of the scheme and he was sentenced to fourteen years hard labour in New South Wales, and Sparrow, whose face, mysteriously, was covered in scabs, was charged with receiving and disposing of the stolen goods, some in excess of five shillings in value. The magistrate noted the wily means by which Sparrow had shifted the loot. He seemed to be in no mood to cast the eye of pity upon the boy. However, the jurors took note of Sparrow's youth, his scab-faced condition and his juvenile infatuation with the charms of Misty Knapp. They recommended a degree of clemency and he was sentenced to seven years servitude, also in New South Wales.

Misty's fate was different. She was branded 'a loose woman who stole from intoxicated pick-ups', but she insisted she had received only presents, 'coin and things to let them lie with me.' She confessed her motives were both 'voluptuous and mercenary' and some of her behaviour – a reference to the dancing – lewd and immoral. But she insisted she was not a thief. She said she had never stolen a thing, 'not a penny, not a trinket, not the merest gewgaw' from the trade at The Dirty Sack, and before the court she implored the Almighty to strike her down if she was lying.

The Almighty duly complied and she dropped dead in the dock and promptly loosed her bowels and there they found an earring, a glint of gold in a loose stool, and all present could but wonder at the wondrous ways of the Lord.

5

Cuff and Sprodd carried Thelma to a wooded slope at the rear of the game hunter's campsite at Pig Creek and Sprodd began work on a grave with the sand shovel from the sloop.

'She was way better than the company that ruined her, I'll say that much,' said Cuff.

'I thought she and Biddie made quite a nice pair,' said Sprodd, pausing for rest.

'Keep goin' Dan, dig it deep.'

The westerly off the swampy ground reeked of putrilage, and something else. Mackie was sniffing at the breeze. 'That's mash, thick as tar,' he said.

'Harp Sneezby, has to be,' said Sprodd.

'Brewing his gut rot.'

'Sad to say I know what's next,' said Cuff. Next they would be stalking westward, intent upon finding an illicit distilling enterprise somewhere on the higher reaches of Pig Creek.

'Leave ol' Harp to his devices I say,' said Sprodd. 'If the fiery poison don't get him the savages will.'

Cuff was pleased to find Dan was, in this regard, his ally. 'It's no crime for a man to make the best hand of his industry, Alister. There's no good sense in sniffin' out mash.'

Sprodd was breathing in deep, his twig-thin lips pressed together. 'That is sour enough to make a pig squeel.'

'I seen a pig suppin' on mash once,' said Cuff.

'What happened?'

'Drank his fill, blew up. Guts came out his arse.'

Cuff had seen the pig undone by its gluttony on a small farm outside Boston, the town where he had come of age. His daddy was, in Cuff's living memory, first a gunsmith, then a farmer, then for a while a deputy-commissary in the Virginia Regiment until it was disbanded in the early eighties and he took his family to Boston. For about nine years he ran a lively tavern, in which time Thaddeus became his indispensable assistant, managing the boisterous trade while protecting the virtue of his much younger half-sisters. He was wont to say it was that solemn duty which rendered him most tender in his disposition to all young women.

Cuff peered into the grave. 'Best finish this,' he said to Sprodd, 'while the chief constable and his famous assistant, eminent among detectors, regulators, man-hunters and so on, venture into the woods in pursuit of a dangerous felon, in his prime at a hundred and four years of age, currently engaged in the devilish business of wasting not to want not . . . to say nothing of saving himself from the commercial snares of the military and their wily agents.'

'The ill use of grain is a transgression that cannot be tolerated in the present scarcity. I quote from the government order,' said Mackie.

'You agree with every government order, that's what butters your bread,' said Cuff.

'I butter my own bread.'

'I'll quote you what I know. I know that a bush distillery is the most reward for the least work round here. What's more, you hire labour without grog, like as not they'll pin you to the wall, the felons the same. It's more than consolation, way more. It's currency in these parts.'

'No grog no work, that *is* the chorus,' said Sprodd.

'It's more'n the chorus, it's the entire refrain.'

'Enough,' said Mackie. He took up Cuff's musket and handed it to him. He looked at the sun and then at the ground where the small gathering hardly threw a shadow.

'I'll finish this,' said Sprodd. He was happy not to be stalking a distiller in the fastness.

Cuff thought of one more argument: 'Alister, if we go up this creek, how you plan to tally the losses further downriver?'

'What's left downriver is hardly worth the bother.'

Cuff knew that the chief constable was mostly right. The country downriver, beyond the Branch, became more steep and rugged with every nautical mile and the only place to farm was on the low-lying floor of the tributary valleys or the slim levees on the fringes, hemmed in by the sandstone scarps. The men who farmed these patches were those who would risk the deluge and the savages to have their solitude. They were few and far between.

'There's Joe at the Branch, Joe Franks,' said Sprodd.

'That's right,' said Cuff, 'he'll have something for the tally.'

'We'll get to Joe's,' said Mackie.

'Not today we won't,' said Cuff.

Sprodd finished the dig and they planted the poor girl and took turns, all but Mackie, to shovel back the dirt. Cuff found some wretched flannel flowers covered in grit and picked them for a posy. He took off his hat. They stood about, awkward.

'Someone ought say somethin',' said Sprodd, so Cuff did.

'She was a good girl, way better'n the trade that ill-used her, and I'll not hear otherwise. Some will frown but I say she helped keep the peace as much as any damn constable, and that with some generosity, more'n most of us deserved. She died a terrible death, abandoned. We pray God she might find better company, and peace, in the ever after. Dust to dust and . . . so on.'

Sprodd was pleased. 'I agree with all o' that,' he said.

They set a fire, ate some corn biscuits and made some tea in the quart pot. They wrapped their hot tin mugs in their sweat rags and blew off the steam and sipped at the tea as it cooled, hardly a word.

Mackie watched the incoming tide, the force of it swelling the river. He felt obliged, duty bound, to survey the devastation downstream and reckon the losses at least as far as the Branch. He thought Joe Franks the only decent man on the lower reaches. He was determined to both ruin this distillery and to check on Joe. 'Take the sloop to Joe's,' he told Sprodd. 'You can go on the ebb and we'll meet you there.'

Cuff was annoyed. 'See Dan, we're like witch-finders, wherever we go we root out evil, even in the damn wilderness where it don't matter a hoot.'

The stubble on Sprodd's face was snow white and he was weathered and deep wrinkled and more weary than usual from the day's exertions. He was not entirely happy with the arrangement but an afternoon's repose was far preferable to trekking west in pursuit of a bush distillery. In his pouch he had twenty feet of horsehair line, some brand-new fish hooks, some pepper for seasoning and some *Hai Seng* tea. 'Them perch just beggin',' he said.

'We ought camp here with Dan, go at first light,' said Cuff.

Mackie appeared most displeased by the suggestion but he, too, was tired and hungry, and he pictured the perch, sizzling in the pan. For once he did not press his case. 'Alright,' he said, much to Cuff's surprise.

They pulled the sloop out of the shallows and made camp near the root ball of the old grey gum, well clear of the stinking ox and well clear of Thelma's grave.

6

In addition to being ruined, materially speaking, and most melancholy about his prospects in all regards, Sparrow suffered from jaundice, or so he was advised by Dr Thomas Woody, who was the resident magistrate and apothecary to the farmers on the river in general and the village of Prominence in particular. Sparrow took this diagnosis to be true, for almost everyone commented at one time or another on the yellowy hue of his skin, and the terrible pains he sometimes suffered were entirely consistent with the malady described by the doctor.

It was therefore no surprise to Sparrow when he was laid low on his damp bed with stabbing pains in his abdomen. He lay there in great discomfort for quite a while, a shaft of blue-grey light upon his writhing frame, the smell of rot and sodden earth in his nostrils.

When the pain finally settled it was dark and he was alone, as ever, with thoughts of Biddie on his mind. Sparrow did not rise. He took the opportunity to think. Perhaps best, he thought, not to hurry to Bet Pepper's establishment, for the cottages on the terrace row below the village would surely have been swamped in the deluge and, like the ruin on the bottoms, there would be a great deal of cleaning up to do. It was near to a certainty that Bet Pepper would conscript him into the clean-up and he was not about to be trapped in that way, for once trapped by Bet Pepper there would be no escape from a multitude of chores and he had more than enough cleaning up to do on his own patch. Better to wait a while, a timely pause, and go see Biddie when the bawdy house was once again fit for purpose.

Sparrow felt a great sense of relief at having thought that through so shrewdly. He tried to get up but he was too tired, so he just lay there, staring at the hole in the roof, that tiny patch of dark sky.

He did not relish the thought of having to go cap in hand to Mackie for seed and stores, nor did he welcome the coming dawn, when he would have to begin his own clean-up, rescue what was left of the corn, search for the ruins of the corn crib and set about bracing his hut and mending his roof and a hundred other chores about the place.

He wished Mort Craggs had told him more about the hideaway on the other side of the mountains. Sparrow had pressed for more information but Mort would not talk further on the subject of the big river, the village or the copper-coloured women on the other side. Instead he chose to talk about the fear and trepidation that possessed the colonial authorities, civil and military, as the word spread among the felons and the expirees.

'Try to follow me here Martin,' he said. 'Our masters tell us there is naught but wretchedness and destruction awaiting those who abscond under the persuasion of a sanctuary on the other side of the mountain fastness. They insist upon the impossibility of a crossing, and the fantastical absurdity of a village over there, but let me tell you, this vested counsel has no foundation in practical knowledge or truth.

'They know nothing of the wilderness, nor of what lies beyond. Their deceit is wickedly calculating and self-interested. They would have us succumb to their mischievous geography, their cruel and cramped little world, as if we was surrounded by a wall of iron bars all the way to the sky. They say we are like children, our minds fevered and our dreams preposterous. They would have us exiled on this alien shore, hemmed in by stone, our most reasoned imaginings pruned back to a stump and our vision framed narrow such that we might plod along like a blinkered carthorse.' Mort paused. Took breath. 'But we will not be blinkered nor deceived, will we Marty?'

'No.'

'You mean yes, as in yes we will not be deceived?'

'Yes.'

'We know they are nothing without our labour, yes?'

'Yes.'

'We know our boldness renders them sleepless of a night, mad with the fear, fear of *themselves* exiled without the means to survive, which is to say without us . . . yes?'

'Yes!'

'Thus their most urgent necessity is to disabuse us of all common sense and reason, to quash our well-founded speculations, to squish all hope knowing that hope is a rudder to all humanity. They tell us we're a colony marooned, marooned they say, on a mere thumbnail on the coast, backs to the ocean and otherwise confined by impassable mountains and all manner of terrors therein and nothing beyond but more of the same.'

'*The big lie!*' said Sparrow, the truth of it like a thunderbolt.

'The big lie indeed! And they would have us surrender to it. They would put the frighteners in us; they would liquesce our bowels with talk of bloodsucking leeches and paralysing ticks, snakes and spiders, savages and cannibals . . . dragons and hydras; they would spin their tale of misery and despair for all who would venture forth; spin it like a web to catch us poor flies and stick us to their purpose; their purpose, Marty, *not ours*. Our purpose is otherwise, liberty, y'foller me?'

'I ain't no fly.'

'Good. So you make up your mind swiftish, or we might just be gone, me and Shug.

'Shug?'

'They're killin' me, I cannot do another winter on that shovel, nor Shug neither.'

Next thing Sparrow heard Mort had disappeared, and Shug with him, and he worried he might have ruined any chance he ever had of escaping the drudgery of his patch, of shedding the shackles of hock to Mackie and easing the pain of his longing for Biddie. Perhaps he didn't have the mettle after all. He wished he had not succumbed to the frighteners. He wished his bowels would not liquesce as they did, sometimes. He wished he'd seized upon hope and bolted with Mort and Shug, for hope is a rudder to all humanity, in that regard Mort was entirely right. He wondered if the copper-coloured women on the other side were like the Otahetians who, like Misty, would dance naked for a song and who, like Misty, were seasoned in the art of love, *the diligence of their affections something to behold.* There was hardly a day he didn't think of Misty, dancing, and thoughts of Misty dancing led on to thoughts of Biddie Happ and when that happened all firm inclination to bolt with Mort Craggs tended to, well, to liquesce.

7

In the morning Sprodd clambered into the sloop and they pushed him into the deep and the ebb tide sucked him away, tacking into a gusty breeze, bound for Joe Frank's patch on the Branch.

Mackie and Cuff followed the creek west, the ground flat and swampy for about half a mile. Higher up the creek fed rills that flowed like ribbing, through the woods, onto mild slopes where wheat or corn would surely sprout in abundance given half a chance. Some of these patches had been worked for a time and then abandoned for fear of the savages. Only the most resolute had persisted, a dogged few, but the horrible enormities of the previous year took a toll and they were all gone, all but Harper Sneezby, who some said was daft as a brush.

At Harp's patch a black corpse hung from a sturdy bough, gutted, the cavity stuffed with grass, the skin on the man crusted and cracked from the punishment of the sun. River rats and crows had all but taken the face away and the feet had been ravaged by sundry wild things.

They searched Harp's hut. The hut was a mess – an ancient straw mattress and a pelt quilt in the dirt; a wick soaked in bacon fat in a quart-tin lid; a small axe and some nails, fishing stuff, a jackknife, an old musket, a clay jug on its side with a handle missing; a tin cup and a spoon and an old chest with the hinges broken.

The coals in the fire were faintly warm. 'He comes and goes,' said Cuff.

Mackie surveyed the flats from the doorway. 'He works this patch to ruin.'

'Poor husbandry ain't a crime.'

'That's a crime,' said Mackie, pointing at the corpse.

'That's a warning,' said Cuff.

He retrieved his musket and they set off, following the scent of the corn mash upstream, flanked by sheer stone and saplings hung with the silvery webs of orb spiders, pea flowers and yam daisies blooming in patchworks of sunlight and shade.

'I can smell it now, like hogwash, sour as the devil's piss,' said Cuff.

'Hmmm.'

'He's small fry Alister . . . why *do* we bother?'

'These brews pickle your brain.'

'Mostly they take you to paradise, least for the afternoon.'

'My charge is to keep settlers off the government account, off the store.'

'Grog's the most tradable thing there is other'n wheat. It's illicit grog keeps them off the damn government.'

Cuff knew he was right. About half the colony was dependent on the government for food and sundry necessities – the military and their families, the felons, the civil establishment and their dependants, the clergy, the orphans and so on. The rest farmed, mostly, and the farmers were dependent on the government store, better known as the commissariat, to take their surplus grain, poultry and pork. They got credit at the store, to barter for whatever was in stock, but others turned their surplus grain to bang-head, for bang-head was a ready currency – labour took payment in bang-head and farmers like Harp happily drank it themselves.

'We cannot have grain going for grog whilst indigence abounds,' said Mackie.

Cuff pointed upstream. 'This damn still most likely paid for the reaping, and you want to shut him down. The grog won't put him on the store, *you will*.'

'It is not one clandestine still, it is dozens and more. They divert grain from the store, boost the price of bread; these stills take bread from the very mouths of the poor who sink to potato loaf or crowdie or hasty pudding or otherwise eat dirt.'

'Alright alright,' said Cuff.

They sat quietly for a time. Mackie looked square into Cuff's countenance, nodding, as if he'd just confirmed what he already knew: 'Seems we're at not so much a rupture as an impasse,' he said softly.

Cuff, as ever, was not inclined to leave off. 'You don't ever doubt these stupid laws, the sad mis'able people we hunt down?'

'I don't.'

'*Yes you do*, save ambition prevails over doubt, that's what happens. This old man, why not just warn him off?'

'I don't give cherries to pigs nor instruction to fools.'

'You're meeting your quota, that's all you're doin'. You feather your nest like everybody else.'

'No one sets me a quota.'

'You sets you a quota and you reap the rewards, being high in His Excellency's favour.'

There was good reason for that favour, and Cuff knew it. As a mere boy, seventeen, Mackie had been convicted for theft of cloth at Jedburgh Sessions and transported to the other side of the world. He was sent to the government farm at Toongabbie and there, amidst a great shortage of honesty, reliability and numeracy, he was put in charge of the men's provisions. He kept a meticulous accounts book, rid the stores of peculation and pilfering and further distinguished himself as scribe to the illiterate. He was appointed to the constabulary a year later.

His Kirk education was deemed a great asset and figured in further promotion. He was ordered to make a survey of the grain harvest around Parramatta and, when he was pardoned in 1798, he moved to the Hawkesbury River settlement, taking with him the duty of grain assessor for the district, along with a government grant of 100 acres. He was then promoted to chief constable and distinguished himself in that post, ably assisted by his two constables. But Cuff and Sprodd were not driven, as Mackie was driven, by fierce ambition. They were not really driven by ambition at all, a distinction that made for lively if sometimes fractious conversation.

Cuff was inclined to press Mackie a little further on the subject of his elevated standing. 'You are the only expiree with a lease in the government precinct, you have a licence to sell spirits in that precinct, you have the lease on the toll bridge on South Creek, you have the store contract for salt and otherwise your damn acreage is government grant.'

'And upon that acreage I grow my own wheat.'

'You never go near that acreage, Heydon does it all.'

'*He's my overseer!*'

'I rest my case. The absentee landlord,' said Cuff.

'I sense the futility of this conversation,' said Mackie.

Cuff sensed that too, though he found it difficult to see why futility should get in the way of a good argument. But this time around he'd had enough. 'I'll just step away, break wind, don't say I got no manners.'

They pressed on.

The breeze was up and they could now smell the mash, full strength. 'Whoever's makin' that batch ain't afraid of old Wolgan,' said Cuff.

'I'm afraid of him,' said Mackie.

'Branch Jack is dead.'

'You kill the son, best kill the father too.'

'Not for want of trying.'

The wheat had come ripe two seasons back, summer 1805, the harvest about to begin, when Branch Jack and his mob took to raiding farms up and down sixty miles of river flats. They raided farmhouses for food and clothes and weapons; others they burnt down with seeming indifference as to contents. They speared men and women and left them to die. Some they brained with clubs, others they mutilated with small axes. They stole pigs and maimed oxen and showered grain boats with stones and spears hurled from cliff tops north of the Branch. They made sport of sheep and goats, setting their otherwise useless dogs on them, and chased down shepherds. They moved on wheat fields with firebrands and burnt out crops and later they came for the ripe corn and carried off the loot in sugar bags and flour sacks. Hardly any farm escaped pillage, violence or some form of menace.

'They brought ruin on themselves,' said Mackie.

'Retribution, swift and pitiless!' said Cuff as if reading a proclamation.

'There was pity.'

'I never seen any.'

'They got the concession, from the Branch to the sea.'

'No one I know, north of the Branch, is going to share that river with the savages,' said Cuff.

'I hope you're wrong.'

'It's the most futile concession I ever heard, the governor's a sentimental old fool.'

'We're back to futility.'

'Yes. Let's go.'

They walked on, into a light headwind, the breeze pungent with the scent of damp bark and leaf rot underfoot, now and then a whiff of the mash washing into their nostrils. Mackie pressed hard on his chest and took a deep breath. The effort made him convulse and he brought up phlegm and spat into his hand, studied the viscous gob, flicked it away and wiped his palm on his trousers.

'You alright?' said Cuff.

Mackie nodded and they moved on.

8

Next day Sparrow was slow to rise. He dithered a while, then got himself up and pulled on his boots and walked his patch, dragging his feet from the sucking mud, his footprints puddling in his wake. He squatted in the corn field and peeled back mud-ridden husks and saw the mould and the borers at work and otherwise the damage done by the ruinous foraging of the wildfowl. He sat on a tree stump and took note of the stumps all about, like bulbous sores on the skin of the land.

Hunger moved him. He rescued a few cobs and went back to his hut and ate them raw. He sat himself on a stump stool, chewing on the corn and staring at the patterns in the quarter grain on the rear wall, the light from the doorway playing upon the ripples and burls, the colour and the movement quite pretty.

Sometime about midafternoon he found his corn crib in the bulrushes on Cattai Creek, not far from the confluence with the river. The crib was a ruin of frame timbers and planking with hardly a shingle to be seen. He was contemplating the wreckage when he heard the voice of the Woody boy, the doctor's son, the one they called Jug. 'Hello, Mr Sparrow,' he called, and looking up Sparrow saw the boy give a wave, a mooring line in one hand, his little boat on the end of the line.

Sparrow waved back. He watched the boy secure the line and he wondered if the boy might help him rescue the crib, what was left of it. He was in two minds, for he did not really want to talk to anyone and if young Jug was to help him he would surely have to offer him something, a cup of tea, a modicum of hospitality. That meant talk.

The boy was eager to help. He hurried along the edge of the creek, the sticky ground unable to slow him.

Together, they pulled bits of frame and planking and some of the footings from the bulrushes and carried them in relay to the back of Sparrow's hut and stacked them loosely. When they'd finished Sparrow said, 'You want some tea?' He was studying the boy. Reckoned him fifteen or sixteen; tall, big ears, a mess of yellow hair like winnowed straw.

'No thank you, I better get home. Me and my brother, we gotta fix the roof on the hen-house, it's half gone,' he said, looking at the sky.

'You get flooded?'

'We got soaked but the run-off's good, further up,' said Jug, pointing up the Cattai.

'Take some corn, may as well.'

The boy surveyed the sorry corn field. He did not want to be impolite. 'Papa says good neighbours never take pay.'

'It's not pay, it's just . . .'

'No thank you.' The boy was about to leave but he hesitated. 'I would like to catch some eels, I believe you know how to weave the traps.'

'I don't catch eels, I don't much like them.'

'Oh I'll catch them. I just need help with the traps.'

Sparrow reckoned he was in something of a trap himself, for the boy had been helpful, never was anything but helpful. 'Alright. Sometime soon but not today. Today I'm a bit . . . flat.'

'Tomorrow?'

The boy was not about to relent.

'You help me tomorrow, help me to clean up and I'll teach you.'

'I can do that. I'll help you tomorrow; mend the corn crib too, if you want.'

Sparrow watched him go.

How long had it been since he'd woven a wicker trap? He reckoned maybe ten or so years. And with that his thoughts turned to Biddie Happ. Why his thoughts went from eels to Biddie Happ he did not know for the two subjects were entirely contrary, like darkness and light. She was light. She was everything he ever wanted. She was even more come-hither than Misty Knapp, in Sparrow's opinion.

He could not help but think of the way she peeped from behind that sweep of hair. He could barely sit still at the very thought of those ample hips shaping like moon-pale baker's dough as she sat her bare arse down on her bed at Bet Pepper's.

At the back of his hut he began to sort through the wreckage of the corn crib, but he was not the slightest bit interested in the work. 'Gotta go see Biddie,' he said.

9

They crossed an offshoot, ankle-deep in the flow, climbed a spur and followed the line of a ridge, which was the line of the creek, westward.

Cuff was first to spot the smoke rising from the canopy ahead. They shifted quietly along the ridge, keeping to the bare stone and staying shy of the brow until Harp was close; heard him scuffing about below.

They inched towards the brow and found themselves looking down upon his freckled and scabby pate; saw him pause and look about. There was a big teakettle on a small fire, an iron pot on a chopping block, the Cape pony hobbled close by, black as soot. A possum lay dead near the fire, the hind leg bloodied, still in the hare trap that ruined its day.

They backed off, stepping quietly on the stone, and walked on until they found an easy way down to the creek so as to come at Harp from upstream. They paused when the still came into view, a crude contraption under a rough-cut frame roofed with bark slabs: a large pot on a stone furnace with a cap bolted onto the pot and sealed with a whiteish plaster of some kind; a pipe from the top of the cap to the condenser, a coil of copper tubing in a five-gallon barrel, a brass cock at the base.

Harp carried the teakettle to the mash barrels by a cleft in the sandstone scarp. He began to pour. The Cape pony cocked its ears and turned its head as the constables stepped up the bank, skirting the still. 'Mr Sneezby,' said Mackie.

The old man had not seen a soul since the onset of the flood, when Griffin Pinney had passed through. His first instinct was to grab his musket but all he could see were the clay jugs at the foot of the scarp and a splay-bottomed stick, upright by the mash bins. He could not remember where he put the musket. Then he remembered it was broke. 'I retain a severe attachment to my solitude and do not welcome surprises,' he said.

He was relieved, now, to see Cuff alongside Mackie, for Cuff was an agreeable presence on most occasions and would doubtless leaven the aggravation on this one.

'We gathered that when we stood, enchanted, at the foot of your gibbet,' said Cuff.

Harp's ancient red coat was threadbare and his chest was a mess of grey hair and the gut splayed over the rope tie on his fustian trousers was considerable. His hands and face were ridged and ribbed like old bark, and his cheeks were a latticework of veins and there was a brutal wound from the middle of his forehead to the bridge of his nose, all the way to the socket of his eye, the work of a small axe, a ripe scar. His features seemed baked and shrivelled. He was altogether a vegetable presence.

Harp tapped high on the bridge of his nose. 'That black devil, he's the one did this,' he said. 'Knocked the eyes out of my head, someone put 'em back, don't know who, maybe it was me. Now I see crooked, I know that much.'

Cuff set himself down on a stump. 'Caught you off guard.'

'He caught me worn-out is what he did. I'd buried what was left of poor old Spider Thornycroft and got myself home, my back in spasm and my senses stricken . . . I just had to put a swift end to my despair.'

'How'd you do that?'

'I drank a bucket of bang-head; left myself near helpless to the moonlight treachery of those devils.'

Harp's story was familiar to the river people, having featured in the *Sydney Gazette* and thereafter spread about, and richer for the spreading. Supposedly it was him who found Spider Thornycroft with a spear in his gut, right through, pinned to the ground, the poor man half eaten by the pet hog called Pig. According to Harp the hog had fled, thus saving itself from the savages but then, upon a suitable occasion, had returned to sup on Spider's corpse, lingered for a time, got lonely, or bored, and thus retired to the bush for good. He'd since become a considerable predator on the upper reaches of the creek, so it was said.

Harp was probing at the scar between his eyes. 'The entire ordeal's fresh as the morning in my mind and I'll defy any man to say I shot that savage in cold blood, he was on my porch! That was hot blood or nothin's hot blood and you can tell that to whoever you like, just don't go sayin' old Harp don't know the difference between hot blood and cold blood.'

'We won't do that Harp, never let it be said we'd do such a thing to a good man *would we, Alister?*' said Cuff.

'You are found in the act of distilling spirits,' said Mackie. He was examining the copper piping in the barrel, the worm, an artful spiral, the work of a skilled smithy.

'Where the pig-fuck is the treason in a man making the best of his own grain by means of his own industry?' said Harp.

'These engines are pregnant with every possible mischief,' said Mackie.

'This engine is a potent motivator, paid the reaping. I am no longer able to do the reaping in case you haven't noticed! My felon won't work but for bang-head. The labour's got it all over us, you know that.'

Mackie did not answer.

'I buy it off them officers and I'm skint entire, that what you want?' said Harp.

'He's right,' said Cuff, 'they pay in bushels of wheat for a few gallons and what starts in trade ends in hock.' He popped the cork on one of Harp's gallon jugs and took a swig. '*Poooo*, scorpion juice, pure fire,' he said.

'*Why, then, are you drinking it?*' said Mackie.

'I dram therefore I am,' said Cuff.

Harp smacked his thigh and chuckled.

'Where is he, your felon?' said Mackie.

'He went with Griffin come the flood, I think.'

'Griffin should have took Thelma when he could,' said Cuff.

'Turns out she's got delicate feet, they blister up something terrible, can't walk a mile,' said Harp.

'It is my duty to seize or destroy the illicit apparatus in this lair of yours,' said Mackie.

'You'll ruin me.'

'The clandestine use of grain and sugar in times of great scarcity . . .'

'I have no grain *but* for liquor, don't he understand?' Harp said to Cuff. 'They won't take my grain at the store, you know how it works Mr Cuff, they got their favourites, the officers.' His voice had lifted to a miserable, pleading whine. 'That's how it works, the military's a damn cabal.'

Cuff reckoned Harp Sneezby was right. The small farmers had no guarantee the commissariat store would take their grain. Favourites got preference and, anyway, once the store had the grain it needed to feed the vice-regal establishment, the felons, the soldiers and their dependants, why, then the store closed. The idea of punishing Harp seemed entirely stupid: 'Harp, you have to understand, the chief constable answers to a higher power with a view to your wellbeing and to the wholesome restoration of us all. He ain't God but he's on a par with the angels,' he said.

'My wellbeing you say?'

'Your rescue from the clutches of evil.'

Mackie growled. 'Private stills are attended with dire consequences, to wit violence, lethargy, blindness, indigence, say nothing of the fatal dysenteries, outright poison.'

'You're wasting your breath, Harp,' said Cuff. 'Might as well attack the devil with an icicle.'

Mackie had dismantled the condenser. He held the coil of copper piping in hands, treating the apparatus to careful inspection. 'Who made this worm?'

'Curse the hide on your bones.'

Cuff took a long look at the dead possum by the fire stones. 'There's a tasty critter for a salty stew,' he said.

'You get your own fuckin' meat,' said Harp, 'come in here with this damn killjoy.'

Cuff reckoned that was a fair comment. He was at ease now. He crooked his musket and walked to the mash barrels and peered into one. 'How do you know the proper degree of fermentation?'

Harp was scratching at his gut. 'I know 'cause I know, an' I don't do poison.'

'Well then, tell me.'

'You put your ear on the barrel. Ripe and ready sounds like pork frying in a pan or rain on shingles maybe. Sweetest sound.'

The pony pricked its ears, uneasy, head high.

Mackie cocked his head windward and raised a hand for silence.

'Not a sound from you, Harp,' whispered Cuff. He levelled his musket and shoved the muzzle into Harp's gut and the flesh folded around the muzzle like dough.

They listened.

'Who is it?' said Mackie.

'Could be ol' Wolgan,' said Harp.

'I think not.'

Cuff put a hand on Harp's shoulder. 'Git down in the dirt.'

'I'll never get up, my knees.'

'Get down, and curb your tongue.'

Harp folded himself over and bent at the knees, trying to squat, only to fall backwards with a grunt.

Cuff and Mackie backed into the cleft by the mash bins. The sun had long passed over. The cleft was shaded and dark, the walls damp with seepage. The pony was treading the ground as Griffin Pinney stepped up the creek bank, musket in hand. His kangaroo dog followed, dripping wet, nose down searching for scent this way and that, quickly finding the possum.

'What's wrong with you?' growled Pinney.

He was a reed of a man, his hair loose and low on the back of his neck, a moth-eaten mantle on his shoulders in the fashion of the savages, and a bandolier across his chest. His trousers curled at his waist over a plaited belt, cinched tight, a hunting knife holstered at his hip alongside a small axe strung on a loop.

Mackie stepped out of the cleft, pistol in hand. 'The senior partner I presume?' he said.

Pinney was so shocked he dropped his gun and stepped back, his right foot sinking into the dead possum. His knee buckled and he fell on his arse. His dog sensed the mood and flew at Mackie. Cuff grabbed the splay-bottomed stick and rammed the splay into the side of the dog's head and the animal went down, cut and splintered, and the deputy punched his heel hard down into the ribs and the dog yelped and then fell silent save for sucking for the breath knocked out of it.

'You cruel my ol' dog I cruel you,' said Pinney.

'Oh I cruelled him alright, that's done, that's history,' said Cuff.

The dog got its wind back and limped over to Pinney and the game hunter began to pick splinters out of its jowls and stroke the grey whiskers, and then he held the head still and stared at the damaged eye. He ran a palm across the dog's ribs and the dog pulled away.

'I will fix you,' said Pinney.

'Who knows the suffering ahead, for all of us,' said Cuff.

'You stoop to this, ruin a man's independence,' said Pinney. 'You put a good man like Harp here at the mercy of the store, them vultures. Why they'd steal the sails off'v their own windmill, you know that.'

'You don't even grow grain, you're worse than the traders, you're a parasite on a poor old pensioned-off soldier.'

'I have no connection here save convivial banter in the course of my perambulations, Harp will tell you that,' said Pinney.

'I got no pension, I got my patch is all I got and now I'm supposed to share that with the savages, *so I hear*,' said Harp.

'You ain't north of the Branch, Harp, so you don't have to share a thing, less you want to,' said Cuff.

'Not likely,' said Pinney.

'As to the stewardship here?' said Mackie.

Harp did not speak for some time. He threw his head back so his misfitted eyes might look as best they could upon Griffin Pinney's face. 'Mr Pinney has no connection here save passer-by, and that irregular,' he said.

'He do that gibbet for you, gut that savage?'

Harp thought hard on the question. 'I did that gibbet an' every damn right I had.'

'Right?'

'The governor's say so.'

'Gut a man and hang him up?'

'Retribution must be summary, so they know what it's for. No killing in cool blood, the governor's very own words,' said Harp.

'Like a dog piss on your tick, you got to whip it there and then,' said Pinney, patting the old hound.

'I tell you now my blood was up, *hot and bubbling*,' said Harp.

'He did say that, the governor, I seen it in the *Gazette*,' said Cuff.

'No forswearing the printed word!' said Pinney.

'Mr Sneezby, my concern is this contraption, nothing else,' said Mackie. 'If you are the proprietor then I must take you to the magistrate.'

Harp stood straight and puffed out his chest. 'I have conferred with my Maker and I know it's no crime to make the best I can of my own industry. What's more this juice is indispensable to almost every expression of river intercourse.'

'Harp, you didn't do all this,' said Cuff, gesturing at the apparatus and the barrels.

Harp hesitated. 'I am the *sole* proprietor.'

'Then you are in more trouble than you deserve,' said Mackie.

'You'd hardly run a tavern off this,' said Cuff, but Mackie ignored him.

'That's a point,' said Harp. 'Chief constable licensed in the way of spirits don't seem right, goin' about like a damn fox rootin' out the competition . . . poor little chickens like me.'

'You got a proprietary interest in this poor man's elimination!' said Pinney.

'Your final word Mr Sneezby, I'll have it now.'

'It's mine, the whole show.'

Mackie stared hard at Pinney. The dog was now prone at the game hunter's side, pawing at its jowls.

'Where is your concubine?'

'Thelma, she's down there, the river camp.'

'That she is.'

'What?'

'She's drowned.'

'Drowned . . . dead?'

'You left her to drown and she drowned, wedged up a tree, doubt-less hoping for salvation,' said Mackie.

'Like a figurehead on a ship marked for doom!' said Cuff.

'What?'

'Up that big ol' tree, that was futile, see, 'cause the river was up, the flow was fierce and the tree keeled over, bent low, and she drowned, wedged there . . . you should have took her with you.'

'She couldn't walk a mile, no point,' said Pinney. 'Drowned you say. Damn.'

Cuff wanted clarification. 'So, come the mighty deluge you was safe and warm in some cave in the fastness, that right?'

'I'm tellin' you, she would not come!'

'You made promises to her you never should.'

'I didn't promise her nothin'.'

'That's not what she told Betty Pepper.'

'Well you'd know about Betty Pepper.'

'I thought you were the Moses to part the mountains, walk her through the wilderness, live a life of plenty. Plenty of her if nothin' else.'

'My damn woman's dead and here you mock me.'

'You told her a lot o' lies to keep her in the camp and keep your wick in, that's what you did.'

'I promised that woman nothing 'cept the pleasure of my company and I'll fuck a dead pig if that's a word of a lie.'

Cuff waggled a finger at Pinney. 'As we speak I picture you . . . deep in pork.'

Pinney looked down at his mewling dog. 'She really dead?'

'We buried her yesterday,' said Mackie.

'You can pick some flowers on your way down, put a posy there if you want, the blossom's considerable in all this heat'n rain; lovely little pea flowers about, petals like butterflies,' said Cuff.

Harp had listened to this talk about floods and death and foolish fable and flowers, and it made him miserable. He was very old, he didn't know exactly how old, and now he was caught red-handed, and the chief constable was about to smash his copper worm or seize it, and him too. 'Why don't you just kill me, I'd be better off dead.'

'You have an unusually sunny notion of dead,' said Cuff.

'Well you tell me, what happens when we're dead?'

'Not much.'

'That's sunny enough for me.'

They sent Pinney on his way with the wounded dog at his heel. The game hunter paused at the creek's edge and stared into the dismantled condenser. Then he headed downstream and Cuff went to the water's edge and watched him go, watched till man and dog melted into the patchwork of timber and stone further down. 'Now we can uncoil,' he said.

Harp seemed to agree. He knelt by the chopping block and took the head off the possum with one blow, and he skinned the rest with a hunting knife and then he quartered the carcass and halved the quarters and they added in some bush parsnips and cooked up a stew in a slurry of ancient dregs in the iron pot.

10

Bet Pepper's cottage was damp and grit-ridden from the windowsills down, a sea-green mould upon the footings. The cottage was flood prone but that didn't trouble Bet. She liked where she was, off the switchback path between the river and the village on the ridge, close to hand for the comers and goers.

Bet liked to sit on her porch, survey the river and the farmlands on the far side, and the woodlands beyond the farmlands, pretty, like a picture, and the low hills grading into the Branch country to the north-west, the mysterious fastness that spawned all manner of strange tales and kept them all wondering.

What did trouble Bet was the fickleness of the trade, the men who made shallow promises to her girls and wooed them away. Thelma Rowntree was not the first to be persuaded to leave Bet's employ and now she too had gone off, gone off with Griffin Pinney, and why any sane woman would go off with Griffin Pinney remained a mystery to Bet, for Pinney was a fearsome sight with a fearsome reputation.

Bet suspected Griffin might have stolen her. Trussed her up in the dead of night and whisked her away with a nod and a wink to the night watch, and perhaps a bottle of something for good measure.

Then again, Bet heard he filled her head with talk of a place on the other side of the mountains, a place where there was no peonage and no penury and no tyranny whatsoever; a place where the waters teemed and the ground was fecund and the game was so plentiful the savages were docile, polite even.

Bet didn't believe it. She didn't believe any of that guff, flimflam, but she did know Pinney could spin a yarn and, if pressed, she would concede the other side of that sad coin – Thelma was dumb as a stump.

Biddie Happ was Thelma's replacement but Biddie was not cut from the same cloth. She was not at all inclined to talk bawdy or to sport her wares, nor did she have wares to sport, not such as to compare with Thelma Rowntree. Biddie was a plump girl with pear-shaped hips and a most distinctive birthmark, a big purple splash across her forehead and left eyelid, and she tried to hide it by pinning a swathe of her long red hair in just such a way.

Bet Pepper concluded it was the birthmark that burdened Biddie with a certain reticence in public, though customers said her performance behind doors was more than adequate. That was music

to Bet's ears, that was all she wanted to hear, and soon enough she
twigged that Biddie's residence was more likely to endure because the
squaddies and the expirees were not lining up to run off with her.

Enter, Martin Sparrow.

When Sparrow arrived he found Bet Pepper seated on the porch as
usual, smoking tobacco in a corn husk trimmed to her requirements.
She was watching the river traffic, Guthrie's boy on the barge, small
boats, the trading scow idle. She appeared to be in a state of contentment, save for the westering sun which compelled her to squint and
shade her eyes.

'You should've come sooner, I could've used you cleanin' up,'
she said.

'I been cleanin' up my own patch all day, nothin' but.'

'You should get some help.'

'I did, I got Jug Woody. We fixed the corn crib.'

Sparrow sensed the bawdy house was empty. His first thought
was Biddie might be in Parramatta where she had a sister, so she said,
or she might be asleep; these girls kept strange hours. He was about
to sit and talk to Bet, hoping to find out, when he heard the sounds of
vigorous humping from within, so vigorous the cabin's sodden framework was shaking and bits of thatching wafted down from the porch
cover. One bit caught in Sparrow's hair and hung lank on his cheek
and made his eyelid flutter.

He flicked it away and scratched at his cheek.

'She's busy,' said Bet.

Sparrow said nothing. He did not wish to display his severe disappointment. To hear Biddie at work at her trade filled him with wrath.
The aggravation he felt was not helped by the noise from within, for
the noise was Biddie, squealing and moaning most pleasurably. She
had never squealed and moaned like that with him. She never made a
sound when he covered her. She'd just lie there, occasionally give him
a smile, and then she would pat at that sweep of hair, fix it just so, and

then she would pat him on the arse and tell him not to be all day at it. 'C'mon now, spend your penny,' she'd say. Sparrow always wondered about that because the expenditure was in fact way more than a penny, whether in coin or kind.

'Who's in there?'

'Marty, you don't ask that.'

'If I sit here long enough I'll see anyway.'

'You'll be sittin' in the dark I'll tell you that now.' Bet looked west, squinting, the sun squat on the mountain rim.

'That long?'

'He's regular. He's layin' close siege to my girl.'

Sparrow was shocked. His hope cracked into little pieces, went to powder like a parched leaf underfoot. 'Tell me who it is?'

'Don't be pitiful.'

'Tell me.'

'If I lose this girl to the military I'll scream.' Bet had turned her attention to the activity on the far side of the river where Guthrie's boy had run the barge onto the mud, an oxcart waiting. She was pleased to have something to watch so she could at least half ignore Sparrow.

'I have to know,' he said.

Bet spoke softly, almost a whisper: 'It's Reuben Peskett and there's no stopping that man.'

Sparrow was shocked. Reuben Peskett was a leathery veteran who had several times been demoted for ill-discipline yet each time rose again in the corps to his former rank of sergeant, following bloody exploits against the savages. He had fake front teeth, carved from a single piece of ox bone but so ill-fitted they jiggled when he talked, thus confounding the vanity that had inspired them in the first instance.

Bet could see that Sparrow's mind was flush with dark thoughts. 'Don't you give Reuben Peskett no trouble,' she whispered.

'Some beggars have all the damn luck,' said Sparrow.

'Luck might visit a fool but it won't take tea with him,' said Bet.

'I can fix him,' said Sparrow.

'No you cannot,' said Bet. 'He'll have your fat for soap and your guts for garters.'

Sparrow knew Bet was right. He was a squirt, and Peskett, though not much bigger, had a fearsome reputation for violence once aroused. Otherwise, and worse still, he had a most confident air about him. Sparrow wished he could be confident like that around women, so he might pay court boldly, the way Reuben Peskett did. But women, most particularly the fetching ones, made Sparrow go to water. They reduced him to a muddy puddle.

He was sure now that women could sense weakness in a man and they despised it, Bet no exception nor Biddie neither. If only he could be charming and not give a damn, like Peskett, or Cuff. But the more he cared the more it showed and that aroused not so much fondness as contempt. If he didn't give a fig, Biddie would probably want him. But he did give a fig, and it showed, and now Biddie was squealing and moaning for an old veteran who couldn't care less so long as he got his wick in.

Sparrow was full of doubt, doubt about everything. He leaned towards Bet and spoke softly: 'Is that her real name, Biddie Happ?'

Bet's face was momentarily contorted as she tried to make sense of the question. 'Why would she have another name, you daft man? Her name is Biddie, Biddie Happ, affectionately known as Miss Happ, and she is a poor ratcatcher's daughter from Diddlebury and that is no secret.'

'I'm sorry,' said Sparrow.

'That's it,' said Bet, 'you're always sorry, if you weren't so damned sorry she might treat you different. Ain't you noticed, Reuben Peskett's never sorry. He's got *panache*, might be rough round the edges but it's *panache* all the same.'

'What is *panache*?'

'It's not bein' sorry is what it is.'

Sparrow was now most seriously deflated. He looked at his hands. Could a woman ever love a yellowy man? He feared another visitation – the sharp pains in his right side were inclined to strike him without notice. He knew it wasn't gas for he could fart all day and half the night and it did not make a penneth of difference. Dr Woody was probably right when he said it was jaundice but, sadly, putting a name to the ailment in no way lessened the discomfort nor did it compromise the wicked stealth of the disorder.

He reckoned he best go. He did not want to suffer a visitation in the presence of Bet Pepper. If he took sick Bet might warn him off, but that hardly mattered this time around. The throb in his pizzle was long gone.

He felt his throat clog up. He did not want to be there when Reuben Peskett stepped onto the porch, happy as a tick on a pig. Nor did he want to couple with Biddie Happ in the aftermath of Peskett's sweaty exertions.

'They got Shug, did you know that?' said Bet.

Sparrow was shocked. 'What happened?'

'Seems they went on the maraud, him and Mort. They killed Gordy and they took his pony, and various oddments, and they took the girl Dot too, the poor thing.'

'Mort got away?'

'Who knows! All we know is they got Shug, that savage found him, Caleb, saved him from a miserable demise and a lonely grave bereft of all Christian consolation.'

'Caleb!'

'The fabled Caleb, yes. Passed him over to Peskett in the foothills.'

'Peskett, again!'

'The very same, he's everywhere,' she said. 'And now he's brung in a bolter, so he'll get the reward.'

Sparrow stared at the cabin wall. 'Shug just didn't have the mettle,' he said with some conviction.

'That'd be right,' said Bet.

Sparrow felt himself sink into yet another slough of despond. He got to his feet, said he had to go, headed back up the switchback path aiming to cross the ridge and take the South Creek track to the vicinity of the bridge, there to spend time at Peachey's Tap and, if possible, drown his sorrows.

All thought of agricultural renewal was now gone. He let go his resolve with no more care than he would a fart. He marvelled how things he held almost firm in his head could dissolve, just like that. He'd commit to something with the best of intentions and for a brief time hold the vision, bright in his mind. Then something bad would happen and the vision was gone and he'd be there, sloughed, left with nothing, nothing but the desire to run away, his heart full of lead, which was exactly how he felt as he passed the pillory and the gibbet and walked on to the Tap.

The pillory made him recall Mort's ordeal, the day they locked him in that brutal thing and Peskett nailed his ears to the framework. The memory hurried him on.

He found some diversion in the sight of the Tap, for the Tap from the ground up showed all the signs of good intentions fading in the course of a prolonged assemblage. The skilling at the back was made of neat-trimmed split log, but the cabin attached to the skilling was rough-cut palings in some parts and wickerwork bedaubed with clay in others, while the southern wall was made of sod with a stone fireplace and chimney. The trade had rallied to assist the Peacheys in the aftermath of the flood. They had righted the frame with bracing timbers lashed to deep-sunk ground pegs but there was still a distinct lean to the tavern. Like the trees all about, the structure had bent to the will of the fearsome floodwaters. The entire building looked like a loving creation from a child's dream or a Jack tale.

11

The night was mild and the sky above Cuff was awash with stars. Harp could not get up so he stayed where he was, his legs twitching and jumping in some sort of agitation until he was deep asleep, whereupon he snored loud as a fog bell. Mackie was already dozing, having commandeered the dry canvas that Harp kept near the mash bins. Cuff made a pillow of his haversack.

Hours later Harp woke up, worried about the Cape pony. 'Need's water,' he said. Cuff loosened the hobbles and led the pony to the creek and fed him a few handfuls of corn mash and then he went back to the fire that was hardly more than a flicker, the flame guttering to ashes.

He sat beside Harp, hungry still, eager for the scrapings of the possum stew. 'Don't mind eatin' this cold,' he said, as he dragged his spoon across the bottom of the pot.

'You can have the leavings,' he said, and he handed the pot to Harp. He cleaned his spoon in the dirt and squeezed the dirt off it as best he could with thumb and forefinger. He wiped the implement on his britches and returned it to the long, thin, fit-for-purpose pocket inside his vest, as if the tailor somehow knew that a man with a spoon would, sooner or later, acquire this particular garment.

Harp worked the bottom of the cookpot with his stick and scooped out the leavings with his fingers, picking possum hair from his lips and then dipping back in. He picked out the possum head, which Cuff had shunned, and he dug away at the recesses of the skull. 'He that wastes naught wants for naught,' he said, and he clamped his lips upon the creature's eye socket and sucked hard on the one and then the other.

Cuff watched. He chose not to comment upon a homily that did not seem to have served Harp Sneezby all that well. He caught sight of a shooting star in the western sky, and spoke softly. 'I've never seen anything so beautiful as the starry heavens off there. I do believe I can make out the Big Fishhook.'

'Not even a woman?' said Harp.

'Say what?'

'Nothing so beautiful, not even a woman?'

Cuff took his time, and then he clucked his tongue and shook his head. 'I can think of one or two women outshined the stars, beauty that almost hurts; beauty to make you cross a ocean or kill a man . . . or wish you was a damn tree.'

'I never seen no woman like that.'

'I don't know if that makes you lucky or unlucky.'

'I'm mostly unlucky.'

'Well you got me for company, there's a turn in your fortunes.'

'Where'd you see these women?'

'The one that haunts me still was quite possibly the mistake of my life, to let her go. I tell you Harp, she was most magnificently distributed in her parts.'

'Why'd you let her go?'

'I'm too tired to tell, 'cept . . . I'll tell you she was Boston Spanish and something to behold, but I cannot say she was untroubled.'

Harp spat, and waited for Cuff to continue.

'When she was little she saw her daddy set her mama on fire, saw her mama burn. She was awful cautious about men, I'll say that much.'

They sat quietly, Cuff looking at the sky and Harp staring at the ground and Mackie apparently asleep, his breathing an irregular wheeze.

Harp looked skyward yet again. He was reflecting on the conversation. 'That woman in Boston, you cross the ocean after her?'

'I did.'

'You find her?'

'Yes.'

'Where?'

'In the burial ground at Sydney Cove. Sad little grave.'

Harp said nothing, waiting for more.

'The sky's like the mountains,' said Cuff.

'How so?'

'It's that impassable barrier between some supposedly splendid dominion and the world we know.'

'She broke your heart, I can tell.'

'She fled Boston, fled the yellow fever epidemic on a whaler bound for the South Seas. She picked the wrong bunch o' fellers . . . That broke m'heart . . .'

That was half the truth. The other half was the ruin of his entire family. The first fatalities in that morbidly hot summer were quickly followed by more; soon half the city was dead. He recalled how his sisters died, their skin an awful sickly colour and their vomit riddled with black clots of blood. Next his stepmother fell ill and his daddy took it upon himself to tend her day and night. One morning Cuff found her dead and his father delirious, pleading for water. When Cuff came back from the pump in the yard his father was already gone. The old man had come down the stairs tearing off his clothes and, naked, he'd crossed the street and hurled himself into the Charles River and drowned without a whimper. And with that, Cuff was free. He was free to go and he did.

It was Harp's insistent voice that rescued Cuff from dark memory: 'Might be pure fire but my brew's not poison. I am a gifted distiller and unashamed to say so.'

'You want some?'

'*You* want some?'

'Yes.'

Cuff got himself up and got hold of a gallon jug, about half full, and sat and shared it with Harp, the two of them taking turns to swig it down. 'I could be dead and this'd bring me back to life, frolicsome as a kitten,' said Harp.

'It greets the palate like an old friend, it's alright.'

'Just alright?'

'I'd say its maker knows none of the arts of adulteration. It's harsh but pure.'

'Thank you, Mr Cuff.'

'You're welcome, Mr Sneezby, it's a compliment way overdue.'

'It's got a fierce kick, I call it *workhorse*, keep a man going all day long, gets the reaping done, that and more. I sure hope my felon comes back.'

'I'd call it *forty feet*.'

'How so?'

'Forty feet, then you fall over.'

Harp chuckled. He turned his attention to Mackie, asleep on the canvas. 'Sworn off it but he sells it to all and sundry and he pokes into every damn nook on the river lookin' for poor little minnows like me?'

'He's good at what he does, sniffs out all manner of culpability.'

'Some of us call him the governor's dog.'

'He's no one's dog, too canny. But he's a loyal servant of the Crown and the Crown has been good to him.'

'I know.'

'Nowhere else in this world you can start off a felon and end up a chief constable with your own farm.'

'And a damn tavern on the square.'

'That too.'

'I hear he bought a ship.'

'He did. He got a ruin for a song, off a bankrupt.'

'He's like a vulture.'

'He's got a nose for opportunity, that's all.'

'Why's he gotta take me in?'

Cuff paused to think, tapping his fingers on his knees. 'I'd say the man's ruled by ambition, and that's harnessed to duty and duty is the key to his elevation.'

'Why's he so damned tired? He's half your age and more'n that mine.'

'Bronchial eruptions lay him waste, now and then.'

'My poor ol' mother had a bronchial rattle. A rattle what took her off.'

'A rattle will do that, take you off.'

12

When he stepped into Peachey's Tap, Sparrow paused and looked about. He tried to pick out the faces in the russet gloom. The task was complicated by the dust motes that sparkled in soft glowing shafts of twilight arrowing through holes in the wasted daub. The dogs came and sniffed at him and found him acceptable and went back to their dusty wallow by the wall, there to sleep some more.

'You look rung out,' said Seamus Peachey.

'I stagger from one calamity to another,' said Sparrow. The lean of the building was not of great assistance to his temper, nor to his placement within the world, which seemed to have tilted five or ten degrees.

'Marty my boy you need some bang-head,' said Alfie Shivers, the felon now visible in the far corner. With him was Griffin Pinney whose face he could not see but whose bandolier was speckled in the light, a thousand particles of dust dancing on the tatty old leather.

'I do need something, the sharper the better,' said Sparrow. He walked to the counter where Seamus Peachey presided over the trade. Peachey was a weasel of a man, even Sparrow thought that. A weasel with a face of sharp, shadowed panes and hollowed out recessions, and broken teeth.

'What calamity you stagger into this time?' he asked.

Sparrow slid his arse onto a stool by the counter. Several tin plates were stacked, one upon another, with a pile of poultry bones in the slushy leavings in the plate on top. He could smell the cooked meat. 'I am deep in hock, and more to come.'

'More?' said Peachey.

'I got to borrow for seed, I got to crop for the store, I got to have a surplus. Yes, more,' said Sparrow.

'That or the road!'

'That or the road, yes, he'll put me on the road.'

'A road perchance . . . of your own choosing?' Peachey winked at him.

Sparrow was searching for a thread of hope in a moment of wretched gloom. He wondered if there might be a meaning here that he was meant to grasp. 'Which road is that?' he said.

Peachey did not reply but Griffin Pinney muttered something to Alfie Shivers and the two of them chuckled and Sparrow reckoned they had to be chuckling at his expense.

One of the dogs, Peachey's game dog, the one called Tool, was twitching and whimpering, off in some dream world of blood and bone. Sparrow could smell the scrapings on the tin plate. 'Slice o' bread, I can mop that up, finish it off,' he said.

Alfie Shivers began to sing, almost as slow as he talked: 'There's a track no man may follow, there's a track the toll to pay, there's a track . . .'

'A track through them mountains, is that what you want?' said Griffin Pinney as he turned to Sparrow, adjusting the mantle on his shoulders.

Every time Sparrow saw Griffin Pinney's face he wished he could disappear down a hole. This time the game hunter had what seemed to be a poultry bone, a wing bone, through the cartilage in his nose and there were cream coloured tufts of hair that curled from the bore-holes of that nose like some sort of filament of horn. Sparrow did not know quite what to say, the words just tumbled out. 'Can you sleep with that in?'

Alfie Shivers whacked his knee and buckled over with laughter. Pinney just stared.

That made Sparrow even more nervous. 'Is it a bone?'

'Why don't you come close and look.'

'I'm just . . . sittin' here.'

'Not quite sitting, up an' down like a fiddler's arm,' said Alfie.

Pinney was turning the bone with his fingers the way a gentleman might turn a moustache in the course of a waxing. 'It is an adornment. Makes me look pretty, would you not agree?'

'I don't know.'

Alfie Shivers was fixed in a fit of the chuckles.

Pinney removed the adornment and put it on the plate with the leavings. 'You can crack it and suck on it if you want,' he said.

Sparrow felt a fool. 'What I want, I want the track through the mountains.' *There, I said it.*

A surge of singular purpose had suddenly occupied his person. He wanted to escape the mean-hearted little world of the ridge and the river; to change his life, lift himself from the servitude of rig and furrow and the hovering menace of foreclosure. Most of all he wanted to get so far from Biddie Happ he'd have no choice but to forget her. He wished he had the mettle to woo the woman, to woo her with *panache*, but in that regard his hope was frayed as old rope for he didn't have much in the way of mettle and he didn't have any *panache*, none that he knew of, none that he could summon upon the occasion. And now it seemed Biddie had surrendered her carnal self to Reuben Peskett and that just about guaranteed she'd go off with him – him with the damn reward *and* the woman – and that was more than Sparrow could bear. He was not about to sit rotting like corn stubble in a fallow field. Given half a chance he would seek out the fabled haven. He might get killed on the way, killed in the wilderness, skewered by the savages, but he did not care.

'I want the track to freedom,' he said, trying to put a little boldness into his delivery.

There was a long silence, save for the game dog called Tool scratching at fleas and Pinney's old dog licking at his own pizzle.

Pinney struck a thoughtful pose, scratching at his chin. 'I'll tell you something,' he said to Sparrow, 'you can hurl a mountain 'cross that river easier'n force the yoke o' slavery onto me, now . . . how you fixed in that regard?'

'Shhhhhh,' said Peachey.

'I'm fixed, I don't want no yoke.'

'You'll have to pay the toll.'

'Yup, ain't cheap,' said Alfie with a chuckle.

'Whose toll?' Sparrow was sure now they were toying with him.

'Talk soft,' whispered Peachey.

'Why, the savages,' said the game hunter. 'How do you expect to get across that devil ridden wilderness otherwise?'

'What do they want?'

'You don't get across cheap, and you don't come back, ever.'

'I won't come back.'

'You say a word, to anyone . . .'

'I won't say a word, not to one soul on this mortal earth I swear.'

'It's a considerable toll.'

'Coin?'

'Noooo, what's a damn savage want with coin?'

'Dumber'n a box o' hair,' said Alfie.

Pinney was pulling at the pierced cartilage in his nose. 'What they want is a dog.'

'A dog?'

'A kangaroo dog, any old dog no good, they's choosy beggars. They want a passable game dog, no less.'

'I don't have a dog.'

'You don't pay the toll you don't get but halfway . . .'

'And they won't just kill you . . . they'll eat your particulars,' said Alfie.

Seamus Peachey nodded: 'It's true, no dog and your particulars go in the cook pot, your liver too – they like liver them blacks, man liver.'

Sparrow glanced at the dog, now at Alfie Shivers' feet, and Peachey noticed. 'That one wouldn't know a kangaroo from a stick o' burnt wood and don't you forget it and he'll take your arm off if I tell him to,' said the taverner.

'As for Tool,' said Alfie, 'our Seamus will gut the man steals Tool.'

'That I will.'

'I am not about to steal your dog, not the one nor the other!' said Sparrow. He could feel sweat on his forehead, the clammy air stuck to him like chicken grease. He didn't dare glance at Griffin Pinney's game dog.

'Shhh,' said Peachey, 'you'll wake up Winnie, then we're all back in the misery.'

Sparrow wondered why he did not feel downcast, not having a dog to pay the savages. He thought it might be fear, for at that moment he could feel something like fear stirring in his bowels. Then he realised it wasn't his bowels stirring but his belly, he was so hungry.

For some reason the proximity of the poultry bones made Sparrow think of Biddie and thoughts of Biddie undermined his resolve to bolt, which was dreadfully confusing because he had resolved to bolt in no small part to scotch his yearnings for that woman, such yearnings being nothing but misery piled upon misery. But the dangers of the fastness were troublesome too. He could see them, the savages, those far-shadowing spears. He could feel their breath upon his cheek, see those brutal axes in their hands, the great bulbous head of resin that held wood to stone.

Alfie Shivers took a swig from a big glass pickling jar, so big his stumpy little fingers could barely get a grip on it. 'Cut yer name across me backbone, stretch me skin across yer drum,' he sang and he winked at Sparrow and took another swig and passed the jar to Griffin Pinney who guzzled down the remainder like it was water, his Adam's apple clicking over like a greasy gearwheel in a public clock. 'Here's to perdition for everyone but us,' he said with a big smile.

'Peachey lit a lamp. 'I can spare you a tot of the skull-cracker,' he said, 'but no guarantees on the morning comin' round.'

'That will do me lovely,' said Sparrow.

Peachey reached into some nook beneath the counter and he came up with a bottle of something dark. 'There's not a lot I can say for this brew, except, if you die, we can embalm you with it, keep you nice for a thousand years.'

'Put y'on the shelf over there,' said Alfie.

Sparrow was not laughing. He drank down the skull-cracker and felt it burn all the way.

'You want another?'

Sparrow nodded and Peachey poured the tot.

The game hunter stepped so close to Sparrow he could feel the man's meaty breath upon his cheeks. 'You're a brave man, Marty, you're drinkin' coffin varnish.'

'It's not that bad.'

'You ready to bolt then?'

'Sure as eggs are little chickens.'

Pinney stayed close. 'That's the thing . . . eggs ain't always chickens.'

'Could be a duck,' said Alfie.

'You reckon you got the mettle?'

'I reckon I do.'

Sparrow lifted the top plate from the stack on the counter and much to his pleasure he found a pair of crusts in the plate beneath and these he put to work, mopping up the leftover juices and sucking on the brittle bones, taking care to set Griffin Pinney's nose bone to one side, and then he licked the next plate clean and pretty soon he felt better for he knew it was not a good idea to drink skull-cracker on an empty stomach.

There was someone rattling around in the skilling at the rear and that someone was Winifred Peachey, who now made her entrance as she always did, bustling onto the stage of tavern life with considerable purpose. The dogs upped and moved away.

In one hand Mrs Peachey held a key thick as a finger and with the other she pushed her husband out of the way. She lifted a wooden box from beneath the counter and unlocked the lock and retrieved a bunch of promissory notes and sorted through them until she found what she wanted.

She handed the note to Seamus. 'He's in hock to more than Mackie and don't you forget it. We are not a poorhouse for your abettors in the art of lolling about and doing so much less than nothing that nothing'd be something if ever you did it and you knew what it looked like.' She turned and snatched the plate from Sparrow's hand.

'Did what?' said Shivers in a whisper.

'I don't forget,' said Peachey. 'The poor man's hardly drinking the saleable stock.'

'See it stays that way.' She poked a finger into Sparrow's chest and nearly knocked him over. 'Saleable is *the* word. You owe this establishment a half bushel of saleable grain, rust free, grub free and no damp nor mould neither and what's more you give it up before you go favourin' the commissariat store or the traders or anyone else, Mackie or whoever, I don't care, you understand me?'

'I'll pay you when I can,' said Sparrow, his voice a whine that seemed to trickle out of his mouth like a pitiful line of dribble.

'You better pay something or I'll crack your damn skull myself.'

'Winnie, don't be like that,' said Peachey.

'Like what, like something other'n a damn loafer?' She poked a finger in Alfie's direction. 'Why's he not otherwise occupied? Why do we need him, why do we feed him if he's useless? Why why why do I have to nag all the time and don't call me Winnie!'

Shivers scuttled out. 'I'll weed them turnips,' he said, Winifred shouting after him. 'You see you do, and chain up them dogs for the night and feed them pigs before they starve to death and be quick about it or I'll send you back to the government and you'll be on the damn shovel where you belong.'

She sucked for air and smacked a hand onto her chest and pressed hard as she succumbed to a terrible coughing fit that seemed like it would never end, but when it did she turned to Sparrow and stared at him. She just stared and there seemed no end to that either. 'I ain't dead and the gripe won't kill me, so you can stop wishin',' she said, eventually.

Sparrow felt like a thief caught in the act. He stepped away from the bottle of skull-cracker. At such times his mind broke its mooring. He felt it happening now. He remembered the first time Biddie Happ checked his pizzle for sores. She'd called him a ridgeling, made him blush. 'I am not,' he had said.

'Yes you are,' she'd said.

'One nut's smaller'n the other, that's all.'

'So small I cannot see it nor feel it, not in your throat is it?' And that was that for he was lost for words, like now, with Mrs Peachey staring at him.

He felt himself a little giddy. He thought he best go, walk it off. 'I best go,' he said. And he did.

13

Mackie was not asleep. He stirred when Cuff took the pony to the creek. He watched as the pony hurried to the water and stepped down and reefed its head free and drank deep. Cuff dropped the lead rope and put his arm over the withers and leant on the pony the way a drunkard might lean on a friend, or a porch post. Mackie reckoned that was typical, for Cuff was naturally given to trusting pretty much anyone or anything, unless it growled or bit or smelt bad.

Cuff secured the pony and went back to the fire. Mackie lay quietly, listening to the conversation, much of which was unnecessary and trivial. Cuff was well schooled, yet he seemed happiest when he was talking rubbish to silly old dupes like Harp, indulging the man's flair for distilling bang-head, praising his product and drinking it too, until the conversation sunk to pitiable and pointless reminiscing about women, the two of them blind to the snare in every pleasure.

Mackie was hoping Cuff might steer the old man into a confession or a slip that implicated Griffin Pinney in the operation of the still. But Cuff, as ever, was talking for enjoyment. There was no purpose in his talk save for the purpose of more talk, a shallow conviviality. His deputy was turning up the best of opportunities, what with Harp half asleep and half pickled and garrulous into the bargain.

Mackie lay there, his eyes now closed. He knew that Cuff meant well, but Harp would be a lot better off were he persuaded to name Pinney the principal in the matter of the bush distillery and stick fast to that. Instead the two men scraped out the possum slurry in the iron pot, slaked down the brew, sang its praises and talked, unhushed, about a certain chief constable, without the slightest concession to his presence. *He's no one's dog, too canny.* Cuff at least had the good grace to concede that elemental truth but, then, he might have known Mackie was listening.

When the two men finally stopped drinking and talking and Harp began to snore, Mackie lay there for a time looking up at the stars. He was sleepy, his mind wandering off track to the subject of irresistible beauty, his own view sharply at variance given the pernicious character of such allurements – the jarring memories a buttress to the constancy of his resolve. He recalled how, before the Kirk, he begged to be forgiven and how, before the court, he begged for nothing. For at the age of seventeen his flesh had turned to stone. And he recalled, too, the ever so odd sense of freedom he felt upon his sentence coming down, for never again would he succumb to the liquid fear and shame he suffered in the presence of the Kirk. He recalled the shocking desire to be away, to cross an ocean, to be on that transport, bound for New South Wales. To be dead, or gone.

14

Sparrow felt a headache coming. He put it down to the skull-cracker but then he thought better, guessing Winifred Peachey was to blame, that menace of a woman, that shrew, that scold, that fishwife, that hag, that that, that termagant.

He crossed the twisted toll bridge, Mackie's bridge, and he followed the line of the creek eastwards, heading for the confluence with the river, gawping at the great wads of flood-wrack in the clefts of trees and searching the banks of the creek for anything to salvage. He found a Magellan jacket in shreds; he found a family Bible all tattered and swollen; he found a dead and bloated pig and a boy's straw hat and he also found a water bottle, a leather costrel, an old thing, battered but quite possibly useful – for a bolter.

Further up he found the high-water mark where the flattened, ghostly grey underbrush gave way to sprightly grasses thriving on the damp, the heat and the natural drainage. The ground was quite spongy but firm enough underfoot, so he kept to the high side of the flood line and walked on, watching the pull of the tide.

The pain in his right side was sharper now, so much so that he had to sit down, but when he sat down he couldn't stay still. He lay back on the grass and clutched at himself and bunched up, wrapping his arms around his knees and rocking to and fro.

Next thing he heard footsteps, that sucking sound, and when he opened his eyes he found he was looking up at the unmistakable mass of Griffin Pinney who stood over him, framed by the night sky.

Pinney's dog arrived and the old thing sniffed at Sparrow with his wet whiskers and licked at his neck and Sparrow let him do it.

'So now you know about the other side,' said Pinney.

'I don't know nothin' about the other side.'

'You know it's there, that's enough.'

'Enough for what?'

'Enough to get your throat cut and your tongue sliced off the bone.'

'Why would you do that?'

''Cause you might tell.'

'I would never.'

'Are you straight on this?'

'Sraight as a rush.'

'Swear, positively.'

'I swear!'

'You understand we don't want improper persons to be knowin' about the other side.'

'I'm proper, I want to go.'

'What about that girl got you moochin' about?'

Pinney stepped away, scratching at his package, and Sparrow sat up and dropped his head and stared at the grass between his legs and flicked at it, back and forth. 'Biddie Happ,' he said.

'Is that her name?'

'I'm finished there.'

'My Thelma's dead.'

'Dead?' Sparrow was shocked.

'That's what I said. Dead, drowned dead.'

'That's awful.'

Pinney sucked up some phlegm and turned his head and spat a long loop of a gob onto the muddy bank below. 'River rat down there, goo on his head. "Where'd that come from?" he says.'

That seemed to take the fix out of the atmosphere. Pinney sat down beside Sparrow and Sparrow smelled the paste the savages wore to keep off the mosquitoes and the cold.

'Autumn,' said Pinney. 'How they have the goddamn hide to call this autumn I do not know. I miss the colours, that's what I miss, the burning flame of autumn.'

'I miss them too.' Sparrow was thinking not about autumn, or colours, but about the gob of spit.

'What was all that groanin' I heard when I come along?' said Pinney.

'Just a bit of colic.'

'Warm ale and a dash of laudanum.'

'Warm ale and a dash of laudanum?'

'Don't repeat what I say.'

'I'm sorry.' Yet again he'd said sorry. He half expected Griffin Pinney to whack him, but he didn't. He continued to be helpful in the medicinal way.

'If that don't work, try three teaspoons of oil of turpentine and ground ginger.'

'Thank you.' Sparrow was so pleased that Griffin Pinney was being nice to him he forgot the problem wasn't colic.

'If we was in the bush I'd find you somethin' better but this ain't the bush, not anymore.'

Sparrow scanned the flats beyond the creek, everywhere the ponding, tree stumps like some sort of eruption on the sodden earth.

Pinney was staring at Sparrow. 'You got eyes like a owl, you know that?' he said.

'No,' said Sparrow.

'And I hear you got but one ball, that true?'

'Where'd you hear that?' asked Sparrow, but he already knew. Biddie must have told Thelma. Or she might have told Pinney herself. 'One's bigger than the other, that's all.'

'Irregularity can be a mark of distinction, like that Happ girl's birthmark. I quite like that, don't you?' Pinney waggled his tongue for Sparrow's benefit and Sparrow was sickened. To think Biddie would suffer to be covered by such a man as this; to think she would tattle to such a man about another man's imperfections.

They sat there for a while, in silence, their world hooded by a darkness speckled with stars all the way to the impenetrably solid form of the mountains far off, black as pitch.

'You understand a secret like this makes for a bond that is tight and a spirit of union that must not be broke?'

'Oh yes.'

'You will swear on thunder and lightning.'

'I do, I swear.'

'You understand prudence will facilitate its own agency and at the same time confound our enemies by means of their ignorance of our design and direction . . . them who would undo us.'

Sparrow had an idea he understood what Griffin Pinney had just said. 'Just tell me what I gotta do.'

'Get a dog, a hunting dog, that's the toll you gotta pay, that is the *sine qua non.*' Sparrow waited, hoping Pinney might translate, but he just talked on. 'You understand there can be no middle state – it's the misery of this mercantile tyranny or by God it's the other side, the sovereignty o' the commonweal, free of the brutish parties that govern us here.'

'I will have it, I'll have that weal, if I can,' said Sparrow.

There was one question that he dearly wanted to ask but he was unsure when best to do so, for the information he wanted was a sensitive matter.

Pinney seemed to know that Sparrow had a question. 'You want to arks me somethin' you can,' he said.

'Is it true there's a river, on the other side?'

'Of course there's a river, has to be, country this size don't make sense without a river over there.'

'You've seen it?'

'It is a river of the first magnitude, as predicted by no less an authority than Mr Flinders in the *Gazette*.'

'I heard about that, what he said.'

'Well there you are . . . even our overlords know it's true which is why they forever deny it.'

The birds roosting in the trees high on the ridge had all gone silent but now the cicadas filled the void, supported by the bustle of the ebb tide, their song grating on Sparrow's ear. 'What about a axe, instead of a dog?' he said.

'Old Wolgan wants a game dog, game dog's gold; we know it, they know it. Get him a game dog he'll lay palms under your feet all the way to the other side.'

'But they already got dogs, the savages.'

'They have and they're fuckin' useless. Thing is, our dogs have bequeathed something of a leisurely turn to the savages' abject plight, see. You want across you pay the toll, same as anywhere.'

'A toll?'

'Yes, a toll, a ticket, a tithe, something to trade, Marty, *are you with me here*? You got that you travel in perfect security, why, you pay the toll you could walk a lady through that country . . . long as she had a umbrella.'

Sparrow was somewhat reassured by the reference to a lady, and an umbrella. A hunting dog surrendered to old Wolgan was like a pass, a ticket of leave to go and work somewhere else, but with no ties. Bondage in all its manifest and wicked formulations left behind. This was a lovely notion and it warmed Sparrow to think on it but he worried it might be too good to be true.

'I heard it said there's a good fifty bolters out there in the fastness, stripped of all but their moulderin' shoes and some of them butchered something awful, their pizzles gone and their livers cut out.' He thought it best to say nothing of tongues.

'That's true, and you need to know it,' said Pinney. 'See, they was lone bolters, or pairs with no compact with the savages. I got a compact with old Wolgan and he is an honourable man, like his grandson young Caleb, a formidable interlocutor, so you trade fair, them savages are true to their word. In short they'd fuck their own mothers for a game dog.'

'Wonder what Mort took, for a toll. Mort and Shug.'

'Nothin', clearly they got no compact.'

'Shug's in the gaol.'

'Shug could've come with me, paid the toll he'd be there now, free as a bird.'

Sparrow looked up to the ridge where lights flickered, a dim glow in sundry windows, but the wattle and daub hovels where the felons slept cheek to jowl were black dark.

'How big is it, the river?'

'It is a river the majesty of which there is nothing to compare.'

'Lord!' said Sparrow.

The cicadas now were very loud and Sparrow's mind turned to one of the big puzzles in his life, which was how come cicadas are ever so loud all about but you never get to see a one? He had not expected Griffin Pinney to offer up any more intelligence on the other side, so he had let his mind wander into the field of natural history and was much surprised when Pinney continued.

'Marty, against the better judgement of my weary bones, and my kidneys, I will extend to you the courtesy of the most complete picture I can paint.'

'You will?'

'Think of it, you reach the final summit, having traversed and prevailed over a most forbidding wilderness and having paid your toll to old Wolgan and partook his hospitality one last time. And there it is: *the* most beautiful grassy woodlands you are ever going to see, and way below, a small village, embosomed in a grove of tall trees by a most majestic river, flowing west, west as far as you can see, and small boats gliding the channels between little islands, and women, knee deep in the shallows, casting their nets.'

'Women?'

'Olive skinned, well-favoured by nature and most pliable and yielding in all regards. Why we suffer the harpies we got here I'll never know.'

Sparrow gave out a deep sigh.

Pinney took a hold of Sparrow at the back of his neck, his finger-nails sharp in the flesh. His old dog was licking Sparrow's hand. 'Now, you're sworn, you remember that or I'll take your tongue off at the bone.'

'I know.'

Sparrow sat for a while, speechless, wondering where a man's tongue did go at the back there. It troubled him to think that Griffin Pinney might know.

The faint glow along the rim of the mountains was gone and the night sky was so full of stars there was hardly space for whatever it was the stars hung on to. Sparrow wished he could feel the brilliance of the heavens uplift him, give him true hope. But all he could feel was Griffin Pinney sitting alongside him, a man who gave off menace the way a pot gives off steam, a man who smelt like a rank carcass, a man to whom he was now bound in a bond of trust, a bond he dare not dishonour lest his throat be cut. There was, however, one compensating consideration: such a man might just get him across the mountains, safe and sound.

'What about the other side, must be savages on the other side?'

Pinney pressed hard on his forehead, like he was pressing up his thoughts. 'What these despots call *improper intercourse with the native peoples* is in my own personal eye-to-eye experience a connection rooted in free and honest exchange, whether in the mountains or on the other side. I tell you these savages practice what I call a certain nobility,' he said.

'You mean they friendly?'

'Of course they friendly, you treat 'em right they will extend to you more geniality and kindly intercourse than you'll ever get in this scabby little garrison.'

'It is that.'

'Indeed, which is why I believe you can appreciate a sphere in which a master-less man is not a put-upon vagabond but a free agent, dignified and reputable in his singularity, safe and secure in a hospitable realm. Over there we got all the comforts o' life without the harshness o' labourin' for them as we must on this side. There's no bondage over there Marty, we share the common lands and the waters and the women, and they yield up to us all we want, we men.'

'I'll steal that dog.'

'You do that and we'll be on the other side before you can say *fuck King George*.'

'I wouldn't go that far.'

'You already have Marty.'

15

At first light they readied to depart for the Branch. Cuff set a familiar tone. 'The pale light of dawn, the cool of the morning, the stillness, the quiet . . . I do believe this interlude twixt sleep and toil is magical, unless you're hung over, or tangled in some pointless reconnoitre up a damn creek,' he said.

Mackie straightened up. He looked at Cuff and almost smiled.

'You agree with me, I know it, you just won't say,' said Cuff.

Harp took the hobbles off the pony and led the way, a bladder full of bang-head strung on his shoulder.

They followed the creek to the gully that ran to the Branch, a narrow defile shaded beneath the deep green vaulting of cabbage trees and tall ferns.

Mackie carried the coil of copper piping called the worm, having put a ball through the pot and pushed it off the furnace and watched it tumble into the creek, thus visiting upon Harp an interlude of severe unhappiness.

For almost an hour they tramped through the chill sandy shallows. Harp was silent all the way, searching for the best line for the pony and brooding on the damage Mackie had done and wondering how he would ever get the apparatus up and running again without the most vital bit of the machinery, the all-important copper worm.

By the time he started to feel better the country was fast changing, as he knew it would. They came out of the gully and followed the creek onto a long stretch of cleared ground that ran to river flats and the waters of the Branch beyond. There was a cabin bathed in midmorning sun on the margin of the forested slope to the west, and there was a small peach orchard and a vegetable garden nearby. Pigs and fowls were fossicking next to a corn crib on log footings and there was a henhouse and a sizeable fold and a byre and alongside the byre there was a slab hut that looked to be derelict and beyond the hut, way beyond, they could just make out the government sloop, beached and roped to a mooring tree with Joe Franks' twelve-footer alongside, but there was no sign of Sprodd, or Joe for that matter.

'Here we are,' said Harp as he tethered the black pony.

'It's a pretty place,' said Cuff.

'Pick o' the patches.'

'Awful lonely.'

'Lonely's what we like round here.'

They saw the gangly form of Joe Franks coming up the valley to meet them, his gait most unsteady. The man called Freddie hustled along behind, an elderly composition akin to a barrel.

When he reached the incoming party Joe sat on a log, a pained look on his face. He nodded hello to Mackie and Cuff. 'That's my limit,' he said. 'A furlong and I'm done.'

'He's not that bad,' said Freddie.

'That's not like you Joe,' said Cuff.

'Well it's like me now, don't take much in the way of effort and I'm a ball of knots and spasms, only God knows why.'

Joe took note of the spiral worm in the chief constable's hand. He turned to Harp. 'Busy as ever I see.'

'You're no good to me,' said Harp.

'That makes me no worse for a neighbour.'

Mackie stepped up to Joe and shook his hand. 'You're not one for neighbours.'

'True enough, Alister, but it's good to see you.'

'And you my friend.' Mackie could not help but notice that Joe's face was fixed in a permanent squint and his eyes, what he could see of them, were awfully bloodshot. 'You and Harp make a pair,' he said.

'I doubt that, I am sworn off the grog,' said Joe.

'Since India,' said Cuff.

'One sorry lapse but otherwise yes.'

'You look most unwell, you ought see Dr Woody,' said Mackie.

'Whatever it is I know I'm riddled with it. I doubt old Woody can help.' Joe closed his eyes and worked a circular motion on his eyelids with thumb and forefinger. 'They burn something terrible. Worst is I cannot read, a hard loss of an evening. I miss my Bunyan.'

'The man's a wreck, he best come with us,' said Cuff.

'No,' said Joe.

Mackie had known Joe Franks for the better part of ten years. He was a decorated army veteran of countless engagements in India, cashiered and exiled for killing a fellow soldier in a duel. He had requested the remote location upon arrival in New South Wales and the governor granted his request, noting on the documentation that the duel was a matter of honour and not in any way criminal in the ordinary sense of the word. The chosen location was described as a fertile patch on the Branch that Catley the botanist had noted on a sketch map and dubbed *Mr Freddie Gitts residence*, unaware that the surname was Giddes, spelt with two Ds, the E silent.

Mackie recalled the occasion of Joe Franks' first appearance at the ridge. He came with the wagoner, from Parramatta. He fraternised briefly with the soldiers and got terribly drunk and took exception to a soldier whipping a stray dog, a sergeant called Reuben Peskett. The outcome was a surprise to all present that day, for Peskett had a fearsome reputation, but that counted for nothing when Joe took to him with a pair of blacksmith tongs, knocked out his front teeth and battered him senseless.

The ordeal hastened Joe's determination to get away. He bought a twelve-footer from Guthrie, the shipwright, a little boat right off the slip, and with Guthrie's help he fitted a mast and sail and took off downriver. He rowed up the Branch on a windless day, rapt in the solitude, the richness of the bottoms and the grandeur of the deep-cut sandstone country beyond.

Mackie put his hand on Joe's shoulder and bent down and looked into the man's bloodshot eyes. 'I'll talk to Dr Woody. We'll send a tonic on Guthrie's scow.'

Word of the trading scow pleased Freddie. 'Some of that candied ginger too,' he said.

'I see our sloop, I don't see Sprodd,' said Mackie.

'They gone fishin' at the traps,' said Freddie.

'They?'

'He went with Caleb,' said Joe. He stood up and steadied himself, a hand on Mackie's shoulder. He waggled his legs, first one then the other. He headed for his cabin, his gait improved by his brief repose. Mackie stepped along with him and Cuff and Harp came on behind, musing on the delights of cooked fish.

In the cabin, Joe and Mackie chose the chairs at the table and the others sat on stump stools, dipping corn biscuits into mugs of *Hai Seng* tea.

Cuff examined the books on the mantelshelf, set between two squared off bits of sandstone – Dickson's *System of Agriculture*, Fontana's *Venoms and Poisons* and several other volumes including the pocket edition of Bunyan. His mind shifted to the fishing expedition. 'Hope Dan's alright, don't want him skewered,' he said.

'He's with Caleb, he'll be fine,' said Joe.

'The gentleman savage, wrested from the wild whence he has returned!'

'What they did, they took him fresh off the tit and gave him a warm bed, taught him the Bible inside out, taught him manners too, and for that he spat in their eye,' said Freddie.

'He went back to his people, Freddie, that's what he did,' said Joe.

'We do that sometimes, we take a pretty one, a little black cherub,' said Freddie, 'but you cannot school the treachery from their black hearts.'

'That's not true,' said Joe.

The name Caleb was fabled at the river for he was old Wolgan's grandson, having spent his earliest years with the Reverend Hardwick in Parramatta. He was clutched to his mother's bosom when they shot her. The ball went through the bone in his little foot and pierced the mother's gut. She died and the soldiers took the orphaned boy and gave him to the Hardwicks to raise and they did that, the reverend and his wife. They raised him until he could run and when he could run that's what he did. He ran away and never came back.

'You've made your peace with the savages I hear,' said Mackie.

'I've made a pact.'

'What kind of a pact?' said Cuff.

'I happily surrender all the maize they want. They don't care for the wheat but they do take my piglets at a whim. They lack an appreciation of animal husbandry.'

'That don't sound like much of a pact to me.'

'It works, enough to keep us safe.'

'They won't chop off your nethers, that's what you need to know,' said Cuff.

'They have a partiality for salted goods; I intend to nurture that, the better to husband my livestock,' said Joe.

Cuff laughed. 'You give them maize *and* pork, salted?'

'I barter my tenure in the soil from some of what I raise, whether corn or stock. That's fair.' Joe looked around the table, weighing up his little audience, wondering was anything further worth saying. 'They *are* the true proprietors of the soil, have been since Genesis.'

Cuff laughed some more. 'Proprietors, a tribe o' savages!'

'They are not a tribe Thaddeus, not anymore, just a ragged remnant prone to desperate acts. I hope to soften their demise, keep my patch and my nethers.' Joe smiled that warm smile and everyone knew he meant what he said.

'For your sins?' said Cuff.

'Yes, for my sins, and more,' said Joe.

'What more?' said Mackie.

Joe came over thoughtful, like he was pondering whether or not to say whatever relevancies were as yet unsaid. 'In my regimental lodge in Calcutta we had a motto: submissive to superiors, courteous to equals, kind and condescending to inferiors.'

Cuff was first to respond. 'That fine vision might cut across class and faction but it can hardly extend to savages.'

'Why not?'

'Because I thought what you masons did was unite good men from throne to cottage, not throne to wigwam.'

Freddie buckled over with laughter, 'Wigwam, that's good.'

'I'm not inviting them to join a lodge,' said Joe, a touch of sharpness in his words.

Cuff picked the tone. 'So you was a mason?' He took a sly look at Mackie who sat, still as a stone, contemplating Joe Franks.

'All too late I was, yes. All too late did I understand we have to be free from party or religious prejudices, unaffected by rank or occupation or even by colour . . . a new sociability, worldly in its embrace, that's what drew me.'

At last Mackie spoke. 'Have you retained a connection with your lodge?'

'I doubt any connection I might assert would be acknowledged.'

'Why is that?'

'I shot our Worshipful Master in a duel,' said Joe.

'Was he a villain?' said Cuff.

'He was, yes.'

'You shoot him dead?

'I did. I put a ball through his eye.'

'Well, good for you Joe. Nobody wants a villain runnin' loose,' said Cuff.

'All I know is I get a terrible fright when they come in numbers,' said Freddie.

Warm gusts were coming through the doorway and dried out corn husks were carrying on the wind across the fallow ground to the east. Joe got himself up and went and got a clay jug and some mugs. 'Peach cyder off the second crop.'

'I will say this, Joe, you are firm planted upon the high ground of virtue,' said Cuff.

Harp was about to skol some bang-head but he paused. 'I think you're a damn fool,' he said.

Joe shook his head. 'What they won't take is the wheat, that is the blessing. A pure accident of ancestral preference. That makes for an accommodation.'

'That's no accident,' said Cuff, 'since they don't farm and they don't hardly cook. They like to pick up the ready things and walk on. I know the feeling every time I slide past a tray of toffees, which ain't often.'

Joe was silent, thoughtful. The company was waiting. Finally, he spoke. 'They do not want our ways, it is that simple, gentlemen.'

'I take my hat off to you Joe,' said Cuff.

'As do I,' said Mackie.

Joe was troubled by the compliment. He didn't want anybody's praise for what he was doing. His solution seemed to him so sensible and so completely necessary that he didn't know what else he could do to survive, given the horrible enormities practised up and down the river by both black and white in recent times. 'The maize travels and keeps. The savages' particularity suits me fine. We've always got maize; it's hardy, never fails. I grow it to share and I'm pleased to share it. I just can't see it any other way. I have what I need, they take what they need; neither party left wanting.'

'Alright, I surrender,' said Cuff. He threw his hands in the air. He liked Joe. He had no desire to step on his tail.

'Yours is a generosity over and above the terms of the governor's concession, you know that?' said Mackie.

'The concession says we must share the fruits and the plenty of the river from the Branch to the sea. For my sins I am happy to do that.'

'Crops is the fruit of your labour, Joe, it ain't the fruit o' the river. Just let them come and go, fish and hunt, nothin' more,' said Cuff.

'We might see it that way but they never will, that's the rub.'

'You let them violate the sacred principles of private property you set a dangerous precedent, that's what people will say.'

'That's what people do say,' said Freddie. 'Thyne says Joe's gunna get us all killed.'

'The true violator was the first man to fence in a piece of land or draw some imaginary line and say *this is mine* and the violators after him were the folk who liked the idea. What then? Crimes, wars, unspeakable atrocities, that's what then. Don't you tell me about private property.'

'You a Leveller or a Jacobin or just a damn silly Frenchman, which?' said Cuff.

'The fruits of the earth belong to us all, and the earth itself to nobody, least of all the miscreants on this part of the river, pardon me, Harp,' said Joe.

'That's just a load of drivel, you're talking drivel,' said Harp.

Joe was not finished: 'If we all shared the river we'd have peace, there'd be no burning, no killing, none of that; from the Branch to the mouth we're obliged to share the river, that's what the governor says.'

'Joe, you need to read the government order, it's in the *Gazette*,' said Cuff. 'The order says downriver, from the Branch farms down, we got to let them fish and trap and hunt game, farm for yams and muscles and such, come and go, la la la, *that's all*, that's the order, that's the concession. Subject to the sanctity of our crops we let them forage, that's it!' said Cuff.

'I marvel they leave the clothes on your backs!' said Harp.

'They do not trouble us,' said Joe.

'They do when they turn up out o' nowhere for breakfast. I come on with the drizzles every time,' said Freddie.

'They do us no harm is what I mean.'

'As to their vices, there's a hundred things a decent man can only hint at!'

'And here we are, you and I, entirely unmolested.'

'How often do they come?' asked Cuff.

'Old Wolgan is regular as the seasons, and he's never alone,' said Joe. 'Sometimes he tells Caleb to bid me trim his beard . . . and I do. I set about him like a damn barber. Napoleon in Egypt could not be more unlikely.'

'Napoleon was in Egypt,' said Cuff.

'That's precisely what I mean,' said Joe.

'What's he want with Egypt? They got nothin' but sand,' said Freddie.

'They got dates, they got pomegranates, they got vipers . . .' said Cuff.

'Well, if they got vipers old Wolgan be in his element I reckon,' said Freddie.

'That old warrior has a presence, I will say that,' said Mackie.

Joe poured them another measure of peach cyder. 'I think they look at me the way they look at a fruiting shrub or a perennial tuber. They know they can come and pick me any time and I'll fruit again so long as they don't chop me down or snap my taproot. So I don't worry they'll do me, not anymore; I worry about my sinews knotted up, my legs gone to custard and my tongue like a desert, and my eyes dry as a sun-struck bone, that's what I worry about.'

'What you need's a wife,' said Cuff, 'a good stout woman who likes hard work. I can see the maids lining up, fresh off the scow, keen as mustard.'

Joe bowed his head like he was embarrassed. 'Same ol' Thaddeus,' he said. 'Anyway, I'm too old.'

'Well, you know what they say about old. The older the violin the sweeter the music.'

'I ain't a violin.'

'And I ain't jokin'. You need a woman.'

'It's a turn in the road I just might take, if I can find one can read.'

'What!' said Freddie.

'Well you can't read.'

'Women don't read neither, mostly.'

'He's a eligible bachelor Freddie, you best know that,' said Cuff. He winked at Mackie. 'Fine acreage, ample surplus weather permitting, the savages eatin' out of his hand like . . . like tame birds.'

Cuff's head had a habit of wobbling like it was on a spring whenever he was teasing.

'He is not egible, and he don't need no woman,' said Freddie.

Cuff was wearing a wry smile. 'I think you should advertise, Joe. A public notice in the *Gazette*.'

'Advertise?'

'Then every lonesome woman in the colony will know you're available.'

Cuff thought for a moment or two. Then he continued, as if dictating to a notary. 'Wanted. Wife or concubine. Must be sturdy and reliable, mild temper and sobriety essential, a commanding presence behind a plough. The advertiser, *a gentleman*, is by no means desperate or embarrassed. His intentions are honourable. He seeks prudent helpmeet for connubial contentment if not happiness. A premium on wholesome character, and a nice bosom.'

'Must have reading,' said Joe.

The gathering was laughing along with Cuff. Even Mackie was sufficiently entertained to add a passage of his own: 'Accustomed to frugality and preferably with a few hundred pounds at her disposal,' he said, as if the line came to him from nature itself, like sap out of a tree.

'Just don't mention the Branch, nor the savages neither!' said Freddie, who took the laughter to mean all this wife talk was a joke, which it was.

They fell to silence, each man contemplating some thread of the conversation thus far.

'Joe, you ain't a gentleman,' said Freddie, finally.

'That's true,' said Joe, 'not sure I want to be one neither.'

'Personally I value my lowly standing,' said Cuff, 'if I was a gentleman I'd been shot long ago.'

16

The dark had set in fast when they heard the sounds of Dan Sprodd and Caleb outside, the clatter and the talk as they set the cookfire beneath the tripod.

They heard the unmistakable cadence of Caleb's English. They went out and gathered around the budding fire. 'Return of the prodigals,' said Cuff and they counted the catch.

'Got some bream and a coupl'a perch,' said Sprodd.

'Good evening to you, Mr Caleb,' said Cuff.

'A good evening, yes sir,' said Caleb.

'How is your grand-daddy, how is the old boy old Wolgan?'

'He is well, thank you.'

'That's good.'

Caleb's only garment was a pair of cotton canvas trousers, torn at the knees and threadbare at the arse and half-mast at his shins. He likely towered over the original occupant, name unknown. His torso was heavily scarred in the ritual way of the Branch mob and his shoulders were muscled in proportion to his long and lean frame and his long hair, matted like the thrums of a mop, was dressed with feathers and teeth.

Joe sat on a stump stool by the budding fire, next to Harp. He beckoned Caleb to sit. 'Big cook up?' he said.

The fire had worked up a sizzle in the heavy skillet and Joe was pushing the fish round the pan with a stick.

As Cuff sat himself down he rested a hand on Caleb's shoulder and Caleb watched the hand as he took the old constable's weight.

'What news, Dan?'

'News?'

Cuff cocked his head in Caleb's direction. 'Yes, news, worldly affairs.'

'Oh that. They don't trust the government, they say the concession is a trick.'

'It is not enforceable, and they know it,' said Joe.

Cuff was warming his hands at the fire. 'The fact is they cannot forage or fish for fear of the muskets, fear they'll get shot like ducks on a pond.'

'It's not right.'

'Just don't you tell me it's their river Joe. If I hear that again, talk of proprietors and such, I might have to emigrate, go somewhere where property's safe, back to America.'

'I think we made the concession so we ought keep to it, share the river and the fruits of the river, what say you, Caleb?'

Caleb rose slowly. He was staring into the dark in the direction of the Branch.

They heard a gravelly voice. 'Comin' in, don't shoot me.'

'That's Thyne,' said Joe, as Thyne Kunkle stepped from the shadows into the firelight.

'It's alright Caleb,' said Cuff, 'he misbehaves we'll shoot him.'

Thyne Kunkle was a former soldier, heavy-set, with the calcified bearing of an old blacksmith. His musket was on his shoulder, a fist wrapped around the lock plate. The firelight sparkled on the silver trimmings on the walnut stock.

Kunkle studied Caleb. 'You lot sup with the devil you better have a long spoon.'

'The devil you say!' said Cuff.

'As black within as without for God's light does not shine within them.'

'I don't see much of a glow comin' out o' you Thyne.'

'You be careful Thaddeus.'

'Careful makes me torpid, I don't do careful.' Cuff beckoned

Kunkle into the circle. 'Why don't you sit and talk, never know what we might reconcile, the family o' man gathered about the fire in the forest primeval.'

'No man's safe with them on the river.'

'*They* ain't on the river; you and the likes of you, you've drove 'em off.'

'We'll do more'n that,' said Thyne. He sat the butt of the flint-lock on a stump stool and took the barrel in his fist. He spied Harp's bladder. 'That bang-head?'

'You want some?'

'Is the Pope a heretic in the devil's pay?' Harp gave up the bladder and Thyne sat himself down on the stump stool and took a prolonged draught. 'Right now I could eat the arse out of a camel through the bottom of a cane chair.'

'You can have some fish,' said Joe.

'That's a beautiful gun, Thyne, where'd you find that?' said Cuff.

Thyne put down the bladder and wiped his chin. 'It's a Swedish flintlock and I bought it 'cause I need it,' he said, staring at Caleb.

'Here we go again,' said Cuff.

Caleb was fixed staring at the fire, attentive to every word.

Sprodd leaned forward in a most earnest fashion, intent upon fur-ther discussion of Joe's stratagems. 'Joe says there's a better way,' he said.

'I think he's probably right,' said Cuff, intent upon argument.

Thyne turned his head and spat into the dirt. 'Joe's gunna wake up with a small axe in his skull. Until then he's a danger to us all.'

'Come on now Thyne, let's break some bread here,' said Cuff.

Thyne made ready to depart. 'I got family, no time to fraternise with savages.'

Cuff got to his feet. 'We'll miss the delicate touch you lend to the conversation. By the way, how's the missus, that little one still on the tit I fancy?'

Cuff could see he'd achieved what he wanted to achieve.

'You keep away from my missus,' said Thyne. 'And you come for them stooks,' he said to Joe.

'I will, soon as I can,' said Joe.

Kunkle turned and walked off into the dark, the little company watching. Cuff spat in his pipe and thumbed it out. He pushed the pipe in his vest pocket, adjacent to his spoon. 'And good riddance to that,' he said.

They were peeling the cooked flesh off the fish and bouncing it in their palms and blowing on it and then taking it on their tongues.

'I suppose you want the losses for the assess?' said Joe.

'I do,' said Mackie.

'Some damage to the corn. Most of it we got in, say ten bushels with some allowance for moisture.'

'Wheat?'

'I'll sow two acres, one for the store; say twenty bushels. The wheat stack, that's gone. Thyne snared that downriver.'

'Wants one part in five for salvage. The man's a brigand!' said Freddie.

'I have to be thankful we have an arrangement,' said Joe.

'Doesn't seem fair,' said Cuff, 'the deluge serving up grain to venomous loafers like Mr Kunkle. Thieves' market on every damn reach.'

'You did not have that wheat stack on the bottoms, surely?' said Mackie.

'Alister, that flood swallowed a lot more than the bottoms, wheat stack and all,' said Joe.

'If it come out o' that gorge, woe betide all downriver!' said Cuff.

'I never seen anything like it, 'twas biblical,' said Joe.

17

Sparrow had several times started for Prominence and then changed his mind about the good sense of attending another execution. Finally, he decided he must go. Better to be seen, absorbing the moral drama for the benefit of his character, for soon enough he would be gone and his absence noticed.

He was curious, too, about how Shug might die. In that regard no two executions were ever the same. A man might meet his death with contrition, with prayers and torrents of tears, perhaps sing a psalm and declare the heinous nature of his crime and the great folly of its commission. Or he might have none of that. He might damn his betters with vile oaths and curses, nothing but insolence and execrations proceeding from his mouth, a degree of boldness that might well shock all present. Contrition or defiance, which would it be from Shug? Sparrow reckoned it would probably be contrition, but who could know what kind of misery or mastery a man could summon on the brink of death?

What the captain might say about the bolters, the fastness and the far beyond was yet another reason for his presence. Captain Henry Kettle would surely speak of the horrors awaiting any man who took off, for the entire colony was imperilled if the trickle became a flood. So Sparrow was eager to hear Kettle's every word. He was eager for any little slip of the tongue, any formulation that might suggest or confirm the existence of a river and a village and a people who lived free, unencumbered and un-put-upon, on the other side of the mountains.

A menace of black cloud hovered in the north-west and distant thunder carried to the the ridge as the soldiers fell in, five in a row, two rows deep in front of the barracks, and Sergeant Peskett thumbed his ill-fitting denture into position and called the muster to order, the last vestiges of the bivouac jostling with incoming settlers and their bonded felons, civil department men, concubines, and others who were victualled on the store and thus compelled by law to be present.

Shug, in double irons, was dressed in the ritual white nightshirt of the condemned and flanked by the Reverend Warrington Abbott and Captain Kettle, his wolfhound bitch at his heel. The head of the stolen pony hung from Shug's neck, bloodied, blank-eyed like some ludicrous talisman, the prisoner hunched over with the weight of it.

Kettle stepped onto a pedestal with the assistance of his walking stick. The wolfhound dropped down beside him, her long forelegs folded under her chest. Peskett stepped away. The Reverend Abbott looked on, vast in his preaching robes, his eyes locked upon the prisoner, searching for signs of his temper.

Kettle rapped the pedestal with his stick and embarked upon his address as the assemblage fell quiet: 'You are gathered here to consider the fate of the prisoner Shug McCafferty, a most bigoted fugitive, plucked by mere happenstance from the brink of annihilation. Sunk to ruin after a mere month on the maraud, having barely escaped a most brutal assault by the savages, his perseverance shattered and his restless disposition perfectly corrected into submission. You must all consider most solemnly this fatal example, a wretched soul tragically deluded by an absurd falsehood; by the notion that a settlement of some kind prevails beyond the mountains. Prisoner McCafferty and select others once among you have chosen to wantonly abandon their security, to wander through country known to be impassable, to endure the terrors of fatigue and famine and finally to curse the propagators of these preposterous conjurings, to repent too late of their gullibility and, exhausted, perish miserably . . . death by starvation or death at the hands of the savages. To perish in that infinite waste, alone, without a friend, no loved ones to pour the balm of Christian consolation upon their tortured bosom; no prospect of a respectable interment, their remains picked over, at leisure, by sated carrion.'

From the store porch Sparrow had a good enough view. He could hear most of what was said, words crafted to put the frighteners into any man or woman who contemplated a bolt and a life on the other side. He could also hear the rattle of the cart coming up the track and the voice of Hat Thistlewaite, the executioner, shouting his oaths at the ox in the traces.

Shug was silent all the while, his eyes downcast. When Kettle's cautionary tale was complete Shug lifted his head and looked about.

He stared at the mustered assemblage on the square and others on the fringing porches. On the tavern porch he saw Fish, Dr Woody and his boy Jug. On the store porch he saw the store hands, the garrison butcher, a few old squaddies and the expiree Marty Sparrow, the very same who Mort said was weak as a puddle. But Shug did not think Sparrow was weak. At that moment, he envied him, for Sparrow had done his time, got his patch and had the good sense to say no to Mort Craggs. He reckoned Sparrow would have to be happy as a pig in muck right now, watching on, thankful for that good sense, thankful he was not tempted by Mort's overtures, thankful he had not succumbed like a damn fool.

Mort believed, firmly, that Sparrow did not have the mettle and Shug had thought that too, but not now. Now, on the brink, he thought Sparrow's caution was entirely prudent.

Abbott bent forward and whispered in Shug's ear. 'Speak as directed, and speak up.'

'There's nuttin' out there,' said Shug, 'nuttin' but waste. There's no crossin' dem woods, for every peak you gain you gain for naught save the sight o' more. More o' the same like. Bit and stung I was, near to madness, and wet through like, and the nights the worst of it, shapes full o' menace and sounds . . . I heard a lion out there I'll swear to that . . . an' I had a rat the size of a cat lickin' at the wounds on me feet and I'm tellin' yez all there's no end to them mountains and there's no end to the misery and I can but hope me sufferin' will but excite commiseration in the mind o' humanity, and the mind of me betters in whose hands I place me life, hopin' like, for some sort o' dispensation.'

Kettle was unmoved. 'The prisoner is the beneficiary of a short shrift and a speedy doom,' he said, 'and he may thank God in his generosity for that small mercy for, in the course of his flight, the prisoner was party to murder, abduction and rapine.'

'That wasn't me,' said Shug, but his voice had sunk to a whisper.

Sparrow watched as the cart circled around and came to a halt. Hat Thistlewaite folded down the weathered panel at the rear, revealing the foot end of the coffin. 'You have to sit up there,' said Hat.

'I sit on me own coffin?' said Shug.

'You do, yes, you know that.'

Sparrow was readying to follow the cart along with everyone else when he saw Betty Pepper and Biddie Happ step from the switchback path and cross to the vicinity of the pillory and the gibbet. The sighting made him entirely uncomfortable. He did not want to see Biddie. Nor did he want to be seen by Biddie. The sight of Biddie made him mad, she who had tattled to Griffin Pinney about his private parts, tattle that was not even true. He reckoned he might whack her, given the chance. He took to a stump stool at the back of the porch, pondered whether or not to make for his patch. He stood again, went up on his toes so he might catch a glimpse of her from his obscure vantage. How could anyone not notice that red hair, that beautiful sweep of thick red hair, that shy sweep across her eye and her cheek? He felt his legs wobble so he sat down again, for it did him no good to stare at Biddie Happ. Her shy beauty turned his resolve to mush and Sparrow well knew this was no time to have his resolve go to mush.

At that moment it occurred to Sparrow he didn't really want to see Shug's pitiful exit. He'd seen such things before, seen them cry, seen them rage. He made ready to go. He snuck away as the cart rattled off the square with Shug seated on his coffin, the official party a step behind, then Peskett, then the mustered assemblage, the miscellaneous comers and goers, the mockers and the mourners and the flanking soldiers.

———

At the gibbet the cart wheeled about and Hat Thistlewaite backed up the ox, tapping the animal's shoulder with the butt end of his long whip, until the tray was correctly positioned beneath the noose. Then he climbed onto the tray and lifted the prisoner to his feet and Shug was made to stand beside the executioner, the condemned man still freighted with the pony's head.

Shug could see the top of tall trees on the river's turn into Argyle Reach. The storm had raced north. The sun now hazed through thin cloud, the river dappled in the light, the current rippling the reflected world. He heard the sweet sounds of the morning birds all about. He searched the crowd for Sparrow whose presence, he knew, would fill him with rage, rage at his own fool self. But he could not see Sparrow.

Abbott patted down his velvet lapels and interlaced his fingers in ritual pose and took charge as the crowd fell silent. 'It hath pleased Almighty God to bring the marauder and bolter Shug McCafferty under the sentence and condemnation of the law. He is shortly to suffer death in such a manner that others may be forewarned. A no less dismal catastrophe can be expected than an ignominious and untimely end and it is much to be desired that his atonement may deter others from impulsive acts that cannot fail to plunge them into the horrors of the wilderness or the torments of the savages or the terror of divine judgement through the machinery of British law.'

Shug spoke softly to Hat, 'If I'm chokin', you give me a good hard tug.'

'That is the prerogative of friends or family,' whispered Hat.

'I got neither,' said Shug.

'I'll do it then,' said Hat and he put a hand on the small of Shug's back and Shug felt the hand, a gentle hand. 'I fear I'll fill my pants,' he said, but Hat seemed not to hear him.

A foot soldier took up the long whip, waiting for the nod, ready to urge the ox forward.

Shug searched the crowd some more, still looking for Sparrow. He wondered if he'd come along to see the finish. Come along to gloat at the gulled fool. He reckoned Sparrow must be somewhere, laughing. The crowd clapped. Some shouted words of encouragement, others shouted insults, and Shug began to pray, his fingers locked together on the pony's muzzle.

Abbott shushed them. He led the gathering in the Lord's Prayer and when they finished Hat tightened the noose at the back of Shug's head and he took the double irons off the poor man's legs and the crowd stood silent waiting for the ritual words of contrition from the prisoner, the assurance that he would submit himself humbly and with Christian resignation to the final judgement. But there were no words. Shug was so much overcome by the dreadful pause that his composure forsook him. He jumped into the arms of death causing the crowd ahead of him to shrink back and fall about, one upon another, the solemnity ruined, the horrible moment transformed into a scene something comic.

They heard Shug's neck crack and his legs bang on the tray and they saw the body convulse. Hat leapt to the ground, ready to tug at Shug's legs if he had to. But there was no need. Shug was dead and the convulsions ceased and the body freighted with the pony's head turned slowly on the taut rope, first one way and then the other, the poor man's neck stretched to extremity.

18

Mackie and company were two hard days getting back to Prominence. On the second day, late in the afternoon, the tide was against them and then the wind swung contrary to their needs and a great deal of unhappy rowing was required to complete the journey, with the corn biscuits gone and the empty demijohn cosied in the prow to mock their thirst.

The dusk was fast yielding to dark as the sloop slid onto the mud beside heaps of salvaged timber. A fatigue party cleaning the mess kettles watched them shuffle off the duckboards and some of the cottagers on the terrace came out of their damp domiciles and watched as the boatmen took to the switchback path, Mackie followed by Harp and Sprodd, and Cuff at the rear.

When Bet Pepper stepped onto her porch Cuff could not resist: 'I'm back, rejoice.'

'Huzzah,' said Bet, her fists planted on her hips.

They saw a light in the doctor's window as they neared the top of the path but they did not stop for they saw the pillory and the gibbet beyond and they were drawn to it, the sight of Shug, his neck horribly stretched, like the body might come away at any moment.

'That should be Mortimer Craggs hangin' there, not that poor pilgarlic,' said Cuff.

'He knew the price you pay,' said Mackie.

Cuff clucked his tongue and shook his head. 'As ever, quick to chide and slow to bless.'

'I feel sorry for the pony,' said Sprodd.

'They could have brung in the ears, just the ears,' said Cuff.

'The ears could be any grey pony,' said Mackie.

'We are not exactly swimmin' in grey ponies here at the river, Alister,' said Cuff.

'As to the eyes, wherever I move they seem to follow me,' said Sprodd.

They crossed the square and set their loads on the tavern porch in the dim light of a swing lamp hooked on a shingle bearing the full title of Mackie's establishment: The Convivial Hive.

Mackie charged the custody of the copper worm to Dan Sprodd and went inside. He took Harp with him for the old man was entirely worn out. A part of him wished he'd left Harp behind but he couldn't do that, and now he hoped Dr Woody in his capacity as magistrate would not put Harp on the shovel.

Sam Rattle was seated in the barber's chair opposite the stairs. He was a he-oak of a man, big in all departments. 'I've torn something,' he said, pressing at his groin, poking in the vicinity of his package.

A lantern hung from a cross beam and a slush lamp sat on a sconce on the rear wall, by the corridor to the lodgings, close to where Sam was resting. In another corner men played at dice in the light of a single tallow candle set in its own wax and further along there were men huddled around an upright hogshead, drinking quietly in their own gloom. The drudge they called Fish was dozing in a chair beneath the stairs, shrouded in the emanations from a smoke pot, like some shabby apparition shaping from another world.

'Can you work?' said Mackie.

'I suppose,' said Sam.

'And the trade?'

Sam looked about. 'Thirsty enough,' he said. 'Reckon I dragged that damn yawl up one muddy bank too many.'

Sam had gone out with Dr Woody's crew in the midst of the flood and they had rowed hard, lifting stranded souls out of lofts and tree-tops and, coming in, time and again, heaving that boat across the sucking mud. Sam knew his pickle traced back to some moment in all that exertion, though which moment he wasn't sure. The pain had come on slowly the next day when he was quite recovered in every other facet. 'Got to get me a truss,' he said.

He stood and fixed himself down below with a poke and a push and he shuffled to the counter, the movement plainly uncomfortable.

The shuffling sound woke Fish. 'You're back,' he said, leaping to his feet and slamming his skull into the underside of the stairs. He fell into the chair grimacing and feeling at his head and looking at his hand, searching for blood. 'I'm alright,' he said.

Sam beckoned Mackie close. 'Some of this trade, their wheat's in the ooze or half way to Santiago, the collateral's mostly rubbish.'

'Barter what we can use and be generous to the traffic. A premium on nails,' said Mackie.

'We short on nails?'

'We're always short on nails.'

Sam nodded solemnly, as if he'd just made a pact to restore goodness to the world.

Harp had followed the conversation with some care, hoping it would turn to matters relating to his immediate sustenance and comfort. The light from the lantern favoured a tuppence-coloured lithograph on the wall behind the counter – *A Splendid View of the Cheviot Hills*. 'You from there?' he said to Mackie. He was pointing more or less at the picture but he seemed to be staring at the timbers above it.

'Near there. Yetholm,' said Mackie.

'Pretty river.'

'Yes.'

'What you call that river?'

'Bowmont.'

'Shame you're not still there.'

'Shame is a hard bed for a loafer.'

'I ain't no loafer.'

Mackie felt the little needle pricks of pity and regret probing his flesh, prompted as much by the memory of the Bowmont river as by Harp's sad mien.

Harp pulled at the skin on his throat. 'I could do with a drink, right now I'll swallow anything won't blind me or kill me or make me bleat like a goat.'

Mackie nodded and Sam poured and Harp gulped down a tot of rhum. He bleated like a goat.

'You saw Shug?' said Sam.

'We did,' said Mackie.

'Who ever heard of a man hung with his horse?'

'It wasn't his horse.'

19

Cuff and Sprodd had lingered outside, sprawled on the tavern porch with their haversacks and their muskets and the empty demijohn. Sprodd had the salvaged harness in his lap and the copper worm on the porch boards by his side. He alone was properly seated. He had commandeered Cuff's rocking chair, so Cuff sat on the step, watching the comers and goers on the square.

Fish brought them some grog on a tray. Upon his head was an unfamiliar hat.

'That's a strange hat, Fish. Looks like a chamber pot,' said Sprodd.

'It's mine, I found it, I claim salvage.'

'So do I,' said Dan, pointing to the harness.

'You want to hear about Shug?' said Fish.

'We know he's dead, we seen him.'

'What about Shug?' said Cuff.

'Peskett snaffled him.'

'Is it a good story?' said Sprodd.

'Oh yes.'

People hardly ever listened to him so Fish was more than pleased to recount what he'd seen and heard: the bolter Shug McCafferty had been saved by Caleb somewhere in the fastness, then delivered up to Sergeant Peskett somewhere in the foothills, and Peskett brought him in, and Shug was made to carry the stolen pony's head all the way because Peskett said the ears would prove nothing, the ears of that particular pony being quite nondescript.

There was more to tell but the constables had fastened onto a detail that required urgent consideration. Cuff scratched at his forehead. 'To think that Caleb never said a word. Ate with us and not a word.'

'There's no knowing the depths of their cunning and deceit,' said Fish, parroting a familiar line, variations on which appeared regularly in the *Gazette*.

'The mystery is why,' said Sprodd.

'Because no one asked him, that's why, a still tongue in a wise mouth. On reflection I admire that young man's restraint,' said Cuff.

'Poor old Shug,' said Fish.

'No mercy for Shug!' said Cuff. 'That crazy notion of a haven, that takes hold we're all in a pickle.'

'Where do they go, that's what I want to know,' said Sprodd.

'They don't go nowhere. There's nowhere to go, there's nothin' west of here less you're a bird. That wild country might go on for a thousand miles.'

'You don't know that.'

'I know I don't know, nobody knows, that's the point,' said Cuff. He was tired, he was heartily sick of the silliness and determined to put an end to it. 'I'll tell you what happens when bolters head west never to be seen again, the likes of Jephthah Big, Tinkerton, Turley Potter, Mary Mingay, them and more – first they get lost in them mountains, then they get hungry, then their feet blister up and bleed, then they get bit by leeches, mosquitoes, damn ticks, you name it. Then they get real sad, then they get tired and giddy, then they pass out, then they get skewered and that's if they don't get bit by a snake. We got a good two dozen unaccounted for and I'll tell you boys, they're all some- where in the fastness, rot in their bones, their flesh picked clean.' Cuff waved a hand westward.

Sprodd thought he might have a trump card. 'Mr Flinders says there's a big river over there, and quite possibly a settlement.'

Cuff stared at his boots and shook his head. 'To the best of my knowledge, Mr Flinders is a master mariner who's never put a toe west of Parramatta, where he's supped with the governor in considerable comfort, played some whist, sipped on Andalusian sherry, slept in a nice soft bed, then took a carriage back to Sydney with a military escort.'

'Yeah but he sailed the whole continent, he should know. Says there's a river over there, a river of the first magnitude, *has to be*, he says.'

'He's a able navigator but he's not immune to a passionate lapse in reasoning now and then, like some I know,' said Cuff, his head waggling like it was set on an old spring.

'Well Mort and Shug bolted and they took the girl, Dot, and Gordy's pony.'

'So?'

'Them Cape ponies, they're like goats,' said Sprodd.

Cuff had to intervene. 'Dan, Shug's dead, the pony's dead, and who knows what's happened to Mort and that poor girl he took.'

'They might be skewered?' said Fish.

Cuff thought there was a good chance Fish was right. If the country didn't get the runaways the savages would. He and Mackie had chased enough bolters to know something of the wilderness – a vast expanse of ravines and gullies, defiles cut through by rivers and creeks, the severe slopes heavily forested, thick and dark, bottomed with rotting flood-wrack knee deep in parts and topped mostly with sandstone ridges. Rifts a thousand feet deep, and a hundred foot and more of sheer stone at the ridgeline, cracked and crenelled like crude fortifications, conforming to no pattern and dooming puny white men to confusion, exhaustion and defeat.

'I don't know why we chase the bolters,' said Cuff, 'either they disappear forever or they come back crawling, mostly.'

'Not lately, that's my point,' said Sprodd, 'they don't come back no more, not a one of a dozen last year.'

'They don't come back because they're dead,' said Cuff. He had a sneaking feeling there could be some truth in this wild notion of a sanctuary – all the more reason to dismiss it emphatically. If it took hold there'd be no staunching the bleed. That was Mackie's point entirely and he had to agree.

They sat quietly for a while, contemplating the mystery of Caleb's silence and watching the activity on the square, the last of the refugees, the laggards, settling for the night, the poultry crated and the dogs fixed to tether weights, lamplight shadows on calico and canvas, a double guard on the store and the granary, the butcher at the mess door, a pair of fowls in his fist, bled and plucked.

'A prodigious concourse in the esplanade,' said Cuff.

'Ain't it more a *cul-de-sac*?' said Sprodd.

'You're out of your depth, Dan. See, a *cul-de-sac* is a refined thing, cobbled and fringed, you cannot have a *cul-de-sac* where there's nothin' but dust or mud. You cannot have a *cul-de-sac* in a wilderness. That's a *non sequitur*, like a pig in a palace or a bull in a *boudoir*.'

'What?'

'See, the bottoms is nothin' but a bog and this here, this is a spongy scab on a prominence, framed for the most part by hasty constructions and poor excuses for civic endeavour. It's a muck heap goin' nowhere.'

'You never said that down the river, downriver you said it was Arcadia.'

'Down river, like here, I have but one purpose in life and that is to leave you all the more nimbleminded for having engaged with me in the *conversazione*,' said Cuff.

'But you said Arcadia.'

'Well what do you want, you want a billet in some fever ridden garrison in Africa?'

'Nooo.'

'Alright then, I rest my case.'

Mackie was standing in the doorway, listening. He would never admit it, hardly even to himself, but he wished he could hold court like Cuff. He wished he could enjoy people, life, the sun, the moon, the stars, a pretty flower, a cup of warm milk, a conversation with a woman, the way that Cuff did. But there was something about contentment that offended him mightily, so much so that it brought disgust, like vomit, into the back of his mouth. 'It is my firm belief, Thaddeus, that you could talk a fish up a tree,' he said.

'If I could find a fish willing to listen I'd do my best,' said Cuff. 'Thing is, Alister, they're stuck in their ways, the fish, like someone I know! You hear about Caleb?'

'Yes.'

'He never said a word about Shug.'

'There's no telling what Caleb makes of us, save we are riven and vengeful among ourselves. I expect his caution curbed his tongue,' said Mackie.

'We agree!' said Cuff, like it was a miracle.

Fish was back. 'I heard he put a balm on Shug's feet and then some rags and then Shug could walk, and he cut him a stick too.'

'What else you hear?' said Sprodd.

'Well, Redenbach was with Peskett and he says Peskett shackled Shug and tied him to a tree, then they went with Caleb and they found the dead pony and the sergeant chopped off the head with a small axe and Caleb went on his way, took a big cut off the rump.'

Mackie took note of the copper worm on the porch boards, safe beside Sprodd. 'Take that to Hat, he's to lock it up and I'll have a docket,' he said.

Sprodd raised himself with some difficulty and took hold of the worm. 'What about Mort?' he said.

'I heard Mort got a compass,' said Fish.

'Big deal,' said Cuff.

Mackie went to the lantern and turned it down to a flicker.

From the barracks windows came a tune, played on a fiddle. Cuff hummed along; then he began to sing:

A master of music
She came with intent
To give me a lesson
On my instrument
I thanked her for nothing
And bid her be gone
For my little fiddle
Must not be played on

The constables clapped and Fish said 'What's that one called?' and Cuff said he had no idea.

Mackie couldn't help himself: 'You've an acute recall for drivel.'

'I see no harm in banter or merriment. You ain't a painted vase, Alister, won't crack your face if you smile.'

20

Biddie Happ unbuttoned her chemise at the shoulder and dropped it to the floor and stood there, naked, watching him undress. 'Well?' she said.

'Well?' said Sparrow.

'What's your fancy?'

'I like to see your face, you have a pretty face.'

Biddie stared at him like he was a fool.

She sat on the edge of the bed with his pizzle in her hand, turning it this way and that, looking for what she called a *venereal distemper*, which Sparrow took to mean sores. She said, 'I find the slightest abrasion I'll nail this thing to a bedpost,' and he laughed but she did not.

Then she lay on the bed, face up, and she spread her legs for him and as ever Sparrow was dumbstruck by the strangeness of her beauty for it was hardly orthodox, that much he did know.

Biddie had a lovely head of thick red hair and quite good teeth, alabaster white skin with a faint speckling of freckles and a lusty pink flush in her cheeks. She had small, floppy breasts and nipples like tiny pink buttons and from there down it was like she was another woman, her stomach heavily wrinkled and her hips ample like the base of a pear, and a muff so mature and so thickly matted as to hide every detail.

'Come on then, get aboard,' she said. She didn't much like Sparrow standing there looking at her. She smoothed the wash of hair that hid the birthmark. She had pale brown eyes, the colour of weak tea and every time she blinked Sparrow saw how the birthmark carried onto that one eyelid.

First time he was with her he almost said 'you got a purple eyelid' but he didn't, he checked himself, luckily. That was one time he didn't say the wrong thing and he was proud of it. He committed that visitation to memory for guidance in the future, firmly believing, at that point in time, that a better future might be within reach.

Sparrow wished his thoughts still but his thoughts would not be still, like snakes in a bag. Eels in a bucket. Biddie was not pleased. She sat up. She wacked his pizzle with the back of her hand. 'Come on, get your wick in and get done,' she said softly.

'Why do you call it a wick?'

'The fuel rises to the flame. I'm the flame, I get you done.'

She did that more than she knew. Many a time thoughts of Biddie had got him done on his own.

But this time, the last time ever, Sparrow did not want to get done, not in a hurry. He wanted to savour Biddie Happ. He wanted the doing done slow. He covered her and fumbled about and got himself underway.

Biddie turned her head and closed her eyes and patted at the hair that concealed the birthmark.

Sparrow moved her hand away and slid his fingers into that lush hair and pushed it back and he began to kiss the birthmark on Biddie Happ's forehead. He reckoned Biddie would know for sure that he loved her if he kissed her birthmark and, if she knew he loved her, well then she might love him back and if she loved him back his life would surely be transformed in ways he could hardly imagine. He could work his patch, harvest a good crop of wheat, get credit at the store, pay his debts and never have to risk the savages.

'Don't do that,' she said, but Sparrow did not stop. 'Don't you kiss me there,' she said, but Sparrow kept on. He began to kiss her eyelid, the purple one. 'Don't do that,' she said again and she punched him in the head with a closed fist, knuckles, and set her hair back to the way she liked it.

Sparrow was shocked. 'I'm sorry,' he said.

'I don't want you to kiss me there, not there . . . not anywhere.'

Sparrow wondered if she let Reuben Peskett kiss her there, or somewhere, or anywhere. He daren't ask, lest she hit him again. The desire had departed his nethers entirely. He was limp as old rope.

Biddie could sense that. She worried she might have lost a customer. 'Come on now,' she said with a voice sweet as syrup, 'you ratchet up that little cannon o' yours and fire your best shot.'

But it was too late. She'd taken the starch right out of him.

That seemed to offend her too, which only made him unhappier. She was never going to come and live with him on his patch. He was certain she would go off with Reuben Peskett, who'd wallop her as ready as kiss her. Certain, too, that he'd made the best decision when he committed himself to Griffin Pinney. Better to go with Griffin than with Mort. Mort's companion was dead and Mort might be dead too, whereas Griffin surely knew the way, and Griffin had a compact with the savages.

'You shouldn't try to be so nice,' said Biddie. That puzzled Sparrow severely but something inside him prevented further inquiry into the mystery of niceness being so unwelcome in the vicinity of Biddie Happ.

'Seems I've pricked your bubble. You might need a splint for that.' She flicked her fingers in the vicinity of his pizzle and she gave him a big smile, hoping to restore the occasion to its purpose.

But it was too late. He tried to focus on his nethers. He tried to think it up. That wasn't going to work and he knew it. 'I'm going now,' he said. He was thinking there might be some advantage in going at that moment. Biddie might reflect on her hard words and the fact that she punched him in the head. She might regret both words and punch. She might begin to understand there was nothing wrong with nice, that nice was a lot better than a black eye or a crooked nose or a fat lip.

'Come back soon,' she said, and she patted him on the arse, this time through his britches. Her voice was tender and this time Sparrow was sure he heard something special in her words. Perhaps he might come back one more time.

Outside he found Bet Pepper on the porch, settled in her chair. 'She's going to concubine with Peskett, I just know it,' said Sparrow.

'Sit yourself down and stop fixin' on your own damn misery. I can tell you about misery if you really want to fix on misery, put you in the shade,' said Bet.

Sparrow sat on a stump stool by the door. The two of them were silent for a little while, after which Bet heaved quite a sigh and scratched at her forehead like she was scratching up a pearl of wisdom. 'Well,' she said, 'misery shared is misery tempered I suppose, you best get it out and I don't mean your pizzle.'

There was such a tired *I've heard it all before* ring to Bet's words that Sparrow felt somewhat unmanned. He felt his head heat up and his cheeks redden. He did not reply.

They could hear Biddie rummaging within.

'She's not my chattel, Marty. She may concubine with whom she pleases if she's fool enough,' said Bet, finally.

'I know.'

'It happens.'

Bet grunted as she shifted in her chair and glanced again at Sparrow's strange eyes, those yellowy whites, and the faint pocking on the skin all about his face. She'd once asked him if it was the small pox and he said no and offered nothing more, so it was still a condition without a name.

She saw a small boat sail into view, a lateen-rigged dhow making its way upriver with a fluky nor' easter in the sail.

On the perimeter of her vision Sparrow was something akin to a beetle. His sadness was the pathetic kind she had seen in many a smitten man. She shaped her hands around her eyes, the better to watch the dhow. 'Marty, you fix on your own misery, what you gunna be?'

'Miserable I suppose,' he said.

Bet smacked her hands together. '*Quod erat demonstrandum.*'

Sparrow did not care to know what that meant. His thoughts were all ajumble, flitting from one thing to another, from birthmark to wick to flame, from worm to axe to dog to gaolhouse to gibbet to the poor hens, to the fastness and the village embosomed on the other side. To the women, dancing, and so on.

He sat there in a state of considerable bewilderment, his pictorial mind in a whirl.

He wished he hadn't kissed Biddie on her birthmark. Somehow he should have found the enthusiasm to have another go in a somewhat more orthodox fashion. He wished he'd not made her angry, his own, lovelorn behaviour driving her into the arms of that damned old squaddie.

———

The helmsman on the dhow wore a dark blue knit cap, tight fitted on the brow but loose on top. 'That's Rupert Chaseling,' said Bet. She studied the rigging. 'That sail's in bad tack.'

Chaseling was shouting at them as the dhow grounded by the duckboards at the foot of the switchback path. 'I got Thyne here, butchered,' he yelled.

Bet and Sparrow got to their feet. What appeared to be a body lay along the line of the keel, wrapped tight in blood-stained hessian.

Chaseling slumped onto the stern board and put his head in his hands, his fingertips on the fringe of the knit cap. He had a wad of wet cloth in one hand. He trailed it in the river and then he bunched it up, squeezing, and held it to his nose.

Bet and Sparrow hurried down the path to the dhow.

'I must o' tacked a thousand times,' said Chaseling, pulling at his chin plait.

Sparrow wondered why an Englishman would choose to wear his chin like a Chinaman but now was not the right time to ask. 'Thyne?' he said.

'Thyne, yes, violated, massacred, done to death.' Chaseling put the wet wad to his bleeding nose.

Sparrow stepped into the shallows and gripped the gunnel. He leant into the boat, close to the shape in the hessian. He thought he might faint if it moved. 'Massacred?'

'Go get the captain,' said Chaseling, but Sparrow was not about to do that, nor Bet.

The two men took hold of the corpse and they carried the lumpy thing up the path to Dr Woody's cottage. The doctor's horse and gig were there, his boy Jug fixing the tether weight.

The doctor emerged as Henry Kettle arrived followed by Mackie and others drawn by the swift circulation of the news.

———

Inside there was hardly room to move. Someone bumped the sideboard and the specimen jars shuddered and clattered and the slender bookshelf swayed.

They laid the shrouded corpse on Dr Woody's surgical bench.

Woody was struggling with the knots. Reuben Peskett got them undone and folded back the canvas from head to toe.

'Jesus wept,' said Kettle.

Thyne Kunkle was black and blue from the blows of the savages' waddies. His scalp was cracked open, his battered face was covered in dried blood, and there was a brutal wound in the vicinity of his private parts, the irregular work of a small axe.

'I thought them finished,' said Woody.

'Not quite,' said Mackie.

'I brung him as I found him, for all to see the barbarous inhumanity,' said Chaseling.

'They do not forget,' said Mackie. The shock had passed and he was looking carefully at the axe wound in Thyne's groin.

'You would apologise for this monstrous savagery?' said Kettle.

'I would say vengeance, like thirst, is common to us all.'

The gathering understood the allusion to a most infamous episode when Kunkle had kept a black girl chained to a hollow tree on the lower Branch, for the occasional gratification of a sensuality most brutal and unmanly.

'The honour of women has loosed the depravity of many a Briton,' said Woody.

'What do savages know of honour?' said Kettle.

'No less than Kunkle.' The doctor pressed his glasses up the bridge of his nose and held up a magnifying glass and peered into the cavity in Kunkle's skull.

'You may depend, this will not pass with impunity,' said Kettle.

Dr Woody ceased his examination of the brain matter and stood straight as he could. His back hurt. He shifted his weight, a hand on Sparrow's shoulder. He saw his own boy, Jug, at the window, peering in.

'I swear you'd pat a mangy dog,' said Kettle.

Woody was weighing whether or not to pursue his difference with Kettle on the matter of the savages. He felt inclined to persist. 'Why did they not kill Shug, you tell me that?'

'How in God's name would I know?'

'Shug never done them harm, that's why. I dare say their own sense of honour has an element of discrimination.'

'They did not kill Shug because Caleb was there, that's the truth of it. That's the one and only reason, which makes you, sir, the embodiment of a most foolish liberality.'

'Enough, gentlemen,' said Mackie.

'No damn expiree tells me enough. I'll say when enough is enough,' said Kettle.

Woody stepped between his friend and the captain. 'We have a common cause here, let's remember that,' he said, but Kettle was not inclined to be mollified.

'I do not approve of former felons rising to prominence in the constabulary. Makes of us a laughing stock,' he said.

'We know your thoughts on that matter, Henry,' said Woody. He turned to Chaseling, hastening to unfix the tone. 'Where is the widow Kunkle?'

'I left her, babe'n all, with Joe Franks. I'd still be on the water . . .'

'She's in good hands then,' said Woody.

'Oh yes sir, he's a good man Joe, but he's mighty rickety,' said Chaseling.

'She's in the hands of the man who caused this with his damn placation,' said Kettle. 'I tell you now, we turn them into porch monkeys they'll be on the porch, every time you turn around.'

Woody had heard enough. He rapped the benchtop beside Kunkle's battered skull. 'This is a man who shot them the way you might shoot ducks on a pond and worse, a case you may recall,' he said.

'Not the point!' said Kettle. 'The point is fear and fear alone inhibits their natural-born inclination to depravity. Every violation argues a depravity of mind that renders the savage obnoxious to society, that much I know.'

'Least we got one,' said Sparrow. He had taken to a chair in the corner by the books and the specimen jars, the better to study Reuben Peskett on the sly.

Heads turned. 'One what?'

'A society!'

'Martin, you are in way over your head,' said Woody.

Sparrow had a book in his hand, the word *Micrographia* on the tattered spine. Woody took it from him. Put it back on the shelf. Mackie stepped close and spoke softly. 'Yet again, on your arse, idling the hours,' he said.

Kettle pointed at the corpse. 'I want this old soldier avenged. The sooner they bend to our will the better for them and us.'

'I'll take a hunting party. I'll make them bend,' said Peskett.

'They'll be days up the Branch, such is their velocity,' said Mackie.

Kettle took two pennies from his pocket and he placed them upon the blank dark eyes of the deceased. 'You will not dissect this man.'

'As you wish,' said Dr Woody.

'He is not some useless felon, some nameless cadaver to be carved up for your morbid curiosity. He is one of us, the corps, do I make myself clear?'

'Well then he's yours, take him, I don't want him,' said Woody.

21

Later that day soldiers under orders from Captain Kettle took the body of Thyne Kunkle for burial.

The doctor was disappointed not to have Thyne's corpse to slice and probe, for Thyne's skull was conveniently rent apart and Woody's foremost interest in the anatomical sphere was the brain: 'With the study of the brain we can unlock the secret places of Man's mind,' he would say, 'and look into the living and breathing chapel of the deity.'

But Dr Woody was not long without a cadaver, for the very next day he acquired the detached head and the body of Shug McCafferty.

He laid Shug's head in a chiseled recess in the benchtop and proceeded to saw off the calvaria, otherwise known as the skull-cap. Then he set the head upright and began to examine the brain, probing with a chopstick and peering at the brain matter through a magnifying glass.

He was entirely focused when he heard someone tugging at the door and saw it was Agnes Archambault. Agnes had acquired her exotic surname when she married a French vigneron whom the gov-ernor had brought to New South Wales to teach vine growing to the colonists. Their assigned felon was Shug McCafferty, his labour to prepare and maintain the ground for the vines. But the venture was a disaster and Monsieur Archambault was returned to France with a bad report, while Agnes and Shug stayed on the failed farm and thereby hangs a tale – for Shug was well enough behaved when mon-sieur was on hand, but he was a different man when Agnes was alone.

'I hear he's here and if he's here I want to see him, *here and now.*' She was staring at Shug's head and Shug, it seemed, was staring back.

'Why?' said Dr Woody, having noted the belligerent tone.

'Because I have something to say to him.'

'Agnes, he's dead.'

'Which is exactly why I am here.' She wrapped her arms about herself and began to laugh heartily, staring at Shug's head. She crossed the room and before the doctor could blink she took hold of Shug by the ears, lifted the head and slammed it down on the bench.

Dr Woody threw his hands in the air. 'Agnes!' He was fixed as a hinge post, shocked and appalled by this most unexpected behaviour.

Agnes held onto the ears and bent low and spoke to Shug's dead face. 'You will never misuse me again,' she said in a whisper. Then she straightened and back-handed the head off the bench, her knuckles sounding on the bone.

Woody hurried after the head and picked it off the floor. He gathered his composure, and his authority. 'Agnes. I am going to put this man's skull back on my surgical bench and there it will stay, unmolested, and I will continue my examination, all the way down to the *arterial anastomosis.*'

'I'll tell you what you'll find deep in there, you'll find the dirty thoughts of a dirty man is what you'll find.'

'Agnes, don't tell me what I will find.'

The woman seemed to have cooled. 'I done what I came to do,' she said.

'It is a relief to hear that!' said Woody.

Agnes was about to leave when an odd bod appeared at the door accompanied by a Cape mule that seemed intent upon stepping inside the cabin. Agnes guessed who it was and Woody knew for certain. 'Hello Mr Catley,' he said.

The man smacked the mule on the nose with the back of his hand and then he took the mule by the throat latch on the halter and bent forward and pressed his arse into the mule's chest, compelling the creature to retreat. 'This mule thinks we're married. How are you, Thomas?' said Catley.

Agnes had noticed the mule was decked out with a pack saddle and a rump harness laden with wicker baskets and panniers of canvas and leather. She knew this man by reputation and what she knew was entirely consistent with what was at the door – a stocky man, built strong, decked in a faded velvet vest with many little pockets over a voluminous white shirt, knee-length britches and thick leather sandals and between the britches and the sandals the most enormous calves she had ever seen. He carried an eyepiece on a lanyard around his neck and small pouches on pull strings hung from his belt and there was an everlasting in a buttonhole on his vest, tiny white petals.

He took note of Agnes and his eyes seemed to lock upon her. Agnes pulled at her hair and looked to Woody for some form of intervention. But it was Catley who came to the rescue. He unstrapped his haversack and took it off his shoulders and set it down. 'Permit me,' he said, 'I am Mr George Catley, explorer and botaniser specialising in the *eucalyptii*, and latterly anatomist for Sir Joseph Banks, whose unfailing servant I am.'

He removed his straw hat and bowed an elaborate bow, thus revealing a tight-cropped head of light brown hair.

The mule had again stepped into the doorway and this time butted into Catley's arse, almost shunting him into the arms of Agnes Archambault and filling her senses with the unmistakable odour of onions.

Catley turned and slapped the mule on the muzzle with such power that the creature shrunk back and almost sat down on its haunches on the porch. The cottage shuddered and they heard the bay mare snorting and stamping.

Agnes stepped clear of this violent turn and bumped the doctor's sideboard and steadied the frame lest something fall. 'Fear not madam, I am a gentleman,' said Catley. 'I did not mean to cause alarm, least of all 'neath these calamitous skies. Moreover, I am glazier's putty in the presence of any gentlewoman.'

'Forgive him Agnes,' said Woody, 'he spends too much time in the wilderness with nothing for companionship but that mule.'

'Not quite,' said Catley.

Agnes was reminded of Mr Catley's reputation. He lived wild in the fastness for much of the year and wore those sandals in all weathers. It was said his only companion, apart from the mule, was the splendid young mountain savage called Moowut'tin, otherwise known as Daniel, who guided him about. He was a slave to science, botanist to Sir Joseph Banks who sailed with Cook on the *Endeavour*. But Agnes Archambault was not a woman to be moved by reputation alone. 'I am no gentlewoman,' she said.

Moreover, she was not keen on onions.

'Words, meanings,' said Catley. 'Kindness is gentility and there is nothing in this world to equal a woman's kindness save perhaps a woman's touch which is, of course, a kindness beyond measure.'

Agnes pulled a face. 'I can whack a mule same as you.'

Woody was ready with a fresh subject. 'You are embarked, George, upon another campaign?'

'I am that, I seek the duckbill *in situ et in vivo* and the answer to one of the great mysteries of anatomical science. Madam, will you dine with me before I gather my provisions and depart?'

'No.'

'Apologies, beauty renders me impulsive beyond measure, whether flower or the flower of womanhood.'

'George!' said Woody.

'What?'

'I am busy here.' The doctor picked up the chopstick and recommenced his probing at Shug's brain matter.

Catley stared. He stepped forward. 'Work of the utmost importance. Forgive me Thomas I was . . . diverted.' His gaze shifted from the specimen on the slab to Agnes Archambault.

He stepped outside and took to fiddling with the harness and the buckles on the panniers. The mule had retreated and was nibbling at bright green shoots by the porch footings.

'You tether that mule clear of my porch, and the mare,' said Woody.

'Have you seen the duckbill?' said Agnes, hoping not to offend two men of science in the one day.

Catley seized on the opportunity for conversation and stepped inside once again. 'I have, yes, but not in her lair, that now is my mission.'

'A new mission!' said Woody.

'I have presently set aside my botanical passions in order to address, for the benefit of Sir Joseph and the Royal Society, and for posterity, the most burning question on the anatomical schedule.'

'I thought you'd finished with the duckbill?' said Woody.

'I seek not so much the duckbill these days as the *modus regenerandi* thereof. I am advised they headquarter in vast numbers on the Branch.'

'How they birth, you say?' said Woody.

'That's it, does she lay her eggs and hatch them in the warmth of her lair or does she hatch them inside herself, in her belly, as some fish do? Is she *oviparous* or *ovoviparous*, that is the question.'

'To lay or not to lay, that is the question!'

'A most damp and uncomfortable mission, I see myself mostly prone on muddy banks, soaking wet. You might say I have forsaken the flint-*lock* for the mat-*tock*. It's most fortunate I have my father's constitution, that of an ox.'

'That will hardly fend off a skewer if the savages stick you in the gizzard,' said Woody.

'I am long ago launched upon a systematic cultivation of amity with the Aboriginals. I have never hurt a one nor they me. What's more I have Moowut'tin with me in the woods, one of nature's diplomats.'

'Well good luck with that,' said Woody.

Catley scratched at his stubbly chin. 'Thank you, Thomas. Like all progress in science, it's the hard-won answers that bring us closer to clarity as to God's design.' He took a raw onion from his pocket and took a bite, the chomping like the sound of a chaffcutter.

Woody had turned to polishing his glasses with a rag. 'I hope that's true.'

Catley turned to go. 'There's a pony's head on the porch, you know that, Thomas?'

'Yes.'

22

The examination of Rupert Chaseling in the matter of the savage murder of Thyne Kunkle, settler, formerly of the New South Wales Corps, took place in the government store.

Kettle and Woody empanelled themselves behind a dry-goods bench, the bench cleared and the entire setting swiftly rearranged by the storemen.

Chaseling sat on a single chair before the panel and Mackie sat by a pile of empty flour sacks and a row of empty meat casks, the lids unsealed. Soldiers filed in. They lined up at the long counter.

Reuben Peskett was there.

From the rear of the store Sparrow cast a furtive eye over the sergeant, saw him thumb his false teeth into place. He was searching for the man's charm, but he could see none. 'He'd be a eel if he had a slippery tail,' he whispered to Bet Pepper.

'A tad more yellow and you'd be a Chinaman,' said Bet and she whacked Sparrow's thigh with the back of her hand.

Sparrow felt entirely hopeless. He sunk once more into a slough of despond. Then he saw another hand, an ancient hand, softly tapping his elbow. It was Harp Sneezby.

Harp glanced about the store, his head tipped back in that familiar fashion. He leaned into Sparrow, shoulder to shoulder. He spoke softly in his ear. 'Griffin says get the copper worm and you won't need no dog for the savages.'

Sparrow looked about, noting the comers busy with conversation. 'Where is the worm?'

'It's in the gaol.'

'How do you know that?'

'Hat and me, we fraternise.'

'What about the axe?'

'Oh you'll need the axe alright, but the worm is the *sine qua non*.'

'What does that mean?'

'It means you better get the worm.'

Sparrow surveyed the scene. It seemed most of the village was packed into the store or gathered on the porch, pressing at the doorway, where Private Redenbach had positioned a hurdle.

The folk there were eager for the details of the most recent terrible assassination and full of talk as to its meaning, but Sparrow no longer cared for such details. He could think of nothing but Bet Pepper's cruel designation. A colour, yellow, a mere word, but enough to confirm in his mind that Biddie Happ would never come to his patch. What girl in her right mind would ever attach her affections to a yellowy man?

'This is a heaven-sent moment, Marty. No time like the present,' said Harp.

Sparrow did not know what to think. He reckoned he might never get another chance like this and a coil of copper piping was surely a lot less trouble than a live dog. He wanted the problem solved, over and done, and he could think of no better way, and no better moment. He got up and made to leave but upon reaching the doorway found himself confronted by Private Redenbach.

'You go you miss the show, best show in town,' said Redenbach.

'I got to piss,' said Sparrow. Redenbach stepped aside and Sparrow shifted the hurdle and pushed his way through the crowd and hurried across the square as the examination got under way. The private watched Sparrow go, then he reset the hurdle and turned his attention to the examination.

The light from the river-side window did not carry far into the store. It lent a pale brown texture to just about everything. The entire atmosphere put Rupert Chaseling, prize witness, at some considerable unease. Nor did the framed print on the rear wall help him much; a wild skirmish amidst flesh and armour and swords and flames, a furious battle betwixt the Israelites and the Amalekites at a moment in the battle when the Amalekites were not doing very well at all.

'This is an informal inquiry, Rupert,' said Dr Woody. 'You do not have to swear an oath but you must tell the truth, do you understand?'

Chaseling sat up, rigid. 'The mere spectre of God's vengeance is enough to keep me straight.'

He eyed the giant Amalekite who had clutched the point of an Israelite pike at the very moment another pike was about to skewer his kidneys. That particular Amalekite was done for. The awful realisation of his doom was clearly evident, written, as it were, upon his countenance.

Chaseling was still studying the besieged Amalekite when Cuff arrived. Redenbach shifted the hurdle just enough for the deputy constable to squeeze through. 'Nothing but a willowy paragon like myself would fit that tiny aperture,' said Cuff. He was patting his stomach. The soldiers laughed. They could not help but like Cuff.

'Thaddeus, we are underway here,' said Dr Woody. Cuff found himself a meat cask, thumping the lid on tight, and he sat quietly.

Woody watched him. Cuff watched back. He saw in the moment an opportunity. 'I know he had a hankering for dark trim in extremis, I know that much,' he said.

Kettle glared at Cuff.

'Resuming then,' said Woody. 'These horrible deeds, tell the panel on what day they occurred, and take off your knit cap.'

'Tuesday last,' said Rupert as he removed the cap and put it in his lap; he picked it up again, then he tucked it into his belt and then he felt for the scabby lump on his head.

'Tuesday, you're sure of that?'

'I'm sure 'cause Thyne's missus, she said to me it's Pentecost, it's the Feast of Weeks, and I said not here it ain't and she said well Rupert, today is Tuesday and it's Pentecost, how she knew that I don't know but that stuck with me . . . ain't often I know what day it is.'

'I believe we have Tuesday for a certainty,' said Henry Kettle. 'Now tell the panel how it came to this, your principal, the late Mr Kunkle, butchered in full view of his family.'

Chaseling took a deep breath. 'Well sir, I would put my blame on no man but instead upon the locality, in the first instance.'

'The locality?'

'Yes sir, the loam is rich but the situation is entirely perilous. They watch us from above, loaded with their weaponry, their cackle something terrible, like geese in season. Then they're gone, then they're back. They come round the point too, in the shallows, armed to the teeth and we're all down to the drizzles.'

'And?' said Woody.

'I do believe my principal's nerves were red raw, as were mine . . . and the missus too and the babe, the poor little thing, riddled with the frighteners.'

Kettle intervened. 'Are you saying that, notwithstanding the liberality with which these beggars are supplied with corn and other comforts, you and the Kunkles were compelled to live in a state of alarm due to their unforgiving harassment?'

'A moment,' said Woody. 'Your principal, how was he disposed to the governor's concession?'

'I believe his feelings were, um, complicated.'

'Go on then.'

Chaseling looked away, an empty stare out the river-side window.

Mackie clicked his fingers. 'Rupert, Thyne is dead and you have been dutiful in your care for his family. Now do not ruin this for yourself.'

Rupert hung his head and scuffed the floorboards with the toe of his boot. 'I guess it don't matter now, can't hurt the dead, can it?'

'No, go on.'

'Thyne said it was all his, even the mussels in the mud, every inch o' that patch, by virtue of his sweat and his enterprise. He said a man might as well condemn his father for fornication as mourn the founding work we do.'

'That might depend on the father's work, whether it was courtship or rape,' said Cuff.

'Thaddeus, enough,' said Woody.

'So, what happened?' said Kettle.

'First light we seen 'em in the shallows, Caleb and the one we call Napoleon in his grey frockcoat, and one other. Them spears longer'n a ten-foot pike and brutally barbed to shred a man's flesh.'

Dr Woody leant forward. 'Did your principal take pre-emptive action of some kind?'

Kettle smacked the bench. 'I venture to say the time for pre-emption was long gone, that moment being no less than a prelude to encirclement!'

'They was turnin' the screws, I know that much,' said Chaseling.

The panel nodded as did most present, being sympathetic to the situation as described.

'A turn too far?' said Mackie.

'What happened next?' said Woody.

Rupert Chaseling looked left and right, and then he looked at the Amalekite. He could not have said the picture gave him courage, but he knew he had to continue with the truth as best he could tell it. 'Thyne was worked up to a pitch, the missus beside herself with fear, the babe screaming, the savages' jabber something frightful and Thyne said to me he said *enough* and he put a ball straight into Caleb and they fell upon us with a fierce wrath.'

The word went around the room: *Caleb, he shot Caleb.*

Woody sat up. He put his hands in the small of his back and tried, as ever, to straighten his upper half and he grimaced as he did so. He said: 'We appreciate your recourse to frankness, is there anything else you would like to add?'

'They will not change their brute ancient ways. They must be kept in subjection and punished wholesale, that's Thyne word for word, more or less.'

'I think we're finished here,' said Kettle.

'Nothing more then?' said Woody.

'The sergeant will take a hunting party.'

'Forthwith!' said Peskett.

'What happened to Caleb?' said Mackie.

'I don't know,' said Chaseling.

'We are finished,' said Woody.

'The Branch mob ain't finished,' said Cuff.

'One more thing,' said Mackie, 'where is Thyne's fancy gun?'

'Carried off, that and more. Corn, the small axe, poultry, Thyne's gun. Weren't nailed down so they took it.'

23

Sparrow departed the trade store and headed for the gaol. He was unhappy enough to feel reckless and that was a most unusual feeling. He would shun the hearing into Thyne Kunkle's death, just as he'd shunned the final chapter of Shug's execution. Why he was something of a shunner he was not quite sure but on this occasion, he well knew, there was method in his meekness.

The heavy panelled door to the gaol was chocked open. He stepped inside, into the corridor, and listened for sounds of life. The air was much colder inside than out. *No stone so cold as gaol stone.* One of the granary cats rubbed against his leg. 'What you doin' here?' he whispered. He wanted to pat the cat but he thought best not. Cats made him sneeze and it was not a good time to be sneezing, nor was it a good time to be patting a cat.

The door to the turnkey's billet was slightly ajar. He peered in. He sensed no one there.

'Hello,' he said, just loud enough. 'You here, Hat?'

There was no reply.

He walked on, softly, to the cross passage and the cells. Set high in the rear wall there were three small openings that counted for windows. Each one cast a sharply angled shaft of grey light onto the stone floor.

He could see the spiral worm there, on a hessian sack in the far corner of the cell to his left, the copper sheen defying the faint light. There was a pile of filthy gaol garb next to the worm and a low pallet set against the rear wall with a lumpy, horsehair tick upon it. He glanced over his shoulder. He listened again. He pulled at the cell door and it swung open.

Sparrow stared at the apparatus, wondering how he might carry off such a thing. He had a feeling this might not be too hard for just about everybody was, at that moment, listening to the interrogation of Rupert Chaseling, and the gaol gang, thankfully, was somewhere on the south road, breaking rocks and filling washaways.

The worm could be carried in the hessian sack and he could hide it somewhere on South Creek, somewhere on the escarpment. Then he could bide his time at Peachey's, drink some skull-cracker if there was any left, and come and get the worm in the wee small hours of the morning and sneak it across the bridge and hurry it home and get himself ready to bolt for the other side.

A shudder went through his flesh. The worm was an awkward thing, delicate too, and just how he might get it across the river and then across country to Griffin Pinney's hideaway on Pig Creek did not bear thinking about, at least not now. *One thing at a time.* He took a big deep breath.

'You don't plan to steal that worm, do you?' said Hat Thistlewaite. Hat was standing not two feet behind Sparrow.

'It's you, on the lock,' said Sparrow.

'O'course it's me on the lock, it's me or nobody. It ain't Marshalsea, Marty.'

'Where'd you come from?'

'I roost up there in the rafters.'

'You do not,' said Sparrow. He was looking up. Almost directly above him was a block and tackle fixed to a crossbeam, the hauling rope hitched to a metal rest on the wall.

'You don't want to know about that,' said Hat.

'I already do. Peskett strung up Mort Craggs years back, near popped his shoulders out.'

'What else you know?'

'Mort said Peskett got, quote, *medieval with his arse.*'

'If it's a quote, Marty, it would have to be *medieval with my arse* as in, *That Reuben Peskett, he got medieval with my arse.*'

'I know what he said.'

'Yeah but do you know what he meant?'

'He wouldn't tell me.'

'We best talk,' said Hat, and he gestured at the pallet inside the cell.

They sat themselves down on the tick, which was hardly softer than the timber underneath it. The cat jumped into Hat's lap and Hat took to stroking its fur and the cat's tail was twitching with delight. 'You want the cat, nice and warm in your lap?'

'No, they make me sneeze,' said Sparrow.

'What about dogs?'

'What about them?'

'They make you sneeze?'

'No.'

The subject of sneezing seemed to be exhausted and the two men sat in silence for what seemed to Sparrow a very long time. Then Hat spoke. 'That worm ain't for you; you don't got the machinery.'

Sparrow felt a little bit like he felt when Biddie Happ inspected his pizzle.

Hat said: 'I seen Harp, we talked, know that?'

'I didn't know that, no.' Sparrow's hands were cold. The cat was purring loud.

'I know you know what Harp knows, and maybe Griffin Pinney too . . . about the other side, this hideaway they got,' said Hat in a whisper. He was leaning forward, close, his breath awfully stinky, and Sparrow could not understand why he would lean so, for there was no one else in the gaol, as far as he could tell.

'I don't know about that,' said Sparrow. He could hear the voice of Griffin Pinney: *You share a secret it is a bond of trust, you understand that?*

He ran his tongue along his teeth. He liked having a tongue secure in his mouth, nicely connected to whatever it was connected to. He guessed it must be called the tongue bone.

'You better know something,' said Hat, 'or you'll go down for theft o' this worm, caught in the act, I'll see to it, I'll see you behind bars, *in perpetume.*'

Hat had terrible teeth, few in number, mostly black, and when he smiled he smiled with his mouth wide open and he held the pose so it seemed like God had cast his face in stone and left Hat gaping for all time.

'You wouldn't do that,' said Sparrow.

'I seen you bag it, I seen you try to carry it off.'

'I never did!'

'You can tell that to the magistrates, your word against mine, and they'll get Reuben Peskett . . . and he'll swing you on that tackle if he has to, he'll sling you on the hook. That or worse.'

'Worse?'

'Worse, yes, Reuben Peskett is, and here we come full circle . . . *medieval.*'

'How so?'

'Well, he has an instrument and it ain't a violin.'

'Tell me.'

Hat paused, ran his tongue across his black teeth and his gums. 'It's a rectal pear.'

Sparrow paused. 'A what?'

'A rectal pear, named for its shape . . . got a one-eighth thread top to bottom and a big wing nut at the fat end and the pear shape is four big . . . um . . . like petals on a rose, and the narrow end has a sharp point all greased up for rectal entry and then he turns the wing nut and the pear, that is to say the petals, they open like a flower and it's hardly decent to say more so I'll keep it at that.'

'That's no rose, a rose a beautiful thing,' said Sparrow.

Hat's voice dropped an octave. 'In the humble opinion of Reuben Jiggle Teeth, so too is the rectal pear. Consider this Marty, long ago, so I'm told, that instrument was reserved for sinners guilty of carnal union with Satan, but Reuben does not consider himself restrained in any way by medieval particularity, he's just partial to their methods.'

Hat smiled that awful smile, like his face was frozen.

'You seen him use it?'

'I seen it up an arse or two, yes.'

Sparrow swallowed hard. 'What do you want?'

'You tell me what's on the other side.'

'I thought Harp told you?'

'You tell me.'

Sparrow knew he had to tell Hat something. 'I'm told there's a village.'

'And?'

'It's embosomed at the foot of the mountains, on the other side. And there's a river too . . .'

'A village, embosomed?'

'Yes, embosomed, so I'm told.'

'And a river?'

'A big river, yes.'

'And the wilderness?'

'You have to cross that.'

'I know that you damned idiot, how do they negotiate the damn wilderness that's what we want to know.'

'We?'

'I, me.'

Sparrow had the twin spectre of Griffin Pinney and Reuben Peskett strong in his thoughts. He was determined not to lose his tongue and he was equally determined not to suffer at Peskett's medieval hand. 'Believe me Hat I wish I knew. I hardly know anything.'

'Who told you what you do know?'

'Harp,' said Sparrow. He did not want to mention Griffin Pinney.

'How would Harp know, he's dumb as dirt. He'd never get across.'

'He ain't dumb.'

'A big river you say?'

Sparrow figured magnitude might add to the verisimilitude of his commentary. 'Makes this one look like a midge,' he said.

Hat shook his head. 'I find that quite hard to imagine . . . in my mind.'

'Me too,' said Sparrow.

They sat quiet for a while. Then Hat smiled again. 'The establishment here at the depot, the establishment in which I am but a humble cog, would like to know how the bolters are getting across and by what means and under whose auspices.'

Sparrow thought hard about the mysterious word, *auspices*. He thought it might be French, it was so damn showy. 'I know Shug didn't get across and you hung him with that pony's head strung on his neck.'

'The body came away; did you know that?'

'I heard. I'm glad he was good and dead when it happened.'

'If I had my way I'd rather've hung Mort, assuredly the principal in that mischief,' said Hat.

'I suppose,' said Sparrow.

'Marty, if runaways are getting across it's on the wing of mutual endeavour, that much is certain.'

'I wouldn't know.' Sparrow sat himself up, stiff and straight, like a ramrod.

Hat's fingers were in the fur under the cat's chin. The cat was an old cat, shut-eyed and content, sinking into sleep, purring.

'I heard there's a lake . . . you heard that?' said Hat.

Sparrow wondered if, perhaps, this was a trick. He did not want to say the wrong thing, as he so often did under pressure. 'I haven't heard that one, you know more than me.'

'I know more'n Harp,' said Hat, nodding. He seemed most pleased with himself.

'What more?'

Hat kept nodding, like he had a big secret he was proud of.

'Tell me, what?' said Sparrow.

'Mr Catley reports there's mountain blacks who swear the western country has a big lake where the water is salt and whales are seen to spout and there's a people there, white people, and they live a most comfortable existence principally on fresh fish and Indian corn.'

'How does Mr Catley know that?'

'I arksed him the exact same question. He said the savages imitated the whales as seen to spout upon breaching. He said the manner in which they did so, imitating the whales throwing up the water, and giving off the sound, was so completely satisfactory as to leave little doubt they could have known of whales but from actual and faithful observation. You may not know it but they are fine mimics the savages, least, that's what Mr Catley says. Him and the wildlife's thick as thieves you know.'

'Whales, Lord!'

'That's what I said.'

Sparrow was thinking, hard. 'If there's whales it must be connected to the ocean, way off, somewhere.'

'Must be.'

'My goodness, think of that,' said Sparrow. For a moment he felt as free as he'd ever felt free, almost as far back as he could remember, back to Misty, at least.

Sparrow was about to depart the gaol but he was compelled to pause in the shadows of the corridor, for the punitive expedition under Peskett's command had gathered on the square, loaded with rations and weaponry, intent upon bloody retribution for Thyne Kunkle, one of their own.

He snuck off when he could, wormless, slipped behind the barracks and sat himself down, hunched against the wall in a thin slice of shadow. But there was no good reason to tarry, so Sparrow hurried across the escarpment and crossed the bridge with not the slightest inclination to stop at the Tap. He followed the creek downstream with all haste, anxious to get to his patch and have a good think, but not far from the river he pulled up sharp. Ahead of him was what appeared to be a scrub wattle, flipping and flopping, angling its way up the slope.

Sparrow approached with some caution until, up close, he could see a dog snared in the cover, its tether ravelled round the stem.

The dog was a wolfhound, long-legged, shaggy, barely a yearling in Sparrow's estimation. He was a mess, battered and bruised. One side of him was entirely muddied up and one eyelid so caked with muck it was stuck shut, like dried blood on a scab. Sparrow worked the tether free and he sat with the pup. He ran his hand over the creature checking for wounds, found a few cuts but nothing in the way of real hurt.

His guts began to churn. This was not just any pup, this one belonged to the wolfhound bitch that in turn belonged to Henry Kettle, the sole brindle in the litter, pretty as a picture save for the caked mud and the weary mien. 'You must be starved,' he said.

The pup was whimpering and squirming about, trying to nuzzle its way between Sparrow's knees and, failing that, it was flailing a paw at the muddied eye. Sparrow took a hold of the paw. 'I'll fix that,' he said, but he knew he couldn't because what he needed was a wet rag. Soak the eyelid and wipe off the slurry.

Sparrow looked around. Not a soul. He shaded his eyes, squinting into the sun, saw a hawk circling most languidly.

At the water's edge he squatted down and dunked his sweat rag and squeezed it out and held it, poultice like, to the muddied eye. The pup struggled to be free and then fell still.

The mud was coming away and the pup began to work the eyelid, blinking, and licking Sparrow's fingers at the same time. That felt nice and it made Sparrow smile. 'Stop that,' he said, but he didn't really mean it.

His legs were tiring, squatting in the mud in that fashion, but he did not mind. He felt a contentment that was most unfamiliar. 'We'll scuttle on home, you and me,' he said. He wondered if, perchance, it was providence wrought this miracle, for surely this was a miracle and surely this was a sign. He held the dog tight and he whispered: 'You and me we're gone, *gone*, bound for the other side.'

Part II

Sparrow's Resolve

24

The long shadows of evening in ascendance marked the ground as four men came off a twin-masted lugger, a forty-footer with a lateen mizzen sheeted to an outrigger. Folk on the terrace did not fail to notice their arrival, for one of these men led a willowy girl on a tether decorated with coloured ribbons.

The newcomers made enquiries as to the location of Alister Mackie's tavern. They took themselves up the switchback path and crossed the square to the Hive.

They gathered within, the girl pulled forward as they made a line at the counter.

Sprodd came in from the kitchen, licking his fingers. He sat himself in the barber's chair. Fish took to his chair under the stairs, rocked back against the wall, his shaded eyes locked on the girl. Sam straightened himself, stood tall as he could behind the counter.

The girl was tethered to a freckly, bull shouldered man with a head of sparse and bristly hair. The tether was a heavy, laid thing, the end of it wrapped around his fist. 'You must be the queen bee,' he said in an accent that Sam associated with flaxen plaits and the pillage of monasteries.

'That's me,' said Sam.

The patrons chuckled and turned away, intent upon their dice and their grog, occasionally scratching at their ankles or whacking the back of their necks, pipe smoke and slush-lamp fumes like tendrils curling into the air.

Two of the newcomers were twins, weedy creatures with pale skin and frizzy brown hair and immature, wispy beards that did not belong on a grown man's face in Sam's opinion. He could tell they had no education for they had mean little eyes that never rested. One of them said, 'If you want her you can have her, she's for sale.'

The girl looked up and Sam saw she had the palest green eyes, with faint bruising around one of them, and a ripe scar on her forehead. She was olive skinned and she had a put-upon look about her that Sam picked in a trice. Her dark hair was wispy to the fore and otherwise fashioned in a knot at the nape of her neck, the bob skewered with a long wooden pin, the head of the pin carved in the form of a feather.

She was uncommonly tall and Sam reckoned she would be quick, like a fawn; quick and ready to flee at the drop of a hat.

'Yes sir, have a good look.'

'Who are you then?' Sam set four small tumblers on the counter.

'I'm Nimrod Parsonage, I'm the twin with the good hands.'

His brother held up his left hand, a bulbous stump with just one stubby finger and a nub for a thumb.

'Who did that?'

'God in his wisdom,' said Crispin Parsonage.

Sam did his best to look unimpressed. He was about to fill the final tumbler when the fourth man, a wall-eyed character, declined, covering the rim with his hand. In his other hand was a pelt, rolled up and tied with twine. 'My innards are cankered,' he said. 'I need a lining for the stomach.'

'Get him some milk,' said Sam. Fish scuttled off down the corridor.

'I am looking for Alister Mackie,' said the abstainer. He was staring at the picture of Yetholm on the Bowmont river. 'I am Jonas Wick,' he said, as if Sam should know the name.

'Never heard of you.' The pain in Sam's groin was ruining his day. He pressed his fingers hard into the bulge beside his privates. He leant on the counter to take the weight off.

'I hear he makes salt wholesale, for the government. I hope that's true,' said Wick.

'That's true, he's got boilers downriver.'

Fish was back with a pickling jar half full of warm milk.

'Exactly where?'

'Near the mouth, you sailed right past,' said Sam.

Mackie surveyed the new arrivals from the corridor by the stairs. He saw the girl and the tether and he picked out Jonas Wick in an instant. The others were foreign to him.

'You look hale,' he said to Wick as he came forward.

'And you look thin and gaunt as ever I've seen,' said Wick.

The girl had taken hold of one of the ribbons and she was chafing the cloth between her fingers. Fish was poised on a stool, lighting a swing lamp as evening came on.

Mackie pointed to the landing. 'Follow me.'

As Wick followed Mackie up the stairs he was reminded of the girl. 'You take that halter off her now, Gudgeon, and you sit her down nice and quiet.'

Gudgeon worked the knot loose and took the rope from the girl's waist. Sprodd vacated the barber's chair and the girl was seated there in the pale grey light of the mullioned window.

From the stairs, Mackie saw her face when she looked up at him. His hand closed on the bannister so he might steady himself.

Later Fish would say he thought the chief constable had turned to stone and Sam would say Alister had briefly lost all colour in his cheeks and Cuff, too, would proffer an opinion only to be reminded that he was, at the time, asleep by the cookfire in the kitchen.

Jonas Wick felt obliged to assist. 'You know her,' he whispered.

'No,' said Mackie.

'Look again.'

A mosquito was supping on the back of Mackie's hand. He swatted it. He pointed in the direction of the barber's chair and spoke with an authority familiar to the trade. 'See no disrespect comes to this girl under my roof,' he said.

His words were sharp and hard whenever he gave orders, but what the girl heard was the borderland burr.

'Small world, Alister!' said Jonas Wick, his hands in the air like a Methodist in rapture. He turned his head close to Mackie's ear. 'That's Beatrice Faa,' he whispered.

She was taller than her mother and not so dark but she had her mother's slender frame and something in that singular face issued forth the likeness of Jeannie Faa such that when Mackie looked at this girl he saw the mother as if it was yesterday, then the daughter, and then the two somehow merged, the one dissolving into the other.

Fish hurried to the girl in the most unhurried fashion he could conjure as the two men took themselves upstairs. He wiped the back of his neck with his bench cloth. He stood close so he could smell her. 'If he's selling you, then he must've bought you?'

The girl did not answer.

'You want a tot I'll get you a tot.'

The girl nodded.

Fish brought her a tot and she sipped at it, closed her eyes.

'It ain't rubbish, we do not sell rubbish at the Hive, we don't water down nothin' neither.'

'Thank you,' she said.

'What's your name?'

'I am Bea.'

'Like a bee, bzzzzzz.'

'Just Bea.'

'I should not make jokes,' he said. 'I do not have the facility to deliver them with any conviction . . . I'm told moreover that I lack the timing.'

She smiled.

Fish found it hard not to stare at her. He found her willowy beauty quite disturbing. His eyes roamed across the folds of her garb, the loose-laced bustier over worn-out linen and the raggedy skirt of faded blue. 'I like blue,' he said.

She seemed not to hear. She seemed intent upon examining the grainy residue in the tot.

Upstairs the two men sat across from one another, separated by Mackie's neat desk, the *Sydney Gazette* beside the accounts book, a little sign plate to the fore: *In Work is Rest.*

'Bea Faa,' said Wick as he placed the pelt carefully on the desk. 'I thought that might snap your hinge.'

'And I thought you'd be dead. I see we are both mistaken,' said Mackie.

'From what I heard I thought you'd be a fox-hunting man with polished boots and a painted lady for a wife and a shiny black chaise and a footman with a horsehair wig . . . perhaps a novel-reading daughter dressed in fine silks or one of them modish skirts that requires a pair of frilly drawers, lest all be revealed.'

Mackie was silent.

Jonas Wick thought best to move the conversation on. He read the words upon the sign plate. 'What's that mean?'

'You don't know?'

'My troubles, I got no time for riddles.'

'It's not a riddle, Mr Wick, it's a verity, and I live by it.'

'I'm sure you do. I hear you got acreage, grain. I hear you got salt too, that and more.'

'Be careful with hearsay.'

Wick drank the last of his milk and put the jar on Mackie's desk, beside the pelt.

The chief constable stared at the jar, such a stare a man would be forgiven for thinking it was a muddy boot.

Wick retrieved the jar and looked about and settled for the floor. He put the jar on the floor.

Fish knocked and the door opened ever so slightly. 'You want I light the lamps?'

'Yes,' said Mackie, and Fish hurried in, fussing at one lamp and then another.

'Do you remember the surgeon on the transport?' said Wick, as Fish departed. He was looking at Mackie's hand, the finger pads tapping on the desk.

Mackie nodded.

'He said the climate here would fix you.'

'I believe the climate helps.' Mackie leant forward and shifted the newspaper ever so slightly. He squared the accounts book in line with the edge of the desk.

Wick got up and stepped to the window and looked out on the square. It was almost dark. 'A prominence indeed, well beyond the reach of your famous flood I heard.'

'It is the best of scarce elevation, hereabouts.'

'They say the waters rose fifty feet?'

'Here and there the tops of trees, little islands, otherwise . . . an ocean.'

'Imagine that.'

'I still do. Now, tell me why you are here.'

'I brought you the girl.'

'You do me no favour on that account.'

'She's the daughter of Jeannie Faa.'

'Why would that please me?'

'You buy her you can do with her as you wish.'

'I do not trade in women.'

'She has talents, Alister, I've never had a skinner quite like her. There's no damage, no nicks, no wastage when that girl skins a seal, you know why?'

Why Jeannie Faa's daughter would have such a skill was not without its fascination. 'Tell me then.'

'She got took in by a butcher's wife. He trained her. Skinnin' lambs for the warden, for the tables of the clergy.'

'Why took in?'

'All I know the girl was motherless. All the more reason I bring her here – I thought you might want her, being there's history there.'

'History's naught but gossip well told.'

'History may lie but blood don't. I see you in her, plain as day.'

'See what you like but keep it to yourself.'

'Oh I will, I'll keep that to myself, that and more.'

'What more?'

'She fled a transport, with the help of Gudgeon. She maimed the butcher.' Wick was chuckling at the very thought.

'A fugitive then?'

'You might say that.'

'And you bring her to me!' Mackie stood up, the chair shunting back on the boards.

'The girl's in trouble, I thought you might take her in, see her to safe passage . . . somewhere, anywhere, I don't know, but I do know Gudgeon's had his fill of her.'

Mackie closed his fists and leant upon the desk. He looked at the pelt. 'Let's to business.'

Wick ran his hand along the pelt, loosed the tie. 'We're enterprising men are we not?'

'It's fifteen years, Mr Wick, I don't know what you are save for the rumours.'

'Alister, you're makin' this hard.'

'Then put your case and be done.'

Wick stared at Mackie, nodding. 'How the wheel has turned. I feel like I have an audience with a potentate.'

'You've done me no favour bringing that girl.'

'She's but a morsel, this is the meal.' He tapped the pelt.

'Then you best serve it up.'

Wick took hold of the pelt and put it on his lap, played his fingers upon it like he'd just sat down to a reed-organ. 'I don't know another soul so ripe and ready as you for the gift I bear.'

He rolled out the pelt on the desk, ran his palm across the fur. 'Ever seen the like? Cured to perfection, better than otter, better than beaver, why, I doubt mink would compare, you just run your hand, *feel*; that my old friend is the finest, softest pelt this dark world has ever seen. I can see the gentlemen and the ladies in all the grand cities, promenading in their long coats and hats and muffles and gloves and fur-lined boots and God knows what else, saddle blankets for soft-skinned Galloways, underlays for bed-ridden nabobs – I say there's a fortune to be made . . .'

'Go on.'

'I've seen islands south of the forties, teeming with the fur seal – rookeries like you never laid your eyes on.' He paused for a moment, noting that Mackie was content to listen. 'To speak of abundance does not convey the numberless sights I've seen.'

The chief constable gestured for the pelt and Wick handed it to him. It was without a doubt the finest pelt of any kind he had ever handled. Wick was keen to talk: 'Note the bristly hair is gone. Gone! Not a filament of them bristles left.'

Mackie nodded. The pelt was a miracle. 'I know of no way to cure the fur of its bristly hair without degrading the product.'

'I can cure pelts to perfection, not the slightest damage to the underfur. You won't find a muff in a nunnery as soft and pure as this,' said Wick.

'You have in mind a venture?'

'I hear you got a ship, a sealer.'

'Hearsay will run a mile before the truth gets its boots on.'

'You don't?'

'I do, in Sydney . . . the ribbing stressed to ruination, the wedges rotten.'

'A salvage?'

'No, a liquidation.'

Jonas Wick sat quietly, taking this in. 'Can it be fixed, and fitted out, for the South Seas?'

'I am advised yes.'

'What I need from you is a ship and provisions and what you get from me is the venture, the cure, profitable beyond your dreams, a quarter of the profit, probably more.'

'A quarter?'

'The owners take half, the officers a quarter and the crew and the gangs split the last quarter in the pot. You and I split the half because I will dress and cure the pelts and you, you have the means to come into a ship and provision the enterprise, salt included. Who knows, it might be more than a half for the two of us.'

'How is that?'

'The crew and the gang is paid out of the catch, paid in pelts – skins and oil – so upon return we buy their share back at the market price, about three shillings a pelt, and most of that they'll want in grog.'

'I have grog,' said Mackie.

Wick sensed Mackie snared. 'You have grog, indeed you do my friend. And I'll have a crew so deep in hock we'll buy their share for nine pence per pelt or thereabouts, less than a shilling let's say. I do sometimes wonder how the common sea rat manages to scratch his cadaverous arse.'

Mackie was contemplating the portions and the figures. 'Nine pence?'

'A shilling at the most.' Wick was pleased they were now talking the figures.

'That is peonage.'

'That is what?'

'Debt slavery. I cannot abide such arrangements and I will not sink to them. We are awash with peonage here and I am its enemy.'

'If you have scruples in this regard . . .'

'I have scruples, and I know fair dealing is lucrative in the long run – some people have trouble understanding that.'

'Seems you demean me at every turn, I had hoped for a better welcome.'

'You live on hope you die fasting.'

Jonas Wick took a deep breath and heaved a sigh. 'This is a perfect pelt right here, no spoilage in the curing, no discount for damage in the dressing or the packing – we can deliver up crated pelts the likes of which have never before been seen in London, knock the beaver out, sink the damned Americans. They can eat cack and drink their own piss and you can go home to Yetholm, you can buy the entire village if you want to, why, you can build a house to make your mother's head spin.'

It was one of Wick's prerogatives to know more of the chief constable's past than most on the river, save for Cuff and Dr Woody.

'I have no intention of going home,' said Mackie.

'The question is, are we in the way of business, you and I? Think of our time on that stinking transport. What a turn it would be . . .'

'I have not forgotten that transport; I owe you my life, I know that.'

For a time on the transport he could barely sit up, let alone walk. But for the attentions of Wick who fetched his ration and fed it to him and gave him water, he would have died, his body, shrouded, slipping from a greased plank into the black depths of an infinite ocean. 'Don't let them bury me at sea,' he'd said. But down he went, the eye of his periodic dream tracking the lumpy, billowing shroud into the depths until he woke, gasping for air, his heart fit to burst.

'A bond forged in obstinate misery,' said Wick, 'and here we are plotting riches beyond our wildest dreams.'

'There is no bond. What debt there was . . . was paid.'

'Them seven florins in the waisting, I never took them I swear.'

'I make no accusation on that score,' said Mackie. He gestured for the pelt and Wick handed it to him. He took his time looking it over once again, running his fingers through the fur. 'I'll see the cure at work before I commit a penny. Every step, every detail, and I'll know the cost per piece from start to finish.'

'You'll see the cure when we have an agreement, not before.'

'The cat is chasing its tail here.'

'What cat is that?' Wick was at a loss. The slack in his leverage had come as a surprise. 'What we have here is an impasse if not a rupture.'

'Every step, every detail. Take it or leave it.'

Only now did the full meaning of the hearsay about Mackie come home to Jonas Wick. He was a man entirely in command of his sphere at the river, content to make no compromise. 'Here is the man, the boy is no more!'

'Correct.'

'As it should be, an agreement between men. Alister, we'll turn the trade upside down, think of it!'

'I'll first have that cure.'

'And I will give up the cure when I have a written agreement for a joint enterprise in the sealeries.'

'You do as you please, as will I.'

'You look a prince's fortune in the eye and turn away?'

'My good fortune began when I stepped off that transport.'

'You'd be dead without me. Why, I looked after you, fed you, cleaned you . . . kept you warm.'

'Don't speak to me of warmth. I paid for the warmth . . . so do not speak to me about warmth, nor debt or obligation.'

'That is the sourest note I've heard in many a long day.'

'Correct.'

'Another impasse?'

'Yes.'

'I'm here but briefly, then I'm gone. And the cure with me.'

'As you wish.'

25

Sparrow had hardly slept since he'd got the pup home to his patch on Cattai Creek, where the Cattai met the river. He worried Dr Woody might visit on his way home, though Dr Woody had gone to and fro in that gig a thousand times and never once done that. He worried Henry Kettle might learn the whereabouts of the pup and send a complement of soldiers to shackle him and drag him all the way back to the ridge and give him up to Hat Thistlewaite who would no doubt think it comical to lock him in that cell together with the copper worm. 'That brindle pup was a big mistake, you shoulda stole the worm,' he'd say, or something to that effect.

In his pictorial mind Sparrow could see Hat's awful black smile.

He worried, too, about Mackie. With every day that passed there was more chance the chief constable might call, or Heydon on Mackie's behalf, the overseer, intent upon scrutinising the acreage in service of his principal's pecuniary interest. That made Sparrow jittery, made him ponder and puzzle over his propensity for prevarication.

Sparrow and the pup were living on a salty broth of cooked-out bones and grub-ridden corn. There wasn't much else, save what he'd packed in the haversack, what he would carry when they bolted for the other side, him and the pup.

The ache in his gut was sharp and it sent spasms all the way to his shoulder and his palms were sweaty as a pig's snout. Several times he had unpacked the haversack and then packed it again and readied to go but every time he got so frightened he had to sit down and when he sat down and contemplated the perilous journey ahead, well, suddenly that journey seemed impossible. Suddenly his patch didn't seem so bad. He would think of Thyne all chopped up or of Shug, dangling, and then he would think of Biddie Happ and wish he could see her one more time but that he could not do, for that would pile misery upon misery, say nothing of humiliation.

The misery and the worry had combined to visit upon him a bad bout of the drizzles, doubtless accentuated by the broth, and he was making regular trips to the hole in the ground that he called his camp latrine.

It happened that on one such occasion, with Sparrow in the midst of a hasty evacuation, the Woody boy came round the corner of the hut with a brace of pan-sized bream in hand. 'I got a fish for you Mr Sparrow,' said the boy.

Sparrow's innards were in no fit state to accommodate fish but he could not say no. In his indigent circumstances he could not say no to any provisions that might come his way. 'Might you hang him up for me, off the porch?'

'Yes sir.'

As ever Sparrow wondered at the strangeness of the 'sir'. He buttoned up his flap and wriggled his parts to a comfortable repose inside his britches. 'You still fish in that little boat of yours?'

'Why yes.'

'Will you come tomorrow, take me fishin'?'

Sparrow half expected the boy to once again ask for help plaiting the eel traps but he did not do that.

'I will if I can play with your dog for a while.'

'You can play with him if you don't tell anyone. He's a secret.'

'That's easy, I don't hardly tell anyone anything anyway. I can tell you one of my own, then we'll be square, I'll have one o' yours and you'll have one o' mine.'

Sparrow thought that was a good idea for secrets exchanged were a binding thing, a compact. 'Alright, you tell me your secret.'

They walked to the front of the hut and sat on stump stools and the dog came sniffing at the boy's fishy fingers and then he prowled beneath the brace of fish that hung from the porch beam until he settled in the crusty dirt.

'Well?' said Sparrow.

The boy hesitated. He beckoned the dog with a click of his fingers and the dog went to him. He looked up at the fish, wondering if perhaps he was giving up too much, a pan-sized bream *and* a secret. He decided in favour of the aforesaid arrangement not least because he'd been taught to keep to his word. 'We got Caleb, at home,' he said, pointing upstream, up the Cattai.

Sparrow had to think about that. 'You mean the savage?'

'He ain't entirely savage, he knows more bible than I do.'

'He was the Reverend Hardwick's foundling, years back.'

'I know, and he's got table manners, I've seen them. Papa even has him say grace.'

'He eats at your table?'

'Yes sir, Mr Sparrow. Has done ever since he got off his sick bed, ever since the fever come off him. He come in with a awful wound. Papa said the ball shattered in the bone.'

'Did you see it, the wound?'

'I did.'

'What did you see?'

'A most grim repose, the ball in the pelvic bone, lodged there and otherwise shattered all about, shards in the flesh, like splinters, and a good deal of pus too. Papa says lucky it didn't rupture an organ and lucky it didn't fester 'cause that part of the human body does not brave infection with any grace at all.'

Sparrow recalled his conversation with Griffin Pinney on the subject of Caleb. Said he was *honourable.*

'Whose ball?'

'Thyne Kunkle's. Papa says *how the world turns.*'

'What does that mean?'

'It means they took Caleb right off the tit when they shot his ma. That's why he limps the way he does.'

'I don't follow.'

'Well, now he's shot again, but Papa says it's a God-sent opportunity to show goodwill. He says the savages are near to finished, says it's pitiful come to this. Says we've done them a most unpleasant service just bein' here, but he says goodwill can redeem all manner of sins.'

'What sins?'

'We steal their land, their wherewithal, their liberty to come and go upon their domain, then we call them brutes.'

'That does sound like your papa talking.'

'Yes sir.'

'You know what they did to Thyne?'

'Oh yes sir, they brained him and near chopped off his nethers, I seen that.'

'And Caleb sits at your table?'

'Papa has him wear a clean shirt and he gets to sit on a goose-down cushion on account of the wound . . . I reckon if that don't conciliate his affections nothin' will.'

Sparrow had no desire to talk on about the savages. It made him queasier than he already was. But the boy's secret was a good one, and something of a comfort. Caleb knew about goodwill, having been restored to rude health by the doctor and allowed to eat at the Woody table and let to sit on a goose-down cushion. That was a lot of goodwill. That meant Caleb would help them if they got in a fix and Griffin Pinney said he would anyway, said he was a . . . *formidable interlocutor*. That sounded to Sparrow like it meant helpful in a fix.

'Caleb says he will return Thyne's gun, the Swedish flintlock,' said the boy.

'I didn't know they took the gun.'

'Yes sir, old Wolgan, he took the gun, and Caleb says for goodwill they will return the gun.'

The idea of the savages falling upon the settlers at harvest armed with guns was too awful to contemplate, so Sparrow was pleased to know about Caleb's promise.

'I must go,' said the boy.

'You will come tomorrow. Do I have your word as a young gentleman?'

'My mama's an expiree so I ain't a gentleman and never will be, but you got my word.'

He stood and took down the fish and separated the two juveniles in the brace and poked a sharp stick through their skulls by way of their milky white eyes and drew a piece of twine through and tied them to the porch beam way clear of the pup. Then he gave a wave and turned and started for home, his catch in hand. 'We'll fish early,' he said.

'Come as early as you please,' said Sparrow.

26

When Jonas Wick departed, Mackie sat back in his chair. He slowed his breathing, thus stifling an eruption. He felt himself suddenly cold and his frame limp and his every muscle weary.

He trolled through his rules of engagement: an unrushed disposition, always; never be captive to a mercantile proposal; seize the high ground with the better information or moral rectitude, or both. He was not unpleased with the course of the conversation. But he was surprised to notice that, for the better part of half an hour he had forgotten about the girl downstairs, daughter to Jeannie Faa.

The girl was motherless. So said Wick.

He'd let that pass.

There was no sign of Bea Faa downstairs. Gudgeon and the Parsonage twins were busy with their dice and their jars, shrouded in smoke and shadow, like the rest of the trade. Mackie went direct to Sam.

Sam leant forward, his voice low. 'I put her out the back with Atilio, away from the prying eyes.'

Mackie found the girl at work in the kitchen, listening to the big cook recount the story of his life, beginning with his vivid memories of long days in the womb. The kitchen was a dark locale lit only by the burnished light around the cookfire and a slush lamp on the heavy trestle table.

The girl was cleavering a boiler into small chunks and feeding them into a stew-pot on the kettle prop where diced cabbage was already simmering in a liberally salted solution.

Mackie sat and invited the girl to do the same, opposite. She put aside the cleaver and wiped her hands on towelling and sat herself down.

In the fire light, the wash of her pale green eyes.

Mackie rapped his knuckles on the table to get Atilio's attention. 'I suggest you take the air,' he said.

'I don't like the air,' said Atilio, his thumbs hooked in his leather apron.

'Perhaps, *tonight*, you will like the air.'

Atilio looked at the girl and shrugged. 'Alright.'

When the rear door closed Mackie spoke. 'You're caught up with Jonas Wick. I count that a misfortune.'

'I'm caught up with Gudgeon, that's the misfortune. He's caught up with Wick.'

'He bought you, Gudgeon?'

'Yes.'

'From?'

'From the sailor who took me for a wife.'

'With your approval?'

The girl closed her eyes and ran a finger softly along the scar on her forehead. 'Better one comer than all comers.'

'And he sold you, the sailor?'

'I suppose he got a good price.'

'Did you have a say?'

'No.'

'What did *you* want?'

'I wanted to be dead.'

Mackie leant back in his chair. 'You fled the transport.'

'I was sold on from one to another and my arts with me. Come or go I had no say.'

For a time, well beyond politeness, he could not look away. He felt himself blush with shame. He could not forget, try as he might, how Jeannie Faa made a pillow of his stolen gift, the cloth, and lay back in the pungent, sorted straw in the waste barn, his tutor in those private things.

He looked away. 'What to do with you . . .'

'I am not yours to do with.'

'I am the chief constable at the river.'

'I know that tale.'

'They gave you up, your people?'

'If you want the story of my life you can have it.'

'How you come to be here is what I want to know.'

'I'm the bait, for Jonas Wick and his proposition.'

'And before that?'

'Long before . . . my mother died.'

Mackie looked down at his hands, his eyes following the bulging blue veins.

'They gave me to a butcher's wife in Yetholm. She died when I was ten and he took to drink, and took me at his whim.'

'What then?'

'Deep in his drunkard sleep I took the killing hammer. I smashed his shin bones. I crippled him.'

'Did he die?'

'He got the rot in his blood.'

'But you did not hang.'

'No.'

'If you have fled a transport, then I am required to shackle you to the wagon and send you to Parramatta.'

'*See no disrespect comes to this girl.* That's what you said.'

'While she is under my roof is what I said.'

'Perhaps then I should stay under your roof.' She smiled. Strands of long black hair swung about her shoulders as she withdrew the wooden pin from the knot and loosed her mane.

'I am sorry to hear your mother is dead.'

He dragged the slush lamp along the table so he could see her more clearly. Straight away he could feel the fumes feathering the back of his throat, stirring him to cough. He slowed his breathing. He studied her in the glow.

She was not as dark as her mother but she was sufficiently dark to pass for one of the Faa. The raggedy scar low on her forehead was not so old, it still carried some of its raw colour.

'You owe me something,' she said.

'Is that so?'

'I know the grief you brought my mother, you and the good people of the Kirk.'

'You have your something. You are safe under my roof.'

'I'm never but a plus on the accounts.'

'I have no need nor want for a woman here.'

'You had want for my mother.'

'For that I paid a price.'

'As did my mother.'

He could hear the spit and crackle of the cookfire, the hum of the chatter in the tavern. He wished them all gone, Wick most of all, for Wick had brought the girl, thinking to sway some commerce in his favour. And the girl, she brought Mackie nothing but a turbulence of the mind, gnawing memories that stirred him in unwelcome ways.

'If you speak of this I will send you down,' he said.

'You send me down and I will speak of this,' she said. There was a copy of the *Gazette* within reach. She pulled it into view.

'You've more cheek than a rat in a pantry.'

'I can work, read . . . tally.'

'The auctioneer can tout all that come market day . . . say nothing of your arts in the butchering department.'

'You'll see me sold, again.'

'A wife sale according to custom. You will have a say.'

Atilio came in rubbing his hands together. He went to the fire and warmed them. 'I have the air,' he said.

'Good,' said Mackie. He was about to rise when the girl leant across and put her hand on his.

'I know the cure.'

Mackie took his hand away and settled back in his chair. 'The procedure?'

'I know the makings, the measures, the soaking, to the minute. I can finish a pelt to perfection.'

'Tell me.'

'I will have that say, come market day.'

'You will have a say, yes or no as to the right or the wrong of it.'

'You'll see me safe, a good man?'

'A good man, yes.'

She wrapped her arms around herself and hunched over the news-paper. She was thinking what she might tell of the cure and what she might withhold. She scanned the columns under the masthead on the *Gazette*, the government orders, the editor's note.

'Go on then, read.'

She read aloud. She did not get far, just a few lines from the orders when she stopped.

'Go on,' he said.

She sat deadly still, as if listening for a storm. She reached into a pocket on her skirt. Her other hand clutched at the rim of the table. 'Help me,' she said, as she slipped to the floor.

Her body went rigid and her limbs convulsed as her eyes rolled back in her head. In the firelight Mackie could see her face, contorted. He dropped to his knees and took hold of her shoulders and felt her body arched and trembling in his hands, taut as a bowstring.

He did not know what to do. Atilio stepped in, the leather strop in his hand. He pushed Mackie aside and knelt with some difficulty and took hold of the girl's jaw and squeezed hard and forced the strop between her teeth and she bit down. The cook pressed on her shoul-ders and held her still and they were otherwise helpless, gathered there, watching, listening to the agitated hiss of her breath, the sound of her teeth grinding, her entire body in a fix of tremor and spasm.

Her hand slipped from her pocket, a wad of leather gripped tight.

Atilio worked his fingers gently upon her cheeks and jaw and he took the strop from her mouth.

Blood was running off her chin. She closed her eyes and lay there, her body quieted, her breath still quick. The cook ran his palm gently back from her forehead onto her hair. 'The falling sickness,' he said.

'Yes,' said Mackie.

He turned to Fish who was standing in the doorway. 'Not a word,' he said.

Fish raised his hands. 'I have no tongue, sir.'

Mackie's sleep that night was restless, stirred by visitations from long ago, when the mob marched to the old waste barn to save him from a Romany girl, *from the arms of Satan in voluptuous guise*, so said the minister and the elders and the congregation, scandalised to a righteous fury. They seized this Satan and carried her as meat on a pole, banging their pots and pans, a ram's horn trumpeting to rally the pious folk of Yetholm to the bridge, where they tied her into a corn basket and roped the basket and dropped her from the bridge, trussed and helpless, into the depths of the Bowmont river. And they told him, later, of how he screamed something horrible, as if shouting Satan from his very bowels as they raised her up and dropped her, again and again, six times over, until he was sure she was dead, how they left her, on the bank of the river. And they dragged him home, the minister talking loud of how the Prince of Darkness never sleeps and of how we go among snares – *a snare in every pleasure* – and how the senses are like open windows, every sense a window to temptation, and ruin.

27

When Sparrow took to his pallet that night he was so wide awake it felt like he might never sleep again. He could hardly lie still such was the agitation in his frame and such was the thumping in his heart and such was the rampant meandering of his mind.

The pup was in a similar state, or so it seemed. He lay down in the doorway emitting a low whine. Then he got up and walked about. He came and sniffed at Sparrow. He ambled back to the porch by way of the cookfire and stared into the darkness, cocked his head and listened to the creature sounds, nature's raucous symphony. Then he lay down, whimpering, and then he came inside again and sniffed at Sparrow some more.

Finally, the world outside fell quiet. Sparrow fell asleep. The pup crawled into the space beneath the pallet and lifted his nose and sniffed at Sparrow's arse through the ticking and promptly dozed off and neither man nor dog woke when, in the early morning, with the dawn stars a faint grey scattering in the east, a human frame stood silhouetted in the doorway.

An arm reached up and rapped the lintel.

The pup stirred and yelped and Sparrow sat up, blinking.

'Good thing my intentions are pure,' said a voice.

Sparrow knew that voice. It was Seamus Peachey. His first thought was declarativical. 'I got no grain, saleable or otherwise.'

Peachey dropped his haversack, squatted on his haunches and clicked his fingers and beckoned the pup but the pup did not go to him. 'I don't want your mouldy grain. If you had grain I wouldn't be here. I'm here 'cause you got no grain, you got no seed, you haven't ploughed, haven't done a damn thing and I know why.'

Peachey stood up. He pointed at the dog. 'You sure as hell gotta run now boy.'

'Run?'

'I'm goin' with you, that or oblivion. I've had my fill.'

'I don't plan to run.'

'Yes you do, Griffin told me. Griffin says we're better pairin' up you and me, pair up and get yourselves to Pig Creek is what he said. He'll meet us there.'

'Why now, you?'

'Because, Marty, contrary to appearances I live in a state of abject indignity, my sex dishonoured, my manhood embarrassed . . . Winifred is a *feme sole.*'

Sparrow hesitated, wondering what this meant. 'She is?'

'You don't know what that means, do you?'

'No. I mean yes I don't know.'

'A woman who comes free with her felon husband – that would be me – is a *feme sole* according to the Civil Court of England. That means the land grant is in her name and she holds the licence to the Tap. That means I am her dependant. I've seen it Marty, I've seen it. I am in the *dependant* column in the government accounts. You might as well cut my balls off.'

'That's not right.'

'She treats me like a dog! What's more there are other *femes soles*, decent, sensible women, who have freely surrendered the property to their husbands upon emancipation. But Winifred do that? I think not. She says I have no claim on her and no right whatsoever to any part of her business, *her business*, and to think, the work I've done!'

'That is shocking,' said Sparrow.

'And that's just the half of it. She's got a legal document, Marty.'

'What does it say?'

'I do hereby aver . . .'

'Aver?'

'Yes aver, I do hereby aver that the said properties were originally granted to me or acquired by me, Winifred Isabel Peachey, free settler, and that the right of possession to the said moiety is now vested in me and only me, signed W I P.'

'That is pure evil.'

'I know, and I am done with it. I intend to renew my manhood in the teeth of the wilderness.'

'I hope it don't come to that.'

The dog had sauntered across to Peachey and had a good sniff around his boots. Peachey squatted down again and took hold of the dog and held him firm and still and talked to the dog like he was talking to a little child.

Sparrow did not like Peachey coddling his dog. 'What you got to trade, you got a axe?' he said.

'No, I don't got a axe.'

'You should have brought your dog, Tool.'

'Tool's not been out for an age, if I take him I give the game away and God help us all if Winnie gets wind.'

'You got to have somethin' to trade, otherwise old Wolgan, he'll skewer you.'

'I brought handkerchiefs, they made o' Irish linen.'

'Handkerchiefs?'

'Griffin says the savages like handkerchiefs.'

'He never said that to me.'

'Well he said it to me, so I snuck off with Winnie's best, she won't notice till Sunday.'

Sparrow had no idea what day it was. He had to assume Sunday was a way off. 'You won't get a toll out o' handkerchiefs.'

'You got a axe?'

'I got the pup, I got the game dog.' Sparrow was surprised at just how triumphal and troubled he felt, declaring that out loud.

'I mean you got a axe, for me to trade?' said Peachey.

'I got a old axe, short-handled.'

'I'll take that, that and the Irish linen.'

'I cannot imagine what a savage wants with Irish linen.'

'Well then, I'll have the axe, won't I?'

The dawn chorus was underway, all manner of bird life sounding out. A faint cool breeze washing into the hut.

They heard the rattle of cart wheels and the steady paces of Woody's bay mare. 'That'll be the doctor,' said Sparrow. They peered out, scanning the track on the forest rim to the east. Soon enough they saw the doctor's gig with the bay mare in the shafts, bound for Prominence. They saw the mare trot on past Sparrow's patch and follow the track into the gully to the south.

Sparrow sat himself down on his bed. 'He's regular to and fro, he don't come in here.'

'What's to eat?' Peachey was on his knees. He turned the coals in the cookfire and loaded fine kindling upon them, blowing softly on the glow.

'Not much, bit o' salvaged corn, bit o' fish,' said Sparrow. He was not at all hungry at that moment but the question turned his mind to food and the immediate prospects for a better life. 'Griffin says there's meat every day on the other side.'

'I heard that too.'

'What else you hear?' Sparrow wanted to know what Griffin Pinney might have told Seamus Peachey.

'I heard there's a river of the first magnitude, runs west, and there's fertile bottoms far as you can see, a most arresting spectacle,' said Peachey.

'What else you hear?'

'He said he said, Seamus, he said, I could scarcely resolve to leave the eminence I stood upon, such was the grandness of the tracts below, and had it not been for the overpowering rays of the mid-day sun affecting my bowels, as they frequently do, I might still be there . . . transfixed in wonderment.'

'Did he tell you there's a village?'

'He did. He says the bolters got a village; says it's embosomed at the foot of the mountains.'

'I heard that too.'

It occurred to Sparrow that he and Peachey had been talking for quite some time. The imminent sun was lighting the timber on the forested rim to the east, the breeze turning dew-soaked leaves that sparkled in the light. Sparrow feared the boy might not come. If the boy did not come, they would have to steal a boat. That complicated the day beyond reckoning.

'You know there's women over there?' said Peachey.

'I know. Griffin says they fish in the shallows and they salt the fish and trade with the savages, they even hunt with them, and some of them, the women, live on islands in the river, it's that big.'

'Well butter my backside, is that what he said?' said Peachey.

'That's what he said,' said Sparrow, though he was not sure that Pinney had in fact said all that, exactly.

Peachey appeared at first delighted at the thought of women in the fishing way, and then sad at the thought of something else. 'First we gotta cross this damn river.'

'I got a boat coming.'

'I was hoping you'd say that.'

'The Woody boy, his boat.'

'What does he know?'

'Nothing, 'cept we're going fishing.'

'Are we now.'

'He's a good boy, he must not be misused or hurt.'

They settled at Sparrow's little table, munching on the mouldy corn.

'Why would I hurt that boy? Why, his father is the only decent magistrate we've ever had. Up to him and poor old Shug'd still be with us, albeit on the shovel in some damn washaway.'

'A good man, yes.'

'A tolerable apothecary.'

'That too.'

They heard the sound of boots scuffing in the dirt and there was a rapping on an upright and the boy's voice: 'Hello Mr Sparrow.'

Jug Woody was wet to the shins from wading and he carried a small bag of scraps for bait. He looked at Peachey and his expression changed to puzzlement.

'This is Mr Peachey, from the tavern by the bridge,' said Sparrow.

'You comin' fishin'?' said the boy.

'We ain't goin' fishin',' said Peachey.

Sparrow wished Peachey had not said that. He had thought the best line was that of least resistance so he planned to mislead the boy at least until they were midstream. 'We want you to take us across the river,' he confessed.

'What's in that pouch?' said Peachey.

'That's the bait,' said the boy. 'I won't leave it in the boat, damn crows.' He saw the haversack on the table beside Sparrow's salvaged leather costrel. 'You ain't about to bolt, are you?'

'We just want to ramble a little bit,' said Sparrow, 'such is the beauty of these parts.'

'I'll take you across the creek, you can ramble there if you want,' said the boy.

'No point ramblin' on the frontages, that just ain't ramblin'. We seek the *sublime*,' said Peachey.

'I'm not allowed across the river, my brother neither.'

Sparrow didn't know what to say, but Peachey did. 'You take us across that river we'll let you have the pup.'

The boy eyed the pup capering at Sparrow's feet. 'He's hardly a pup anymore, he's grown. Papa says the captain leaves them on the teats way too long, says that litter wore the old bitch right out.'

'You can put things right, take him back to Kettle if you want,' said Peachey. 'He might give him to you, he's a bit runty that pup.'

'He might at that.' Jug squatted down by the pup and began to pet him and talk to him and the dog licked his face and made the boy laugh.

'So, you'll take us across?'

The boy hesitated. 'Yes.'

'It's another secret, you'll have to keep it,' said Sparrow.

'Why is it a secret?'

Sparrow was lost for an answer. Peachey said nothing.

'How you goin'ta get back?'

'We'll ramble away till we see the trading scow, give old Guthrie a hoy,' said Sparrow. His throat was awfully dry. A considerable thirst had snuck up on him. He drank from the leaky leather costrel.

Then he took a gourd from the water bucket and filled the costrel once again.

He felt bad, deceiving the boy. He had a few small coins in a biscuit jar, coins for which he had no further use since the savages had no interest in currency and exchange on the other side was likely all barter, and anyway, his haversack was heavy enough. He tipped up the jar and the coins came to hand and he took the boy's hand and fed the coins into his palm and he tried to look him in the eye. 'Not much but you can have them, for the rental.'

'I'd rather you teach me to weave them wicker traps,' said the boy.

'That will have to wait,' said Sparrow.

They loaded into the little boat, dog and haversacks and fishing poles and bait pouch and all, and what was left of the ebb tide pulled them to the mouth of Cattai Creek and thence into the river and the boy rowed across the tide as they drifted downstream with Peachey and Sparrow on the back board and the dog perched on its hind legs, forepaws on the gunnel, watching the water as if transfixed in wonderment.

Words came to Sparrow, from where he could not recall: *in gallant trim the gilded vessel goes, youth on the prow and pleasure at the helm.* He liked those words. There was more to that verse but the more was lost to his memory.

There were baitfish jumping in the shallows and the dog was whining and stepping from one hind leg to the other as they reached midstream, the boy pulling hard. Sparrow was impressed. He seemed a lot stronger than first impressions had ever suggested. Peachey was impressed too. 'A formidable oarsman, who'd have guessed,' he said.

The boy smiled.

Not a one of them was ready for what happened. The baitfish stirred. An entire shoal took flight and shot like arrows into the deep, going with the tide, their flight so close to their vessel the dog could not contain himself. He leapt overboard and paddled in pursuit. Jug did not hesitate. 'I'll get him,' he said and he lunged for the dog and tipped in. 'Watch that boy,' said Peachey and he pivoted with unforeseen agility and took to the oars, rowing hard while Sparrow watched the boy swimming in much the same fashion as the dog, as boy and dog washed downstream.

'Please no!' said Sparrow.

'What?' said Peachey.

Sparrow had seen a dark fin surface and cut through the water towards the boy. Now the fin disappeared. He held his breath, his hand to his mouth. He had forgotten about the dog. The waters erupted as if blown by some volcanic force. The vertical mass of the bull shark hit the boy from below and lifted him clear up. They crashed down into a broil of pitted froth, and the spray came down upon them like rain. The bull shark was frenzied, tearing at the boy's thigh. Sparrow saw torn cloth and shreds of pink and bloodied flesh. He saw the churning waters colour to mulberry, he saw the monster thrashing, and then he saw it no more.

The bull shark disappeared into the depths, leaving the torso bobbing, the small agonised face, the lank blond hair afloat in the turbulence in a welter of blood and viscera. The waters settled and the ebb tide took the blood and guts away.

Peachey had abandoned the oars. He saw the boy rocking ever so gently on the waters, as if cradled by some melancholy spirit with naught but the agency to coddle and console. The boat drifted close, close enough for Peachey to grab the boy's arm and his shredded shirt and pull the remains onto the gunnel and there they studied the ruin: the startled eyes, the lips in motion but not a word, the savaged innards, the right leg gone, torn from the socket.

They could hear the quick breaths sucking for life and Peachey felt the boy shudder and then the breath was heard no more. The slender arm coloured to bone grey as the last of the blood departed the extremities. The boy was dead.

'It just happened, it just . . .' said Sparrow.

'O' course it happened . . . if it didn't happen it wouldn't a happened,' said Peachey.

'Oh dear Lord, what have we done?'

'We have to bury him or someone will find him, washed up.'

He had let the boy's lower half, what was left of it, slip back into the water. He beckoned Sparrow to take the boy's wrist but Sparrow recoiled. 'I don't want that,' he said.

'You take him this minute or you'll hang or worse, they'll hang you bound in chains,' said Peachey.

Sparrow reached out and took hold of the boy's wrist. He felt shaky and weak and the boy, trailing in the water, seemed heavy as a blacksmith's anvil, the fingers like some strange, fleshy succulent.

Peachey was braking with the one oar and rowing with the other and then he was rowing hard for the west bank. 'Fuck me but we need that dog,' he said.

Sparrow was staring at the water sloshing on the keel, trying not to look at the boy. He felt his eyes tear up. He was thinking about Biddie. He wished he'd never ever considered bolting for the other side even if there was a village, even if that village was embosomed in a beautiful spot by a big river at the foot of the mountains and the living entirely un-put-upon.

He looked to the shore as the keel skimmed onto the mud. 'This is Monty Bushell's patch, we can't bury him here.'

Peachey looked about as if he was entirely surprised. 'Monty Bushell?'

'Yes, don't you know downriver?'

'I'm a damn taverner on South Creek, why would I know the river this far down.'

'You're not really a taverner. You're a dependant, on the *feme sole*.'

Peachey stared. 'Make you happy that, say that, remind me?'

'No, I just . . .'

'Don't talk about that.'

Sparrow was silent for a while. Peachey seemed so angry. He wondered if Peachey thought he was to blame for the boy, which he knew was not fair. It just happened. 'We cannot bury him here,' he said.

Peachey scanned the bank of the river. 'One good thing.'

'What?'

'We keep the boat. Take it all the way to Pig Creek, sink it there.'

'And the boy?'

'We have to find a big rock, Marty. Weight him down and bury him at sea, so to speak.' He was pointing at the river.

Sparrow did not reply. Peachey was a different being altogether in the absence of Winifred. In fact, in the absence of Winifred, it seemed to Sparrow that Peachey was just like Winifred. He wanted to blame Peachey for the entire disaster but the more he thought about it the more he was glad Peachey had come along. Else he might be sitting here in the mud with the remains of the boy, alone. But then he thought otherwise. Then he thought if Peachey had not come along he could not have promised the dog to the boy and then the boy might not have lunged for the dog and by now Jug would be safely on his way home. And poor Mrs Woody, doomed now to eke out her life in the weeping world, and the good doctor upon his rounds, miserable, a life sentence.

Peachey was examining the boat. 'The mooring rope will do the job, sure as hell we won't need that.'

Sparrow could hardly bear to look at the boy, but he did. The eyes were open, sightless, indifferent to the blue sky above; the gut exposed, the viscera trailing in the mud, the ravaged hip socket speckled with grit and gore.

They hauled the boat and the boy into a patch of yard-high river reeds. They sheltered from the hot sun beneath the awry canopy of an old she-oak bent low by the flood, the root ball half torn from the ground. They watched, still and silent, as the dark-ribbed government ketch slipped by, the sails set near to square for the light southerly.

'That was close, least somethin' went right,' said Peachey.

'That's Guthrie, Sydney bound,' said Sparrow.

'I know who the fuck it is.'

'If this wind don't pick up he'll have to lay over.'

'They lay over they might see us.'

'Further down?'

'Where else but further down!'

Sparrow was unreservedly thirsty. He drank from the costrel, tipping it for the last of the contents. Peachey snatched it from him and finished off the dregs. 'If you'd a waxed it proper it wouldn't leak.'

'I didn't have wax to spare. I feel awful.'

'You look awful.'

Peachey lay down and turned on his side, his back to Sparrow. He fell asleep in no time at all, but Sparrow could not sleep. Every minute seemed like an hour and every hour seemed like a day, and so the time went by, and Sparrow lay there, looking up at the sky, watching the flood tide, fanning the flies and worrying about bull ants, leeches and snakes. Most of all he worried about the pup, for the pup was gone. He lay there listening to the sounds of the tide and the jumping fish and the birds, and watching the sea hawks circling into view, circling the fringes of the river, searching for meat.

He worried more about snakes than he did about bull ants. Every rustle in the reedy grass stirred his blood. He scrutinised his surrounds with a regularity that kept him even wider awake than he might otherwise have been. Snakes were too much like eels.

Sparrow felt the long, thin line of scab on the inside of his arm; recalled the crows in that coffin, the hen coop and the dead hens massed within. And Cuff's advice. *A wise man does not burn his bridges till he knows he can part the waters.* He stared at the boy, pale as tripe, dead on the bank. And the waters, quietly flowing, indifferent to all time and all occasion. 'I can't part nothin',' he whispered.

The sun was almost gone when the flood tide was peaking. Peachey awoke and sat with Sparrow and they watched the rose-petal pink of the twilight sky fade to grey. The cloud shadows on the silken flow turned from pink to black, every one of them shimmering into the shape of a shark fin, then running, like ink, into some other form, the shape of something else, some other monster from those murky depths.

'I never heard of a bull shark this far up,' said Sparrow.

'Well, you know what they say about never,' said Peachey.

'What?'

'It's never till it happens.'

'Didn't know they was even true, I thought maybe they was a story for the children, keep 'em in the shallows.'

'Like the duckbill, just a yarn?'

'Oh but the duckbill is true, I seen the one Mr Catley hung up on the store porch one time. Hung it on a hog-hook.'

'Noooo.'

'Yes.'

28

Late in the afternoon the wagoner Dudley Boggitt walked into the Hive with two copies of the *Sydney Gazette* in his hand.

'Hey ho, the wind and the rain, what news?' said Cuff.

The wagoner put his hands on the small of his back and arched himself. 'The governor, the gout's got him again; he's a ruin, I'm a ruin.'

'That ain't news, that's scuttlebutt,' said Sam.

'It's suffering is what it is, brings tears to the poor man's eyes,' said Boggitt.

'That's just what we need, a blubberin' governor,' said Cuff.

Boggitt arched his back once more and sat himself down. 'As gout is to the patrician so rheumatism is the distemper of the coachman. Seems I'm destined to shake to death.'

'You're no coachman, that wagon's no more than a rickety old dray,' said Cuff.

'Muggy as hell out there, where's that damn nor'-easter when you need it,' said Boggitt. He handed the newspapers to Mackie and Mackie laid them on the counter, smoothed them with his palm and set to reading the government orders beneath the masthead.

'The weather's like people, Dud, unreliable. Ain't that right, Gudgeon?' said Cuff.

Gudgeon was chewing on a mouthful of Atilio's flatbread layered with a preserve that was sufficiently sour to complement his mood. He did not reply.

Enter Fish, with maize bread on a tray. Gudgeon glanced at Cuff and then took hold of Fish's arm and pulled him close. 'You tell that cook to keep to his pots and pans.'

'What's that mean?' said Fish.

'He wants to touch her he can buy her, tomorrow. You tell him.'

'She's been sick, he tended her needs.'

'You tell him to leave her *needs* alone.'

Sam intervened. 'You best let go of Mr Fish right now.'

'You button your lip,' said Gudgeon. The Parsonage twins looked at Sam then at Gudgeon and they smiled, as one.

Sam took hold of his truss straps and adjusted the padding on the bulge Dr Woody said was a hernia. He planted both palms on the counter. 'Let him go.'

Mackie flipped the *Gazette* to the shipping news on the back page.

Gudgeon let go of Fish and Fish straightened up and fiddled with his collar. He stepped away, a safe distance. 'He won't touch her and he won't buy her neither,' he said.

'Gudgeon, you'll have your day but it ain't today, it's tomorrow,' said Cuff. He was seated at the doctor's regular table, by the window near the tavern door, writing a letter with a small wooden implement of some sort, an implement that required neither quill nor ink. He resumed his task.

'What is that?' said Fish.

'I reckon it's charcoal,' said Dan Sprodd.

'It's a invention,' said Sam.

Cuff raised it up for all to see. 'It's a stick o' graphite bound between two splints. It's called a *pen-cil* and mark me boys, it's the future. This one off a Nantucket whaler.'

'Americans, ever meddlesome with our ways!' said Fish.

'Wrong,' said Cuff. 'It was the English what was meddlesome. All the Americans ever wanted was the old arrangements, run their own affairs, which they had done for the better part of a hundred years, maybe more I don't know, so, let's be clear about meddlesome, it was the English decided to get meddlesome.'

'I thought we were talking about a *pen-cil*,' said Sprodd.

'We are that, and by the way it's from Glasgow, not America. The Scots invented it 'cause they like words more than anyone and they like numbers even better, especially with a pound sign in front of them, *ain't that right Alister?*'

Mackie did not shift his eyes from the *Gazette*, but the trade was entertained. They liked it when Cuff got going, spicing the conversation with a little dose of mockery. They liked to hear Cuff talk because he knew a lot about a lot of things, and they liked to hear his jokes and they especially liked it when he ribbed the chief constable and made him scowl.

Cuff knew his audience wanted more. 'Know how to wake up a Scotsman boys?'

'No,' said Sprodd, like it was urgent.

'Wave a penny under his nose.' Cuff clicked his fingers. 'He'll come round just like that.'

'I met a man once,' said Sam, 'told me he bought his wife for a bottle of ale and a glass jar full of pennies.'

'How big was the jar?' said Nimrod Parsonage.

'I did not inquire,' said Sam.

The conversation turned to variation in the magnitude of glass jars. Nimrod Parsonage said, 'If it was one of them big jars it might have been a poor bargain, depending of course on the charms of the woman, the diligence of her affections and so on.'

'That's a lot of pennies, one of them big jars,' said Crispin.

'That is my point entirely. She'd want to be generous with her bounties.'

Mackie crossed to Gudgeon's table and sat himself down, pulled his chair close. 'The custom is an agreed third party,' he said.

'We are going to auction,' said Gudgeon.

'It is customary for the parties to agree to the transaction. *All* parties to the exchange.'

'That is not my custom.' Gudgeon straightened in his chair, sat up tall.

Mackie spoke softly. 'This transaction will follow our custom as custom requires.'

'No. The auction will decide.'

'If you, and she, do not have an arrangement with a third party, then the girl must have a right of refusal and otherwise confirm publicly that she is agreeable to the exchange.'

Gudgeon laughed. 'You would defy the market.'

'I will see the market bow to custom, as we know it in the old country and as we have it here.'

'You will see stars, is what you'll see, if you persist,' said Gudgeon.

Sam was listening, every word. He grabbed a cudgel from some nook beneath the counter and slammed it down. 'You want stars Gudgeon, I'm your man,' he said.

She had rested much of the day and she was hungry all of a sudden.

Atilio put together a plate, a slice of maize bread and a spread of lard, a boiled potato and a half mug of small beer and she wolfed it down like it was her first meal in days. She was sipping on the small beer when Mackie came in with the seal-fur pelt in hand. He set the pelt on the bench. 'I have sent for a good man who needs a wife.'

'Will I have a say?'

'As custom requires you will have a say, and I will have the cure.'

The girl smiled. 'This too is business?'

'Yes.'

Mackie listened as the girl recounted the detail of the curing process. She looked drawn and tired but her memory was sharp, good on the particulars.

'Are you certain about the wash?' he said.

'As to the mix, yes.'

'Who else knows of the cure?'

'Outside this tavern no one, Jonas saw to that.'

Mackie rested his elbow on the table and ran his thumb along his jaw. 'Soft soap and pearl ash?'

'In that measure, yes, and the water as warm as your hand will stand and the soft fur perfectly retained in the combing out.'

Mackie took a deep breath and the girl heard the gurgle in his chest. 'I'll see you right.'

'Not a word to Jonas, please.'

'Jonas has gone. He's bound for Sydney Town on Guthrie's ketch.'

'He'll do his business there, with the cure.'

'No he will not.' Mackie seemed entirely sure of himself.

'No?'

Mackie leaned forward and spoke softly. 'No. He will not.'

'I am not sorry.'

'Nor I.'

She nodded. 'Will you see me clear of Gudgeon?'

'Yes.' Mackie handed the pelt to the girl as he stood to take his leave. 'There's not a hard bristle in it.'

'I know, I cured it,' she said.

As Mackie departed Fish hurried in, slid into the chair opposite the girl.

'Just so you know. He sent for Joe Franks at the Branch. Says Joe needs a wife,' said Fish. 'He's a old man lives quiet on the Branch. Even the savages like him.'

'*Like* him?'

'So I hear.'

'Would he share me round?'

'Joe won't treat you bad.'

'Does he still have his teeth? I've had my fill of gummy tosspots coverin' me.'

Fish's lips stopped moving. 'Did they do you regular, that lot?'

'You are a one for the particulars.'

'Did they hurt you?'

'They took me as occasionally as they took one another.'

'Well, they better not do that here. As for Joe, he's straight as a rule and he's no tosspot neither, he's sworn off it.'

At that moment Gudgeon walked in.

Fish abandoned the chair and stepped away.

Atilio straightened up, put his fists on his hips. Fish thought of the old saying, *you can have but one bull in the yard.*

Gudgeon picked up the seal fur and waggled the fur at the girl.

'He gave that to me,' she said. She snatched at the fur but Gudgeon was too quick.

'I will have none of your fits and spasms on parade, you understand me?'

'That is my pelt now.'

'You turn up them eyes and wriggle round like a damn seal and I'll skin you like a damn seal.' He took her by the throat with one hand and pushed the pelt into her face so hard the girl could hardly breathe.

Atilio crossed to the fireplace and picked up the fire tongs. He turned and cracked them down upon the sealer's skull and Gudgeon sunk to the floor. Blood was leaking from his head.

'You killed him,' said Fish.

'I don't care,' said Atilio.

The cook dragged Gudgeon along the hallway and sat him down in the tavern. Nimrod Parsonage said, 'He better not be dead, he won't like that.'

Sam sent Fish for the doctor and Cuff, in the interim, took charge of medical matters. He put a wad of brown cloth, soaking wet, on the bloody wound on Gudgeon's skull and he lifted the man's eyelid and saw nothing to indicate a stirring mind. Beads of water ran down Gudgeon's forehead and some ran into the corner of his eyes and down his face and one bead ran all the way to the end of his nose and hung there, poised, but the big sealer did not stir.

When the doctor arrived he addressed the entire assembly: 'My boy's missing, has anyone seen my boy?'

'Boys will do that,' said Cuff.

'They will,' said Sprodd.

'Not this boy,' said Woody. He lifted the wet cloth and looked at the wound. He lifted Gudgeon's eyelid and stared into the blankness. He said nothing.

He crossed to his regular table by the front window but he did not sit down. He leant forward, fists planted on the table, and he peered out the window, first left, then right, searching the square. 'I need help,' he said.

'We'll find him,' said Sprodd.

'His little boat's gone,' said Woody.

'We'll find him, Thomas,' said Cuff.

'He was supposed to be fishing . . . with that n'er-do-well Sparrow.'

'Sparrow wouldn't hurt a fly,' said Cuff. He joined the doctor at the window, hoping to see the boy, but what he saw was the Reverend Abbott in full flight heading for the tavern. 'Uh oh, it's the minister at a gallop.'

When the Reverend Abbott barrelled through the doorway he was so distracted by the shocking news of the wife sale that he seemed not to notice the stupefied Gudgeon, nor the agitated doctor. He saw the harness and the plaited tether decorated with coloured ribbons on the arm of the barber's chair. He crossed the tavern floor and picked up the tether and closed his fist upon it and shook that fist as if he was strangling a duck. 'It's true then, a woman is to be sold at market, auctioned off to the highest bidder in defiance of everything civilised and godly?'

Fish had scurried up the stairs to get Mackie and the chief constable was now on the stairhead, silently rehearsing the essentials for the conversation to come. 'The girl will have a right of refusal,' he said as he made his way down.

Gudgeon stirred, his eyes flickering. Abbott stared at him, briefly, but the wounded sealer was of no concern to the minister. 'This rope would be better employed thrashing the parties to this transaction,' he said, 'the girl no exception if she is a willing cog.' The great collar of fat on his neck was convulsing as if, like some nesting dove, he was about to regurgitate the macerations of his stomach.

'That girl is caught between a rock and a hard place.'

'There is no more wretched, no more gross a violation of decency than the sale of a woman at a beast market.'

'The beasts are scarce just now,' said Boggitt.

'That's true, it's likely a poor turnout,' said Cuff.

'What is this but wickedness consorting with debauchery, a merger of unclean purpose, to sow adultery ever deeper into the warp and weft of our virtue – even unto its fringes, unto the very wilderness, under the guise of a scandalous perversion of the most solemn ritual occasion.'

Sam spoke. 'You bring any hutch rabbits, for market?'

'Yes,' said the minister.

'That's good, they're good eatin',' said Sam.

Abbott turned on Mackie. 'This, constable, is a pagan thing, a proof if proof is required of the besotted ignorance and brutal feelings that preponderate in the absence of seemly society. A woman on a tether, led about and bartered like a prized cow before the leering assemblage. You must think again constable. This is an infamous transaction, akin to pugilism with nailed boots and metalled gloves or naked racing or carnival gluttony; beastly excess, outside the law of man and God, a violation, a rot in every footing in the house of holy wedlock.'

Dr Woody was fit to burst. 'You want no transaction at all? You want her abandoned, prey to every marauder from here to the wastelands? You want licence unvarnished by ritual, free of vows or obligation of any kind, is that what you want?'

Abbott was about to reply but Mackie intervened. 'Common law and custom admit of a man selling his wife if he so chooses.'

'So does the Bible!' said Sprodd, nodding.

'For the good of both parties the transaction will take place in a public manner and the people hereabouts will know the husband, be she abused for no good reason,' said Mackie.

'*Hereabouts!*' said Abbott. 'It is my firm belief this rustic habit is by and large confined to the picaresque occupations: bargees, timber getters, hunters, men of considerable mobility, no fixed abode, sealers and sailors, men whose *hereabouts* is mostly *thereabouts*. Such people have no care for obligation, they nomad like savages, their women snared in the most transient of arrangements, prey to the corporeal excess of the most debased of appetites. So, tell me constable, what good is *hereabouts*?'

'She will have a written contract, a copy of her own, and the resident magistrate will hold a copy in perpetuity and the public as witness will be her vindication.'

Woody smacked the table. 'You would prefer we cast her to the wind, and the wolves?'

Abbott would not be moved. 'I would prefer her dead in the ground,' he said. He took his leave.

29

When the tide finally turned it was dark. Peachey wandered off. 'I'll get some ballast,' he said as he departed. He was away for what Sparrow thought was a long time. He came back weighed down with a sandstone slab and the pup at his heel, all muddied up again and stinky with the smell of the river's putrilage.

Sparrow dropped to his knees and the pup cantered to him, high stepping, his tongue lolling, his every movement suggesting complete happiness.

Peachey put the sandstone slab on the mud. He was puffing hard, bent over, hands on knees. 'That's ten pounds of stone if it's an ounce.'

The pup licked at Sparrow's fingers and tried to clamber onto his thighs, his coat all wet. Sparrow searched in his pocket and drew out some crumbs and the dog licked them up, seemingly ravenous.

Then the dog put his nose to the ground and sniffed his way to the savaged boy, licking at the bloodied wounds. Sparrow leapt up and grabbed him and pulled him away.

Peachey said: 'You may as well let him do that. He's gotta eat and we gotta trade.'

Sparrow knew that Peachey was right. The pup was their legal tender, so to speak, in the mountains; he was the toll they would pay, that and the short-handled axe; and the handkerchiefs if it came to pass the savages wanted handkerchiefs. Giving up the pup was not a pleasant thought but Sparrow knew it might be necessary so he suffered the thought in uneasy company with his growing affection for the animal.

He let go and the pup ambled straight for the dead boy. He began to lick at the boy's entrails and then to eat them, gnashing hard. Sparrow could barely watch but he had to listen. Just once did he glance. He saw the pup had carried away a good yard of gut and he was devouring it the way a game dog might devour a snake, his long legs splayed, his snout to the ground, his whiskers soaked in blood.

Sparrow watched the river, the sparkle of the starlight on the budding ebb. 'We have to go.'

He wished there was another way, but he could not think of one. It seemed a lot more decent to bury the remains of the boy somewhere along the banks of the river but that course was loaded up with peril as both dogs and floods were prone to lift a body from its resting place.

So they took the boy or what was left of him and roped him to the sandstone slab and lifted their horrible cargo into the boat and pushed off, the boat going with the fresh tide, the farm country slipping by, silhouetted in the night light, first one reach then another, the tide doing most of the work, Sparrow holding the boat on a steady line, the pup short-tethered, Peachey rowing in bursts and resting in between.

When they reached the stone country Sparrow secured the tiller and the two men stood gingerly and bent over and lifted the boy and the sandstone slab and Peachey counted 'one, two, three' and they dropped their heavy burden sideways into the water and it disappeared with hardly a ripple, like a pebble into treacle.

The two men sat themselves down swiftly. They drifted for a time, not a word. Then Sparrow said what he had to say. 'You never should have give him that dog.'

'I give him the dog so he'd take us across.'

'That was a lie.'

'What are you, some kind o' fuckin' saint?'

'We should say a prayer,' said Sparrow.

'Too late,' said Peachey.

Sparrow swivelled about and looked upriver to where they had dropped the boy into the water. He did not think it was too late to say a prayer. He put the tiller under his arm and put his palms together, the way you do in church. 'He was a good boy, generous to a fault. Please God take him to your bosom. He did not deserve what happened. I wish he'd never brought me them fish, I wish he'd never come.'

'You gunna say amen?' said Peachey.

'I pray God will forgive us. Amen.'

Peachey heaved a sigh. 'That's a good prayer, Marty.'

The ebb tide was running strong. The pup had tired of the excitement and he was bloated on his feed. He was dry-retching for a time, that awful sound. Then he was curled up against the ribbing, his forepaws in the keel wash. Sparrow was leaning on the tiller, thinking how the river was like the bull shark: it would swallow you up in a trice.

They coursed along in silence, just the faint presence of a moon behind a fugitive cloud. They took turns to row but the ebb tide quickened and they were carried along at their ease.

Reach after reach, watching for the camp site at Pig Creek helped to keep Sparrow's mind off the dead boy, but his watch was not entirely effective in that regard. He saw eels skimming the riverbed, a frenzied gnawing at the boy's tattered entrails, and his face. Then his wayward thoughts slipped back to the memory of the shark spearing out of the water and then they switched, like a coin flipped over, to the torso on the sandstone plate, and then to the moment when that horrible cargo slipped into the depths, and those eyes. He could not keep the awful memories at bay, no matter how hard he watched for Griffin Pinney's camp. And now his thirst was back and there was naught but a trickle in the leaky costrel. He uncorked it and sucked hard on the mouthpiece, hardly enough to wet his tongue, which felt like the tongue of a cat. He dipped his hand in the river and drank from his palm, one briny mouthful, not much sense in that.

Their progress had slowed, the tide waning. They gave thanks for the night sky, hardly a cloud. The stars lit the banks of the river just enough to pick out the Pig Creek outflow and the clearing Sparrow knew to be Pinney's river camp. He tillered for the beach.

They secured the boat to an old tree bent low by the flood, a vestige of the rooting still anchored in the ground.

The camp site was strewn with driftwood. The pale grey carcass of an ox had slipped into the creek and the flowage now curled about the twisted frame. The dog paid the carcass no heed. He drank his fill from the creek, then he capered about, nose to the ground, fixed on some other scent.

'We follow the creek, I suppose,' said Sparrow. Only now did he consider Griffin Pinney's directions to have been somewhat minimal.

'We follow it till we get to Harp's hut. If he ain't there we go on till we find the machinery,' said Peachey.

'Alright.'

'First we gotta scuttle that boat.'

'That's a capital crime!'

'It's a capital crime to steal a boat!'

'But we never stole it . . . swear on anything.'

'You can swear all you like, we gotta scuttle the boat.'

Come the morning they inspected the grave, Thelma's grave, and they followed the line of the creek for some miles, until they saw the hut and the gibbet and the horrible freight hung thereon, just the faintest movement in the breeze, some long-dead savage, gutted and stuffed with grass. The dog had picked both the shape and the faint movement and he was feet planted, all hackles and bark. Then a voice: 'Don't tell me that's your game dog, he's hardly more'n a pup.'

Harp Sneezby was almost upon them, buttoning his flap as he waddled along.

'He's pure game blood, and he's a year old, almost, I reckon,' said Sparrow.

'I'm sure old Wolgan will be delighted to have you run through the pedigree. More'n likely he'll eat him so don't get attached,' said Harp. He turned his attention to Peachey. 'Griffin never said nothin' about you comin' along.'

'Well he should've, 'cause here I am,' said Peachey.

Harp turned to Sparrow. 'You finally did it, you been talkin' it long enough.'

'I hope they don't eat him, they better not,' said Sparrow. The thought of anyone hurting the dog loosed a surge within him, a most unfamiliar churn. Made him think of Geraldine, too.

'They ain't gunna teach him tricks I know that much. They don't teach nothin' betsept skullduggery,' said Harp.

'He sniffed you out didn't he?' said Sparrow, though he knew that was not true.

'Might be he did.' Harp waved them onwards to the hut. They passed two graves, a small cross and a big one, each of them awry and weathered near to ruin.

'Who's that?'

'That's my missus and my boy. Why they call it *small* pox got me beat, by God it has.'

'I'm sorry,' said Sparrow.

Peachey whacked him on the shoulder and said, 'Pssst.'

'Not a soul but me shed a tear back then, no point doin' it now,' said Harp.

'Where's Griffin?' said Peachey.

'He's gone back to Prominence for the wife sale. Says he'll buy this woman so long as she's hardy and pliant and still got her teeth; says she better have a civil tongue or he'll be teachin' her what for. I said complication, he said fornication. His priorities are clear I'll say that much.'

'How'd he find out?'

'Guthrie on the river, a most untimely quirk of chance.'

'I heard she's a Romany,' said Peachey.

'So they say,' said Harp.

'I hope he comes back soon, whatever,' said Sparrow.

'Don't we all, seems all I do is sit around waitin' for Griffin,' said Harp.

At Harp's hut they were not invited inside. They sat by a cold fire, cross-legged in the dirt, and they drank bang-head for the better part of the day and slept into the early part of the evening.

When Sparrow woke he poked at Peachey and the two of them sat up and brushed off the dirt and looked about, stirring the quantum of recall that survived the assault of the drink. They could hardly hear themselves talk for the cicadas. 'I got a hell of a head,' said Peachey.

'Me too,' said Sparrow.

Harp lit the fire as the light sunk from the western ridge into the pit of the night. He made some hearth cakes and baked them in an iron pot with a heavy lid. They were speckled with little green bits of something. Harp said it was bush parsley.

They ate the cakes. The cakes were good, lots of salt. They drank some more and drew themselves closer to the fire, warming their hands and their legs as the chill of the night set in.

The pup lay down against the fire stones and warmed his back and they passed around a big jug of bang-head and sat quietly for a time and listened to the creature sounds and the sound of the stream that carried to the river, the sound of Pig Creek.

Harp was looking hard at Sparrow's eyes, the yellowing of the whites accentuated by the firelight. 'You look sickly you know that?'

'Dr Woody says I got the jaundice,' said Sparrow. He wanted no further discussion on the matter of his appearance. He hurried to change the subject. 'He let you go, the doctor, the magistrate?'

'He did that,' said Harp.

'Why?'

'Said he knew I weren't no principal. Said the tinsmith at Toongabbie made that copper worm for Griffin. Woody knows more'n me. Said I'm to look out for his boy, too.'

A lantern flickered on the table inside the hut, a lumpy haversack visible in the glow. 'When do we go?' said Sparrow.

'We wait for Griffin, drink the proceeds in the meantime . . . hope he don't turn up with another damn woman,' said Harp.

'Best hope she got no teeth then,' said Peachey.

'What I hear she got all the wiles to make a man stupid,' said Harp.

Sparrow thought of Biddie's teeth. They were by no means perfect, but they were quite lovely in his opinion. Then he thought of Biddie's softness and the sweet plumpness of her limbs and those thoughts led on to sensations, tender sensations in his breast and tingling sensations in his nethers. He thought about the woods and the savages lurking therein, black as burnt bark and still as stone. He thought about the dead boy slipping into the depths. He wondered why he himself, personally, was so stupid. He wished he'd never come.

30

Atilio walked the corridor with the girl. He shepherded her to the barber's chair and she sat herself down. Fish took to sweeping as close as he dared.

Gudgeon had stirred. His eyes were open, the fog clearing. He saw the girl. He saw the beribboned tether on the floor by the barber's chair. He saw the hazy form of the big cook close by.

'Put him on the porch, get the man some air,' said Cuff, loud.

They were helping Gudgeon outside when Griffin Pinney stepped into the tavern, his old game dog at heel.

'That her?' he said.

'That's her,' said Sam.

'That's her indeed,' said Nimrod Parsonage.

Pinney crossed the floor and stood over the girl. He passed his musket to Fish and Fish took it as he stepped away, well clear, staring at the gun like it had come out of nowhere, like it might smoke and wriggle and turn into a snake.

'Stand up,' said the game hunter.

The girl stood, her eyes downcast.

'Are you sound, girl?' She did not reply.

She sensed Atilio's presence by her side.

'You got a tongue in that pretty head?' said Pinney.

The sight of the man made her skin crawl. She nodded.

'Show me your teeth.'

Atilio wiped a filleting knife on his leather apron, thereupon depositing a line of fish scales and watery secretions on the floor. 'No,' he said.

'You show me them teeth right now.'

'No!' said Atilio.

'I have every right to check this girl for soundness.'

Sam stepped from behind the counter. 'Not in here you don't.'

'Custom says I do.'

'Well, custom ain't here just now, I'm here instead,' said Sam.

'That's not right,' said Nimrod Parsonage.

'She is not a beast,' said Atilio.

'That's for you to say and me to find out,' said Pinney.

'No!' said Atilio, louder this time.

Pinney weighed the odds, Sam at his back and the big cook with knife in hand.

He snatched the musket from Fish.

'Lovely day!' said Cuff, as the game hunter departed.

There was something of a crush on the porch as the girl readied to leave the tavern with the tether tied about her waist. The porch crowd parted as Fish led the way, followed by the girl.

Gudgeon got to his feet with help from Nimrod Parsonage and the two parties came together in full view of the busy scene, market day in the offing, the comers on the parade, trestle tables, a few sacks of produce; chickens cheeping in wicker cages, a hutch thick with rabbits; a single basket of greens and a batch of eggs and a lone tray of river prawns and scarce but a dozen fresh fish laid out, blood oozing between fingers, and a few half ducks cured like hams and a single flitch of pork on a hog hook on the trade store porch, and flies on everything.

Gudgeon took hold of the tether as the wagoner, Dudley Boggitt, took to the centre of the precinct and declared the wife sale imminent. Under his old brown hat Boggitt was decidedly bald but he was otherwise well endowed with a booming baritone voice that carried into the deep reaches of every building on the square and made of him a suitable crier.

As he opened the proceedings Boggitt saw the hunting party led by Reuben Peskett come off the switchback path, a raggedy force, footsore, filthy, and thirsty into the bargain. 'Just in time to buy a wife,' he shouted.

The soldiers threw down their haversacks on the trade store porch, set their muskets against the wall and sat themselves on the porch boards.

Someone said, 'You get 'em?'

'We got 'em,' said Peskett, patting his haversack. 'Proof within.'

Boggitt beckoned Gudgeon and Nimrod took him by the arm and walked him onto the parade ground. The girl followed on the tether. At that point the big sealer seemed to regain a modicum of steadiness and he shrugged off his assistant. He fixed the tether in his hand, wrapping it once around his fist, and he led Bea Faa in a circle in full view of the folk gathered, the way a breeder might strut a brood mare at a county fair.

The soldiers passed a gallon demijohn up and down the line, gulping the contents as Boggitt called first for word of the doctor's boy but no word came forth so he urged all present to keep a keen eye, particularly on the river.

Moving on, he let it be known that the sealer Gudgeon Ketilsson, formerly of Reykjavik and more recently the Firth of Clyde and more recently still the fur seal rookeries of the Southern Ocean, was about to offer for sale by auction a wife, the girl Beatrice Faa, a girl of Romany extraction from the Scottish borderlands.

On completing the first circuit, the crier called for a chair as Gudgeon was faltering. 'Don't pay to cross Atilio,' said Cuff, chuckling.

They put a chair in the middle of the square and Gudgeon slumped into it, the tether still in his hand, dribble spilling from the corner of his mouth.

Boggitt kept on, now reading from a script drafted by Mackie: 'Be it known, a man may lawfully sell his wife to another man provided he deliver her over, in full view of the public gathered, and she haltered, the exchange of said halter to signify the solemn public mark of the transaction; said transaction to be confirmed in writing, witnessed by a lawful magistrate, copies to all parties concerned. And be it known the arrangement must, as custom requires, be congenial to all parties. Thereafter said parties will retire to an establishment conducive to *conviviality*, solemnisation and cheerfulness, all welcome.'

Someone shouted: 'Be you willin' missus?' It was Agnes Archambault.

'Yes,' said Bea but hardly anybody heard.

'Do I have an offer, the bidding is open,' said Boggitt.

'Any bad habits?' said Redenbach.

'She got a civil tongue in her head?' said Pinney.

'That husband looks booted and spurred to me,' said Alfie Shivers.

'Will she submit in a wifely way?' said Redenbach.

Abbott was heard to gasp.

'All indicators confirm an obliging young woman,' said the crier.

'Three guineas and a dozen pelts, prime pelts,' said Griffin Pinney.

'Kindly specify the pelts,' said Boggitt.

'Wallaby,' said Pinney.

'Lord help that girl,' said Sprodd.

'Four guineas!' Joe Franks walked onto the square, his britches muddied to the shins. He dropped his haversack and bent over, hands on knees.

The girl heard the murmur: *Joe Franks, old Joe, well well...*

She studied him. Watched as he leant against a cartwheel and took the weight off, his arse on the hub.

Cuff was relieved. 'There, see! Ye of little faith,' he said to Mackie.

'Four guineas don't best three guineas and all them pelts,' said Pinney.

Cuff was not inclined to agree. 'A dozen pelts at a shilling a pelt, you're a bit short.'

'I'll match the guineas with the pelts then.'

The crier looked to Joe. Joe said, 'Four guineas and a Whitney woollen blanket.'

Cuff was warming to the contest: 'Mr Wallaby makes the better blanket but Mr Whitney carries the treasured mark of distinction.'

'Dead heat, might have to cut her in two,' said Alfie.

'Four guineas! That's a year's bread for a man,' said Monty Bushell.

Pinney wanted this girl. He wanted her even more than he wanted Thelma Rowntree on first sighting. He did not intend to lose to an old dog like Joe Franks. 'Five guineas, and the pelts.'

Fish was upset to think the most horrible man on the river might get his dirty hands on Bea Faa. He felt safe enough standing at the chief constable's shoulder. 'You don't hardly got a hut, even.'

'An' he smells like a savage,' said Cuff.

'Enough of the badinage,' said Boggitt, 'the bid is with Mr Pinney, the call is with ex-sergeant Franks, veteran of the American wars, of Mysore and Seringapatam and Travancore and more . . . Joe?'

Joe had enough credit at the store to bid more. He had the receipts in his pocket. But at that moment in time he felt his purpose dissolving. He was staring at his boots but his boots were a blur. The eyes of the gathered folk and the half-drunk hunting party were upon him. *Silly old man, old fool.* He thought himself pathetic and sad, say nothing of exhausted. How was it that Guthrie had persuaded him, at Mackie's behest, to bid for a wife? He blamed Cuff, for what had begun in jest was ending in farce.

Joe shook his head. 'I'm done,' he said. The assembly seemed to groan in unison, whether at Joe's misfortune or the girl's was hard to say.

'I say Joe's still ahead,' said Cuff, loud.

'Here's the equation,' said Boggitt. 'The blanket's a Whitney woollen so it offsets all them the pelts, but on the cash money Mr Pinney is ahead.'

'What we gunna do?' said Cuff.

Mackie walked to the centre of the square where the crier stood by Gudgeon, who had hardly moved though he managed, still, to hold the tether. The chief constable talked and Boggitt listened, and then he walked back to the Hive porch and the crier started up again.

'The bid is with Mr Mackie. The bid is twelve guineas. Six to cover the purchase, on Mr Franks' behalf, and six to cover Mr Gudgeon's convalescence whereupon he will depart the precinct in the company of his gentlemen companions, Messrs Parsonage and Parsonage.'

'What's that mean?' said Crispin.

'Means we ain't welcome,' said Nimrod.

Boggitt was not finished. 'Here she is, dark as mystery, pretty as the morning, nimble as a bean, uncommonly tall, useful in a orchard, a picture, what more is there to say. Last chance, gentlemen.'

Cuff was chuckling to himself, recalling the conversation at Joe's patch when they composed an advertisement for a wife. 'By God I never thought I'd see the day you bid for a woman, Alister.'

'I bid for Joe, no more nor less.'

'Here's hoping rumour gifts that interpretation to posterity.'

Griffin Pinney stood hands on hips, a look of puzzlement on his face. 'Why'd he do that?' he said to no one in particular, the old dog asleep at his foot.

Abbott spoke softly in Mackie's ear. 'We are a nation sinking into muck and mire in the eyes of the world. This will carry, mark my words.'

'Let it carry, let all parties know to whom she belongs.'

Woody could not restrain himself. 'I know a church, and my shame for a part of it, where annulments are swapped for gold and the blessed poor have, in that regard, no redress at all,' he growled.

'It would seem sir that you have but two temperatures: mild and infernal.'

'I have an infernal sense of forsakenness is what I have.'

'In the cause of peace I will retreat to the rear of the assemblage, forthwith,' said Abbott as he moved away.

Bea Faa reckoned Joe Franks might be fifty, but it was hard to tell. He was, perhaps, not as old as the doctor but he was just as wearied in appearance and rickety in his motion. In his face she saw a steady, contemplative man, a man quite unlike Gudgeon. She could but hope.

'I am closing,' called Boggitt. 'The bid is with our chief constable on behalf of the ex-sergeant.'

Pinney kicked the ground and marched off, bound for Peachey's Tap, the sleepy old dog hastening at his heel.

Boggitt paused, his forefinger pointing to the heavens. 'Done! The girl is transacted for six guineas and six for the convalescence of the vendor.'

Mackie beckoned Joe Franks and the interested parties joined Boggitt in the centre of the square. They gathered about Gudgeon and the girl. Agnes was there too, as were Cuff and the Parsonage twins. Agnes took the girl by the arm and squeezed. 'You can count your blessings, better dead than Griffin Pinney,' she whispered.

Cuff peered into Gudgeon's blank eyes. 'Let's hope the relinquishing party can follow the procedure at this customary juncture.'

'I gave this girl my word she would have a right of refusal, as custom requires,' said Mackie.

'I do apologise for my late arrival,' said Joe, 'the river near beat me.'

'Ask him, whatever you want,' said Mackie.

'I will not be ill-used,' she said.

'You can be sure of that!' said Joe.

Agnes rested a hand on the girl's shoulder. 'Hear hear!'

'Is this forever?' said Bea.

The crier chuckled. 'Would you like a fixed term?'

'I will not be sold on, save here, in public.'

Joe Franks had not, not for a moment, considered such an eventuality. Nor had he anticipated the startling, limpid green of her eyes. His mind went to particles and the particles flew about in confusion, like straw in the winnowing. She was tall, and taller than she'd seemed at a distance, though by no means as tall as Mackie. Thinking about tallness he lost his train of thought. He was uncertain as to what further he might say.

'I have a farm on the Branch,' he said. 'It's downriver. Not too far.'

'A most handsome setting, a fine peach orchard,' said Cuff.

Gudgeon twitched and jerked as if startled and he snatched at the girl's hand but she pulled away for he had not the strength to hold her. His eyes were wide open and the strangest look was fixed upon his face, like he was possessed of some comic demon.

The girl wondered how far downriver was *not too far*, but she did not care to ask. She had decided she would go with this man Franks. It was not so much what he said; it was the sound of his voice that made her inclined to trust him. She could hear in that voice a fathomless sadness. Mackie said Joe Franks was a good man, as did Fish, and Atilio too. All she could see in the game hunter was ill-use and misery.

'Will you do your share girl?' said Joe. 'That's all I need to know.'

'Yes.'

'Can you read?'

'An elaborate interview, an avalanche of enquiries!' said Boggitt.

'Yes.'

'I mean *read*, out loud, to me, with some fluency?'

'Yes.'

'A transaction or a courtship I no longer know!' said Boggitt.

The girl cast a fierce look at the Parsonage twins who were much pained by the dawdling sentimentality of the epilogue and wanted the sale over. 'I ain't had a drink for twenty minutes,' said Crispin.

Cuff handed the tether to Joe Franks and the onlookers applauded what seemed to be a successful conclusion to an uncommon entertainment.

Agnes spoke softly to Bea: 'He treats you bad you come to me.'

'Where are you?'

'I'm over there,' she said, pointing. 'Freeman's Reach.'

The crowd dispersed, some to their duties in the precinct and some to the Hive and some to their boats and some to the south track, thence to the Tap, and the soldiers decamped to the mess there to drink some more, and reminisce on the hunt.

Bea untied the halter and let it drop to the ground. 'You have an orchard?'

'We have a small peach orchard.'

'A most agreeable peach cyder,' said Cuff.

'We?'

'My man, Freddie,' said Joe.

'Freddie's a good man, simple soul, don't go worryin' yourself about Freddie,' said Cuff.

Nimrod Parsonage grinned at Mackie. 'You gunna lodge him, Gudgeon, till he mends?'

'I will lodge him, you will tend him.'

'We don't tend nothin', 'cept what we kill and cure, same as her!'

'Pick him up.'

With some difficulty the Parsonage twins helped Gudgeon to the Hive and settled him on a cot in a small room near the kitchen.

Late that night Atilio appeared in the hallway with a coarse muslin cushion in his hand. He stood for a moment, listening to the quiet. He stepped into the small room. He moved silently to the head of Gudgeon's cot. He stood listening once again. There was naught but Gudgeon's irregular breath. He put the cushion lightly on Gudgeon's face and heard him suck for breath. He jammed the cushion hard down, stretching it wide, his knuckles pressing into the tick, the shape of the face taking form through the muslin like a bloated mask, a spray of feathers wafting to the floor, the sealer's hands clawing at the big cook's forearms. The upper body rose up and slammed down, and the hands clawed at the assailant some more, but to no avail.

The kicking and the clawing subsided. The body beneath him went limp. Atilio took away the cushion and saw the face of the dead man, white as winter's goose down. He bent low, close to Gudgeon's face, picked feathers from the floor and closed his fist upon them. 'No more,' he said. He stood and listened, once again, to the silence.

31

The pup lay sprawled in the dust, wide-eyed, listening, watching, as Harp stepped from his hut, scratching at his parts. The sun sat squat on the forested rim to the west, an orange glow along the horizon, as if the great orb was cut and bleeding out.

Sparrow and Peachey stirred, but they did not wake. They lay in the dust, in a restless half sleep abetted by a surfeit of bang-head.

Harp did not mind. He plonked onto the chopping block by the fire stones. He beckoned the dog and the dog came to him and sat at his heel and they sat there, quietly.

When the darkness crept in, Harp set about fixing the kindling, ready for the fire. He sparked some dry grass into flame and put the grass to the kindling. 'Alright,' he said and smacked his hands together.

Sparrow and Peachey sat up, brushed themselves off. They felt the tiredness that comes from doing very little in the course of a long day drinking.

Harp cocked his head right back and he saw the moon and everything else. 'Like a jewel box,' he said. He searched the heavens for the only constellation he could ever pick out, albeit something of a blur to him. 'There it is.'

'Is what?' said Peachey.

'The Hydra, don't you know the Hydra?'

'I gotta piss, that's all I know.'

Peachey got himself up, stretched, wandered into the trees at the back of the hut.

Harp heard a thud, as did Sparrow, and then another thud like a man going down and the sounds of Peachey in extremis, groaning and cursing.

They found him on his knees near the tethered pony, his arms wrapped around his ribbing. 'He's broke my ribs,' he moaned.

The pony was treading ground, snorting, stirred by the commotion. 'Never trust a Cape pony, Africa no exception,' said Harp.

'Africa?' said Sparrow.

'That's his name.'

'He give me both barrels. There I was, pizzle in hand.'

The pup was there too, licking at Peachey's ear and Sparrow had to pull him away as Peachey was quite unable to let go of his ribs.

'You flash your pizzle at me I'd kick out,' said Harp.

They helped him back to the cookfire and Peachey went down on his knees again.

'You give him a big fright,' said Harp.

'He don't know fright like the fright I got, he's black as pitch.'

'He's snapped them ribs like a dried twig, that's my guess,' said Harp.

Peachey didn't know what to do. 'I don't know what to do,' he said.

'Nothin' we can do, short of a gentleman's corset and that I do not have,' said Harp.

Sparrow looked down on Peachey with the eye of pity, though privately he was glad it was Peachey and not him.

'Why, why'd I ever listen to that man, all that commonweal prattle,' said Peachey.

'Why do birds sing after a storm?' said Harp.

'Why?'

'I don't know.'

'What are we gunna do?' said Sparrow.

'I don't know that neither,' said Harp. 'Come light there's some berries he can chew, if I can find 'em, fix the pain.'

Peachey bent low like a Mahometan, so low his forehead almost touched the ground. 'Get me some now.'

'Not now, not in the dark,' said Harp. 'That boar's out there.'

Peachey lifted his head and stared into the dark. 'You seen him?'

'I seen him alright, I caught him rootin' out a mash barrel one time. I stood off, hoped he'd eat his fill and blow up but he didn't.'

'Get me them berries.'

'You know what he did to Spider Thornycroft, that boar? He tore out his throat and ate his tongue and miscellaneous other parts I'll not deign to nominate.'

'You think he might come back,' said Sparrow.

'He's around, that I know.' Harp stared into the darkness along the creek. 'It's round the mash you got to worry. Come next corn I intend to build a sleeping place, like a burial platform with a ladder but.'

'What's a ladderbutt?'

'I mean . . . but with a ladder.'

'Oh.'

Peachey was still contorted but somewhat diverted by Harp's idea. 'What if you roll out of bed?'

'I'll buckle myself in, sleep like a snug foot in a shoe.'

'You mean like a foot . . . snug in a shoe?' said Sparrow.

Harp took on a look of unhappy puzzlement. Sparrow noticed. 'Sleep like the dead?'

'That I will. I'll shoot him from up there if he comes for my mash again.'

They made Peachey stand while Harp dragged the old straw mattress from the hut and laid it in the dirt near the fire. Peachey sunk onto the mattress and rolled onto his back.

Harp threw a tatty blanket over the invalid. 'I might have to shoot you.'

Sparrow reckoned Harp wouldn't do that but Peachey wasn't so sure. He took to suffering in silence, just the faintest groan now and then as he rocked to and fro and stared into the twinkling infinity above. 'How could I possibly know about Africa,' he said.

That set Sparrow to thinking about the vast river on the other side. He now knew, on the authority of Mr Catley by way of Mr Thistlewaite, that the river flowed to a lake where whales were seen to spout and that meant the river must flow on, out the other side, a waterway to the ocean. And on that ocean a man might go anywhere if he wanted to, or had to, even Africa. But Sparrow had no thought of going to Africa. If the commonweal on the other side was all that Griffin Pinney said then he would stay there with the men and the women of the village embosomed at the foot of the mountains. Sparrow could picture himself looking down from the crest of those mountains, his bowels in good order, his mind transfixed in wonderment.

Peachey was quieter now.

Harp appeared with a musket in the crook of his arm and a lantern in his hand. 'I'll have a little look for them berries,' he said, pointing. He wandered off, past the gibbeted savage, into the dark.

The pup ambled to the fringe of the firelight, his attention divided between the tavernkeeper in his misery and Harp's form as it melted into the darkness on the creek, just the lamplight moving through the trees.

Sparrow clicked his tongue and beckoned the pup and the pup crossed to Sparrow and crawled onto his lap. He was no small thing, not anymore. He was a sprightly young dog, as good a companion as a man could have. As ever, the animal licked at his hand, wanting the salt in his sweat. Sparrow patted him and took hold of the loose skin on his neck and felt the warmth of that coat. He wondered if, perchance, the pony had done more damage to Peachey than just the ribs; if Peachey might have a burst liver or a busted spleen or a slivered length of gut, something deep within, something bad, prospects-wise.

It occurred to Sparrow that if Peachey was to die he might reclaim the short-handled axe and give that to old Wolgan, that and the handkerchiefs, and if that was toll enough he might keep the pup for his own.

Sparrow liked the pup. He liked him very much indeed.

32

The high tide was due a little after sunrise. A small crowd of well-wishers gathered near the waterline to watch Joe Franks and his new wife depart. They heard the rattle of the doctor's gig, heard him whoa the bay mare and saw him fix the tether weight by his porch step, his every move observed by Caleb on the box seat.

When he'd fixed the tether the doctor pulled a water bucket close but the mare showed no interest.

The doctor called on Caleb to step down and the two men walked the switchback path down to the small gathering, Caleb limping, same as ever, a clean white shirt worn loose over his raggedy trousers, Mackie close behind, armed.

The doctor spoke to Joe. 'You'll see he gets to his people.'

'I will that.'

'And Joe, keep an eye out for my boy.'

'I will.'

Joe unravelled a fit-for-purpose oilcloth and threw it over the provisions and set about lashing it down. 'Thank you,' he said to Mackie.

Mackie nodded. 'Good luck to you both.'

The doctor was anxious to hold Joe's attention. 'Whatever's happened to my boy it's happened on this river, I know that in my marrow.'

'I'll keep a keen eye,' said Joe.

'Do, please.'

'Caleb too, he's sharp.'

Cuff pointed a finger at Caleb. 'He knows the ropes Joe, he can help you with the boat. Right, Caleb?'

Caleb nodded, said 'yes sir', and the girl wondered if perhaps this fabled Caleb said that every time.

Franks readied the sail for the light sou'-westerly, figuring the setting might do, trimming here and there, all the way to the sharp turn at the end of York Reach. They moved off, pushed into the deep by Cuff, who never seemed to care about muddy boots and slosh between his toes. Some of the watchers clapped and waved as the sail took the breeze and the boat slid downstream.

Cuff did not wave. 'Somebody should've made a speech, I should have made a speech.'

'No one stopped you,' said Mackie, as Woody took off, labouring his way up the switchback path, bent low.

'No one asked me neither.'

'Since when do you need prompting to pontificate?'

Cuff was briefly silent, his thoughts on another tack. 'You pay the wife price, provision them up . . . Why'd you do that?'

Mackie hurried after the doctor. Cuff hurried along by his side. 'Well?'

'She will serve Joe well, he's a good man; that's our ethic.'

'You serve another you serve yourself, every time, Alister.'

'You're the one said Joe needed a wife.'

'That was a joke, long before them sealers come in draggin' that girl.'

'Perhaps, then, you are a prophet?'

'The only time you resort to what you think is humour is when you want to change the subject, I suppose you know that?'

'No.'

'Well, you're not changing the subject.'

They crossed the square, bound for the Hive.

'What is the subject then, you tell me.'

'The subject is you and Beatrice Faa; the subject is that girl's green eyes. She's got your eyes, Alister.'

'That's entirely foolish.'

'They're the palest green eyes I ever seen, same as yours, down to the last detail.'

Cuff took hold of Mackie's arm and stopped him just short of the Hive porch. He was pointing at Mackie's left eye. 'Little black spot, flaw on the iris, same as hers.'

'I note you've been looking at her most carefully.'

'Who wouldn't?'

'I'll hear no more of this.'

'Her age is about right.'

'I said *no more*.'

'And she's willowy too, like you.'

'Enough! I made a bargain with her and I kept it.' Mackie stepped onto the porch.

Cuff was not finished: 'Hear no more, speak no more, shut it out, but you cannot shut it out, which is why you paid the bride price and why you provisioned them up. And one thing more. The legalities will catch up with that girl. She's fled a transport, God knows what else.'

'She's way clear of the legalities.'

'What cunning hides time will reveal.'

'Who said that?'

'Me.'

33

Caleb stood in the prow with his back to Joe Franks and Bea Faa. He surveyed one side of the broad waterway with some intensity, then the other.

He had removed the white shirt, folded it neatly and jammed it under the lashing.

Joe noticed Bea looking at the young man, her gaze searching after his to the fringes of the river, left and right. 'It's his pantry,' he said as he trimmed the sail to a close haul.

The girl turned to Joe, unsure of what she'd heard.

'Pantry,' he said. 'Most of what they live on, or should or did, you'll find in this river, or no more than a stone's throw from the river. Thus, the river is the object of all contention.'

Joe contemplated what more he might say. There were things the girl would have to know, the sooner the better. He settled the boat on a course, beating to windward. 'Shellfish, roots, tubers, the fruit of the traps, bream and bass, soapies, catfish, all washed in by the hand of providence, that being the tide, and there for the taking till we drove them off, his people.'

'Are they many?' she asked.

'Their numbers are diminished.' Again Joe Franks found himself working hard for words. 'Come what may this river steers our lives.'

The girl watched Caleb. She could not tell if he was attending to the conversation, nor how much he would understand if indeed he was listening. He seemed intent upon watching the western riverbank.

'When they come in they get punished,' said Joe. 'They tried to take back the river, harvest time last year, but for that they paid a terrible price in retribution.'

Joe had put the tiller in her hand for he was trimming the sail more or less constantly, tightening and easing the sheet, glancing at her, discreetly, whenever he could. He guessed he might be older than her grandfather. 'The wind takes the sail, quickens the spirit, so I find,' he said. The muscles in his forearms were aching just shy of dreadful. He was grateful to have her by his side.

They skimmed past Cattai Creek. The Cattai brought Woody's urgent words to Joe's mind. 'Keep a sharp eye for that boy's dinghy,' he said.

Caleb nodded.

Come midafternoon their progress was much slowed by the flood tide. The landform had changed, the gentle hills replaced by steeper, sandstone climbs that were heavily forested and dappled with the pink and grey of rusty gums, their roots like glue spill on the stone, and higher up glimpses of caves and ledges from which a proprietorial eye might overlook the fertile patches on the margins of the river below, rimmed by the tidal flow and flanked by tributaries coming out of gullies and gorges. Idylls nestled in the embrace of water and stone.

'First sight of my patch I thought of paradise,' said Joe, 'cosseted away like a downy nest in a thicket. I sat on a big flat stone, made it my hearthstone; imagined a corn crop tall as young Caleb there.'

Neither of them was ready for the shriek that came at that moment from Caleb. Bea had never heard a sound like it. He stood in the bow, waving, and Joe and the girl followed his line of sight to the west bank, a low, marshy point thick with reeds.

The figures stood, three in a line, native to their element, shin-deep in the shallows, watching the boat as if transfixed, the two young men armed with barbed spears, the old man with a musket in the crook of his arm. They began to shout and wave. Caleb waved back and shouted some more.

'Will you put him off?' she asked. But already the savages were trekking into the timber, northbound, their lower legs stockinged with grey mud, their chatter ecstatic, the young men leaping and pirouetting through the underbrush, the old man scuttling along, keeping up as best he could.

Caleb turned about. 'My grandfather,' he said.

Bea was momentarily lost for words. 'He is happy to see you,' she said, finally.

'He is my grandfather, thus he is happy to see me, yes.'

'That's ol' Wolgan,' said Joe.

Bea was thinking back over the subjects traversed earlier in the journey. She had been cautious enough to make no comment on Caleb lest he have some small grasp of the language. Now it seemed his grasp stretched all the way to *thus*.

'Caleb spent some years with the Reverend Hardwick in Parramatta, did you not, Caleb?'

'That ol' bugger,' said Caleb.

'Brought in by soldiers, orphaned . . . sometimes they salvage a handsome child.'

Caleb chuckled. 'A pretty one.'

'And God help the rest,' said Joe.

'Do you know his grandfather?' she asked.

Joe nodded. 'The boy is home, replenished, for that we ought find favour in their sight.'

'My grandfather will return the gun, for goodwill.'

'In that case we better have a cook up.'

The wind had swung about and the flood tide was building. 'We have to lay over,' said Joe. He pointed to a sandy spit a way ahead.

On beaching, Joe took hold of the mainsail boom and the gunnel and he tried to step out of the boat but his legs were liquid and his stiff arm on the gunnel failed to hold him. He fell sideways onto the sand and rolled onto his back.

They helped him up. 'I am naught but a ball of knots and spasms,' he said.

The girl watched the river, the tide at work, a vast ocean pushing the flow contrary to their needs.

They stretched out on the warm sand and closed their eyes.

———

Bea woke to Caleb's singing. The sun was almost down, lost behind the serried timber on the ridge, tiers of blood-orange clouds.

Caleb sat cross-legged, singing quietly, a lullaby perhaps. In his lap were a bunch of pale taproots, dripping wet. He began to eat one of these taproots with some enthusiasm. He leaned forward and his entire frame rose up, erect, as if lifted on some hydraulic principle.

Joe shook his head. 'I wish I could do that.'

Caleb threw a taproot to the girl and he handed one to Joe.

'As do I,' said Bea. They laughed and Caleb smiled and repeated the manoeuvre in reverse, crossing his legs at the ankles and lowering himself to the sand with not the faintest shudder.

'I call them bush parsnips,' said Joe.

'They are sweet,' said Bea.

'They are sweet,' agreed Caleb, and he named a name that neither of them could repeat let alone remember.

The air now was crisp and cool.

Joe felt better. He got himself up and went on shaky legs, retrieved the water bladder from the boat and drank like he'd not drunk for days. 'The heat, does me in.' Then he handed the bladder to the girl and she realised she'd not had a drop since they departed the ridge and she too drank her fill.

They departed as the slack tide surrendered to the ebb and they sailed on.

They heard the sound of frogmouths and boobooks and night-birds unknown to them, and they heard the whoosh and smack of fish jumping in the shallows and the constant sound of the tide chafing the banks and far off a dog howling, and they saw river rats scurrying for cover and myriad shapes in the dark recesses of the forest and higher up they saw great bands of ancient sandstone, moonlit, cracked and fissured by the chisel work of ages.

———

Some hours later they ploughed up the Branch with the habitual nor'-easterly in the sail, the bow cutting through the failing tide. The moon hovered over the black rim to the west and the stars marked the silken black flow of the Branch with a speckling of silver.

At Joe's patch the girl tillered the boat to the mooring by a big old she-oak and they helped Joe climb out. He sat himself down on the gunnel, smacked at his thighs, worked his fingers into his cramping flesh and muttered his displeasure.

Bea recalled Joe's words – *a downy nest, cosseted away.* Her most fearful notions were tempered by the starlit vision of the cabin and the byre on the slope beyond the flats, and by the scatter of yards and shelters, the old hut, and the sight of the vegetable garden and the peach orchard; the sense of something carved out by epic toil, a working farm in the embrace of wilderness.

She looked down at Joe and she thought about what she'd learned. He did not drink for he was sworn off it, save for his peach cyder. His voice was gentle and his conversation welcome, being for the most part practical. He wanted her to read to him – she would do that with pleasure. As for his weariness in the form of his affliction, that she did not find burdensome at all, that she could see to advantage. *I will not be ill-used,* she had said. *You can be sure of that,* he'd replied.

She could see a man barrelling towards them, followed by a goat. 'That's Freddie, he's a fixture,' said Joe and he put out his arm and the girl helped him to stand.

Freddie circled around Caleb and scuttled past Bea as if she wasn't there and he threw his arms around Joe Franks and buried his face in the old soldier's shoulder. 'Lucky I'm here,' he said, 'else you'd be sayin' where's ol' Freddie.'

'I'd know you were somewhere hereabouts,' said Joe.

'Ain't goin' nowhere, not me,' said Freddie. He was tugging at the worn-out bit of linen that passed for his waistcoat and brushing down the slop cotton shirt beneath it.

Joe folded back the oilcloth with some care and retrieved a sack of salt, pulling it upright against the gunnel. He beckoned Caleb. 'Please,' he said, and Caleb hefted the sack onto his shoulder and headed for Joe's cabin. An ox tethered in the corn stubble lifted its head and watched him limp by.

Joe watched Caleb until the boy was well on his way before hauling the oilcloth off the provisions. He peered into a corn sack and flashed a smile at Bea. 'Pork belly in linen, cured.' He folded the corn sack tight around the hefty lump of pork and pulled a half bushel sack of seed wheat upright on the gunnels. 'Old Wolgan's comin' for the boy,' he said.

'Hide things!' said Freddie.

'Freddie, where's Mrs Kunkle?'

'Back on Thyne's patch, Rupert come got her.'

'Is she alright?'

Freddie paused. Then he giggled. 'They got in the byre, I could hear 'em humpin' in the hay . . . I had a good listen.'

'I'll bet you did.'

'They sure as hell weren't missin' poor ol' Thyne.'

'One way to mourn,' said Joe, but his attention hardly strayed from the job at hand. 'Get along now Freddie, put your fowls inside, put your axe and adze inside, lock the swine in the byre and get yourself to the tripod and we'll set a fire.'

'Big old stewin' hen?'

'As we do.'

'Feed 'em and they go away,' said Freddie, staring at Bea. 'You the wife I s'pose?'

'Her name is Beatrice, Bea,' said Joe.

'I hope your intentions are honourable,' said Freddie.

'I believe they are,' she said.

'Mild temper and sobriety essential,' said Freddie, parroting the words he remembered.

'Yes,' she said. The goat was butting gently at her knee.

'Her name is Beauty,' said Freddie.

'Take a bag of wheaten flour while you're at it,' said Joe.

'Wheaten flour, smell that bread.' Freddie hefted the bag onto his shoulder like it was a feather.

Joe took the bagged pork belly and the girl hefted the sack of seed wheat onto her shoulder and they followed the track that edged the field of corn stubble. They crossed a faintly perceptible flood line and moved on up the grade to the cabin on the western side of the tributary valley where the trees rose thick to the ridgeline.

Bea stood in the doorway. A fireplace on a generous hearthstone, a table and a pair of chairs and stump stools; a keg; on the mantelshelf a button box, books and a bayonet set in a scabbard; butchering knives and meat hooks racked on the rear wall; a dividing curtain, pulled back; a bed in the recess, a seachest by the bed.

Joe put the bagged pork belly on the stone. 'No home without a hearth,' he said.

She saw the faint outline of his smile.

Outside Caleb and Freddie were setting the fire.

Joe took a meat hook and the bagged pork belly and sunk the hook through the cloth and the flesh and he knelt by the fireplace and reached up inside, a good arm's length up the chimney, and hung the meat out of sight.

She glanced outside at the scene by the cookfire. Caleb was seated on a stump stool, plucking the old boiler. She could hear the crackle of fat in the pan.

'Will you kindly bring me a taper,' said Joe.

She went to the cookfire and picked out a taper and came back to Joe and he lit a fat candle on a sconce above the keg and the flame gave off a soft, mustard coloured light. Then he sunk a dipper into the cornmeal in an earthenware jar and put it in a wooden bowl, mixed in some water and spooned in a liberal quantity of salt and set to kneading dough for dumplings. 'I am romancing their palates,' he said.

'Ah!'

'I would hold my patch. Give me that and my wants are met.'

'Will they come tonight?'

'I believe they will. They'll come for their young man.'

34

Next day, on the trudge to Harp's distillery, they saw a bloody patch on the seat of Peachey's britches. Harp reckoned it might be a big leech but there was no leech. When Peachey dropped his trousers they discovered he was bleeding from his arse. Worse still he had a bad case of the drizzles and he blamed the berries that Harp said would fix the pain, for the berries had not fixed the pain but had brought on terrible cramps and had loosed Peachey's bowels, thus revealing the extent of the damage within.

When they reached the clearing on the creek Harp found the distillery much as he'd left it: disabled, the apparatus strewn about by Alister Mackie.

He tethered the pony and Peachey propped himself against the stone furnace. He called for water and Sparrow filled the leaky costrel in the creek and set the vessel by Peachey's side.

Harp worried Peachey might fade away, for the invalid was unable to hold onto his food. 'You have to eat when you're like this, when it's pourin' out the other end,' he said, and he set about making a corn broth just as soon as he'd checked the mash barrels.

He got the quart pot on the warm and sliced in the corn fresh off the cob, stirring a thick flour paste into the broth with a pinch of salt. 'Just a pinch, help it go down.' He dropped the corncobs in for good measure.

Peachey watched him, grateful for the kindness but certain he could not hold down a watery soup. He felt weak, weak as poorhouse gruel. He could not think how he might brave the wilderness in his present condition.

Harp sensed the failure of will in his midst. 'You go back now, Seamus, you might be alright, no law against payin' old Harp a visit.'

The suggestion was a turn in the road that Sparrow had not foreseen. He waited for Peachey's reply.

'I ain't goin' back no matter what.'

'Winifred is a *feme sole*,' said Sparrow.

'And she won't give it up neither.'

Harp scratched at his pate. 'That is a outrage, front to back.'

'I know,' said Peachey.

'He's gunna renew his manhood in the teeth of the wilderness,' said Sparrow.

Harp was stirring the broth, waving the steam in the vicinity of his nostrils, taking in the aroma. 'I knew one of them once,' he said, 'one of them *femes soles*.'

'You did?'

'I did yes. Her name was Lydia Izzy and so, of course, we called her Lizzy, most fondly. She was a came-free, like your Winifred, but she surrendered the agency of her property to her husband, dutifully, upon his emancipation, and she faithfully took up her God-given role as his dependant and mother to his children. She was a good woman.'

'See, Winifred won't do that,' said Peachey. 'I've tried but she won't do it.'

'You obviously haven't tried hard enough,' said Harp. 'Now, if Griffin was here he'd give you some advice. He'd say Seamus, he'd say, you gotta get physical with that woman, you give her the birch is what he'd say. The full flail.'

'What do you say?' said Sparrow.

'There's little in this world that would stir me to violence against a woman, but property, that's the line in the sand, that's another matter, that's tooth and claw, Mr Sparrow, *tooth and claw!*'

'We can't go back anyway,' said Peachey.

Harp had set a thick cloth on the rim of the quart pot and tipped it, the pot, so as to pour the corn broth into the mugs. 'Why's that?' he said.

'We killed the boy, the doctor's boy.' Peachey lay back and groaned as he pressed his palms on his ribs, testing his predicament.

Sparrow was shocked to think Peachey would say this to Harp, who was an unsteady quantum at best and most likely a leaky vessel under any kind of pressure at all.

'We did not kill him,' Sparrow said. He felt obliged, at that point, to tell Harp the true story, the story of the pact struck with Jug Woody, of the little boat and the bull shark and the agony of those hours, laid over with the dead boy on the river bank, and then the very sad burial, the torso on that slab, slipping into the depths as they coursed downstream, hardly time for a prayer.

'Lord, you gotta run now!' said Harp when Sparrow was finished.

'We know,' said Sparrow.

Peachey could but groan at the thought of having to tackle the country to the west with broken ribs and cramps and a bad bout of the drizzles. He sipped at the broth until it was gone, as did Harp and Sparrow. Then they passed round the bladder and drank bang-head, Harp declaring the spirits would surely kill the pain if nothing else would, and Peachey declaring he was ready to drink anything, even rat's piss, to achieve that end.

The dark had set in. Sparrow built up the fire and the clearing was bathed in a halo of light, camel coloured, the glow off the sandstone scarp.

They stretched out on the ground, close to the fire, all three, and soon enough they fell asleep and they slept that uneasy sleep for which Harp's bang-head was notorious, up and down the river.

35

Freddie heaped up a bed of red coals, thick for the heavy skillet, and he watched as Caleb plucked the boiler like an old hand.

Bea cleavered the naked bird into good-sized chunks and fed them into the skillet. She cast the head into the coals and watched it shrivel and bubble as if manifesting some horrible disease. Then she sat herself down on a stump stool and poked around the contents of the skillet. The night chill had set in, she could feel it all around, and she was grateful to be close to the fire. The red-hot glow of sparks as they soared into the night sky.

She could imagine Joe and Freddie on a warm night, feasting on the out of doors, the twinkling heavens, the forest silhouetted against the sky, the two of them, quietly talking; long, comfortable silences, staring into the flames, perfectly alone, entirely at their ease.

She spooned more lard into the skillet and watched the lard slide about and the chunks sizzle. Freddie poured in a lumpy liquid from a jar. 'The unrivaled fat of the wild duck.'

Caleb snaffled a sliver of half-cooked meat from the sizzle and tipped it from one palm to another and took it on his tongue and sucked in the cold air and began to chew. He walked away, beyond the reach of the firelight. He studied the forested ridge beyond the cabin.

Bea swiveled about and stared into that same darkness. The cicadas in full song. The swine, penned away, muzzling into a swill. She scanned the ridgeline. She did not fail to see the two lithe figures as they came over the rim and then disappeared into the darkness of the timber.

Caleb saw them too. He hollered with delight and went to meet them.

Soon enough the boys stepped into the firelight. They were thin as wisps, the two of them, mostly knuckle and bone. They were naked, save for generous mantles of fur on their shoulders and belts of plaited fibres round their middles. They carried spears barbed with shark teeth, their hair dressed with the teeth of dogs, small bones and the claws of some crustacean.

Joe stepped into the firelight. 'Cook up!' he said, and he shook hands with the two boys.

'Cook up, yes,' said Freddie. He tipped a quartered onion into the skillet and proceeded to liberally salt the meat.

'Nice big bird,' said Joe.

'Good table bird,' said Caleb.

Joe returned to the cabin to ready the dumplings. He worked his hands into the sticky dough. He heard Freddie's shout, the alarm in his voice, as Wolgan stepped into the cabin followed by Napoleon in his grey frockcoat.

Their matted black hair was tied off at the forehead, the locks bedight with turquoise feathers and incisors torn from some carnivore. Napoleon wore the fawn-coloured tail of a dog in his hair and old Wolgan the claws of a lizard and the jaw bones of some honoured fish.

The old man's skin hung on his frame like a fiercely weathered parchment. He stepped to the fireplace and turned about and stood with the beautiful musket, Thyne's musket, in the crook of his wounded arm. Much of the flesh on his shoulder had been shot away and what was left was part scabbed over and otherwise raw.

He stared at Joe Franks' floury hands. He glanced at the knives racked on the rear wall and he looked at the bagged salt on the table. He waved his free hand through an arc from right to left. '*Nula*,' he said.

Joe didn't know the word, but he read the gesture as entirely proprietorial. 'You have me at a disadvantage my friend, somewhat unmanned,' he said, as he wiped the sticky dough from his fingers. He set the dough pats aside, that plan scuppered.

Wolgan handed the gun to Joe and Joe studied the silver trimmings on the walnut stock. 'Thank you,' he said.

Caleb and the two boys pressed into the cabin, leaving Freddie and Bea to see what they could see from the cookfire.

Napoleon sat at the table and the others followed his lead, seating themselves on the stump stools. The ladder-back chair at the head of the table they left vacant, as if ceremonially, for Joe.

Joe took a loaf of maize bread from a sack and put it on the table. They cut open the salt sack. They shredded the bread, sucked on the pieces and dipped them into the salt, sucking and dipping, now and then a word.

Outside Freddie had ceased to stir the makings of the meal. He could see the savages, crowded in, their features almost lost in the dim light of the withering candle. He saw the coated one, moving about. He turned to Bea and whispered: 'Some poor ol' pale ol' Saxon dead in a dell, coatless.'

Bea nodded.

Napoleon took a small book from an inner pocket of his coat and placed it on the table. He wiped flecks of shag tobacco from his fingers.

Joe leaned forward, squinting, trying to see the words embossed on the cover: *Somerton's Natural History of Birds. A Rambler's Pocket Guide.*

'You may have this book,' said Caleb.

'Thank you,' said Joe.

Freddie arrived with the skillet in hand. Put the skillet on the table.

Joe gathered up his tin plates and his spoons and he began to ladle the meat and the juices onto the plates. Napoleon took the ladle from his hand and served himself, being entirely familiar with the procedure. He shifted the skillet to the centre of the table and his companions shared the ladle around, dishing out the stew for themselves.

The meal was gone within a few minutes, save for the bones they sucked on. Joe helped himself to the leavings and did as they did with the bones.

When they finished, the old man directed Caleb to the chimney, a word, just a word, and Caleb obeyed, squatting on the hearthstone. He reached up the chimney and brought down the bagged pork belly. He removed the meat hook and the bag, the linen sticky with the fat, and he put the prize on the table. The meat hook he surrendered to Joe.

Freddie put his hand over his mouth and muttered something.

'No matter,' said Joe.

'No matter?'

'By long forbearing is a prince persuaded.'

'I don't see no prince.'

At the table they tore the linen off the pork. They peeled strips of the smoked meat from the slab and dipped them in the salt. As the feast proceeded Wolgan beckoned his grandsons and sent them from the cabin with instructions that neither Joe nor Freddie could fathom.

Joe went to the door and peered after the boys. He saw the girl by the fire, alone. He bid her stay with a motion of his hand, heard the commotion in the byre.

Before long the boys returned, each with a piglet by the hind legs, the skulls cracked open, their catches twitching and jerking, the blood sketching shapes in the dust.

Wolgan got up and the others followed, stood as one, readying to go. The old man spoke words that were kindly in tone. Caleb provided the meaning. 'My grandfather is happy to see me returned.'

'Tell your grandfather that I too rejoice upon your safe return, in rude health,' said Joe.

Caleb paused. 'You may have the gun, for goodwill.'

'You tell your grandfather I will return his goodwill in kind, corn of an autumn, melons in summer; winter potatoes if you want.'

They left swiftly, loaded up with their weapons and a bag of bread and a sack of corn on the cob and the pork belly, what was left of it, and the meat on the hoof, the blood still dripping from the snouts.

The fire beneath the tripod was a bed of dimming coals. The savages strode past the fire, past Bea, into the dark, and they were gone.

Joe watched them go. 'That went well,' he said, as Bea stepped into the cabin.

'I'd hate to see what don't go well,' said Freddie.

'I have seen what don't go well,' said Joe. He could feel a tremor in his legs and he felt as if he could barely stand. He was tired enough to fall over but he kept his tiredness to himself, unaware the girl could see it at a glance.

She took a rag and dabbed at the fat stain on the table, blotting up the pork grease. Then she folded the rag, twice over, and wiped the surface as clean as she could. The residue of the grease put a shine on the timber. 'Vinegar would do better,' she said.

'We had some vinegar, once,' said Freddie.

Joe studied the table. 'Used to be,' he said, 'you got a leg of smoked pork upon a year of happy marriage.'

'A custom long gone,' she said.

'Custom is a frail thing, frail as life itself.'

36

Doctor Woody saw no signs of mischief upon Gudgeon's corpse. No markings on the sealer's face or his throat or his upper body, just brain matter oozing from the crack in the dead man's skull.

The Parsonage twins hovered, peering over Woody's shoulder. Cuff took charge in the absence of the chief constable. 'Move away,' he said, and they did, shuffling back to the wall.

The doctor took hold of Gudgeon's jaw and forced the mouth open and stared down the gullet. He pressed his glasses up the bridge of his nose. He beckoned Sam and Sam moved close, adjusting his truss as he bent over the intimate scene. 'There's long tweezers there, find them will you Samuel.'

Sam rummaged in the doctor's medicine bag until he found the tweezers. Woody took the tweezers and he searched deep in the sealer's gullet and drew out a downy feather. 'Gudgeon did not swallow this for his amusement,' he said. He glanced at the twins, who said not a word.

'You reckon they did it?' said Sam.

'We never did!' said Crispin.

'The cook did it, he brained him, everybody knows that,' said Nimrod.

'A vigorous interrogation might loosen your tongue,' said Woody.

'All we ever did was feed soup down his throat like a pair o' mother terns, we never did him no harm.'

'You are to reside in the gaol until further notice.'

'We got the Magna Carta, we got rights!'

'Not just now you don't.'

'Sling 'em on the hook!' said Sam.

'Do as required,' said Woody. He took pleasure in the consternation of the twins, the shrill bleat of their protests. He felt himself fixed in a most uncharacteristic frame of mind.

'You take 'em, Sam,' said Cuff.

Sam stepped up to the twins and grabbed the two of them by the scruff and they both yowled as he led them away, bound for the gaol. 'You boys know about the rectal pear?' he said.

As Woody stepped into the corridor he almost collided with Alfie Shivers, Winifred close behind him. Winifred had Alfie by the ear, the bonded felon bent over in pain. She waved a menacing finger at the doctor. 'If you don't get answers from this river rat, I fully intend to drown him this day; that will do nothing for my misery but it might just quell the fury in my kidneys.'

'What answers?' said Woody.

'What answers?'

'What answers, Winifred, that is what I said.'

'Well you're the magistrate!' Winifred was staring at Dr Woody like he was a fool.

'Winifred, what is the question?' said Woody.

Cuff stepped into the frame. 'Let him go, Winifred.'

'Why am I talking to you? Where's Mr Mackie?' she said.

'He's seein' to the wheat; sow early, beat the grub, *et cetera*,' said Cuff.

'I rest my case!'

'What case?'

'I esteem that man, an early bird, a man of ambition, someone like me!' she said.

Alfie Shivers was still yowling as Winifred Peachey twisted his ear.

'Let's just sit Alfie down, shall we?' said Cuff.

'I am a free woman, a *feme sole* with not a blemish on my name so don't tell me what to do. My Seamus is gone.'

Dr Woody took hold of Alfie Shivers' unfettered ear and turned it somewhat fiercely and Alfie squealed some more. The manoeuvre surprised both Cuff and Mrs Peachey.

'Your Seamus is gone, Sparrow's gone, my boy's gone, and they did not go fishing,' said Woody.

'Where did they go?' said Winifred.

'I believe they've bolted, and took my boy.'

'I knew it, I knew it!'

'Knew what?' said Cuff.

Winifred smacked her chest and cleared her throat. 'His comportment was most strange some days prior; I should have known there was mischief afoot.'

The doctor twisted Alfie's ear a little more. 'Did they take my boy?' he said through grinding teeth.

'I don't know,' said Alfie.

'We'll know what you know soon enough,' said Cuff. 'Get him out the back.'

They sat Alfie down in front of the cookfire in the kitchen and Cuff took hold of the fire tongs and waved them in Alfie's face. Atilio watched on, wiping his palms on his apron.

'You have a choice,' said Cuff.

'I'll take it,' said Alfie, like he'd just been offered a prize.

'I can crush your pizzle in these grips or twist the nose off your face . . . which one, you choose.'

'You won't do that, not you, I know that.'

'Rumour of my gentle disposition precedes me,' said Cuff. He handed the tongs to Atilio. 'He'll twist the nose off any living thing you care to name, any livin' appendage that takes his fancy.'

Alfie looked at the tongs, held firm in that big dark hand. Atilio lifted the tongs. He rested the grips on Alfie's shoulder.

'I'll tell you what I know, which ain't much,' said Alfie.

'That's a lie first up,' said Winifred. 'He's party to all their whisperin' I know that for a unvarnished certitude.'

The doctor came up close to Alfie Shivers and bent low and whipsered: 'There's no need for Atilio, is there?'

'No?'

'Because *I* will twist the nose off your face myself if I don't hear something true about my boy in the space of this unfinished minute.'

Alfie was breathing loud through the nose in question, his jaw set, his lips pressed hard together. He had never in all his time at the river heard the doctor speak like that. 'All I know is Griffin said Sparrow was going to bolt; he said they ought pair up, Sparrow and Seamus . . . to get across.'

'They spun my boy some lie about fishing.'

'I swear I don't know about that I just know Griffin . . .'

'What?' said Winifred.

'Griffin what?' said the doctor.

'Nothing,' said Alfie.

'Do not doubt my resolve in this for in this I am the fourth horseman, the pale rider with hell on my heels,' said Woody.

'I cannot help you,' said Alfie.

Woody took the tongs from Atilio: 'I'll see you wheeled out with Gudgeon, I will crack your skull and spill your brains and I'll feed 'em to the government pigs, I swear.'

Alfie liked Thomas Woody, as did almost everyone on the river. He knew this was most uncharacteristic behaviour. He felt pity for the father's anguish. 'Griffin says it's a paradise over there . . . that's all . . . no governors, no chains, no gaols, no soldiers, no . . . tongs. He says it's a refuge for the plain folk, a haven . . . he says they want for nothing . . . over there . . . but I don't know nothin' about your boy I swear to that.'

Winifred threw her hands in the air. 'He's gone, bolted, my Seamus!'

'He said the legal document was the last straw, *aver* this, *aver* that,' said Alfie.

'That weasel!'

'They've took my boy,' said the doctor. 'They've bolted and they've took him.' Woody turned to Cuff. 'You have to get after them, you and Alister, someone has to go. If you don't go I'll go.'

'You can hardly shuffle across the damn square. We'll go.'

'I would not trust the military. Conjure some tale for my assuagement, whatever suits.'

'Thomas, we will go, Alister and me.'

Cuff turned to Alfie. 'Where's Griffin Pinney right now?'

'I don't know.'

'He's gunna waltz them two fools into that devil-ridden wilderness ain't he?'

'No.'

'No?'

'Not first up.'

'What then?'

Alfie did not reply.

Cuff bent low. He rested a hand on Alfie's shoulder. 'You esteem the doctor, his good works?'

'I do, most certainly, yes.'

'That boy of his is gone, Alfie, that good boy is gone.'

'I don't know nothin' about that.'

'Well where's Griffin Pinney, you tell me.'

Alfie stared down at his shoes and shook his head. 'I swear the man gives me the squirts.'

'You are pathetic,' said Winifred. She whacked the back of Alfie's head. Cuff held up a quieting hand, waved her away. 'Where is he, Alfie?'

Alfie took a deep breath. 'He's gone for the woman, the Romany girl, the one Mackie bought for Joe.'

'What!'

'Griffin don't like to lose out.'

'Did he go alone?'

'Just him and that dog I'd reckon.'

Cuff pulled a chair close and looked hard at Alfie Shivers, weighing the truth or otherwise of what he'd just heard. He took it to be true, not least because the tale fitted the man – he would expect no less of Griffin Pinney.

37

Bea Faa worked in the vegetable garden for most of the morning, some of it with Joe. They had risen early, for the warmth of the previous evening and a thin veil of low cloud promised a hot and sticky day. They had not slept much, the savages vivid in their drowsing reflections and their fitful dreams.

They worked alongside one another for an hour or so but once the sun was up, the sweat dripping from their foreheads, Joe could work no more. His limbs gave out. He tried to work on but spasms wracked his arms and legs and he had to sit down in the shade. 'The heat, does me in,' he said.

Bea worked on, readying the ground, and when it was right Freddie wheeled in barrows of good rotten dung from the henhouse and the pigs and this she spread in uniform thickness all over. She dug it in as best she could and then she dug out the furrows, row after row, *one blade deep* said Joe, and she sowed the onion and Freddie sowed the cabbage.

Around midday Joe Franks slumped into his chair at the table. 'I must be a horse, I could sleep on my feet.' The chair warped a little, sideways. 'Salvaged this from the flood before last,' he said, patting the seat.

'It needs a brace,' she said.

'Like me.'

She nodded, and he smiled.

She took the cork lid off the green glass demijohn and filled a mug full of peach cyder and passed it to Joe and he took it with shaky hands and drank like a man who had just crawled out of a desert. 'Good work this morning,' he said.

She nodded. 'I like the garden.' In fact she liked the work and she liked Joe, the way he was, better than anything she might have hoped for. She now knew something of his time in India, a tale unadorned, or so it seemed; and he knew certain details about her conception and her birth, her youth, her schooling at her stepmother's knee and her fate at the hands of the widowed butcher, and more. A brief exchange, fragments of their lives.

Joe wanted to know if she'd heard of Mackie before she came up the river with Jonas Wick and the sealers.

'I grew up with that story, never let forget it,' she said.

'What story?'

So she told him about the waste barn, how the young Mackie, besotted, had traded wares from his own mother's loom in exchange for the charms of Jeannie Faa, and how the pious folk from the Kirk had taken the poor girl for a ducking in the ducking chair and near drowned her; and how the boy's own family had taken him and bewailed him before the congregation with talk of his wickedness; of his dying father, *your own dying father*, and how they gave him up to the severe hand of the law and disowned him forthwith; and how he did suffer it, craven, only to spite them, famously, as the sheriff took him down.

Joe drained his mug and reached for more and the girl took the demijohn and poured him some more, and he drank it down. 'He was want, was Mackie, to see you safe,' he said.

'For that I am grateful.' She smiled at him, a smile she knew would not deliver her into peril, as a smile might otherwise do.

She helped him to the bed. 'Are you sure you won't eat?'

'I'm sure, go ahead,' he said, as Freddie arrived, ravenous.

They mashed some boiled potato onto their bread, cold, and talked farm as they ate, the bread coming apart in their fingers. Freddie declared the peach orchard in need of trimming before it was too late in the season. Joe advised against it, knowing he could not help. 'Too hot,' he said. But Freddie was untroubled by the heat. He departed, with the goat at his heels.

Bea sat with Joe.

'Freddie has the constitution of a bull elephant,' he said. 'I'd trade my left foot for a measure of that.'

'I can read you some more Bunyan,' she said after a while.

'Not just now. Might remind me there's a way to hell even from the gates of heaven,' he said. He closed his eyes and seemed to doze off.

There was a chisel and a whetstone on the lid of a toolbox by the cabin door and Bea looked about to see what she might sharpen.

She took a boning knife from the rear wall, set it on the table and retrieved the whetstone and spat upon it and began to work the long thin blade on the stone with some proficiency. The boning knife brought back memories of butchered lambs on the hook and massacres on the sealeries.

She was a world away when Griffin Pinney stepped into the cabin, musket in hand. He looked about. He saw Joe Franks throw his legs over the edge of the bed and try to rise and Pinney stepped up to Franks and slammed the butt of the musket into the old soldier's forehead.

The girl rose up. She hurled the knife and the blade struck low and deep in the meat of Pinney's thigh.

Pinney hardly moved save to turn his head and lock his eyes upon her. He made no sound. He spat a big brown wad of something onto the floor. His old dog ambled forward somewhat rheumatically and gobbled it up.

Pinney looked down at the handle of the boning knife and saw the blood soaking into the cloth of his trousers. He made no attempt to remove the blade. He moved to the table and sat. 'You sit back down girl,' he said. He tore the gash in his trousers wide open.

The girl did not move. Pinney spoke softly. 'If you do not sit down I'll kill that old man this instant.' He closed his fist on the bone handle. 'I'll cut his throat from ear to ear an' I'll take his tongue off the bone and feed it, *root and branch*, to my old dog.'

Bea sat.

Pinney's old dog came to him and licked at the wound all about the blade. 'Mind now.' The game hunter pushed the dog away and set his jaw and sucked in his breath as he drew the blade from his flesh and banged the point into the table and the blade quivered along its stem and a fine spray of blood dappled the rough-cut surface, the colour leaching away as the blood soaked into the wood.

Pinney scratched at the back of the dog's ear and with that the old dog resumed licking at the wound.

'He wants the blood,' said Bea.

'This dog is devoted, like no damn woman,' said Pinney.

The girl made no reply but studied the old dog as it dutifully licked at the torn cloth about the game hunter's wound.

'Why'd he pay for you?' said Pinney.

She did not understand the question.

'He bought a share in you, Mackie.'

'He helped Joe, that's all.'

'Against me.'

'Yes.'

'He bought a piece o' you, that's what he did.' Pinney smiled and nodded at her as if to say *I know the secret here.*

The girl said nothing.

'You're his bit o' trim downriver, ever so discreet. They say the man has an ethic, well, there's no ethic I know ain't got shit on the underside.'

'He wants no share in me.'

'I despise such falseness in a man.'

'I am Joe's.'

'Mackie ain't gunna have any, and that old ruin won't have you neither,' said Pinney, gesturing a thumb in Joe's direction.

'I will not go with you,' said the girl.

'You will, or I'll cut his throat here and now.' Pinney wrapped his fist around the bone handle of the knife and let the blade bend to and fro, the sway like a lone reed in the wind.

Joe was on his feet, a run of blood on his forehead. He shuffled forward, shaky on his legs. Pinney pulled the knife from the table and stood and whirled about and slammed the butt end of the handle into the wound on Joe's forehead, and Joe went down like a stone.

The game hunter stood astride Joe, his own blood drying on the blade. The girl lunged at him and Pinney turned and took her by the throat, one hand, crushing her windpipe, and backed her up against the table. He dropped the knife. She went up on her toes in search of breath. He seemed to lift her without effort onto the table's edge and he stepped between her legs and unbuttoned his flap and pushed her down and threw back her skirt and took hold of her nest. 'Well well well, a man trap in the bush,' he said, and he chuckled as he fumbled about and got underway.

Bea Faa clutched at the edge of the table. She sucked for air. As Griffin Pinney entered her she went rigid, her back arching, her eyes rolling in her head and then, first, a tremor, then another, then she convulsed, time and again and Pinney was leering. 'You're doin' me a treat,' he said, and he pushed a fist onto her pubic bone and pinned her to the table and he went at her with that awful rhythm, and he saw the whites of her eyes and he felt her rigid, like a plank, and he did not care. He went at her until he was done.

She heard words, words beyond grasp, a jumble, and she saw needles of light come at her and her skin crawled with something, sweat, fear, and her ears hummed a low whining sound within, like steam through a cracked lid, and she could taste blood. She had folded her lower lip into her bite and bit down, bit through her lip. Blood was running on her cheek and her chin as she opened her eyes and tried to sit up. She could not sit up.

She heard the scuffing of boots and she rolled her head to one side and looked to the doorway. She saw the hazed outline of Freddie there, as if through clearing fog.

Freddie was leaning into the cabin, staring agape, his hands on the door frame like he was ready to push off and run for his life. He saw Griffin Pinney wipe his member on the girl's skirt. He saw the blood-soaked gash in Pinney's trousers as the game hunter buttoned up his flap. He saw the girl, dishevelled, breathless, bloodied at the mouth, her eyelids flicking like the wings of a stuck moth.

'Nooooo,' he said.

Pinney was tucking in his shirt tails. 'What a fine fit you aaaare mistress Faaaa,' he said.

The goat buffeted its way onto the doorstep, pushing vigorously at Freddie's knee. It looked upon the scene in the cabin and bleated softly.

'You still got that stupid goat I see,' said Pinney.

Freddie stared at the goat.

Pinney seated himself and he spread the tear in his trousers and poked at the wound in this thigh.

'How'd you do that?' said Freddie, peering close.

'Never you mind.'

'I got a swathe.'

'A swathe o' what?'

Freddie took a small jar off a shelf and handed it to Pinney. Only then did he see Joe bloodied on the floor. He went to him, swiftly.

'Folk goin' down like flies.' Pinney took the top off the jar and sniffed at the gummy solution.

Freddie helped Joe onto the bed and Joe laid back, blank-eyed, his forehead coloured with bruising and streaked with blood.

Bea felt a rude churn in her guts. She rolled over to vomit but somehow she held it down, all but the taste of it. She struggled to sit up, shifting her legs, turned side on, steadied herself on the table's edge.

Pinney took hold of the green glass demijohn. He uncorked it and drank down the cyder, wiping his mouth on his sleeve. He returned his attentions to the balm. 'What is this?' he said.

'It's honey and sugar, dries up the blood and drowns the rot in the goodness, would our world laboured on such a principle . . . my mother used to say that,' said Freddie.

Pinney glared at him. 'You some kind o' imbecile?'

'Noooo, it's true, good for leeches too, helps with the itch.'

The game hunter dipped a finger into the jar and sniffed at it and pasted the balm onto the wound. He upended the demijohn and drank some more. 'What's he done here, mix piss and toffee?'

'That's peach cyder.'

'It's kitten piss.'

'We got no kittens.'

'What else he give you, Mackie?'

'He give us seed wheat, for two acres I think, and some cocoa.'

'Cocoa?'

'Quite lovely of an evening.'

'What else?'

Freddie stared at the chimney. 'Pork belly.'

'We'll take that.'

'It's gone, the savages gobbled it.'

The old dog had dropped down on the hearthstone and the goat came sniffing. The dog snarled and growled and the goat backed away. Pinney turned to the girl. 'You run I'll set that old dog on you . . . you want the particulars?' he said.

'Yes,' she said.

'I truss you up, I cut a hole in your gut and he'll tear out your innards. That's the wolf in him.'

38

Mackie and Cuff left the village, first light, sailing into a fading flood tide, effectively slack water, tacking interminably from one reach to the next and one hour to the next, intent upon the entirely perishable convenience of a south-westerly breeze and the ebb tide in full flow.

It was midafternoon when the boat skimmed onto the sand south of Pig Creek. They reckoned they might miss Pinney if they went straight to Joe's. A better chance to intercept him at Harp's. Mackie slid onto the hull and leant against the back board, his eyes closed. Already the air held the cool fresh smell of evening with more than a hint of rain.

They followed the line of the creek into the back country with as much haste as the chief constable could muster.

Cuff found a modest shelter, a shallow cave, among dappled grey gums and grass trees like squat sentinels hatted for extravagant show. They sat, listening to the creature sounds and the patter of the light rain.

'Frogs,' said Cuff.

'That sound, like a ratchet?' asked Mackie.

'Well it ain't a ratchet.'

'You know your frogs.'

'Yes I do.'

'I suppose that hoot is a frog?'

'That's a owl.'

'I was hoping you might credit me with knowing the call of an owl.'

'Hope is physician to misery.'

'As ever, we come to a proverb . . . from frogs to proverbs.'

'Never let it be said I'm a miser with my wisdom.'

'More's the pity.'

'I was imbibing gainful proverbs when you was still suckin' on the tit in Yetholm, and they done me no harm.'

'Gainful?'

'Yes, gainful. You ought thank me.'

'I thought it was just minstrels and songsters craved applause.'

They sat quietly for a time, but Cuff was not finished. He wanted to make a point. 'Nature's a gift, Alister, and you ought soak it up, broaden your mind, not least since it's free. The simple things, a seashell, a wildflower, a feather on the sand, the sounds wondrous, the frogs. You cannot reduce such things to a squiggle in that double-entry book o' yours, things of immeasurable mystery, and wonder.'

'I have no interest in a *mystery*.'

'That's my point. You're too busy plotting your ambition like some crazed navigator. People like you are forever getting ready for the future, I don't know why. The future ain't gettin' ready for you, it don't even know you're comin'. That's a hard fact in case you need one.'

'That fact, so called, I don't need.'

'The point is, there's joy to be had in things other than the practise of virtue. You think work is a remedy against sin, I think it's a rude interruption.'

'Are you ever likely to stop?'

'I don't know why I start . . . waste the riches of my ruminations on you.'

They heard the guttural bawl of a cullawine. 'There's no wonderment in that, like a pig in a bad dream,' said Mackie.

'They're poor meat too,' said Cuff.

The rain was faltering. Their recess was dry. They untied their bundles and rolled out their blankets and wrapped them round. They pressed themselves against the stone and set about trying to get some sleep.

In the morning Mackie woke coughing, his lungs heavy with muck. He got up and spread his legs and bent low and coughed up what he could, some of it into his hand for closer inspection. Trying to settle his chest to some sort of equilibrium, he breathed slow and deep. Then he swallowed hard, wincing as he did so. He longed for a draught of claret.

'You alright?' said Cuff.

'I'm alright.'

They made a small fire and ate some hard biscuit, washed down with a mug of tea, packed their bundles and resumed their westerly course on the sodden gravels of Pig Creek.

They stopped briefly at Harp's hut and then pressed on, upstream, until the wreckage of the still was in view. They saw the pot and the cap had been rescued from the creek and the pot now lay on its side near the stone furnace. They saw Harp rooting around in a haversack and Peachey prone on the ground.

The pony stirred.

Mackie stepped up the bank and crossed to the firestones in the centre of the camp.

'Not again!' said Harp.

'Where is Griffin Pinney?'

Harp paused. Cuff intervened: 'Don't think, Harp, just tell us the damn truth.'

'He's gone, you're too late.'

'Gone where?'

'He come with his dog, and that girl, and he took Sparrow and the pup and they've gone and you won't catch them.'

'What pup?' said Cuff.

'You don't know about the pup?' Harp was chuckling. 'They got Henry Kettle's brindle pup.'

'What of the girl?' said Mackie.

Harp angled the carriage of his head severely upwards. He seemed to be looking into the canopy beyond the chief constable. 'You here for the girl?' he said.

'No.'

'I hear you and Joe bought her for a wife. That's against the law, ain't it?'

'Joe bought her for a wife and that is law according to custom.'

'Well, you missed her, they've been and gone.'

'What's wrong with Mr Peachey here?' said Cuff.

'Got kicked in the guts and he's come down with the bloody drizzles and the rest is history,' said Harp.

'Well, history and the drizzles is close cousins,' said Cuff. 'There's a great deal of fluid prejudice in the both of them.'

Peachey raised himself onto one elbow. 'I'll tell you the history, Harp's up and poisoned me, that's the history.'

Harp waggled his forefinger in the air the better to stress his emphatic denial. 'I did my best, medicinally speaking.'

'And my guts in violent spasm, cramped to buggery. I been to the underworld and back, you cannot imagine the night I've had, the torments.'

'You give him the wrong medicine!' said Cuff.

'I did no such a thing.'

'And here I am, my ribs broke, my bowels in startling eruption.'

'Build the fire, we'll wash him out with buckets of tea,' said Mackie.

Harp got busy at the fire. Cuff squatted down beside Peachey. 'Seamus, we know you took the boy's boat. Now, where is that boy?'

'We took his boat, that's all. We took it and went.'

'He gave you the boat, knowin' you couldn't bring it back?'

'We told him we was ramblin'. That boy had every expectation we'd come back with his boat. I swear we left him hale and hearty on the Cattai.'

'You know he's missing.'

'I don't know nothin'.'

'And his daddy, the good doctor, he is in purgatory, and the missus too.'

'I can't help that.'

Cuff searched the crags and recesses of Peachey's countenance. He looked him in the eye but Peachey looked away. 'Did you pay him for his trouble?'

'Yes. I believe Sparrow paid him some coin.'

'How much coin?'

'I don't know but I know he gave him some coin.'

'But you weren't comin' back, and you were stealing his boat. That's a capital crime in this neighbourhood, we hang you for that.'

'We gave him money for rent,' said Peachey. He was most grateful Cuff had reminded him of Sparrow's coin.

'You took it, you used it and you scuttled it,' said Mackie.

'We never did.'

'What then?'

'We moored that boat on the river, for all the comers and goers to see. There to be found forthwith, Guthrie on the scow or someone.'

'There's no trace of it,' said Mackie.

'That is a mystery to be sure,' said Peachey.

'Seamus, the boy is gone, lost. And you and Sparrow took his boat from him and you lied to him,' said Cuff.

'That's all we did I swear.' He lay back and wrapped his arms tight around his ribs and rocked to one side and then the other, his face contorted with what appeared to be real pain.

Harp had made the tea. Mackie passed a steaming half-pint mug to Peachey and Peachey pulled his sleeve over his fingers and took the mug.

Cuff turned to Harp. 'What they do with that boat? What they do with the boy for that matter?'

'I don't know nothin' about the boy,' said Harp.

'You help them scuttle that boat?'

'Lord no, sink a boat's worse'n ravishing your own mother.'

'What of Mr Pinney and his little company? They on the Branch now?'

'They are now, yes, and well along.'

'Bound for the other side?'

'Griffin follows that river every time, all the way to the headwaters, that's all I know.'

That night Seamus Peachey felt, yet again, a stabbing pain in his guts and the now familiar stirring in his bowels. Harp woke, watched him go, bent over and clutching at his middle. The constables did not appear to stir.

Peachey followed the creek downstream with some difficulty, dragging his feet through a tangle of ferns and pushing through thickets of slender saplings. Dim grey slivers of light from the night sky.

There was hardly any wind at all, just the faintest north-easterly that stirred the canopy and eddied around his extremities as he shuffled on.

He found a snug nook and brushed off an old log and fumbled at the big buttons on his flap, stepping from one foot to another, his buttocks clenched, his guts in loathsome revolt. He sat himself over the log and let go and a flood of thin bloody stools poured from his arse; he put his face in his hands and gave out a deep sigh and as he did so the log gave way, its fibrous rigour long gone.

Peachey fell backwards into a sodden bed of rot and shit, his ribs buzzing with pain. Exhaustion flowed through him. He was panting like he'd run a mile. His mouth was dry and he was desperately thirsty. The shit was warm on his thighs and his bare arse, the warmth and the cool in some strange, sweet equilibrium. He lay there, breathing heavy, bound to the earth, drifting into light sleep, shapes and voices and strange sounds weaving dreamlike in his head, slipping ever deeper into a netherworld, whereupon he felt himself shunted, brutally, his shoulders ploughing up the leafy rot.

He lifted his head and screamed. The black shape of the boar was between his legs. The snout shunted into his loins and the teeth tore at his private parts and ripped at the cheeks of his arse. He felt his flesh coming away, torn from his frame. He was on his elbows recoiling, kicking. The boar moved with him, the vast poundage forcing forward. Peachey screamed for help. He made to rise but the boar leapt forward and pinned him and tore at this throat.

Peachey was so cold now. There was no fight in him. He heard a voice, Harp's voice, far off, 'We're comin'.' He heard a woman's voice, he saw her lips make words but no sound. He saw a hornless deer take flight, a hound give chase, the deer all pearly white, save one red ear.

He felt the boar's snout deep in his throat and the smell of his own shit rose into the back of his nose. He thought to say, 'What a terrible mess I am,' but he could not talk.

39

They buried the mutilated remains of Seamus Peachey in the morning. A shallow grave. They dragged the remnants of the rotten log onto the loose-packed earth and paused briefly.

Cuff was about to say a word, a forgiving word, but his thoughts turned to the missing boy, and to Dr Woody, and he decided he could not speak kindly of Seamus Peachey so he would not speak at all.

Back at Harp's camp they drank some bush tea and readied to leave. Mackie's departing words were sharp. 'Do not mend this contraption.'

'I got no worm,' said Harp.

'In that, count yourself lucky.'

'Let's hope you find your girl.'

'Mind yourself, Harp. That boar, he's sharp as a rat's tooth,' said Cuff.

'I'll shit with my pistol primed,' said Harp.

They followed the creek upstream until it disappeared under a thick covering of prickly fern, and they crossed over the headwall and went down into a valley to a swamp that drained north to the Branch.

They skirted the swamp and climbed a steady grade and followed the forested ridge to a high point where they could see the stone country to the west, ever more angular and sheer. Serried bluffs folded like braids to the ragged horizon that met the sky far off.

Cuff studied the raw spectacle. 'If there's somethin' on the other side of that devil's waste I'll never know, 'cause I ain't goin' there.'

'Nor I,' said Mackie.

The ridgeline they followed was serpentine, the drop-aways severe but the ground lightly timbered, thin cover, wattle and bottle-brush, and the going easier than climbing in and out of gullies so they kept to the contour until the pattern was broken by a descent to another swamp and a scramble up the far side. When they reached the top they could see the Branch, perhaps an hour's walk from where they stood, the line of the river cutting ever deeper into the country beyond.

They made their way by ridge and gully until they met the river, the afternoon sun poised in the western sky. They trekked upstream keeping to narrow levees forested with she-oak and slender water gums, stopping occasionally to drop down and drink, or to rest on shaded sand, swatting at flies and plucking the odd leech off a leg and scratching at day old scabs.

They passed through a ceremonial ground where squares of bark were cut from old trees, and carvings were incised within the frame – the weathered shape of emus and fish and wombats and other creatures. Further along they came upon an awful assemblage: wasted black bodies, a woman on the ground, shot through, and two men hung by their necks from a single bough, their ears removed, their torsos riddled with shot.

'The righteous vengeance of the military,' said Cuff.

'We've done worse,' said Mackie.

'Not for sport we haven't.'

'I picture our heroes in the mess, recapping the chase, the story slipping to fable.'

'Mawkish tears, Thyne avenged, the world a better place.'

'The worst of what we are, dressed up as virtue.'

'As ever, the redemptive ending.'

'As it must be.'

'The tyranny of the musts, yet again.'

Cuff was staring at the back of his hand, his thumb bunching up the skin. 'It's because we're the first.'

'First what?'

'It's the first settlers do the brutal work. Them that come later, they get to sport about in polished boots and frockcoats, kidskin gloves . . . revel in polite conversation, deplore the folly of ill-manners, forget the past, invent some bullshit fable. Same as what happened in America. You want to see men at their worst, you follow the frontier.'

'I suppose you're right.'

Cuff surveyed the dead. 'Damn right I'm right.'

They walked on the rest of the day, pushing through thick swamp heath and flood-wrack and wading through the shallows, skirting the tumbledown stone, keeping to the levees where they could.

They slept that night on the sand, beneath the canopy of a broken old red gum deeply rooted in the stone, the shattered limbs calloused with tumourous growths.

Twice Mackie woke Cuff with his coughing, his frame convulsing as he raised himself on one arm and turned away to clear his chest, spitting on the sand.

'You ought get up, cough it out good and proper,' said Cuff. He could hear Mackie's quick, sucking breaths.

The chill predawn found them further along the river, stepping from sand to shallows to sand again and otherwise picking their way along the bank through dense stands of fern and she-oak, patches of hare's foot rooted in the crevices of broken stone, the pendant pale green blossoms of the fuchsia, scrub wren and tiny finches winging swift across the water.

By the afternoon they felt the quickening flow against their shins, the gradient sharper now, the river carving its infinite way out of the stone country, the forest dense and cramping, the waterway strewn with boulders and the cataracts somewhat more forceful.

They checked their lower parts for leeches and pressed on. They found a game track on a contour above the flood line. They took to the track and followed it for some miles, ducking and weaving through needlebush and wattle. They had long ceased talking and each man was ready for a rest when Cuff put out his arm and signed for hush.

They squatted down, Mackie onto one knee. Cuff pointed upriver where a savage lay upon his back on a pillar of stone. A cloth covered his face, a lace cloth as fine as woven wind, and there were teeth and feathers gummed into his long hair. His arms were by his side, his palms lay open, cupped in a sacrificial pose, and upon the puckered scars on his chest was a spread of entrails from the gut of a fish.

The sweat on his frame; his skin shone like the richest amber set in glass.

Cuff looked to the sky and saw an eagle, circling. It lifted on a gust and rose into the sky and circled some more.

They watched. The eagle banked and spiraled down once again. The great bird landed close, perched in a tree, watching the deathly still form upon the pillar of stone.

'No,' said Mackie.

'Pssh,' said Cuff.

The eagle spread its wings and flew off a way and swept around and coasted back, skimming the water before it banked and lifted, landing by the prone form.

The great wings folded away. The creature did not move, nor the savage. The creature, emboldened, hopped forward. It picked at the viscera. It picked again, the head bobbing, its beak skyward as it swallowed.

The open palm snapped at the eagle's legs, seized them and tipped the bird as the great wings spread wide and the bird shrieked and the other hand seized the neck and snapped it with a most violent turn of the wrist.

'You see that?' said Cuff in a whisper.

The lace cloth was on the breeze, wafting to the sand like a feather. The savage was on his feet, the great bird hung upside down in his fist, the claws like some primeval bouquet.

They heard him chuckle. He threw the bird upon the sand below and leapt from the pillar and landed much as the eagle might have landed on some previous occasion: lithe, sprung, weightless upon impact. He picked up the bird and the lace cloth and jogged off, upstream, and twice he spun about, scouting the rear, before he disappeared into the cover at the far end of the reach.

The white men stood and stared after him. They saw the footprints in the sand, proof, assuredly, of the spectacle they had witnessed.

'You seen him before?' said Cuff.

'Yes,' said Mackie.

'That's Daniel, that's Mr Catley's man.'

'Moowut'tin?'

'Yes . . . The earth their bed, the heavens their canopy . . . they are something else.'

They stood there, silent, for a time.

'Don't ever tell me we know what we're doin' out here Alister,' said Cuff.

'I'll not do that,' said Mackie.

They walked on until the footprints in the sand disappeared. Late in the afternoon they sighted a cave in a tributary gully where elkhorn and fern flourished under a dense canopy of coachwoods and turpentines. In the forecourt, they found bones and tools, digging sticks and tattered basketry on the sandy floor. Further in they found withered corpses in tortured poses, sallowed black skin sunk onto bone, riddled with the puckered scarring of the small pox and preyed upon by quolls and lizards and lesser things.

———

They returned to the river as the light began to fade. Hurried along in the rain. They found shelter further on, beneath a ponderous forehead of rock some twenty feet or so above the floodwater mark. A smoke-blackened overhang, the floor thick with the grit of ages. The residue of an old fire in a shallow pit, animal droppings and a little pile of grassy vomit, the vomit covered in a faint blue membrane. They settled there behind a forest of tall trunks, the bark curling and shedding like burnt skin.

Parrots were massing in the canopy, a shrill, manic disharmony, the prelude to a collective subsidence.

'Worse than cats in a box,' said Mackie.

'You'd think they'd learn,' said Cuff.

'Learn what?'

'You'd think one of them would say *why do we squawk and squabble every night, it always gets settled, why don't we just . . . discuss this, calmly, save a lot of aggravation, save aggravating those two poor, lost gentlemen in the cave yonder.* Why don't one of them say that?'

'It seems so obvious when you say it,' said Mackie.

They both chuckled.

'We're not lost, moreover,' said Mackie.

'I'd have said we're not gentlemen, notwithstanding the ambition of one amongst us,' said Cuff. He had gathered some wisps of dry grass and rotten touchwood, kindling for a fire so they could have some tea.

They ate some corn biscuit, saving their cut of smoked meat for days to come, and they sat for a while listening to the calls of night birds and scrutinising the cliffs on the far side of the river until the dark snuffed out all things in sight save the patchwork of the canopy against the night sky and the lithe black shapes that moved through it.

On a cold breeze came the faint sound of rapids upstream. Cuff set the quart pot on the flame. 'Why are you here?' he said, his comment on ambition fresh in his mind.

Mackie pondered the question. 'Why?'

'Are you here for the girl . . . and what if you manage to snatch her from Griffin Pinney's claws, what then?'

'*We* are here to find Thomas's boy, to collar the villains, the more so if they've hurt that boy, and we are here for the girl, for Joe's sake.'

'You wanted her off your hands, gone, and Joe came along all needy, his ailments heaven sent, for you that is. Might be you care more for your reputation than your own blood.'

'She is not my blood.'

'There's every chance that is a masterly deception of your own self.'

Mackie scratched at his neck. He took a burnt stick from the fire pit and drew a line in the sand. 'I expect there's a warrant for that girl, inbound. She has escaped a transport. She's lived wild with the sealers, who knows what else.'

'So why didn't you give her up, send her off to Parramatta?'

'I had my reasons.'

'You got her well placed instead, well placed and well away, at Joe's.'

'I did.'

'You got her well clear of you, the least you could do to the most advantage – to you that is.'

'She was safe with Joe.'

'And you are cunning as a rat in a barn.'

'What would you have me do with her?'

'If she was mine I'd keep her close and her questionable past closer still, and to hell with the gossip.'

'That's your loins talking, as usual.'

'Well your loins may well have done some talkin' too, Alister, there's no way that girl's a full blood Romany. And there's that black spot upon her iris.'

'A fact so random as to be thoroughly hollow.'

'I've not seen that on another living soul save you. She's cut out like you, long and lean. As to her earlobes, you look at 'em. Everyone knows earlobes are passed on, my own earlobes for example: identical to my dear pappy's. And I'll tell you something else.'

'Spare me!'

'My second toe on my right foot is longer than my thumb toe and my papa's second toe on his right foot the same, so don't tell me.' Mackie threw his arms in the air, gesturing to the heavens for urgent assistance. But he made no reply so Cuff went on. 'This much I can tell you about jizzum: if it's not a slave to precise replication, it is a servant to the tiniest particulars.'

'Well, you'd know about that particular fluid would you not?'

'I would that, I've spread enough of it about.' Cuff was chuckling at the thought for it made him happy to contemplate his busy life in that regard.

'There's more to life than skirts and quim.'

'I'll grant you that's true, but it's a poor heart that never rejoiceth, and a sad life that finds joy in nothing but the practice of virtue.'

'And grief it is that walks upon the heels of pleasure.'

'Yes, and talking to you a man might think pleasure was a poison brewed in the sink of the bowels.'

'You have a poor opinion of me.'

'You're a sad case,' said Cuff. He was pouring the tea into the mug.

Mackie shook his head. 'I have not the pliability to reform myself as you require.' He stared up at the projecting mass of rock above the forecourt of the shelter, a formidable tonnage.

Cuff noticed. 'Yes, and if that drops on your head you won't have any more worries.'

Mackie failed to repress a smile. He looked down at the line in the sand. 'I've done what I can.'

'Done is the operative word. You're done with her save for the off chance a load of seal fur comes your way, then she's altogether handy.'

'You think me a wicked schemer?'

'I think you fashion a way such as to serve yourself when you think you're serving others. It's an art form peculiar to the overlords of this world, them you seem to envy *and* despise.'

'I seem to rank low in your estimation.'

'On this matter yes, mighty low, and one thing more.'

'Say it and be done.'

'The blood you have, the blood you share, you ought count precious while you can. There's faith, hope and charity, and there's love, and the greatest of that bunch is love, that's in the Bible, I know that much.'

'And I know the meek do not inherit the earth, nor the indigents nor the layabouts. I know the Lord does *not* temper the wind to the shorn lamb, Thaddeus.'

'What I know is life is short, and all too quick it's too damn late. Commerce might fill your pockets but it will not fill your heart.'

'The heart is a perilous guide in this world.'

'Well, a rudderless heart has its perils too.'

The wind was up and catching in the trees. The black phantom shape of bats arced through the darkness, the sound of the river eddying about the cave.

'I wonder how we'll find them in this damn fastness,' said Cuff.

'We stick to the Branch.'

'*That* is our elaborate plan?'

'Yes.'

Cuff took another sip of the tea and handed the mug to Mackie. He heaped more wood on the fire and sat contemplating the flames. Mackie sipped on the tea. The rain was easing. Neither was inclined to talk. Cuff pulled his jacket tight and made a pillow of his haversack and closed his eyes. Mackie stared into the blackness for a while, sipping at his tea. He buttoned his coat to the neck. He pulled his blanket tight around his shoulders. It was cold in the cave, cold but dry.

Next morning Cuff made his way up a gully through a tangle of ferns and a forest of coachwood and wattle to the heathland above, a vantage colonised by dwarf gums and bottlebrush rooted in ancient sands and stone. Small birds skittered from the heath to the cover of the woodlands on the slopes below. Far off, the morning light on the ridges, the dark folds of shadow in the valleys.

'Weather looks promising,' he said upon his return to the shelter.

They followed the river all that day, and the next, the meander shifting ever more to the north until late in the afternoon they halted at a creek that snaked its way down to them through more of the same, thick scrub and stone. They rested there, studying the scene upriver, a gathering of she-oaks, the towering cliffs of the gorge beyond.

A cheerless dusk. A coal-grey sky.

'You look tired enough to fall over,' said Cuff.

Mackie nodded.

40

Seamus Peachey had begged Griffin Pinney not to go. He'd begged him to wait, just for a day or two, when he'd be well enough to walk, to keep up, which he would, so he said.

Harp was sympathetic, for he was keen to get Peachey off his hands, but the game hunter would not entertain the proposition, he would not have an invalid on the trek, and they left Harp's camp the same day, Pinney and Sparrow, and Bea Faa and the dogs, the young dog and the old dog.

The game hunter set a pace, Thyne Kunkle's Swedish musket in hand. He pushed them hard, through swampy country draining to the Branch, until they met with the Branch above the tidal limit. They drank deep on hands and knees and with that they took to the river, sand and shallows, the cluttered banks, or game tracks higher up, whatever worked best. Griffin Pinney was in no mood to dawdle.

Sparrow had temporarily lost the power of speech. He thought Bea Faa a beauty, more beautiful than Biddie Happ. He tried not to look at her, for when he did it was hard to look away. Like a spell. She might be more beautiful, even, than Misty Knapp, the woman who first sparked his manhood, dancing the way she did, at The Dirty Sack on the river Irk, so long ago.

He wondered where she'd come from, this Bea Faa. Perhaps she was an Otahetian, though he'd never seen an Otahetian, not even a picture. He'd just heard the stories and he reckoned she was about as dusky as what he'd imagined, thinking about the Otahetian beauties, sporting their allurements, dancing and so on.

He felt awfully diminished in the presence of this tall girl. He, Marty Sparrow, expiree, failed farmer, sad sack, yellowy man with no panache.

When his tongue came back to him, he did try. He asked her questions but her answers were curt, just a yes or a no. Only when he asked her about the cut on her lip did she provide something more. 'That happened when he raped me,' she said.

Pinney took Sparrow by the arm. 'Go on,' he said to the girl and they watched as she walked ahead, keeping to the slim track. 'You want some o' that you can have some o' that.'

'You mean . . .?'

'I mean, you stick with me we can share the quim.'

'I don't do that.'

'Tell me then, what is Bet Pepper's little venture if it ain't the sociable sharing of the quim?'

'That's different, that's um, contractual.'

Pinney stared at the ground about his boots, scratching at his forehead. 'You disappoint me Marty,' he said.

The game hunter foraged on the move and they watched him, Sparrow and Bea, and mimicked him when they could, uprooting the tubers he called bush parsnips, picking wild berries and edible greens. A feed, now and then, of the little mushrooms he called milk caps and the climber that he called snotty-drops, and they watched as he gobbled down the little snots, so-called. They did as he did, for they were hungry.

They passed through the ceremonial ground and further along they came upon the murdered blacks.

They did not tarry for long.

Bea stood off. Sparrow moved as close as he dared and looked up at the two men hung from the bough, the dogs sniffing at the feet. 'You know them?' he said.

'I know they're Branch,' said Pinney.

'We still got a compact?'

'O' course we got a compact! We are as much at variance with the military as they are; *are we not?*'

'I suppose we are.'

'Suppose! Suppose! You're trouble Marty, you're lukewarm, you're tepid. Not like this girl. She got the grit you need, stuck a knife in me to prove it.'

The game hunter spread the tear in his britches and put the wound on display.

'I didn't know that,' said Sparrow.

'Well, now you do, so take it in. There's no place for *suppose* out here.'

'No, yes.'

'One more thing. She puts a foot wrong, I'll punish her like you ain't never seen.'

'I do hope you won't do that.'

'Depends on her. She's a good girl she'll be alright.'

They trekked for two days, their course bearing ever more northward, and they paused at a confluence, studying the scene ahead, a forest of she-oaks and the towering cliffs of the gorge beyond.

They walked on, sand and shallows for much of the afternoon, here and there weaving thickets on the banks, until the half-light of dusk settled into the gorge, a faint moon.

Beneath that moon a wild dog stepped from a fracture in the cliff wall. The dog surveyed the scene and then picked its way down the scarp to a thicket of water gums by the sand and there it stood, cloaked in the shadows.

Griffin Pinney put a hand on his old dog and the animal dropped down. Sparrow took hold of the pup, anxious to soothe the creature, keep him quiet and still. Sparrow was tired and footsore, and so was Bea. And they were hungry. They were keen for meat.

Pinney went down on one knee. He primed the Swedish musket. He checked the flint and the flint screw and he put the cock from half to full and raised the gun, settling the stock into his shoulder.

The wild dog stepped cautiously from the cover. The dog stood there, fear and thirst commingling, still as stone save for the slow, watchful turn of its head. Then it moved to the water and began to drink.

Pinney took aim and fired in one movement. The sound came back at them off the cliff walls as the ball took the dog in the shoulder and brought him down, but he was up again, frenzied, spinning about, snapping at the wound, squealing with pain. Then he made for the timber.

In that instant, the pup leapt forward, broke free and galloped across the sand, drawn on by the distressed wails of the prey. Into the shallows, long, swift strides, born to this, his rhythm untroubled neither by the run of the river or the bedrock as the wild dog scrambled up the wooded scarp.

Pinney was reloading as the pup took to the timber, bounding up the slope, snapping at the shot dog's heels. The shot dog turned and stood its ground, teeth bared, the near foreleg soaked in blood, the pup inching forward, itching for engagement, when Pinney fired a second shot.

The wild dog plummeted onto a bed of scree among the water gums. It twitched and kicked and fell still.

'This gun's alright and that pup's a natural,' said Pinney. The observation made Sparrow uneasy. No one save Seamus Peachey had ever said a word good or bad about the pup.

'I might have to have him. He's a certifiable game dog, *heart and snout.*'

'He is not for sale,' said Sparrow.

'Well, don't get too attached.'

Pinney turned to Bea. 'Put a fire.' He threw her a piece of flint from his haversack and she caught it. 'Lose that and you'll be sorry.' Then he snapped words at Sparrow. 'Go get that meat.'

Sparrow found the wild dog among the water gums, dead as mutton. He took the carcass by the hindquarters, the head joggling in the shallows as he crossed the river, the pup cavorting in the wash, snapping at the dead meat and sniffing and licking at the bloodied fur.

Bea gathered old flood-wrack and tufts of dry grass from sheltered nooks in the stone. She lit the fire. She sat with Sparrow as the pup shook out the wet in its coat, pleased as punch.

'He'll chase a fat duck to hell and back that one,' said Pinney.

Sparrow was pleased the pup had come good. He was a blue-blood game dog. He was swift and brave, plain to see. Now he stood foursquare, his flanks heaving, his eyes locked on the dead meat, his shaggy coat soaked and ridden with grit.

Pinney threw the carcass onto a hip-high block of tumbledown stone.

'I'll ready the dog,' said Bea.

'Why?' said Pinney.

'Because I can,' she said.

The game hunter considered the offer. He put his axe and his knife on the stone beside the bloody carcass and stepped away with a bow and a flourish of his arm across his middle, like a Dutchman on his way to church.

'Keep your eyes on her,' he said to Sparrow.

He walked downstream a short way and fumbled about and began to piss.

The girl watched. 'If he covers me again I'll slice his jugular,' she said.

'What with?' said Sparrow, as Pinney returned.

She said nothing more. She severed the dead dog's head with the axe and took off the lower legs above the knuckle bones, chopped off the tail and threw it to Pinney's old dog. Then she took the knife and cut a line from the neck to the belly through to the bumhole. She took hold of the carcass at the scruff, fingertips in the raw stump. She waded into the watercourse and stood for a moment while the water washed round her ankles and cooled the itch in her scabby leech wounds.

She slid her hand into the cavity and closed her fist on the innards and dragged down to the dog's rear and took all the gut away and dropped it into the flow and washed out the cavity. Then she washed her hands and came back to the block as the pup took to the water, snapping up the guts.

She peeled the hide off the neck and the forestumps and gripped the raw flesh in her hands while Sparrow jerked the hide off the ribbing and the rear end.

Downstream there were crows at the water's edge and some tall wading bird in the shallows, picking at the innards on the flow. Dark settled into the gorge.

Pinney snatched up the axe and quartered the skinned dog with heavy blows, and they cooked portions on hardwood skewers fashioned from the branches of a turpentine tree. They turned the meat as required, the smell inciting their hunger.

Sparrow marvelled at the skewers for they did not burn through. 'Hard as iron,' said the game hunter.

They ate all they could, not another word, peeling the charred black flesh from the skewers and tipping it from one palm to the other and taking it on their tongues, sucking in the cold night air and flicking the grease off their fingers while the pup prowled for the dregs and Pinney's old dog watched on, drowsy.

They slept that night on the sand beneath the arc of a shallow cave. Somewhere to the west a lightning storm cracked the sky, filling the gorge with flashes of blue-grey light and charging the ridges with a faint blue tracery, but not a sound to overlay the murmur of the flow.

That night Bea dreamt they were sleeping, much as they were. A dark figure came silently across the sand and stood in their midst and she feared for her life but she could not move and neither could she speak. She saw a bone-handled knife and she saw the dark figure drop to one knee beside Griffin Pinney. Her fear was gone, for it was Joe. Pinney opened his eyes. His lips mimed words but he gave out no sound, like a fish grounded, and Joe spoke to him. 'You can't talk Griffin, I just cut your throat,' he said.

In the morning, a shadow crept over the river as dark clouds moved in from the west and banked like some grim fortress in the northern sky.

They made bush tea on the rekindled fire and they picked over the carcass one last time, and fed the leavings to the dogs.

Pinney led them upstream, the old dog labouring along at his master's heel, the pup splashing through the shallows, lunging at shoals of tiny fish, tiddlers.

The girl watched the pup. 'You cannot keep a cat from mousing.'

Sparrow was caught unready. He did not quite hear what she said for she had not hitherto spoken to him, save to answer his questions.

'He's a natural,' she said.

'I know, he's special.'

Now the wind in the gorge was cold and seemed to whirl about them and they noted the surge in the river's flow. They could hear the drum of the rain miles off when they felt the first light drops, heavier by the minute. High above they saw wood ducks in formation, like the head of an arrow. They noticed Pinney limping, his hand on the leg wound, his gait hurried as they turned onto a long straight reach, hardly a crook in the river's line.

Pinney searched the timber and the ridges on either side of the gorge and saw no relief. He hurried forth, the old dog keeping up as best he could, the pup in his element.

The heavens opened and the rain harried into the gorge and before long the river swelled some more, the quickening flow thick with silts from the uplands. The levees were crumbling into the flow, slender saplings bowed down in the rain, the ridges mantled in the black of ages, like ruined battlements, silvered cascades pouring through fractures in the cliff wall.

At the far end of the reach the river took a sharp turn and they picked their way through a muddle of boulders to a sliver of sand high on the shoulder. They went higher still, through old flood-wrack and scrub, into the trees, and they perched there in the downpour like ticks on a mammoth, watching driftwood hurtle into stone, the torrent banking and churning, the white water crashing into the boulders and lashing the timber on the fringe, saplings coming away, the runnage downstream sucking them on, them and all things loosed by the force of the flow.

Pinney said something but his words were lost in the sound of the waters on the bend. He stood and turned and limped away and Bea and Sparrow followed, shivering, and the dogs with them and the old dog stumbled and Sparrow helped him up and pushed him on.

They followed Pinney onto the next reach. The track narrowed as they went higher. Higher still they spied a shelter beneath a prodigious overhang. They edged their way to the shelter and there Bea and Sparrow dropped down, soaked and shivering. The dogs shook themselves and set to and fro, sniffing out the scents in the grit, devouring whatever they could find, lime-white dung and shards of cooked bone.

Pinney stood beneath the cover of the overhang, watching the torrent below, the incessant boom percussing around the shelter as the waters banked and crashed on the turn.

The night came on with great swiftness, as if the light was sucked away on the flood waters.

The old dog came and stood beside Pinney. He tried to cough something up, but in that he failed. He walked slowly to the rear of the shelter where he dropped down and sunk deep into sleep.

41

It was dusk when they heard the two gunshots in quick succession, a musket, the sound confirming for Cuff and Mackie that Griffin Pinney's party was not that far ahead.

They sought cover in a shelter high up, above the uppermost gatherings of old flood-wrack, nestled among coachwoods and turpentines and tangles of anchor vine.

Small birds fled from nests in the honeycombed stone. Mackie leant against the wall and slid to the ground. He checked his parts for ticks and leeches.

Cuff stood on the lip, staring into the gorge. 'All we need's a hubble-bubble and a songbird in a cage, this could be Babylon.'

Mackie was in no mood to be cheered. 'I'd sell my soul for a tot of claret.'

'It's still yours to sell, that's good news,' said Cuff.

Cuff scanned the shelter and spied more than what he needed for a fire – a scattering of dead wood and leaves eddied into a heap so neat you'd swear they were sweepings, and little piles of lime-white dung, likewise useful. He set about making a fire upon a spread of antique coals as Mackie stretched out on the cave floor, his head propped on his haversack, his eyes closed, his breathing laboured.

'I thought you'd struck a truce with those lungs.'

'A truce of uncontracted length.'

'Want some biscuit?'

'No.'

Cuff sat close to the lip of the shelter. He ate some biscuit and contemplated making some bush tea but as Mackie was dozing he chose instead to sit quietly, watching the scene fade as night came on and then a lightning storm, bathing the ragged shelves and the fault lines on the far cliff wall in flashes of blue. When the cold began to bite he retreated to the fire, stoked it once again and made some tea. He could hear the river. In the firelight he could see the sweat on Mackie's brow.

Several times in the night Mackie woke with a start, convulsing, sucking for air. His neck was spongy to the touch, the glands swollen, as were his legs below the knee. For some hours the sweats came and went, swift visitations that left him soaked through.

———

In the predawn Cuff made some tea and rationed out a biscuit, one each.

Mackie got himself up. He shuffled to the lip of the cave and spat into the void and tried to cough up some more of the phlegm that rattled his every breath. He declared the very thought of solids made him ill, but he was desperately parched. He drank the tea, catching his breath between gulps, the warm mug romancing his fingers. He grimaced as he swallowed. His joints ached and there was hurt in his throat and he could hear the gurgle in his chest like bubbles up through water. He wished he had some claret, for claret alone seemed to calm his throat and placate his mood.

Cuff was pleased when Mackie dozed off. He dozed for much of the morning. Cuff dozed too and otherwise sat by the fire, sipping at lukewarm tea and pondering their predicament.

Rain set in, then heavy rain, sheeting into the gorge. Cold gusts swirled about the cave, stirring the firesmoke. The sound of the river drew Cuff to the edge of their shelter to view the spectacle below, the swollen river thrashing the banks.

He studied the river, and he studied the prone form of his companion; reckoned they would have to relent and head home. He did not want to abandon the chase for the gunshots to the west had been as sweet and clear as a message in a bottle. They knew they were making ground. Pinney could not move swiftly with a pair of novices in tow, and there was the Woody boy to consider as well. Cuff had a feeling in his gut the boy might be alive. He went back to the fire and squatted down. 'That boy just might be alive,' he said.

Mackie stirred. 'I think not.'

'Well, we can but hope.'

'You live on hope you die fasting.'

'And you'll die fasting if you don't eat my biscuits.'

Mackie coughed some more, propped on one elbow, bringing up

what he could and spitting into his palm so he might inspect the red droplets from the depths of his lungs.

'I've heard it's called the sad passions, that clears me and puts you square in the frame,' said Cuff.

'It is hereditary, nothing to do with passions sad or otherwise.'

'Like monarchy?'

Mackie did not answer.

Cuff would not relent. 'I reckon melancholy plays a part.'

'Well then, perhaps I am doomed.'

'Perhaps you am, 'less you cheer up. Remember that old Chinese proverb.'

'Alright, tell me the proverb!'

'You cannot stop the birds of sadness from passing overhead, but you can sure as hell stop them nesting in your hair.'

'That's very helpful, thank you, Thaddeus.'

'We have to go back, we cannot go on.'

'You mean I cannot go on.'

'That is exactly what I mean; listen to yourself, you sound like a Persian hookah.'

'I wouldn't know about that.'

'No you wouldn't, you wouldn't take the time to sit quietly and contemplate the world if your life depended upon it, which it well might! That's why I recommend a pipe to any man I deem worthy of my counsel.'

'Why?'

'For to sit in quiet contemplation of all things. A pipe helps.'

'Whether quiet contemplation or sheer indolence, who would know.'

'Who cares what anybody knows or thinks they know.'

'I care.'

Cuff shook his head and chuckled. 'Alister, you're ill and you have to rest, that's it.'

'It will pass.'

'Only a fool would go deeper into this gorge in your condition, knee deep in the flowage, them glands o' yours puffed up to buggery. I'm hoping you're not a fool.'

'We all know about hope,' said Mackie.

'What is it this time?'

'It's grief's music.'

'That's the melancholy talking.'

Mackie stared at his companion. 'You never miss a chance.'

'We've missed ours. We have to go back,' said Cuff.

'Tomorrow.'

'We'll go when we can; when you can and not before. Could be days, settle in.'

Mackie took a deep breath. He felt himself convulse, his lungs erupting, but he managed to hold it down, lips pressed tight. He ran his tongue over the ulcers on his gums. He gathered his blanket tight about him and closed his eyes, slept, and the sounds of Cuff moving about were like faint echoes from afar and the sounds of the rain and the river the same.

42

The thunder of the floodwaters in the gorge had settled to a hum somewhere deep in their skulls. When they woke the rain had stopped but the river was angrier than ever. The old dog staggered to the shelter's edge and stood beside Pinney. A faint grey mist carried to them on a swirl of updraught from the rock and wreckage on the turn. The mist enveloped the shelter like a shroud.

The old dog was shivering. Pinney bent down and worked his cold fingers into the creature's fur. Then he gave him a whack on the flank and took hold of his collar and gave the old dog a shake, rattled him, ready for the day.

He looked about and saw the pup and he beckoned the pup come. The pup ambled over and stood there, sniffing at the wound in Pinney's thigh.

Sparrow took a drink from the costrel, the leakage running down the long, thin scab on his forearm. His eyes locked on the game hunter. 'I won't give him up,' he said. 'Not for trade, not for nothin'.'

Pinney stood the dog up straight, hind legs aligned, a finger under the animal's chin, like he was some kind of gentleman breeder. 'I might have to fashion you an offer,' he said.

'No,' said Sparrow. He called the pup and the pup ambled across the shelter and rested his snout in the crook of Sparrow's arm.

The game hunter led them up the face of the escarpment, to a vast upland of pitted rock and heath dissected by thickly forested ravines and gullies, forming no pattern, cutting in all directions, chaotic work.

Sparrow studied the vastness. He wondered how a man would ever find his way if he didn't stick to the Branch or otherwise to some known track. 'Where are we goin'?' he said.

'We're goin' over the top, 'less you can part the flood like some damn Moses,' said Pinney.

They trekked all day through the prickly heath, stopping to drink from small pools in the rock and resting whenever the old dog fell too far behind. They hardly spoke a word.

Late in the afternoon they took in the view from a fiercely weathered peak. Far to the north they saw sandstone cliffs that ran west to a point where the country was lost in a haze.

'That's the upper Branch,' said Pinney.

'How far?' said Sparrow.

'Too far for now.'

They followed him through dense heath that stood shoulder high, along a well-worn track that led down from a headwall into a sheltered gully, tall bloodwoods and scribbly gums and here and there the extravagant lily the savages called *gymee*, with leaves like the blade of a broadsword and a spear-like stem way taller than a man. A swarm of ghost moths swept over them, downy soft wings, like kapok in a whirlwind.

Further down, Pinney pulled up sharp and signed for quiet. They watched a black snake move slowly through scree and leaf-rot, half hidden. It slithered into a hollow log and was almost gone when Pinney grabbed its tail and dragged it out and stepped on its swollen neck.

He took his axe and severed the snake's head with one blow, held up the remains, four or five foot of snake, red-bellied, still twitching. He dropped the meat and picked up the head and squeezed a frog from the severed neck. 'Silly ol' frog,' he said.

'Should o' held his breath,' said Sparrow.

Pinney chuckled. 'Give up too quick.'

They found a cave nearby and took to it and Pinney told them to set a fire for the meat.

He gutted the snake and chopped it into chunks. The grey shades of the coming night flooded the gully and the cave like a soaking dye.

The old dog did not eat but otherwise all present feasted on the cooked meat, the plenteous chunks, the pup gulping down the tail.

Pinney took up the old dog's portion and tried to handfeed him but to no avail. 'He's off his food,' said Sparrow.

'First time for everything,' said Pinney.

When they'd finished they watched the fire burn to nothing much, the flames but a flicker in the coals. The cooked meat had blocked out all the creature sounds, locked them in a world oblivious, but now the sounds came back to them, carried to them over the dull *whomp* of the floodwaters below.

Pinney spread the tear in his britches and pressed at the swelling around the wound. He was grimacing like someone was poking him with a sharp stick, hissing through clenched teeth. He glanced at Bea. 'You'll pay for this, times over.'

'You got the poison,' said Sparrow.

'I know what I got,' said Pinney.

Sparrow saw a tiny white grub at work on the gash, busy in the seepage.

'What's that?' he said.

'That's what'll eat you if I cut your throat, that'n whatever else.'

Sparrow wished he was anywhere but where he was. Cuff's words rang in his ears again: *Don't burn your bridges if you cannot part the waters*, he'd said, and Sparrow knew Cuff was right.

He thought again of the bull shark and the boy Jug, the bloody torso bobbing in the river, the skull thudding on the blackbutt planking as Peachey hauled the remains onto the gunnel. He recalled the boy roped to the slab of stone and tipped into the depths of the river. In his mind's eye he saw the whole horrid thing slipping into the deep, settling on the bottom, a knot of eels tearing at the meat, savaging the boy's face.

He thought of the doctor, who would probably never know what happened to his son. The doctor was a good man, a decent magistrate, un-bought, no one's instrument. The doctor did not deserve the unforgiving misery of never knowing.

Sparrow wished he could banish such thoughts. He feared he might be tormented, all his life, by that one terrible event on the river. Such torment – a man could lose his mind. He was most anxious for some diversion. 'What's it like, on the other side?' he said.

'You'll see, soon enough,' said Pinney.

'Tell me now.'

'You want the other side in a hurry, I'll point you the way. The girl stays with me, the pup too,' said Pinney. He was grinning a grin that might be described as a sly grin or perhaps a very cruel grin, Sparrow could not be sure for he was not endowed with the faculty to read faces with any precision.

He did not want to reveal the panic in his heart at that moment, nor the fear he felt, curling around his vitals. He thought best to continue the conversation as if untroubled by Pinney's taunts. 'I doubt I'd find the way,' he said.

'Get a picture of a compass, pin it on your hat, you'll be fine,' said Pinney.

Sparrow could see the pleasure the game hunter was taking, making a fool of him in front of the girl, and he did not fail to notice that Pinney had once again made a proprietorial reference to the pup. He worried, now, that everything Pinney had said, *everything*, could be untrue. 'Is there a village, on the other side?'

'Yes.'

'Jephthah Big, Tinkerton Hides, Jack Chitty, they there?'

'I don't know about Jephthah, but Tinkerton's there and Jack Chitty too.'

'What about Tom Snape?'

'What is this, the fuckin' inquisition?' Pinney pressed his fingers into the hinge at the back of his jaw and he worked his jaw open and shut. 'Swear I been hit with a block o' wood,' he said.

In the morning the old dog did not stir, laid out. Pinney woke and sat there, close to the dog. He rested a hand upon the animal's frame and felt the sag of cold and lifeless skin between the ribs. He sat there for a long time, looking down upon his dead companion, his sole companion for as long as he'd been coming and going in the wilderness, shepherding the bolters to another world.

Bea and Sparrow and the pup watched on. Pinney looked at them like they'd done the deed, like they'd murdered the old dog in his sleep. He stood over them, staring at Bea, scratching at his package.

He grabbed Sparrow by the collar and pulled him to his feet.

'Go forage,' he said, 'and don't come back less you got somethin' to eat.' He handed the small axe to Sparrow and waved him away.

Sparrow beckoned the pup and he was surprised that Pinney made no objection as they left the shelter together, taking to the lower part of the gully.

'Get on your knees,' said Pinney.

Bea did not move.

The game hunter rested the blade of his knife on her cheek. 'I'll give you a smile all the way to your ears, girl, if you don't kneel and get about.'

Bea knelt and Pinney holstered the knife and motioned her to turn about. He knelt behind her and pushed her forward onto her hands. He threw up her skirt and growled like a dog as he pulled her onto his shaft and thumped at her with a frantic rhythm, so loud, so rapt, he neither heard nor sensed the presence of Sparrow at his rear.

Sparrow was all atremble. But his mind was clear.

He raised the axe, two-handed, and thumped the blade into Pinney's skull so hard he rent the skull in two, a declivity so deep that Pinney's eye sockets parted ways and he crumpled and rolled and lay in a stupor, the sockets angled away, the visage like some kind of strange fish, the eyes blinking.

Sparrow threw down the axe. He went numb. His legs failed him. He dropped to his knees, his eyes locked on Pinney and the blood that now soaked into the grit like some kind of painted halo.

Bea threw down her skirt and turned about. She fell sideways onto the sand. She could but gape at Sparrow's handiwork. For a time there was no movement in that cave save for Pinney's arms and fingers twitching and the young dog licking first at the blood and then busily pushing his nose into the cleft skull, licking at the game hunter's brains.

'Come away,' said Sparrow, but the pup paid no heed.

Sounds were coming back to them – the *whomp* of the floodwaters, the wind, an agitated quoll, the liquid banter of currawongs.

Sparrow stared at Pinney's cock, limp now, beside his buttons. He muttered something that was indecipherable to Bea, something about a compass. On hands and knees she pulled herself close to Pinney's face. She took the hunting knife from his holster. She put the blade in his mouth and cut him from the corner of his mouth to the bone beneath his ear.

She dropped the knife. She wiped her bloody hand in the grit and rubbed her hands together until the grit was off. She remembered the wish dream, the dream where Joe had rescued her. She bent low to Pinney's ear, the eyes still blinking. 'You will rot with that stupid smile on your face,' she said.

'Pup, come away,' said Sparrow. He was trying to think what they might do next but his mind was a muddle, entirely deprived of direction by the awful scene and the horrible doings that had caused it. He thought he might faint. He thought he might be in a bad dream. Then he saw Bea straighten, he saw her thrust her hand into a pocket as she fell backwards, her body arched, convulsing, her eyes like marble.

She'd reached out to Sparrow as her body went taut as a fiddle string and she was all aquiver, trembling and jerking, her knuckles ivory white, a leather wad in her hand. Sparrow wrenched the wad from her fingers and tried to force it between her teeth but he could not loose her jaw. He took hold of her, held her tight and the tears loosed from his eyes. And all the while the pup, untroubled, was feeding on the blood and brains of Griffin Pinney.

Part III

The Cave House

43

When it was over the girl was limp as a rag and her skin was slick with sweat, arcs of dull pain twisting in her flesh. Sparrow dragged her a little way towards the mouth of the cave, away from the horrible mess, her heels furrowing the grit. He laid her beneath a blanket and there she slept, fitfully, for much of the morning.

He sat close to her, close enough to hear her fitful breath and to watch her bosom rise and fall in what appeared to be a troubled sleep. He noticed a trickle of blood on her chin. He studied the old wound in her lip, the scab undisturbed. The leather wad he returned to her pocket and there he found a piece of bone from the leg of a dog, knuckle at one end, sharply splintered at the other, like the point of a needle. A weapon perhaps, something to pierce a jugular. He left her to sleep.

He stood over the carcass of Griffin Pinney, recalling with some wonderment his resolve in the moment when he drove the blade of the axe into Pinney's skull. He'd done it without forethought, without hesitation, without fear. He wondered how he'd done that, for now he felt fear. Now they were alone in the fastness, alone but together, he and Bea and the pup.

Late in the morning she woke and asked for water and there was hardly a drop in the costrel. He went for water and came back and she sat up and drank her fill. Then she lay down again, not a word, and she rested, in and out of sleep. She woke yet again and lay there, silent. Several times Sparrow caught her looking at him. On one occasion she looked away, studied the prone form of Griffin Pinney. 'We are, perhaps, a formidable pair,' she said.

Sparrow didn't know if that was mockery or truly meant. 'We are, yes,' he said, more in hope than conviction. He promised her he would get some food. He went down the gully looking for things edible, axe in hand. It was hard going, the slope severe, the ground sodden and sticky, boulders dressed in staghorns and mantled in lichens; spider webs like gossamer wheels, shuddering in the breeze.

He found native currants and he ate some and put the rest in his pocket. He searched the ground for the edible tubers but he found none and nor could he find bush honey, nor the snotty-drops he seemed, now, to crave, nor the sweet-tasting grubs that Pinney had found with ease, chopping into rotten wood.

Not wanting to be long away, he settled for the meagre ration and hurried back to the cave. On his way he spied a little crop of mushrooms, the ones Pinney called milk caps, their caps a milky orange colour. He ate one and pocketed the rest and hurried up the gully.

Bea was sitting up, her back to the wall of the cave, the blanket around her shoulders.

He filled her palm with the currants and the two mushrooms and he fanned the fire and half-filled the quart pot with water and got it cooking for a mug of tea, and when it cooled a little, the tea, they drank it down.

Bea put her head between her knees and vomited the currants and the one mushroom she'd managed to get down. She sipped at the tea and drank the acid taste away. Then she got to her feet, steady enough.

She rummaged in the game hunter's pockets and commandeered the pot of balm he'd taken from Freddie, and Sparrow took the powder horn and the bandolier and they took the axe and the knife and the musket too, Thyne Kunkle's musket.

They went up the gully to the heathland above the cave. They walked west for about an hour and then took rest, sat themselves down on the lip of a basalt outcrop fringed with tea-tree and spider flower. They searched the scene to the north and the north-west, the upland dissected by the maze of ridgelines and valleys to the far horizon.

Sparrow wondered how they might ever find their way should they press on. The country so abrupt and warped and altogether infinite, the patterning so random, a man might succumb to a most morose and hopeless bewilderment – like Shug. He tried to sight the valley of the upper Branch but he could see nothing but the hazy blue-green sameness of the forests and the endless confusion of sandstone rimrock. He was awfully glad to be with Bea and the long-legged pup, but he worried about pressing on and he worried, too, about not pressing on.

The foremost ridge was lightly wooded with strange trees, the skewbald limbs bent low, tortured and twisted by the onslaught of the elements year-round.

'What if the savages come?' he said.

'We give them what they want.' The ache in her was an ache all through, an ache for which she had no word.

'They can have an axe,' he said. 'But I keep the pup.'

'They'll take what they want, brigands mostly do.'

'I never thought a brigand might be a savage.'

'What matter the colour?'

'You ever met a brigand?'

Her first thought was the sealers but she would not speak of them. 'I've met Caleb and I've seen Wolgan, and the one they call Napoleon.'

'Met?'

'They came to Joe's. He's faithful to the governor's concession. He says they are the true proprietors of the soil, so he pays them a tithe.'

'A tithe?'

'He says the time has come to pay the tithe.'

'What's he like, old Wolgan?'

'He's ancient but he's sharp as a pike.'

'Joe's pretty ancient too.'

'I know. I have to get back, see to him.'

'I cannot go back, and I ain't even a bolter, strictly.'

'No?'

'No, that's Seamus, he's on a bond, see, and Winifred, she came out free and he's bonded to Winifred and she's a *feme sole*!'

'And now he's a ruin. He can hardly walk.'

'That's Seamus, betrayed by a woman and kicked by a horse.'

'And you?'

'I done my seven years, got a grant, my own patch, thirty acres.'

'And that's not good fortune?'

'It's endless toil, the stumpin' nearly killed me, and I'm deep in hock too. It ain't freedom.'

A faint sun hazed through thick grey cloud. They stood there, on the ridgeline, gazing across the valley, the far cliff walls fissured and scarred like the hide of an old dromedary.

To the west the mountains appeared to shudder, dappling with the shift of cloud, a land remote and alien, empty as the voids of space, so it seemed to Sparrow. 'You think he told us a pack o' lies?' he said.

'Pinney?'

'Perhaps there's nothing over there.'

'It's of no import to me.'

'I have to see.'

'And I have to go back.'

'Why?'

'Because I owe him that, Joe. He treats me decent. I only hope he's alive,' she said.

Sparrow didn't wait to think, he just said it. 'I would treat you decent,' he said.

Bea Faa smiled. 'You would?'

'Oh yes.'

'Then come back to Joe's.'

'I don't know if I can.'

'But you won't tell me why?'

He shook his head, stared down at his boots.

'Is it too awful?'

'It's worse than awful, it's the other side of awful,' he said.

'You don't have to tell me.'

'Thank you.'

'Thank you, too . . . for what you did.'

'Did he hurt you bad?'

'Not so as new to me.'

'I am not sorry I killed him.'

'Nor I.'

Bea was still thirsty. She took up the costrel and drank till she could drink no more and Sparrow watched her drink, every drop.

He worked his fingers into the young dog's scruff and the dog sat, content, and they with him, and that made Sparrow feel a little bit better though by no means untroubled.

The pleasant moment was all too brief. Sparrow felt the young dog bristle and rise on all fours, his hackles up, every muscle taut as an archer's bow. Bea sensed it too. They were not alone. They heard something pushing through the heath. A mongrel dog quick-stepped onto the rock, a big dog, poor design, bulldog shoulders and duck hound legs. A dog muscled like he was fired in a kiln, jowls quivering, pacing to and fro, a guttural rumble up from his innards like he might erupt and spew red hot lava and cook the soles of their feet.

That heath was a fount of unpleasant surprises for it quickly came to pass the dog was attended by a tall savage who followed in line, his hair much matted and richly gummed with eagle feathers and shark teeth. The claws of the great bird hung from a fibre necklace, the talons upon the scarring on his chest.

The savage barked a command and the mongrel dog stood alert yet at ease, uncoiled, so to speak.

Bea searched the scene before them for every detail that might count towards their deliverance. She could see naught but severity in the eyes of the savage and the mongrel dog. Sparrow swallowed hard and wondered why it had to be a savage *and* a menacing dog, why not just one or the other. He remembered various sermons from his childhood wherein the Lord was forever visiting trials upon this man and that, not just Abraham, but just like Abraham the trials seemed always to be somewhat excessive, *Kill your son!* and so on. He had once discussed this puzzling matter with Mortimer Craggs and Mort had proffered the observation that God might be a maniac. It was not a thing that Sparrow, personally, would ever say out loud, but now that observation came to Sparrow's mind as his gaze flicked from the savage to the mongrel dog and back to the savage again.

Much to his surprise and to Bea's surprise as well, he spoke.

'Good afternoon,' he said.

Bea was wide-eyed. 'Hello,' she said.

'I am Daniel.'

Sparrow held tight to the pup.

Then they heard singing and they were now thoroughly bewildered if somewhat relieved, for the song was unfamiliar but they were, Bea and Sparrow both, conversant with the genus.

Oh don't you remember sweet Alice, Ben Bolt,
Sweet Alice whose hair was so brown
Who wept with delight when you gave her a smile
And trembled with fear at your frown . . .

It was on 'frown' that a compact white man, a man of square frame and quick parts, stepped into the scene like some impresario. The man threw down his field haversack and removed his straw hat and he bowed an elaborate bow, thus revealing a tight cropped head of light brown hair.

'Permit me, I am Mr Catley, explorer, botaniser specialising in the *eucalyptii,* and latterly anatomist for Sir Joseph Banks, whose servant I am . . . Are you lost?'

'I don't know,' said Sparrow, studying the man's sandals.

'We are probably lost, yes,' said Bea, thinking a confession of lostness might bring forth some assistance.

The savage toed the mongrel dog in the ribs and the dog sat down and the savage squatted beside him, watching them, the tips of his fingers fanning over the pitted rock.

Catley looked them over, these two lost souls. He noted their sorry condition. 'We must see to your needs . . . what are they?'

'I am Joe Franks' wife,' said Bea.

'Well I never. You're Mr Mackie's ward,' said Catley.

'I am nobody's ward,' she said.

'You're the Yetholm girl, sold into matrimony?'

'Yes, times over.'

'I am Martin Sparrow . . . single,' said Sparrow.

Catley took note of Sparrow's marital status, nodding as if Sparrow had touched a chord. 'I sympathise . . . it is my misfortune to have a bachelor patron who, notwithstanding his eminence and virtuosity, has a strong belief in the incompatibility of marriage and field work in the cause of natural science. Thus, here I am, nose to the grindstone, shoulder to the wheel, but truth be told I wouldn't be anywhere else, for what few talents I possess are *not* to be exercised upon a fine Axminster carpet nor beneath the glass panes of a conservatory, nor upon the gravelled pathways of a manicured garden, no no. No no no.'

Catley turned about and waved his arm in an arc, gesturing to the wilderness. 'Let me be tried upon the lofty mountains, the dark and intricate wood, the sun-drenched uplands, the marsh and the peaty bog, the intricate weave of precipitous chasms . . . and so on.'

The savage called Daniel rolled his eyes from left to right as if to say *not again*. Sparrow saw this and he smiled and the savage smiled back and it pleased Sparrow to think a savage as tall and fierce as this one could smile like a civilised man.

'So here you are, hungry, yes?' said Catley. He seemed to be addressing his question entirely to Bea.

'Yes,' said Sparrow.

'Are you hungry?' Catley said to Bea.

'Yes, ever so.'

'Well then, follow on. Moowut'tin, Daniel, he'll lead the way.'

44

Catley hustled them into the wild hedgerow so he might take up the rear. 'Mr Pinney's bandolier,' he said, as Sparrow walked by. He winked and Sparrow wondered if he should wink back but he didn't. He followed on, behind Daniel and Bea, with Mr Catley taking up the rear, the pup ambling along, sniffing at the mongrel dog.

They followed Daniel across the uplands, traversing gullies and tributary creeks where necessary and skirting the headwalls of deep-cut gorges where possible, and correcting where they could to hold their north-west line, closing on the upper Branch.

Catley was a good talker, happy to convey to them his various achievements in the wilderness and pleased to keep them informed as to their whereabouts while delicately probing for information in return. He was walking close to Bea, Sparrow now a little way behind. *If he was a dog he'd be sniffing her arse.* That was Sparrow's foremost thought at that moment. Bea's foremost thought was onions – the man reeked of them.

'The Branch forks sharp west above the gorge,' Catley said to her. 'Notwithstanding the vicissitudes of the fastness, we shall meet with the upper reaches in an hour or so.'

'That soon?'

'The upland's a mere bagatelle; a doddle compared to that gorge . . . Griffin Pinney would know that.'

Bea was unsure as to how to respond for she was committed to silence on the subject of Griffin Pinney and the succession of horrible doings in the cave. 'I suppose he would,' she said.

'The man's an unspeakable villain, but I'll tip my hat to his bushcraft,' said Catley.

Both Bea and Sparrow were pleased to hear Mr Catley's dark take on Griffin Pinney, Sparrow especially, for it was he who had – and this he still found hard to believe – actually killed the man.

'Swift now, we're almost home,' said Catley, and with that he strode off, munching on a raw onion, passing Daniel, only to stop again while he examined the underside of the narrow lanceolate leaves of an upright little shrub he had formerly named *Cistomorpha lanceolata* but had never before seen, until that moment, in anything but a moist and sheltered rift.

He got up and brushed himself off and leant close to Sparrow. 'We are trekking in a garden of infinite wonders, you do know that?'

Sparrow took this in, looking about, searching for the wonders. He could but nod. It seemed the polite thing to do.

They walked on through the heath. Soon they were there, standing four in a line atop sandstone cliffs, a sheer drop to thickly timbered slopes that flattened to a valley floor perhaps a mile wide, the river there flanked by irregular patches of forest and wild meadow and game feeding on the grasses – emu and wallaby, a wild dog loping along and wildfowl breaking from the reeds. They saw a flock of parrots skimming the canopy, their colours coursing down like windswept rain. They saw a wedge-tailed eagle, those ragged wings, wheeling, slow, hypnotic, in the heavens above.

'That is a wonder,' said Bea. She was trying to take in the valley, every detail.

'It is beautiful, like a poem,' said Sparrow. It occurred to him that perhaps Griffin Pinney was not all lies for, at that moment, he was, indeed, transfixed in wonderment.

'A river with many faces,' said Mr Catley.

'Yes,' said Bea. She was thinking of the gorge.

'It is the sublime incarnate, except for the mosquitoes in the heat, say nothing of sandflies and leeches. In spring it has no rival, nowhere in the world that I know.'

'What of autumn?' said Sparrow.

'Autumn, as ever unpredictable, can be hot like summer running on and cold like winter, altogether bracing.'

'It don't run west?' said Sparrow.

'It's the Branch, runs west to east, to the Hawkesbury thence to the Pacific, the infinite flow.'

'Is there a river runs west, on the other side?'

'I'm advised there could be, but I much prefer to have the answer firsthand, exploration being one of few categories within the small frame of my genius, botany the other.'

Sparrow looked puzzled. Catley came to his assistance. 'I am good at exploration,' he said. 'I have the vanity to think God has gifted me a pre-eminence as a traveller in this country.'

'I see.'

'Beyond that I might say no more of the other side.'

Daniel led them west along the cliff top. Late in the afternoon they followed him down a slot gully, picking their way on a narrow track through elkhorn and bird's nest fern and tumbledown stone mottled in bright green moss that glowed in the pale grey light; honeyeaters and silvereyes darted away and a hulking lizard flashed its forked tongue at them and paced off, fearless, claws the size of a man's hand.

Further down the gully opened out and they walked onto the timbered slope and followed along at the foot of the sandstone cliffs, eastward through stringybark and waratah and a carpet of fern.

'Almost there,' said Catley over the din of cicadas and parrots roosting somewhere close.

They passed by a small army tent strung on a rope between two trees, the sides fanned out with pegs on twine, the words TAFT DUCK faintly there, the near side blemished with a gaping tear, the canvas splashed with bat droppings.

Ahead of them they saw a Cape mule picking at the underbrush and a crude stairway up to a cave beneath a basalt-capped overhang. The cave was walled off with stone; a dry-stone wall with a window framed square with split timber and a door hinged with leather and fashioned to a similarly unrefined standard.

Sparrow was delighted. He could see a big old teapot sitting on the windowsill. He saw a raggedy old pair of boots by the steps to the door, the flaps and tongue all gnawed and dog-eared. 'It's a cave house,' he said.

'What a most astute fellow you are,' said Mr Catley.

'A snug in the fastness,' said Bea.

'I suppose so.'

'You built this?'

Daniel laughed a raucous laugh and shook his head at this highly improbable suggestion.

'He of little faith,' said Catley.

'You did!'

'No.'

'Who built it?' said Sparrow.

'I don't know, some bolter,' said Catley. 'It was here, teapot included . . . entirely convenient.' He threw down his field haversack and Sparrow rested the musket on the stone wall.

They followed him up the steps, single file through the narrow doorway. They stood blinking, their eyes adjusting to the faint light within. There were strings of wild figs and tubers hung like chimes from a centre beam recessed in the walls, a swing lamp in the middle. There were plant specimens and seed pods and bird skins laid out on bark fragments on the floor and a flintlock and a short-handled mattock against the wall and a small table to one side, upon which Bea could make out what seemed to be a blowpipe, a salt pouch, a bird's nest, a little pile of fishhooks, small bottles and jars all in a row, and a tubular vessel, a strange thing with a hinged lid and woven cotton shoulder straps. To the rear was a sleeping place, set snug in a niche, crypt like, thickly bedded with grass and fern fronds and draped with a pelt rug.

'My sabbatical digs,' said Catley.

'You live here?' said Sparrow.

'As required by Sir Joseph, I seek the duckbill *in situ*, something of a digression given my botanising inclinations but there you are. I don't pay the piper I just play the tune.'

The girl had picked up a cork-stopped jar in which she could see a large black spider pierced through with a long black pin. She lifted the cork top and peered in.

Sparrow figured this creature would hardly fit on the palm of his hand, considering the legs extended. 'What is that?' he said.

Catley peered hard, squinting at the jar until he recognised the content. 'That is a mountain funnel-web, which Moowut'tin assures me is deadlier than a brown snake, day or night, happy or sad, utterly fatal!'

'Worse than a brown!' said Sparrow.

'There is no known means of assuagement whereas, swift to the task, his people have means to deal with a snake bite.'

'They do?'

'They do, yes. In some regards they humble us.'

'What happens?' said Sparrow, scrutinising the jar. He noticed the long pin, the spider speared through, perhaps to minimise contact in the course of embottlement.

'We'll have to ask Moowut'tin that one,' said Catley.

They could hear Moowut'tin outside, the snapping of twigs and the crackle of the cookfire. 'Come and sit, warm yourself,' said the specimen hunter. But he went first to the niche and retrieved a flannel jacket and he put on the jacket and then he took up a fur cloak and he gave it to Bea. She put on the cloak as they exited the cave house.

They settled themselves on a damp log beside the fire, watching Daniel turn square cuts of pickled meat in the cookpot, the cuts mixed with possum bones from another meal, the smell of it all a pure delight.

Bea noticed a bark hut on the far side of the clearing, the bark positioned loosely on a frame of cut saplings. Sparrow sat quietly, wondering about his prospects for a cosy sleep in the hours to come, in the cave house. He wondered, too, about the canvas tent on the fringe of the camp. 'Whose tent is that?' he said.

'That's Sergeant Peskett's tent, somewhat diminished.'

'Does he come here?'

'Chasing Nabbinum he did, once.'

Sparrow fell silent. He was surprised to know the soldiers came this far into the wilderness.

Moowut'tin set some baked onions in the warm coals at the fringe of the fire. The smell rose up and filled their nostrils.

Catley spoke to Moowut'tin in the tongue so harsh on the ears of most white men. Moowut'tin replied and Catley translated for the benefit of Sparrow and Bea. 'On the matter of the funnel-web spider, my good friend advises the poison is swift and the symptoms irreversible – first goose flesh all over, then tingling around the mouth and tongue, then the face will twitch and the agitation will spread until the body is convulsing. He says it is pitiful, the poor pilgarlic will lapse into babble, he'll vomit and pant as if running and then his system will slow and the symptoms with it, ere death release the poor soul.'

'That is dreadful,' said Sparrow.

'Yes,' said Bea.

'They are the bearers of much treasured wisdom passed down through the ages and we are but children in their world,' said Catley.

'What do they call it?' asked Bea.

'*Marryagong* is their word for the funnel-web,' said Catley. 'I call it *montes glabella robustus*, the first and last of this designation is self-evident; as to *glabella*, that means hairless, for the distinguishing feature is the hairless carapace covering the cephalothorax. The fangs can penetrate leather or even fingernails, according to my learned colleague.'

The girl was working Freddie's balm into the scratches and leech wounds on her legs. She handed the balm to Sparrow and he did much the same.

Mr Catley took the opportunity to scrutinise Bea Faa in the firelight as she watched Sparrow work the balm into his ankles. It saddened him to think of his failed connection with the widow Wise, for those interludes were blissfully warm for a time, until she tired of the coming and going at his convenience.

Catley thought the girl a most lovely specimen. He could only assume that Griffin Pinney, true to form, had had his way with her. 'Did he hurt you, Pinney?' he said.

The question hovered in the stillness. Bea appeared to be considering her words with some care.

Sparrow noticed how Catley held the girl in his gaze, his eyes coursing over her, tracing her form. He could restrain himself no longer: 'He did more'n hurt her, he rutted on her and I killed him for it.'

The words spat out, Sparrow took a deep breath.

'Well there's an unlikely turn,' said Catley. 'A fact best confined to this small circle, I imagine. I cannot say I'm sorry.'

'You won't tell?' said Sparrow.

'I am a still tongue in a wise mouth, Mr Sparrow.'

'Thank you.'

'That man was known for unvarnished brutality and something of a deficit in the sphere of chivalry. His fate is best consigned to a murky realm of obscurity. Anyway, I cannot abide waggling tongues, they're worse than wicked hands, in my view.'

Sparrow was quite unsure as to why he trusted Mr Catley, but he did. He felt sure the man would not blab. 'I do hope you catch that duckbill,' he said.

'My objective, oddly, is not capture, not anymore,' said Catley. He was hoping to return to the subject of Griffin Pinney without seeming hasty.

'What then?' said Bea.

'I am to address *the* most burning question on the anatomical agenda.'

'What is that?'

'The Royal Society and Sir Joseph wish to be acquainted with the manner in which the duckbill genus breeds, its internal structure being so very similar to that of birds that I do not think it impossible that they should lay eggs, or at least hatch them in their bellies as snakes and some fish do. Thus capture would only confound my purpose for I must seek the lady duckbill *in situ et in vivo*. I must go in pursuit of her lurking places, her maternal lair to be precise, invade the hatcheries on the river, this river being, so I am advised, a duckbill paradise.'

'Hmmm,' said Moowut'tin.

Catley scratched at his stubbly chin. 'Thus, you might say, I have forsaken the flint-*lock* for the mat-*tock*,' he said.

Sparrow's mind usually wandered when someone talked on in the way Mr Catley was talking on. This time was no exception. His mind had wandered, as it habitually did, into the *my troubles* department. He was troubled about many things, but two things in particular were agitating the glands and the ventricles in his cerebellum. First, Bea seemed intent upon going back to Joe's patch and, second, he had no choice but to go forward. Thus it was that Mr Catley's mention of 'paradise' brought him up sharp.

'If they are like a bird inside, why are they not like a bird outside?' said Bea.

'That, Mistress Faa, is a commendable question. The answer is a piece of the puzzle we do not have but must have, for one can only conclude that, like all progress in science, understanding brings us closer to clarity as to God's design.'

Sparrow had no interest in this Sir Joseph, gentleman, nor in the insides or the outsides of birds. He was thinking about paradise. He remembered Griffin Pinney's talk about a beautiful grassy woodland and a village embosomed in a grove of tall trees, and a majestic river that ran west, that and more. Now he had seen Mr Catley's valley with his own eyes and it seemed to Sparrow that talk of a paradise to the west was entirely believable. He wanted to ask Mr Catley more about the other side but he thought best to be polite and wait for the man to finish, whenever that might be.

'I have asked the natives how they copulate and they have answered like a duck,' said Catley, 'but they are generally ignorant as to how these creatures produce their young, save one astute fellow who assured me they go a long way underground and there they lay eggs. That, sadly, is of no consequence to the learned world, for I have to see it with my own eyes. What is more, the savage examining the afterbirth in an unearthed burrow would hardly understand the limits of his discovery, for the residue of shell cannot disclose whether hatching takes place within Mrs Duckbill or without, the eggs in the latter instance having been expelled *intacto*. In short I must find an expectant duckbill busy in her lair, hatching post birthing or birthing post hatching, thus to establish whether she is, respectively, *oviparous* or *ovoviparous* . . . that's the Latin you understand.'

'Is there a village, further along, westward?' said Sparrow. He could wait no longer.

'Pardon me?' said Catley.

'Do you know Mort Craggs?'

'Only by reputation,' said Catley.

'He's out here somewhere, might be on the other side.'

Mr Catley gave Sparrow the strangest look. 'You seek the village, freely, of your own will?'

'There is one!'

'I doubt the bucolic connotations of the word *village* would bear the weight of the hideaway I once stumbled upon, nor the headcount.'

Sparrow was uncertain as to Mr Catley's meaning. 'I heard it's a paradise, I heard it's a little commonweal.'

'If it's a commonweal it's a piratical commonweal, a lawless place, a terrible despotism where man is wolf to man, as complete in his savagery as any Indian you might encounter in Tierra del Fuego or . . . Ethiopia.'

'Ethiopia!'

Daniel passed Sparrow a piece of charred meat on the point of a stick. He did the same for Bea and the young dog gave up on Daniel and came and sat before them with begging eyes, the mongrel dog watching on.

'Yes, Ethiopia, and there you'll stay, enslaved till you drop, and this poor girl, a slave to their base passions with nothing in the way of a civilised code to restrain them, naught but a grotesque and indolent liberty qualified neither by decency nor compassion, a savagery to suit the likes of Griffin Pinney.'

'I caught him unawares.'

'Martin was brave,' said Bea.

'I suspect you've done our little world a favour,' said Catley.

The delights of the widow Wise seemed a lifetime gone, though they were gone but a season. Catley could but hope his colourful discourse on the horrors of the piratical commonweal would be sufficient to prevent these two from pressing on, westward or anywhere else. He hoped Bea Faa might stay a while but he had to bring a halt to his galloping ruminations, for they were running riot in his head. They had ventured as far as a shimmering vision of her inner thighs. He was certain now, being sufficiently aroused, that he would have some trouble getting to sleep.

'Thank you,' said Sparrow, to Bea. No one had ever called him brave before. He felt a little bit better. He felt a little shaft of colour resting, like a butterfly, upon his heart.

45

Mackie did not rise that day and he was feverish as the dusk began to fade. He would take no solids and only with the greatest effort did he raise up to sip at the warm tea that Cuff prepared for him. It pained him to swallow. He grimaced as the tea went down and the motion brought on a coughing fit.

When the coughing was done, Mackie got up. He shuffled about the cave, wrapped in his blanket, trying to get the cold out of his bones and the stiffness out of his joints. He took himself to the lip of the shelter and there he leant forward, hands on knees, coughing up the phlegm.

Cuff watched on. 'You move like a rickety old cat.'

'All parts conspire against me.'

'A will of its own, the corporeal body.'

'A will most obstinate.'

'More's the pity.'

Mackie's lungs were crackling like kindling taking to the flame. He wanted to rest some more but rest was a cruel bargain: the more he lay prone the more his lungs filled with muck.

He spat blood onto the thicket of fern fronds below the shelter. He watched as it mingled with dew drops and hung there, in the dim light, seeping onto the milky white petals of some flower, the stem anchored in the finest fracture of stone, the roots like the claws of a fine-boned water bird. Drips from the overhang pattering on the back of his neck.

'Come and sit,' said Cuff. 'Dip some biscuit if you can, save on the jaw.'

'I am not an invalid.'

'You will be if you don't take some solids.'

Mackie took in the view below, knowing the light would soon be gone. The floodwaters from the storm had dropped away, laying bare the wreckage beneath the high-water mark. Trees uprooted, wedged in stone. Great wads of detritus pinioned in crack and crevice and matted shrubs and grasses in the unyielding scrub cover like witches shawls and ancient beards, the scene coated in the dull grey particulate of the wash-down.

He went back to the fire and sat and sipped at his tea. He stirred the tea with a twig and watched the tiny leaves tumble about in the bottom of the mug, rising up and falling away, like everything. The fire smoke made him cough. He moved away, sat himself against the shelter wall; probed at the ulcers inside his mouth, felt a weighting in his core, like lead.

'I'd like to know what they're doin' right now,' said Cuff.

'Who?'

'That girl and that damn woodsman.'

'And Sparrow.'

'He might be dead, and the boy too.'

Mackie waited for something more by way of explanation.

'No place for a faint heart out here,' said Cuff.

'And the girl?'

'She saw it through with them sealers; starch in the blood, like someone I know.'

'If I had starch I'd be on my feet.'

'What you got's a infirmity; starch is another matter.'

'Well starch is a great stiffener, you'd be the one knows about that.'

'I cannot deny my capacity in that regard.' Cuff chuckled, picked up the water bladder and shook it. 'I'll go for water. Probably slip and break my damn neck, all silt and putrilage down there.'

'I'll drink the tea.'

'We're goin' back, you understand that?'

'Yes,' said Mackie, but he could not imagine how, such was the lassitude in his frame.

Cuff went for water, the gully mottled in starlight and shadow. He returned with his boots slaked with mud and his rear end soggy. He put the water bladder down and turned his arse to the fire and brushed the gritty wet with his hands.

'It will be hard going, Alister, when we go.'

The wind had picked up, whistling down the gorge. The eddies whipped the smoke around the shelter. The last light slipped away. Mackie sat with his lapel pressed to his ulcerated mouth, his body convulsing as he tried to smother the eruption in his lungs.

Cuff watched, his resolve fortified by the scene. He was intent upon getting Mackie home. His thoughts were back at the ridge. He saw the doctor at his table in the Hive, devouring the *Gazette*, staring out the window; Sam probing his pelvic region and fiddling with that damn truss; Bet Pepper on her porch. He thought he'd like to spend more time with Bet. He had no objection to amplitude or maturity in a woman so long as she humped with enthusiasm and liked to talk in a leisurely fashion afterwards, and perhaps share the gossip and a pipe.

It was a pleasant line of thought but it did not last. His mind shifted back to the doctor, whose situation was truly horrid. He wondered if they would ever know just what happened to Woody's boy. The subject of disappearance hastened his thoughts yet again to another mystery. 'What did Guthrie say to you, about Jonas Wick?' he said.

Mackie hesitated. 'He said they played cards late in the night as they sailed down the coast, drank a lot of rum. He said Jonas went off to his cot. He said next morning he was gone. They searched the boat and he was gone.'

'Overboard?'

'I have nothing else to set at variance.'

'The man's a veteran sealer, the swell was moderate, so they say.'

'He was sworn off the drink but he lapsed, paid the price.'

'And the crew saw nothing?'

'So it would seem,' said Mackie.

'The question is foul play,' said Cuff.

'The answer is lost overboard.'

'That suits you.'

'It does me no harm.'

'I thought you might pair up with him, cure pelts and make a princely fortune. That's what he thought.'

'Well, you know what thought did.'

'He thought he followed a wedding but it was a muck cart in the wheel ruts.'

'He got it wrong is what he did.'

'You had no intention of pairing with him.'

'I'd pair first with the devil.'

'The trade, then, is yours for the taking.'

'The trade requires the sanction of the governor and a licence from the East India Company. I have neither sanction nor licence, nor shipshape vessel.'

'You get one you might get the others.'

Mackie nodded. 'That is my hope.'

'So, you do deal in hope.'

'When there's nothing else I am reminded it's the mainspring of faith,' said Mackie.

'Faith! Only book you worship is that ledger,' said Cuff. 'I'll tell you one thing: if you cannot keep your accounts on your thumbnail your life's got out o' hand.'

'My accounts are the least of my worries.'

Cuff's head waggled in that sardonic way, indicating he was listening to rubbish. 'Since when!'

'Since we have to face Thomas Woody and tell him we failed.'

'We just have to hope the boy turns up.'

'Such is the futility of so much we call hope.'

'I know.'

'We agree!'

'Yes.'

'Well there you are.'

'What?'

'There's a miracle.'

46

They sat for a time, took turns to spoon the fatty slurry from the cookpot.

Mr Catley seemed to be deep in thought, which he was. He picked up a stick. He scratched a few lines in the dirt by his feet.

The fire threw out just enough warmth. Wisps of bark flared aglow on the heat, wafted into the canopy and faded into the blackness.

Daniel had some yams in the coals, on the fringe of the fire, there with Catley's onions. Occasionally he pushed them about with a long stick. When he spoke to Catley he did so in his own language and Mr Catley spoke back in kind. Bea and Sparrow could but sit and listen in wonderment.

Catley took bones from the cookpot and fed one to each dog. The mongrel dog disappeared into the dark. The pup dropped down by the cookfire much to the pleasure of his audience. They watched the pup go to work, listened to the crunch of back teeth on bone.

'You may stay a while, if you wish, long as might be convenient subject to your needs and wants, and so on,' said Catley.

'I cannot go back,' said Sparrow.

'Word of one G. Pinney's fate need go no further.'

'It's not even that.' Sparrow had sunk into a profound melancholy.

'You can come to Joe's patch, with me,' said Bea. 'And the pup too.'

She liked the pup and she found Sparrow easy enough to tolerate and, no small thing, he had rescued her from Pinney. What's more she had no idea of Joe's condition, nor of his prospects. She might need Sparrow. She might need him along the way and she might need him once home. She thought him a pliable fellow, pliable by any meas-ure she cared to contemplate, any measure she knew. He was a most unlikely champion but that, surely, was his greatest strength, for who would ever suspect. *Go forage*, Pinney had said, and he put that axe into Sparrow's hand!

Sparrow looked about. Night had settled in but it wasn't that dark. The sky was bright now with countless stars. There was a faint breeze and the light played through the trees all the way to the grassy bot-toms, from whence they could hear the sound of the river, running east. 'Are you sure that's the Branch?' said Sparrow.

'A rose by any other name,' said Catley.

'Huh?'

'It might be one of the headwaters that feed the Branch, I cannot yet say for sure. So much to see so little time.'

Whether it was the Branch or not Sparrow wished he could stay here forever, with Bea Faa, and perhaps with Mr Catley and Daniel too. For Mr Catley was clearly a learned gentleman and Daniel seemed to be a most accommodating savage and his fierce demeanour could hardly be anything but helpful in a fix.

Sparrow felt tears pool in the sink of his eyes. He felt one of the tears roll down his cheek.

'My dear Mr Sparrow,' said Catley.

'I'm sorry,' said Sparrow.

Bea patted Sparrow's arm.

Catley smacked his palms softly onto his thighs, drumming his fingers. 'Confession may not be absolution, Mr Sparrow, and far be it for me to give that to anybody, but it does lift a weight from the shoulders. Tears might be words the heart cannot say but words in this instance will, surely, be a balm to the troubled soul. Why not tell us, we shall do our best to help and we shall swear it go no further. Call it a pact.'

'A pact?'

'A pact to hold close, to honour, never to share beyond ourselves, a true mark of character and friendship.'

'Cross your heart and hope to die?'

'And stick a needle in my eye.'

'Alright.'

So, Sparrow told them. Everything. How he and Peachey had gulled the Woody boy they called Jug; how the bull shark had savaged the boy, killed him; and how they tied his remains to a slab of sandstone and sent it to the bottom of the Hawkesbury River. How they chopped a big hole in the bottom of the little boat and sunk it; how Pinney came through Harp's camp with Bea Faa and the old dog. Stood over poor Seamus, ridiculed him, called him *weak as rank piss*, and how they left poor Seamus behind. And further, how they went up the Branch till the rains came and the gorge flooded and then how they went over the top all the way to the cave where Pinney's old dog died, and Bea on her knees, put upon, and so forth.

Sparrow told all, almost. He took the narrative all the way through to the killing of Griffin Pinney with the short-handled axe and there he left off. He said nothing about Bea Faa going to work on Pinney with the hunting knife though the cut and the outcome were still vividly pictorial in his mind. 'I find it hard to believe I did what I did, but I did; I did it,' he said. It seemed like a story about someone else. It seemed most un-Marty to Marty.

'You surprised yourself,' said Catley.

'I did that. I recall, I shook like a leaf.'

'The greater the fear the greater the triumph.' He was pointing straight at Sparrow.

'Thank you.'

Daniel loaded up the fire. The yams were ready. They each took one, skewered on a burnt twig, and they ate the vegetable as it cooled.

Catley fed the young dog a lump of gristle from the edge of the fire. 'Does he have a name?' he said.

'I call him pup,' said Sparrow.

'He's grown beyond that. Would he like a Latin name, I wonder.'

'Latin?'

'Yes, you could call him, let's see . . . you could call him *amicus amico*, Amicus for short.'

'What does that mean?' said Sparrow.

'It means a friend to a friend,' said Catley.

Sparrow liked the meaning. 'Amicus, Amicus Amico . . . yes.' He liked the sound as much as the meaning. He called the dog and the dog rose and hurried to him, the tip of his tail working the ground like a broom.

Sparrow had noticed he felt better after his confession and, since he had confessed to the axe murder of the game hunter and the loss of the boy, he could think of no reason why he should not confess to finding a lost pup and keeping him, albeit he knew whose pup it was. He could see no reason, sitting here among confidants, why he should not tell the truth and he almost did, but he could not quite bring himself to confess all.

Catley was still contemplating the terrible truth about the boy Jug. 'If you go to the good magistrate and tell him as much of the truth as you can, at least his torment will be over; he will know the boy is lost, gone. He will not be forever looking and wondering, and he will be able to sleep at night and his good wife too; and he will know you were not to blame. I picture the scene. You may well shed a tear together. He may even thank you, the relief being such as to overwhelm his heart. He is a good, kind man and if there is an eye of pity at the Hawkesbury River establishment it's his eye. Speaking of which, he might have some advice for you.'

'Advice?' Sparrow was stroking Amicus Amico, thinking how much he liked the name.

'Why yes, that yellowy complexion, something wrong there,' said Catley.

'It's jaundice,' said Sparrow.

'Let's hope the mountain air's a tonic.'

Sparrow did not put much hope in the mountain air but he knew Mr Catley was trying to lift his spirits in that regard. Then it struck him that his ailment these past days was in fact less troublesome than it had been for some years. Perhaps Mr Catley was right, perhaps the wilderness was a tonic?

Catley's thoughts turned once again to the charms of Bea Faa. He wished he could rut her himself. His mind held the moment in all its fleshy detail. Why was he smoothing the path for Sparrow? He did not want them to depart for the river and if they did depart he hoped they might come back. Upon this reckoning, he formulated the following commentary and delivered it without review: 'As to the headwaters, I should say this – any one of them might mark the way to another Eden. The magnitude and the magnificence of the land to the west can hardly be imagined. If you do find yourself compelled to seek it out you might base yourself here and venture forth, to and fro as weather and wellness permits.'

Catley said this while poking a stick at the onions in the fringing coals, hardly daring to glance at Bea Faa lest he betray his deepest yearning. He was intent upon being the good fellow he knew himself to be.

'Have you seen it, the other side?' said Sparrow.

'I cannot be sure,' said Catley, 'for the mountains go on and on.'

Sparrow was tempted to mention the whales but he thought best not to digress at this moment. 'I wonder could we build a cave house, somewhere?'

'Beyond a doubt, most assuredly,' said Catley. He was smiling at Bea. 'This country is a garden of stone; any number of capacious hollows might be fashioned and walled as you see here. Water and game, and soil so rich you can sing a bean up a trellis; a man could want for no more. All that is here for a verifiable certainty but beyond here one can only surmise as to unseen complications, the want of society for one thing.'

Sparrow had no want for society. His only want was Bea Faa and Amicus Amico. He swivelled about and scrutinised the cave house in the firelight, the stone frontage, the door, the window frame, the teapot.

Catley was anxious to make make the best of the moment, to impress Bea with his knowledge of the far beyond. 'The country to the west is very hard and very strange.' He paused, searching for the words. 'It is a land of thickly wooded valleys and brutally weathered stone, of precipitous ravines and fractured cliff lines sheer to the sky and towers of sedimentary rock and ironstone, like chimneys or ceremonial pagodas from some ancient world, amphitheatres for a confederacy of giants, the sculpted work of a vanished people, the work weathered beyond all recognition, weathered into serried ledges and caves and crags, exquisitely beautiful from a vantage, deadly cruel if you're lost in there. I tell you both this: the wilderness to the west begs a certain reverence and demands a certain humility.'

Bea had hardly noticed Daniel slip away, into the dark, like a shadow into shadow fold. Now he was back with a half-rotten piece of damp wood. He sat by the fire cross-legged with the wood in his lap. With a sharp stick he picked grubs from the hollow in the wood and gobbled them down with relish.

'What is that?' she said.

'They are *cah-bro*, which Daniel cherishes as a delicacy but for mine they are loathsome,' said Catley. He put a quart pot on the fire. 'Let's have some *Hai Seng* tea.'

'Shall I get the teapot?' said Sparrow.

'Whyever not.'

Moowut'tin took another stick, thin as a feather shaft, and he skewered a pair of *cah-bro* and handed them to Bea. He chuckled as he did so, said something in his native tongue.

Bea took the offering and looked to Catley.

'He says they're husband and wife.'

'Who?'

'Those two grubs on the stick, the very picture of marriage.'

Bea examined the wriggling grubs on the skewer. She had the flavoursome taste of the cooked meat in her mouth and she was inclined to dwell on that. But now Daniel was watching her, as was Catley, and Sparrow too, teapot in hand. She had no intention of appearing faint of heart. She took the grubs in her mouth and chewed and searched for the taste and she found them to be not unpleasant. She nodded, and Daniel smiled. 'Nice!' he said.

'They are sweet.'

'They're ravenously fond of these things, his people,' said Catley.

'Who are his people?'

'Why, Nabbinum's mob, the mountain blacks.'

'Is he truly seven foot tall?' said Sparrow.

'No.'

Sparrow tried to remember if Griffin Pinney had ever specified who it was who collected the toll, the Branch mob or the mountain blacks, but he could not remember. He was, however, certain that Pinney had not mentioned the name Nabbinum. From that he deduced it had to be the Branch mob, old Wolgan and company, who traded select goods for safe passage, and it followed that there was, most likely, no such understanding with Nabbinum. Any progression further west was therefore fraught with a new and distressing complication.

The girl was scratching at the leech scabs on her legs.

'You need some trousers,' said Catley.

'I have none,' she said.

'I have trousers, for Daniel, but he won't wear them; they're long in the leg, they'll fit.'

'Thank you.'

Catley fed the young dog another small bone. 'I must say, your Amicus Amico does bear a startling resemblance to Henry Kettle's brindle pup.'

'I found him, that's all I know.'

'The dog's good fortune.'

'I won't give him up, not to Henry Kettle, not to anybody.'

'Are you aware Mr Mackie is on the Branch?' said Catley, quite out of the blue.

The information startled Bea and Sparrow both.

'No,' said Bea.

'He's stalled by the rains but he's coming, or was, he and Mr Thaddeus Cuff, the latter a *true* gentleman by nature if not by birth.'

'How do you know they're coming?'

'Daniel.'

Sparrow had a very big urge to be done with all the worry. 'I might just surrender,' he said.

'Will you take us to him?' said Bea.

'I'm told you have a history, you and he,' said Catley.

'My mother knew him, briefly, long ago. Before I was born.'

Bea did not want to discuss her mother or the strange unfolding of her life, the twists and turns that took her from the travellers' camp on the outskirts of Yetholm to the butcher's snare and thence across the world to the Southern Ocean sealeries and on to New South Wales and thence to Joe's patch and from there to Catley and the cave house. And Mr Catley was gentleman enough to know this was no time to probe further, though he was quite curious to know more. 'Mackie is straight, straight as a mason's rule. Though others might choose the word *unbending*. He'll look to your interests with some zeal, most particularly if his own interests are concerned.'

'Will you take us to him?'

'When the river's safe, dropping sufficient to permit my search for the duckbill, then I'll take you.'

'When will that be?'

'Not long, the sandbars will be tricky but Daniel knows the woodland tracks above the flood line. If you know the tracks you know the history – not long ago this wilderness was busy as London.'

'That busy?' said Sparrow.

'A slight exaggeration, Mr Sparrow, busy nonetheless.'

'Oh.'

Bea and Sparrow slept in the cave house and woke in the still dark to the clatter and the alien jabber of Catley and Daniel outside, and the sounds of the pup cavorting about the mongrel dog.

They spent the day much at their leisure, save for Moowut'tin. He departed early, in the company of the mongrel dog, and did not return until midafternoon. Catley was most attentive to Bea Faa and Sparrow could do nothing about that so he did not try. He went off with Amicus Amico and they followed the cliff line west for several miles, way past the slot gully, pausing now and then to sit and survey the valley and the river and the sandstone ridges beyond, and Sparrow took the opportunity to ponder the mystery of the other side and to meditate on his many troubles.

With the dog at his heel, he hastened back to Catley's camp in the early afternoon and Moowut'tin returned a little later, dragging a big dead lizard by the tail. 'Big cook up,' he said. He set him close to the fire pit, the tail thudding in the dust.

They feasted that night and they slept, all of them, a deep sleep.

47

Next morning, they departed the valley as they had come, climbing to the upland through the slot gully and from there they retraced their steps, much the same course as before.

Daniel led the way. Catley brought the mule, loaded with the mattock and miscellaneous stores plus the tin vasculum with the woven cotton shoulder straps in which, he said, he would cosset any duckbill eggs he might extract from womb or lair, hoping, in the event, to hatch one.

'I thought we was goin' to follow the river,' said Sparrow.

'Patience Mr Sparrow, soon enough we meet the settling Branch,' said Catley.

An hour later, the track veered south-east and further along it shifted course yet again for now they were following the southward line of the gorge. Catley reefed the mule's lead rope and stopped the hybrid just short of a sandstone ledge. Moowut'tin stepped around the creature totems etched in the stone and stood on the brink. Sparrow and Bea followed in his steps. A faint morning sun was playing on the honeycombed cliffs beyond the Branch when they heard a musket shot, a single shot, downriver.

Moowut'tin led off and they followed him, through dense scrub for something like an hour until he drew to a sudden halt, sniffing woodsmoke in the air. 'Cookfire,' he said. And he led them down a gully into the hooded coolness of rainforest, onto a cutback that angled to a rock shelter, where Cuff was cooking a fat goanna, hoping that Mackie might take some meat for his breakfast.

Cuff had heard them coming and Catley spied the shelter as the deputy stepped into view. He called to Cuff to put him at ease: 'Hey ho, Mr Cuff,' he shouted.

Mackie was getting to his feet with some difficulty. 'It's alright, it's Catley,' said Cuff. 'Hey ho to you sir,' he shouted back.

Cuff watched them come, single file. 'It's Catley and his eagle man and Sparrow and the girl, if they had a horse it would have to be Christmas. I don't see the boy.'

'We have a horse of sorts,' said Catley. 'He's tethered back there.'

'That's good,' said Cuff, 'because we have a man here much in need of a horse of sorts.'

'What's on the spit?'

'You grown particular with the years?'

'Not about meat.'

'Thank you, Mr Catley, I do not need your mule,' said Mackie.

The mongrel dog and Amicus Amico were at the fire, drawn to the butchered meat on the flame. Cuff shooed them away.

Mackie chose to ignore the girl and watched Sparrow as he set Kunkle's musket against the wall. 'Where is Dr Woody's boy?' he said.

Sparrow hesitated, thinking on what he might say and what he might not say and trying at the same time to remember exactly what he had confessed to Mr Catley. He squatted by the musket, stared at the ground, Amicus licking at his hand.

'Mr Sparrow, you really must,' said Catley.

'We didn't hurt the boy, we never ever hurt him, I swear.'

The chief constable moved close, that foul breath. He smacked the dog away, spoke softly. 'I will visit torments on your flesh if needs be. As for the doctor, he will deliver you up to the military.'

The rectal pear came to Sparrow's mind, the worse for never having seen it. 'You don't have to do that.'

'They'll sling you on that hook, Marty. You seen the hook?' said Cuff.

'Yes sir.'

'Where is Dr Woody's boy?' said Mackie.

The question chilled Sparrow to the bone as he recalled how they tipped the remains roped to the stone into the depths of the Hawkesbury River. The truth was the most awful thing but it was the truth, a truth for which neither he nor Peachey could be blamed, not entirely. 'The pup went overboard and the boy tipped in, and a bull shark took him and that's the truth. Bit him near in half and it's a torment forever that memory and I'm sorry beyond all measure I truly am Mr Mackie.'

'A shark?'

'Yes.'

'A shark took the boy and not the dog, that's a queer thing.'

'This one didn't take the dog he just didn't. He took the boy.'

'Perhaps this one never yet tasted dog?' said Catley.

'You've nothing to prove the truth of this,' said Mackie.

'I would not conjure this in my worst dream.'

Beyond the shelter the sun had disappeared and the day coloured to grey, light rain falling, beads curling around the slick black brow of the overhang, poised there, like a string of pearl drops.

They sat for a time, in silence, picking at the oily meat and drinking their tea.

'With God as your witness you will look the doctor in the eye and tell him what happened,' said Mackie.

'I will.'

'If it is a lie you carry it to judgement and the terrors beyond.'

'It's not a lie.'

'On that you will be tested.'

'Don't sling me on the hook, please.'

'That is for Dr Woody to weigh in the balance.'

'Where's Griffin Pinney?' said Cuff.

'He went off, never came back,' said Sparrow.

The dogs were still prowling about the fire, drawn by the sizzle and the smell of meat on the flame, Cuff backhanding them away.

Bea wanted to help Sparrow. She trusted to Mr Catley's vow of silence. 'He went off to forage and he never did come back,' she said.

'Maybe the savages got him,' said Sparrow. He cast an uncomfortable glance at Daniel who had called the big dog and sat with him, at one remove.

'Have you seen Joe?' said Bea.

'No,' said Mackie.

'Was he not there, on his patch?'

'We came by way of Pig Creek, joined the Branch upstream,' said Cuff.

'Joe is sick and hurt,' said Bea.

'How so?'

'Griffin Pinney hurt him.'

'Did he hurt him bad?'

'He's bedridden.'

'We'll see you safe to his patch, swift as we can.'

4 8

Having delivered Sparrow and Bea Faa into the safekeeping of the constables, Catley and Moowut'tin headed north on the Branch, deeper into the gorge, in search of the duckbill *in situ et in vivo*, while Mackie's party rested through the remains of the day and slept warm enough, and dry, through the night.

The next morning Mackie declared himself fit enough to trek to Joe's and they set off downriver, forcing a track above the flood line and resting every hour, the rests lengthening as the trudging took its toll.

The journey took the better part of three days, and it was late in the day when they reached the lower Branch and walked on to Joe's patch and made for his cabin.

They found Joe in his bed, much diminished. He had lost the capacity to speak.

The girl sat on the bed and took his hand and tears ran down Joe's cheeks. He tried to talk but his speech was slow and slurred, a word here and there and otherwise garbled sounds and his limits in this regard filled him with anguish.

'He got up for the necessaries and he took a turn,' said Freddie, 'and I told him, I said Joe, you are gunna break my heart.'

'What'd he say?' said Cuff.

'He don't like his predicament. He gets angry.'

Joe heard this and, plainly, he understood. 'Hmmmm,' he said. The wound in his forehead was scabby now, black and crusty. He looked so worn and so sad. Bea wiped away the tears on his cheeks and with the back of her fingers she stroked the stubble on his chin and Joe put his hand to hers and held it to his cheek. He was panting, the upset stressing his heart.

The company looked on, lost for words.

Mackie found his eyes drawn to the curve of Bea's neck. Her hair was tied as ever in a knot at the nape and held there, for the most part, with that long wooden pin, the tip carved as a feather. She wore that hairpin exactly as her mother did, long ago. The memory put a shudder through him. He felt the need to retreat and did so. He sat himself on the ladder-back chair by the table, the scene in the recess like a painted tableau.

Outside the goat called Beauty and the dog called Amicus Amico had took to play and the sounds of their scampering carried to the company indoors. Freddie was happy to be diverted. He stood in the doorway watching, a hand upon the low-set lintel. He was pleased he'd yarded the fowls for he was unsure of the dog in that regard. 'You be gentle with my Beauty,' he said. But he was not truly concerned for he knew play when he saw it and he knew stalking too.

Sparrow was bound for the doorway when Mackie beckoned him sit. He sat hunched, his hands clasped between his knees, sensing something bad.

Mackie spoke softly. 'You will tell that boy's father what happened, every detail.'

'I already said I would.' Sparrow did not want to revisit the subject. He heard Freddie chuckling at the door, saw Bea patting Joe's hand. 'She says I can be here, the pup too. I can help, I'll work, hard.'

He wanted to scream it out loud, he wanted to say it. *Griffin was doin' her and I killed him and now Joe's an invalid and I can help.* That's what he wanted to say, but he couldn't. He knew he could never say that, not least because he was in enough trouble already, the boat, and Jug, and the stolen dog – a trinity of troubles, all that and more. If only he could say it he could explain, he could tell the chief constable: *Griffin was doin' her and I killed him and we're a good pair, her and me, and the pup too, she likes the pup.*

'Whatever happened to Miss Happ?' said Mackie.

'Who?

'The strumpet.'

'I don't know and I don't care,' said Sparrow. He was shocked to hear himself declare he didn't care about Biddie Happ and to know it was true.

'You will tell the doctor everything.'

'I will, I swear I will, I did no wrong.'

Mackie looked hard at Sparrow. 'A piece of advice.'

'Thank you.'

'Don't say you did no wrong, not to Thomas Woody. Whatever the rights or wrongs, his boy is dead because of you, is he not?'

Sparrow could but nod. He thought the forewarning good advice. He thought best to say no more even though he wanted to insist he did not force that boy into the water nor did he conjure that bull shark, nor did he in any way cause the terrible happenchance of shark and boy that followed.

'You have your own patch to farm, and debts to meet, have you forgotten that?' said Mackie.

'Forgive the debt and you can have my patch. I will sign a paper, I will sign over to you,' said Sparrow.

Mackie sat, silent.

'I ain't cut out for . . . bein' alone,' said Sparrow. He was going to say he wasn't cut out for endless toil but he didn't because he knew that wasn't quite true. He knew, now, that he could toil hard if he was toiling for Bea, and Amicus Amico.

At the bedside the girl stood to make way for Cuff, who sat with Joe and took hold of his hand, noting the tears that welled in the old soldier's eyes. 'My good friend,' he said.

Joe's face was set, his lips pressed together, breathing hard and loud through his nose, trying to summon up the words he needed but no longer having the wherewithal to speak whatever was in his mind, the strange moaning sound indecipherable. His head dropped and he slumped there, propped on cushions, ashamed to look up, his fists closed hard.

THE MAKING OF MARTIN SPARROW

Cuff wrapped his fingers around Joe's fist. 'Is that all he can say?' he said to Bea.

She nodded.

He turned his attention back to Joe, wondered what, if anything, Joe had understood. He took but a moment to compose his thoughts.

'Joe . . . Joe, look at me now,' he said. Joe lifted his head, his eyes wide. 'You'll come good Joe, you just gotta . . . take your time, y'understand?'

Joe closed his eyes, the tears welled there in the rims. He nodded.

'You are a good man Joe and we'll see you right. *Won't we, Alister?*'

'Aye, yes.'

'Alright then,' said Cuff. 'You rest up, my good friend.'

Sparrow leant forward, across the table, and whispered: 'I can help here, I know I can.'

It was midafternoon and Cuff was hungry. 'You got a bird we can eat?' he said to Freddie.

Freddie weighed the situation, recalling Mr Mackie's generosity. 'I got a big ol' boiler, and I got potatoes for just such a occasion, or for winter, whatever come first.'

'Seems we beat winter by a comfortable margin.'

The girl took no part in the meal at the table. Instead she sat with Joe. She fed him a corn broth enhanced with poultry bones and the fat from the pan, now and then taking a spoonful for herself as she listened to the table talk. She heard Cuff speak of the killings on the Branch, the shot woman and the crucified men – horrible doings she'd seen for herself. They spoke of Reuben Peskett's aptitude for such doings. They mused as to the governor's dim view of killing the savages in 'cool blood', so called.

Sparrow could summon no interest in these worldly matters. He no longer felt languid and lazy. He marvelled at that. If only he could stay here he might be safe and happy. He no longer wanted to bolt for the other side; he was inclined to think Mr Catley's account of the piratical commonweal might be true. He wanted no part of that, and whether or not there was a big river, a river of the first magnitude, or a lake where whales were seen to spout, who could know? What he knew for certain was Bea Faa was back on Joe's patch and she intended to stay. That he knew for certain. He recalled her words: 'We are perhaps a formidable pair.' *Pair.*

When Joe was done eating Bea took the bowl to the table and set it down. 'What of the garden?' she said to Freddie.

'We can sow cabbage right now, and potatoes for summer, fresh dung and straw to mix, old rotten dung's no good, not for potatoes.'

'Are you right till harvest?' said Mackie.

'I think we are,' said Freddie.

'Well then, all's well with the world,' said Cuff.

'I sure hope so, but there's the weather and the savages and the grub, you just never know with the grub less you plant awful early. The grub's one big fly in the ointment.'

The girl stepped outside. Sparrow followed. Freddie kept talking, farm talk.

It was almost sunset and the clouds to the north sat flat, as if on a straight edge, and they were lit bright pink on the underside and the sky beneath was the palest petal blue.

'I have to go back, tell the doctor,' said Sparrow.

'You have to say what happened,' said Bea.

'Will you take care of Amicus?'

'I like that young dog.'

'I hope to come back if I can, if you want me.'

'You think the doctor will forgive you?'

'Hope's all I got.'

'The little songbird in the well of our troubled soul.'

'What?'

'Hope.'

'Oh yes.'

'I will take Amicus,' she said.

'I can help you work the patch, when I come back.'

'He may say you murdered his boy.'

'I will tell him the truth, that's all I can do, I never murdered any-body except . . .'

'Well now you know,' said the girl.

'What?'

'How to do it.'

That surprised Sparrow. She said it like it was a knack or a trade, once got never lost. And she was right. A small axe brought down with the full force of the forearms would split a man's skull like a hunting blade through lard.

49

They were a long day on the river, some of that laid over for the dura-tion of the ebb tide in full flow. Once back at the ridge Mackie was in no mood to waste time. He marched Sparrow to the gaol and deliv-ered him to the custodianship of Hat Thistlewaite and promptly sent for Dr Woody.

Sparrow watched the evening light slip from the slot window, high in the rear wall of the gaol, the leather costrel in his lap, the soggy seam rendering his britches a little damp. His heart began to bang in his chest when he heard footsteps in the corridor and saw the company attending Dr Woody. He shifted his legs off the tick and stood up as Hat Thistlewaite unlocked the door and the doctor stepped into the cell, stooped as ever, followed by Sergeant Reuben Peskett and Private Redenbach.

An audience gathered, the Parsonage twins in the adjacent cell attentive to every word. 'Best show in town,' whispered Nimrod.

'I doubt I can watch,' said Crispin as he waddled to the bars, somewhat bow-legged.

The blanket fell from Sparrow's shoulders and he felt the cold air. Redenbach was carrying a pot of grease. Peskett had a corn sack in hand. He dropped the sack on the floor beside the grease and it went *clunk* and Sparrow reckoned it had to be the rectal pear. The lump in the sack had the look of a small bird, about the size of a wren, as best he could make out. But the *clunk* suggested something other than a wren.

He did not want to look the poor old doctor in the eye. In that regard the evening gloom was helpful. He felt so sad he reckoned he must, somehow, have taken on the doctor's sorrow and stowed it in his own heart, tucked away in one of those little ventricles.

The taptoo sounded. He could hear the clanking of skillets, the faint thud of boots on stairs, and the government pigs whipped along, bound for the butcher's pen. The sounds did not help Sparrow's composure.

'We'll sling you like pork on a hog hook if we have to,' said Peskett. He pointed to the block and tackle in the rafters.

The doctor raised up a hand to quiet the sergeant. 'Sit down, Martin,' he said.

Sparrow did as he was told. He smoothed the blanket and sat on it. He glanced upward, the block and tackle fixed to the beam in the corridor. He could hardly bear to contemplate the tackle and the pear in action, together. Snatches of Hat's words came back to him: *the narrow end, the sharp point, all greased up for rectal entry, the wing nut at the fat end, the petals . . . like a flower,* something to that effect.

This time Hat Thistlewaite brought the doctor a chair and the doctor shunted the chair close and then sat down. 'I am going to ask you a question, Martin, and I want you to think carefully before you answer me, for if you tell me a lie I will know and I will not persist. I will leave you to the tender mercies of the sergeant, you understand?'

'I won't tell you a lie, I swear.' That was bound, sooner or later, to be a lie, but Sparrow had to say it.

'You tell me then: what have you done with my boy?'

At that moment, the worst possible thing came to Sparrow's mind, most pictorially. He saw the pup on the riverbank, gnawing at the entrails. *I, me, Marty Sparrow, I did that, I let that happen.* That was his foremost thought and he could not banish it.

He felt his eyes tear up and he thought of Joe, who could no longer speak save a half-strangled word or two, and who cried because he was so addled and helpless, and he recalled the enchanting aspects of Bea Faa and the pleasant sensation when Amicus licked his hand and all of that, being there, on Joe's patch, all of that seemed impossible now.

He tried not to blink for he knew that a blink would send the welled tears running down his cheeks. Peskett and Redenbach would despise him all the more if they saw tears, and they would relish a free hand to do with him as they pleased. They were like hunting dogs on the leash, straining to be free. He blinked and wiped away a tear as it ran onto his cheek, quick as he could. He guessed the doctor had already heard Mackie's account of the bull shark story so he determined to tell the story much as he'd said it to Mr Catley and much as he'd repeated it when they were in the shelter on the Branch.

The hardest thing was to begin. He did not know how to begin so he just did. He poured out the bull shark story, every detail except to say whose dog it was, and the old doctor watched him all the while. Sparrow was hopeful that the dog would be of no consequence to the doctor. He hoped the doctor might be so focused on his boy such that all details about the dog, save the dog was party to the tragedy, would be overlooked.

There was a long silence, broken only by Redenbach who felt obliged to say, 'Bull shark my arse!'

The doctor sat hunched over, staring at the cell floor. He made no sound but the sound of grit under his agitated soles.

'More likely you killed him and buried him somewhere,' said Peskett.

'I want my boy back,' said Woody. 'I want proof of life or proof of death, one or the other and I will have it no other way and my missus will have it no other way, do you understand me, Mr Sparrow?'

'He is not alive. The bull shark took him and I'm sorry beyond measure I truly am.'

'How do we know that?'

'Too neat for my liking,' said Peskett.

'Give him the pear!' said Crispin Parsonage.

'Where did it happen?'

'Not far downstream o' the Cattai.'

'How far?'

'I don't know.'

'You told Jason you wanted to fish?'

'Jason?'

'You don't even know his name?'

'I called him Jug.'

Woody's stare was so hard that Sparrow thought he might have shot his bolt there and then.

'You don't even know his name,' he said again.

'Yes sir I do, it's Jason, I know that, I do.'

'You ridicule my boy?'

'We were going to fish, we changed our mind.'

'You and Peachey decided to bolt, that's what you did.'

Sparrow had the powerful sense that he might just survive a small lie here or there but a big lie here would sink him sure. 'That is true,' he said. 'Me and Peachey was bound for the other side.'

'There ain't no bull sharks that far upriver,' said Redenbach.

'Oh yes there is, and I'm haunted forever. The rest o' my days.'

'There ain't too many o' them days left 'cause you'll hang for this.'

'You in league with Mort Craggs?' said Peskett.

'Noooo.'

'Griffin Pinney then?'

Sparrow thought carefully. 'I just did what he said.'

'A dog you say?' said the doctor.

Sparrow paused. He wondered if, perchance, Mackie had revealed the truth about the dog. 'Yes sir, a stray dog, that is, he found me is what I mean, and I took him with me.'

'Why would you take a stray dog?'

'For to trade . . . Mr Pinney said the savages require a toll, else you don't get across. They'll trade for dogs and hatchets, that's what he said.'

'Did you know they like handkerchiefs?' said Redenbach.

'So you tricked my boy?' said the doctor.

'We wanted to cross the river, that's all.'

'And then you took his boat and then you scuttled it, yes?'

'That alone is a capital offence,' said Redenbach.

'Add to that facilitating a felon to bolt,' said Peskett.

'I never scuttled that boat, God's truth. That was Peachey and I tried to stop him. I told him, we moor it and someone will pick it up, Guthrie on the scow, or someone, that's what I said but he wouldn't listen.'

'And now it appears Mr Peachey is dead, which is entirely convenient. Like this bull shark,' said Woody. He was still staring at the ground, shaking his head. He sat bent over, his forearms resting on his thighs, his hands clasped together, his knuckles ivory white.

Sergeant Peskett took the opportunity to intervene. 'Let's see now, we got a bull shark eats a boy and a pig eats Seamus Peachey – there's a lot of doubtful eatin' going on, wouldn't you say Mr Sparrow?'

'You know it's true for Seamus, for Mr Mackie saw it with his own eyes,' said Sparrow.

'I think he's tuggin' the collective squirrel,' said Redenbach.

'It's the wild, the woods, things happen, they just happen.'

'The cruel serendipity of the wilderness, that it?' said Woody.

Redenbach chortled. 'You see this boar?'

'No I did not.'

The doctor swivelled about, glaring at Redenbach. 'What on God's earth is the relevance of that to me?'

'Nothin', just —'

'Just what?'

'Just, I heard he was awful big.'

'Will you shut up,' growled Woody. 'Now, tell me about this bull shark, you saw it plain as day I'm told.'

'I did sir, yes, more's the pity, he was awful big too.'

Woody was staring into Sparrow's face yet again, searching for the truth or otherwise in the expiree's countenance. Occasionally he would look to the patch of floor between his boots and sit in silence, shaking his head.

'Tell me this,' he said, finally, 'was there not a scrap of my boy left, for to retrieve, for to bury, for to show me? No resting place, not a thread, not a button, not a shred of flesh nor bone?'

Sparrow felt awfully cold as the full meaning of this question settled in his mind. He did not want to give up the most terrible details, the worst of them entirely beyond the bounds of merciful sensibility and thus the bounds of possible telling. He could say nothing of the boy, the torso they towed to the river bank; nothing of those vacant eyes, wide open; nothing of the terrible transgression that he permitted – the pup supping on the boy's entrails. He could say naught but the boy was gone, entirely gone. 'There was some . . . leavings . . . on the flow, but we did not think to collect them . . . I believe they sunk to the bottom . . . we was in the middle of that river and we was numb with the shock, believe me, please,' he said.

Woody looked away sharply, as if he could not bear to look at Sparrow again. 'Leavings . . . leavings,' was all he said.

Sparrow could hear heavy exhalations through the doctor's nose.

'I am no wiser now than when I sat down. Leavings, like grease on a plate,' said Woody.

'Not like that, no,' said Sparrow.

'On the word of a waster and a backslider I am to be tormented for the rest of my life,' said the doctor. He stood up and he stepped outside the cell and he beckoned Hat to follow. He spoke to Peskett. 'Put Mr Sparrow's narrative to the test.'

Sparrow leapt up, he took hold of the bars. He was not at all sure about that word *narrative*, but he was quite sure that the doctor was departing, leaving him in the hands of the military, so he could only assume that *narrative* had a meaning somewhere in the vicinity of *untruth*. 'It's the truth, I swear,' he said.

But already Woody was shuffling away with Hat in his wake. He was almost gone from sight when he stopped and turned, waving a finger at Sparrow. 'That good man tried to salvage you from the wreckage of your miserable life.'

'Who . . . who?' said Sparrow.

'What are you, a damn owl,' growled Woody.

'No sir.'

'He is not here, Mr Sparrow, because he has forsaken you. He was your port in the storm and more fool him I said at the time. I told him, I said, that man will never do honour to a generous benefactor, I told him you were nothing but an idler, a worthless recidivist. *And here we are.*'

'I know, I know,' said Sparrow. He was trying to look as sad as he could possibly look which wasn't hard because he was, truly, very sad.

'Let's to work!' said Nimrod Parsonage.

Dr Woody was waggling that finger again. 'Mr Mackie extended to you a benevolence founded upon good principles if not good sense. He invested in you and your patch a most charitable faith, a most liberal generosity, and you owed him a dutiful subordination say nothing of hard work and a modest tithe come harvest. What chance now? Your patch in ruins, weeded up, neither ploughed nor planted; your liberal patron most grossly insulted. You ought be ashamed.'

'I am, I see that now, life can take such a turn, a revelation. I'm sorry beyond measure truly I am . . . don't go.'

Woody stared at Sparrow like he was some alien thing. 'It's a sad day when a man's past is what he is,' he said.

'I'm sorry,' said Sparrow.

'Sorry will not do it. This will not wash away, none of this will wash away,' said Woody. He was colouring up, his anger stirred by more than his pain, and Sparrow did not know what to say for it was true – the doctor was condemned forever.

And then the doctor was gone and Sparrow was there, in the cell, with Redenbach and Peskett. He felt very much alone, notwithstanding the company.

50

Peskett thumbed his false teeth into place, moved close. 'See what happens when you do something bad, Marty? It's like an echo, it carries to and fro, doin' hurt in all directions.'

Sparrow had never heard of an echo doing hurt to anybody but he understood the point that Reuben Peskett was making. And he knew the crusty veteran was right. They had bolted, he and Peachey, and that one act had done hurt hither and yon. Peachey was dead, the boy Jug, Jason, he was dead too, and Griffin Pinney was dead but that was a secret. Also, the chief constable's investment in a certain expiree had turned bad and that expiree was now, according to the doctor, *forsaken*, and his patch was a ruin. 'Forsaken, that's all I need,' he said.

His eyes followed Redenbach who had stepped into the corridor to untie the hauling line that was hitched to a big iron ring in the stone. Redenbach glanced back at Sparrow. 'That patch is the least o' your worries now, you don't tell us the truth.' He lowered the tackle rig to hip-high and tied it off.

There was a big hook on the movable block, and the block turned ever so slightly in the chill air. They took Sparrow from the cell and tied his hands behind him and stood him in the corridor with the block at his back. Sparrow's heart was pounding like a big sea onto a beach.

The Parsonage twins stood watching through the bars. 'If I was you I'd tell 'em the truth, front to back,' said Crispin.

'Truth could be worse,' said Nimrod.

Sparrow wondered about the strange serendipity of having Reuben Peskett for his torturer, him with whom Biddie Happ was now, in all likelihood, concubined. He no longer cared for Biddie so why this troubled him he did not understand.

He wished old Joe was dead. If old Joe was dead Bea might just go with him, if ever he got away, if ever he got the chance to run. If he could not stay at Joe's and he had to run, he did not want to run alone. His mind was deeply troubled, turning about, worse than a bucket of eels.

The cat was walking a figure eight around and between Sparrow's legs, rubbing against him all the way. For a moment the purr was the only sound to be heard.

Peskett shunted the cat away with his boot. He stood almost nose to nose with Sparrow as Redenbach took hold of the moveable block and fitted the hook into the rope that now bound the prisoner's wrists tight behind him. 'What are you goin' to do?' said Sparrow, but he already knew. Peskett took up the slack on the hauling line. Redenbach joined to the task, the taut rope straining, lifting Sparrow at the wrists until he was tottering in that dark, cold corridor, his toes barely touching the ground, his arms hauled up behind him, almost shoulder high, the strain on his shoulders most unkind.

At that point Peskett called a halt and Redenbach took the hauling line and hitched it to the iron ring.

Hat Thistlewaite came with a taper. He lit a slender candle set upon a sconce on the wall. Then he glanced at Sparrow and just as quick he looked away. He bent low and swooped up the cat, and he left. Sparrow took Hat's sombre mien and swift departure to be a sign of the turnkey's humanity. That or he was busy.

'He's in a great deal of discomfort, I see that now,' said Nimrod Parsonage.

'That's nothin' to what's comin',' said Crispin.

Peskett moved close again. 'You'll be feelin' the strain on your uppers and your lowers.'

He was so close that Sparrow felt himself doused in the man's stinky breath. It was bad but it was nothing like as bad as Mackie's.

'Is it true what I hear about your nethers?' said Peskett.

Sparrow was stung. He knew the origins of the knowledge hidden in the question. He reckoned he might punch Biddie Happ in the ear if he ever got the chance, just as she'd punched him, only harder. Helpless as he was, strained at his extremities, he had no desire for the conversation to shift to his private parts. Every answer he could summon seemed loaded up with dangerous implications.

'I hear you got but one ball. Perhaps we should have a look?'

Sparrow did not want his britches to come down, not for any reason. 'I don't believe the doctor will condone this,' he said, but straight away he knew the futility of his words for, notwithstanding the doctor's celebrated moderation, he would surely tolerate any means towards the end of knowing what happened to his boy Jug, Jason.

Sparrow could hear Crispin sniggering. 'He's quiverin' like a hare in a trap,' he said.

'They don't care about you anymore, they done with you,' said Redenbach.

'They?'

'Why, the good doctor and Mackie both.'

'What I said was true: a bull shark took the boy.'

'You killed him and you buried him and you hid him away somewhere,' said Peskett.

He was leaning against the wall, working the end of the hauling line between his fingers, a thoughtful pose. 'Proof of life or proof of death, one or the other, Marty. Nothing less will do.'

'Everyone knows a shark will take a dog big or small any day,' said Redenbach.

'Well he didn't,' said Sparrow. The ball of his left foot now had a little more purchase on the floor but his shoulders were still terribly pained. He took some relief by leaning forward and dropping his chin onto his chest and shifting a little more weight onto the better situated foot. His heart pumping hard, he could feel the blood wooshing in and out of his ventricles, he could hear it. His legs were fast tiring. He feared his muscles cramping up. He dreaded the thought they might raise him higher and hang him entirely from his fettered wrists and go to work on him. In his pictorial mind he could see himself hauled high, almost head-high to the beam, his britches around his ankles, the military below. His arms might come away from his shoulders, there to dangle, his body hanging by naught but ligament and sinew, the sockets popped, the flesh stretching like a dough pour.

He heard someone's footsteps, one foot scuffing the ground every time. He knew that sound. It was Henry Kettle. The soldiers looked sharp.

Kettle stopped directly behind Sparrow.

Sparrow felt the captain's walking stick probing the small of his back, gently pushing at him, compelling his shoe leather to drag through the grit on the floor.

'What about my dog?' said Kettle.

'Sir, we will get to the dog, make no mistake,' said Peskett.

'What's that mean, make no mistake? If anyone's to make a mistake here sergeant – should your best endeavours fail to confirm the whereabouts of my dog . . .'

Confirm! Sparrow could only assume the whereabouts of the dog were already known. Mackie or Cuff had likely told the captain that Amicus Amico was at Joe's, with Bea.

He felt such a fool.

'We'll find the dog,' said Peskett.

'Do that,' said Kettle. He gave Sparrow one last jab with his walking stick and then he departed, dragging that lame leg.

'What about this dog?' said Peskett.

Sparrow did not lift his head, He could not look the man in the eye. 'I found him, a stray, that's all. I found him half dead on South Creek.'

'A stray you say?'

'For to trade, yes. Thus to pass, unmolested.'

'Young dog, perchance a brindle?'

'A stray, that's all, to win the good grace of the savages.'

'Did you see 'em, the savages?' said Redenbach.

'Only Mr Catley's Daniel. I never saw old Wolgan nor Caleb neither. Nor the one they call Napoleon.'

'You see any of them hangin' from a tree, suitably neutralised?'

'We did.'

'Quite a sight. You approve?'

'I don't know.' His shoulders pained him something dreadful.

'Why'd you come back?'

Sparrow reached for the most noble explanation he could think of. 'Bea was captive to Griffin Pinney but he went off and he never come back, and Bea said she had to go home, to look after Joe.'

'There's a lot of unlikely mystery pilin' up here,' said Peskett. He was undoing the knot on the iron ring.

'Please no.'

'Griffin ain't a man to disappear, not with a woman in hand, not that woman.'

'Well he did.'

'An' the better half o' your nature took charge and you nobly chaperoned her all the way to Joe's, that right?'

'I went back with her, yes. Please don't haul me up.'

'I'm surprised Catley didn't make that girl an offer, he's a randy one, don't the widow Wise know it,' said Redenbach.

'Where is the boy?' Peskett beckoned the assistance of his fellow tormentor.

'He's lost to the bull shark I swear.'

'Where's the brindle dog?'

'I wouldn't call him brindle, exactly.'

'Where is he?'

'He's with Joe.'

They took the weight on the hauling line and began to heave. Sparrow's arms lifted behind him to the point where they could flex no more and he felt his body weight shift entirely to his shoulder joints as his feet left the ground and he turned, slowly, the pain in his shoulders like fire. He could hear the strain on the block, the rope chafing on the sheaves. Stretched to extremity, his shoulders assaulted by his own dead weight, levered beyond the limits of God's design, bone on bone, a sharp, cruel pain that pulsed into his brain like a needle.

Redenbach was below him now, looking up. 'Did he fuck her, Griffin?'

Peskett pushed Redenbach aside. 'Proof o' life or proof o' death, that's it, then you come down. You can hang there till your arms come away for all I care.'

'There's nothin' left, nothin', truly.'

Peskett reached up and took Sparrow by the throat and squeezed hard on the windpipe, his own face reddening with the effort. The sergeant squeezed harder still, then he let go. 'I've just about had enough o' you!'

Sparrow was gasping, his body rocking, his shoulders loaded with hurt.

Peskett walked about. He circled his captive. He came back into view with the corn sack in hand. He dropped it on the floor beneath the iron ring. *Clunk.*

'Give him the pear like you give it to me!' said Crispin.

'If one more time you deny me the answer I want . . .' said Peskett. 'One more time, I will take down your britches and go to work on your arse, do you understand?'

Sparrow could feel sweat all over, so cold on his skin. He was faint. The walls were shifting, straight things warping into twisted form. He eyed the corn sack. He stared at the pot of grease. He knew at that moment there was naught but one thing to do.

'Alright,' he said.

The Parsonage twins clapped their hands. 'Another narrative,' said Crispin.

'Perchance a counter narrative!' said Nimrod.

'Oh goody', said Redenbach.

Sparrow wanted them to let him down, but they would not let him down. Peskett moved up close once more. 'We'll have the truth while you're up there.'

'I can't talk up here.'

'You best find a way.'

Sparrow was trying to think. He had hoped the real truth would suffice. Now he knew that only a false truth would do, a big lie, masquerading as the true account of the boy Jug's demise. Proof of death in the wilderness would require a sighting, confirmation. He would have to take them there, and there in the fastness . . . in the fastness he might escape. He might even get to the other side, if he had to. 'There is a cave in a gully off the Branch,' he said. He was thinking of the cave where Griffin Pinney and his old dog lay dead. 'I believe I can find it if I try.'

'The boy is there?'

'Yes.'

'Go on,' said Peskett.

'He's there, the boy is there,' said Sparrow. His arms ached like purgatory, the weight on his shoulders heavy as a horse.

'Dead?' said Peskett.

'Let me down, please.'

'Who killed him?'

'Nobody.'

'Nobody?'

'A spider.'

'A spider?'

'A mountain funnel-web.'

'Psssssh,' said Nimrod Parsonage.

'Now *that* is a narrative!' said Crispin.

Redenbach growled. 'You tuggin' my squirrel, laddie?'

'It's true,' said Sparrow. 'They make their burrows in the most unlikely places where you might sit down, or fossick, and they got fangs that cut through fingernails even, and a man once bit has no recourse but to die, that's what happens, and this one bit the boy, and he's dead in that cave.'

'A spider in a cave?' said Peskett.

'No,' said Sparrow. *More.* 'The boy picked up some wood on the way in, the spider come in with the wood and bit him on the back of the hand before he could even blink and when he threw down the wood it was too late.'

'You left him for dead,' said Redenbach.

'We tended him as best we could until he left us, left this world.'

'You understand the doctor will require some exacting detail,' said Peskett.

'Yes.'

'Well then, you describe to me the boy's suffering, swiftly now.'

'I can do that.'

'Do it.'

'Please let me down.'

Peskett looked away. 'Let him down, somewhat,' he said to Redenbach and they lowered Sparrow until the balls of his feet touched the floor and took weight enough to moderate the agony in his shoulders.

'That's it. Talk,' said Peskett.

'It was awful.'

'Doubtless.'

'First thing he dropped the wood and sat and held his hand and we saw the puncture wounds and they were big and deep and red raw. Then he said he was giddy and we propped him against the cave wall and his skin was like a plucked fowl, and his brow was run with sweat. He said his mouth was tingly and his tongue too and his face began to twitch and his eyes to water. He was panting hard and the twitching spread, his entire body agitated and he vomited into his lap so we laid him down and he began to talk, confused talk, babble; and then everything seemed to slow, the twitching, the breathing, the talk . . . and then he was dead.'

Peskett was staring at him, weighing the particulars of Sparrow's tale.

'Please let me down.'

'You bury this boy, you do the right thing?'

'We buried him.'

'You take us out there on a wild-goose chase I will nail you to a tree and skin you alive, do you understand me?'

'I do I do, yes, please let me down.'

Redenbach stepped up. 'Skin you, the bull ants come in droves. Don't we know it.'

'Why'd you contrive that stupid shark story?' said Peskett.

Sparrow was stumped. Why a bull shark when a funnel-web would do just as well? His mind searched in all directions, turning at a gallop. The answer was as much a shock to Sparrow as anyone. 'The boy was hell-bent to come with us,' he said. 'He begged us. I couldn't tell the doctor his son was ripe to bolt, I just couldn't.'

Peskett stared at Sparrow for quite a long time. 'Why would that boy want to bolt?' he said, finally.

'Said his daddy at home was something else, nothin' like his public face.'

'You let him tag along, the boy?'

'He said he'd follow us anyway.'

Peskett seemed to be greatly saddened by Sparrow's revelation as to the boy's intent. 'Damn,' he said, 'that's cruel.' He slapped Redenbach's shoulder with the back of his hand. 'We're done,' he said.

'What!' said Crispin.

'That ain't right,' said Nimrod.

Redenbach took the weight on the hauling line and fed it out and Sparrow felt his feet plant firm at last but his legs would not hold up. He slumped to the floor and he lay there, his shoulders on fire.

He recalled what he'd thought before, about small lies and big lies and just what he might get away with and now, in the blink of an eye, he had told a big lie and was compelled upon the telling to make it bigger still. Where had it come from, this monstrous deceiving lie? There was no sense in which he had actually thought it up. No sense in which this lie was wickedly deliberate, meditated upon, nourished in the womb of the *pia mater*, so to speak, and put together with malice aforethought. No sense in which it was delivered ripe, upon a considered mellowing. No. It just happened into his head, without volition, like ducks in flight shifting into formation. And so he'd said it, and that under no small degree of duress. The big lie was totally absent and then, suddenly, it was present –

a most necessary and entirely unavoidable lie. To save him from the rectal pear.

His pounding heart was settling, the heat in his shoulders moderating, somewhat.

'You give me the pear, why me and not him?' shouted Crispin.

The inquisitors did not answer. They departed the gaol, ordering Hat as they went: 'Lock him up.'

Redenbach had in mind a column from the *Gazette*, one of the little settler tragedies that the editor never failed to report with a marked degree of poetic tenderness and a sizable quantum of fateful resignation as to the mysteries of heavenly intent. 'There was that feeble boy in Parramatta got bit by one of them funnel-webs. He was dead in a trice.'

'I know,' said Peskett.

51

Cuff observed the felons unloading the ketch from Bet Pepper's porch on the terrace. He liked the early morning hours, the chill air, the sweet purity of the unsullied day. But the stillness of the predawn this particular morning was somewhat disrupted by the bustle on the water.

He was packing his pipe when Bet brought him a nip of something. They sat for a while, watching as miscellaneous boxes and baskets were lowered onto the barge and secured there by Guthrie's boy.

'Better go,' he said.

'Better get dressed first,' said Bet.

Cuff was naked save for Bet's long winter coat and her slippers. 'Suppose I better,' he said, as he got himself up. Some of the felons were buckled up laughing, as Cuff posed for their benefit, in full view, hands on hips.

He dressed, slipping the pipe into his vest pocket, there to cohabitate with his spoon.

'Come again,' said Bet.

'Never fear,' he said, taking to the switchback path.

He made his way to the duckboards at the water's edge.

The laden barge slid onto the mud with Guthrie to the fore, his boy on the long ore. Guthrie handed the mail pouch to Cuff and he tipped his hat to Bet on the terrace and the two men talked briefly.

Cuff tucked the mail pouch under his arm, the duckboards squelching in the mud. He stepped to one side and waved on the felons with a flourish, watched them heft the supplies up the steep slope.

He followed on their heels but only as far as the doctor's cottage. He stepped lightly onto the porch and looked through the window, saw the doctor prone on his cot, dead to the world. He pushed at the door, the slack hinges no longer fit for purpose.

Woody woke with a start. 'Damn,' he said. 'What time is it?'

'You with him all night?' said Cuff.

'Not quite.' The doctor scratched at his whiskers. 'He'll tell you it's winter bronchitis. I'll tell you it is pneumonia, again.'

'I tell him he looks like death warmed up. I swear the man wheezes like a concertina.'

'Those lungs crackle like fat in the pan.'

'That too.'

'He was delirious half the night and weak as a wet chicken,' said Woody.

'Did he surrender any secrets?'

'I doubt he'd surrender a secret in the extremities of a *terminal* delirium.'

'It ain't terminal, that's something.'

'These pulmonic bouts worsen every time.'

'Did he say anything?'

'Just wild talk, kept saying he was late for something kept saying *it's gone it's gone* and he blathered about the grub in the wheat somewhat obsessively.'

Cuff laughed and smacked the mail pouch on his knee. 'He doesn't wander far does he, not even in a delirium.'

'That's hard to know,' said the doctor.

Woody sat up and put his feet on the floor and put out a hand to steady himself with Cuff's assistance. His wispy grey hair was mussed as waste straw. He put his glasses on and pressed the bridge firm on his nose, picked his coat off the floor and pulled it on, crossed the room and peered out the window. He was no longer chilled. He pulled on his trousers and tucked in his shirt.

'You ought sleep,' said Cuff.

The doctor took off his glasses and rubbed his eyes. 'My boy is dead in some cave.'

Cuff already knew the content of Sparrow's confession. Another story entirely. 'I know you need finality, Thomas, but pray be careful what you believe.'

'He says the boy got bit by a funnel-web spider and died, in a cave, on the Branch.'

'Do you believe that?'

'I need a sighting I can trust. Will you go? I cannot, Alister cannot, and I would trust Reuben Peskett only to confirm whatever is convenient to himself, or to Henry Kettle . . . conjure some tale for my assuagement. I expect he'll spend more time finding that dog than he will the cave.'

'Sparrow's story might be true,' said Cuff. 'Nature is pitiless cruel, indifferent to all pain not least the pain that passes on to grieving hearts.'

'I need someone to sight my boy, or not, as the case may be. Someone I can believe, someone who will not invent a fable for to give me and mine naught but never-ending doubt. Do you understand me, Thaddeus?'

'Of course I do.'

'Well?'

'I'll go. I'll take Sprodd.'

Guthrie was on the porch, peering in, his arms freighted with a box of medicine bottles and phials, the glass clattering, the cork stoppers like a little sea of top hats. 'You'll have to catch them, they're gone,' he said.

'Who's gone?' said Cuff.

'Peskett and Redenbach with Sparrow in tow, rationed up for quite a tramp,' said Guthrie. He put down the box and readied to depart. 'Can you sign for these?'

'Not now,' said the doctor.

Guthrie departed as Woody lifted the bottles, one after another, reading the labels side on. 'Sparrow to guide them?' he said.

'I know, God help us all,' said Cuff.

'He tells Peskett this cave is on the Branch.'

'That don't make it simple.'

'The unknowing – eats at me like a tapeworm.'

Cuff had almost forgotten. 'The mail's here, you want I open it?'

'I want you to find my boy.'

'There's warrants here for the girl and the sealers, the whole bunch.'

Woody worked thumb and forefinger upon his eyelids. 'Alright, read,' he said.

Cuff opened a warrant bearing the girl's full name and read silently for a few moments. 'Lord,' he said.

. . . All persons in the territory of New South Wales and its Pacific neighbourhood are hereby required to aid and assist, by information or otherwise, in apprehending or causing to be apprehended the convicted felon Beatrice Faar. Fled convict transport Sea Stag in Rio. Tall, five feet ten inches, age seventeen, dusky, limpid green eyes, black hair, good teeth. A pleasant countenance and a lowland

brogue. A party, subsequently, to brutal murder on the southern sealeries, a rival crew with prior right of occupation butchered while sleeping, save for one survivor, a Boston negro. The greatest caution advised . . .

The doctor was on his feet, searching for his glasses. 'Limpid green,' he said.

Cuff clucked his tongue. 'With a little black dot on the iris!' He scanned the rest of the document, then he tapped the papers with his forefinger. 'They're all here: Jonas, Gudgeon, Nimrod, Crispin.' He read the conclusion out loud:

Any person harbouring, secreting, or employing these individuals will be punished with exemplary severity . . .

'By command, et cetera, et cetera.' He folded the warrant and returned it to the batch in the pouch.

'How much of this does Alister know?' said Woody.

'I know he gave Jonas Wick short shrift. I know he's got the girl neatly sequestered on the Branch, again. I know he'll use her for the curing if ever he gets pelts to cure . . . but if she imperils his rank or reputation in this little world he will cast her adrift quicker than a rat up a drain.' Cuff stepped onto the doctor's porch and surveyed the river. 'Better go see Alister.'

'I'll come too.'

At the Hive, Sam provided a brief account of Mackie's night while Fish scuttled up the stairs with the mail pouch. 'He's had a good doze, last few hours,' said Sam.

At the end of the counter was a wicker basket with a blue ribbon tied into the weave. 'What's that?' said Cuff.

'That is a squab pie, courtesy of Agnes Archambault. But I wasn't about to let her see him. As a consequence she called me an ill-mannered oaf, but I never deviated from civility.'

'A slice of pie will do him good.'

'Did he sleep, finally?' said Woody.

'He did, yes, he took the laudanum.'

Woody drummed his fingers on the counter. 'Samuel, you are to confiscate any laudanum you find up there. The man has to cough. In that regard laudanum is a most devious elixir for what appears to be improvement is in fact the veiling of the problem, *thus* its augmentation.'

'Alright!' said Sam.

'We may all wilt in extremis, Thomas, even Alister,' said Cuff. 'Here's a man who swore blind he'd never take the laudanum, said he valued his faculties more than his life.'

'He wilts at his peril.'

'Shoulderblades like chicken wings. I tell you, he eats but the weight's comin' off him,' said Sam.

Mackie was propped up in bed, his greatcoat over his nightshirt. The warrants lay open by his side. The doctor peeled back the coat and put his ear trumpet to the chief constable's chest.

'The thing is, the more purulent and copious the matter the higher the temperature and the greater the frequency and violence of the cough, for the body is now in a loop, but the coughing is most necessitous for to expel the superfluous phlegm.'

'Otherwise what?' said Cuff.

'Otherwise the patient drowns in his own fetid muck.'

'Now there's a delicate formulation.'

'This is no occasion to paint the lily.'

Woody waved a finger close to Mackie's nose. 'No more laudanum.

Contrary to the quackery, it hides the problem, allows it to congregate in the sink of your lungs, you take it at your peril. Alister, *you have to cough.*'

'Claret?'

'Claret yes, laudanum no.'

Mackie nodded. Not the slightest ripple of defiance. The rattle in his breath was readily audible at all points in the room.

'You look wasted and you sound worse than you look,' said Cuff.

'*And I'm the sharp tongue!*' protested Woody.

'I doubt I could pull a damp weed,' said Mackie.

'What's he need if not laudanum?' said Cuff.

Woody was poking at the glands in Mackie's neck. 'What he needs is what he will not have: a long sea voyage. See, the ship as she rolls, the muscles of the body are required continually to brace and relax, thus the viscera in the belly is massaged by repeated friction and gentle kneading, a cleansing action, the motion simultaneously stirring the lungs, the vigour thus acquired facilitating the expectorations, say nothing of the sea air.'

'I'm not about to wander the oceans,' said Mackie. He was reading the warrant again – the warrant bearing Bea Faa's name in full.

Cuff pulled up a chair. 'We got a fair breeze, Alistair. We gotta go, me and Dan.'

'Don't get your hopes too high, Thomas,' said Mackie.

Cuff agreed. 'He's right. Sparrow's a rudderless vessel save for one cause, the salvation of his wretched self.'

'You think he made it up, the cave, the spider?'

'I think Peskett's gentle arts gave him no choice. And yet . . .'

'What?'

'It might be true.'

'What I want is finality,' said Woody. 'If there's anything in that cave —'

'Thaddeus will find it,' said Mackie.

'I'll find Peskett first,' said Cuff. 'Sparrow too.'

'Peskett will stop at Joe's for that dog. Bless the dog, for that will slow him,' said Woody.

'His priorities are indisputably Kettle-ish, but ours, what are ours?' said Cuff.

'What do you mean?' Mackie's voice was barely audible.

Cuff picked up the warrant and smacked it into his palm. 'The rule of law or the song of the heart, Alister, what's it to be?'

Mackie did not answer so Cuff continued. 'This is a young woman who has played her part. Put to the test she's cared for Joe, kept her nose clean, why, she's even given you the cure for the pelts and wants nothing save to be free o' them mangy sealers. This business on the sealeries, say nothing of the transport . . . she could hang.'

Mackie did not respond and Cuff did not miss the opportunity to continue.

'There's more at stake here than your enterprise. I say if you can sequester that girl for your own convenience come the curing business then you can call her for what she is. That alone could save her, the vice-regal discretion being most partisan.'

'Me being the governor's dog.'

'I don't think that and I never said that.'

Woody wrapped his arms around himself and hunched over and Cuff took this as the doctor's submission, like a hedgehog rolled up in a ball, all prickle but no punch. 'You can wash your hands of this, Alister, but I say you got a chance here; not just any old chance, somethin' special,' said Cuff.

'Take them some flour and tea, and some cocoa.'

'What's that mean?'

'Joe likes cocoa.'

'What I mean is . . . *what does that mean?*'

'It means see to their needs, *as you think best.*'

Cuff shook his head and made a clucking sound. 'You can count on that.' He had what he wanted, a free hand.

Cuff picked up the warrant. He folded it and shuffled it into a pocket. 'I'll see to the girl and one way or another I'll sight this cave in the fastness.'

'Thank you, Thaddeus,' said Woody.

'Proof o' life or proof o' death.'

'Please God.'

'I'll do what I can.'

They crossed the square, Cuff and Woody, bound for the doctor's cottage. They stood at the top of the switchback path, the sun on their backs.

'What of the girl?' said Woody.

'Who's asking, the doctor or the magistrate?'

'I'll not pretend to judge her.'

'And I'll not drag her back here to get punished, get pilloried or hung, damned if I will,' said Cuff.

Woody put down his medicine bag and straightened himself, his fingers pressed into the small of his back. 'You have to understand, Alister's one of very few to have risen from the felonry to the seniority, the property, the favour, such as he now enjoys. That's everything to him, *everything*. He cannot conceive himself ever again tainted in any way. The shame's rooted too deep.'

'Well, we all know about shame. First cousin to guilt.'

52

They had put in turnips, long rows adjacent to patches fresh sown for onions and cabbage. Freddie managed to talk his way through the entire morning, mostly about the merits of potatoes and the shortcomings of the turnip. Bea sensed he would talk in this manner whether she was there or not, but he clearly knew his subject so she was happy to listen as she worked, occasionally straightening herself to check for Amicus Amico, who was prone to strike out for the Branch if not sighted and called back.

Freddie spoke a great deal about the turnip. He declared it a poor excuse for a vegetable, save fodder for pigs. In this regard he spoke bitterly of a man called Turnip Townsend whom Bea had never heard of. He spoke, too, about the partialities of the sprouting potato and the unsuitability of very rotten manure as opposed to fresh manure mixed with old straw or thatch. He conceded the former had its applications but not, he said, in the vicinity of a sprouting potato for the eyes were most particular as to dung. Better, he said, to have no dung at all than to have the eyes coated in old rotten dung.

They sat Joe nearby, in the sun, with a broad-brimmed hat on his head and a blanket on his knees. They sat him with a view over the corn stubble on the flats and the Branch beyond, but when they checked he was mostly dozing.

Once when she called the young dog he ambled his way to Joe and sat beside him with his long nose on the old soldier's knee. Joe seemed not to notice and the dog was content just to be there. After a while he dropped down, his forelegs folded beneath his chest, warmed by the sun, dozing with Joe.

In the afternoon Freddie put the ox in harness and ploughed the stubble ground for wheat and Bea Faa followed along behind, shaking out the weeds and bagging them in a corn sack because, according to Freddie, they would greatly impoverish the soil if left to grow in the company of the burgeoning seed.

He told Bea that early sown wheat yielded better, being less subject to the grub and smut and rust and blight to which late wheat was always liable in the close, hot, sultry weather that marked the coming of summer on the river. He vowed to plough some more in the days to come, get as much of Mackie's seed into the ground as early as they could, for wheat meant credit at the store.

Late in the day the last of the westering sun bathed the flats and the banks of the Branch. It was hard to see menace in this scene, and they did not at first see menace when a skiff skimmed into the frame with the familiar nor'-easter in the sail, beaching on the flats by the big she-oak.

They had put Joe to bed.

Freddie was fixing the fire, anticipating a cool evening come the dark. He was grumbling about autumn's slippery cunning. Bea was sipping at a mug of tea on the doorstep, the dog by her side. 'A boat, three men,' she said.

She watched them as first they folded the sail and tied off the boat and headed across the patch, skirting the fresh ploughed ground. She recognised Sparrow the moment he was off the mud and squared up, walking his walk. Amicus tried to force past her but she grabbed him and held him tight.

Freddie was behind her now, his feet in motion like he was treading grapes or mushing the makings for a sod house. 'That's Reuben Peskett,' he said.

She watched Joe come sharply awake. He pointed at the mantelshelf. 'The gun?' said Freddie, reaching for Thyne's musket on the pegs, but Joe's agitation did not affirm the gun.

'The bayonet?' Joe nodded and Freddie took the bayonet from the mantelshelf and handed it to him. 'One time Joe give him a thrashin',' he explained to Bea.

Joe fumbled at the leather scabbard until he drew out the blade. He worked his fingers on the scalloped handle he had carved to measure. He put the weapon under the blanket, touch close to his hip. He straightened up a little, ready as any stricken old soldier could be.

The girl moved aside, held tight to the dog, as first Peskett, then Redenbach and then Sparrow filed in.

All the way down the river Sparrow had worried about what Bea Faa might say to Peskett. She knew the truth about the boy's death, as he had told it to Mr Catley and Moowut'tin, and Mr Mackie too, and she had no notion of the story he'd told Peskett to elude the rectal pear and get himself off that hook in the gaol and into the woods. He fully anticipated his plan would fall apart in the course of their stopover at Joe's.

He said hello as he filed into the cabin, and she said hello back, but there was not the moment for another word. She let go of the dog and Amicus pranced about Sparrow and nuzzled into his hand.

Peskett was staring somewhat triumphantly at Joe. 'Well well, the celebrated duelist, the great conciliator. Let's all coddle the damn savages.'

'What's wrong with him?' said Redenbach.

'He got up for the necessaries and he took a turn,' said Freddie. 'He can't hardly talk anymore.'

'No damn use to anyone,' said Peskett. He handed his musket to Redenbach. He looked the girl over. 'Here she is, the sealer's whore.' He was thumbing his false teeth into the lock position that never quite locked.

He squatted down and called the dog and the dog came to him. 'This is Mr Kettle's kangaroo dog. I am *formally* requisitioning this dog and charging you, Marty Sparrow, with theft thereof.'

He took the dog by the scruff of the neck and closed his fist and pulled the skin tight and lifted the animal off its forelegs.

Amicus snarled and snapped at Peskett's sleeve and the sergeant let go and pulled away and smacked the dog's snout with the back of his hand. 'He does that again, I'll take his balls off.'

Sparrow made a silent vow that he would not suffer more than the mild chastisement of Amicus Amico from that moment forth. He felt a tingle in his fingers, the finger memory of the weighty helve, the small axe, in hand. *Now you know how.* He felt himself a sovereign power, silently sitting in judgement. He sensed a shift in the order of things.

'I want a good firm collar on this dog as of now,' said Peskett.

'He don't need a collar,' said Sparrow.

Redenbach was warming his hands at the fire, peering into the pot. 'What you got here?'

'Corn and cabbage and some fish heads on the warm,' said Freddie.

'Well then, put out the plates, we're starved.'

Bea sliced what bread there was and floated a slice on Joe's serve and took it to him.

Joe took the plate. He smiled at Bea like he didn't have a care in the world.

Peskett rapped the table. 'You get back here.'

The dark had crept in and took a hold all about them, save for the glow in the fireplace. Freddie put a taper to the fire and lit the oil lamp on the mantelshelf, beside the empty scabbard.

'Now, girl, how'd that boy die, the doctor's boy?' said Peskett.

The girl looked to Sparrow and Peskett thumped the table and rattled everything. A centipede scuttled from a crack in the tabletop, pausing near Sparrow's hand.

They watched.

'*You* tell *me* how that boy died out there,' said Peskett.

'A bull shark,' she said.

'We know that's a lie,' said Redenbach.

'Shut up,' said Peskett.

Sparrow took a knife and laid the blade across the centipede and pinned him to the table and they watched the creature wriggle and rear.

'If you like scarin' people you'd come back as one o' them,' said Redenbach.

'He's sure got a lot o' legs that one,' said Freddie.

'Jesus wept, can we just keep to the matter at hand,' said Peskett.

Sparrow said: 'If I had a long black pin I could stick this one right through, keep him in a jar, way clear of his deadly venom and his vicious arts.'

'Like Mr Catley?' said Bea.

'Yes.'

'How did that boy die?' said Peskett, loud.

She hesitated. She wondered if Sparrow could be that shrewd.

'A funnel-web spider,' she said.

Peskett sat up straight, his palms pressed together, his thumbs tapping the one against the other.

'On the Branch?'

'Yes.'

'He said off the Branch.'

'Close to the Branch.'

'The doctor's boy's out there, dead?'

'Yes.'

'Was it quick, did he die quick?' said Redenbach.

'Yes.'

'You tell us then, what happened when he got bit?' said Peskett.

Bea had no trouble recalling Mr Catley's words or, to be precise, Moowut'tin's words as translated by Mr Catley. Such was the peril of her recent years that she was practised in her attention to detail, any detail that might navigate her out of peril. 'The poison is swift . . . the skin went like goose flesh, plucked, then his face began to twitch and his body shook, horribly. He lost the power of speech and began to babble and vomit and pant, and then his breathing slowed, 'ere death released the poor soul.'

'Swift you say?'

'Yes.'

'You got any bang-head?' said Redenbach.

'No,' said Freddie. 'Joe won't have it.'

'Get the flagon,' said Peskett.

Redenbach departed for the skiff and he came back with a gallon flagon in wicker and they drank for a while, just the soldiers. The
wicker was worn out and frayed. Redenbach was folding the frayed
ends back into the weave. Peskett watched. He whacked Sparrow's
elbow. 'You weave that stuff?' he said.

'Not any more,' said Sparrow.

'I thought you was a eeler on the Irk?'

'That was long ago.'

Freddie took the cookpot to the water barrel at the back of the
byre and swilled it with a dipper's worth of water and gave it a good
scrub with dirt and then with a handful of straw and then he swilled
it again. He was relieved to be free of the somewhat fixed atmosphere
in the cabin.

Redenbach was drinking steadily. 'Get a lamp in there girl, I'll see
that bugger's eyes.'

'Joe's worn out.'

'He's more'n worn out, he's useless,' said Redenbach. He stood up
and kicked back his chair and went to the bedside and bent down and
stared into Joe's eyes and saw the old man was wide awake. 'What you
up to you randy old bugger?'

Joe said nothing. The girl could hear him breathing, heavily,
through his nose. She stepped to the bed's end and saw Redenbach
had a handful of Joe's nightshirt in his fist and he was shaking Joe,
demanding some sort of reply. 'You're gunna talk to me one way
or another.'

The dog was close by, watchful. Peskett was entertained.

Bea saw the veins in Joe's neck, thick as rope. She saw Joe's left
hand pull slowly at the blanket, the blanket coming away and Joe's

fist, secreted there, wrapped tight on the sculpted handle of the bayonet. She saw him swing up the blade and ram it through the meaty
part of Redenbach's chin.

Joe let go off the bayonet and slumped back as Redenbach reeled
away, his mouth chocked open, the sound a guttural squall, like he
was gargling nails.

He worked the blade free.

The dog inched forward, licking at the blood on the floor.

'Come away now soldier,' said Peskett, getting to his feet.

But Redenbach was beyond recall. He stood over Joe, raised the
bayonet as you might a hatchet over a wood block, and he chopped
down at Joe and struck him at the juncture of the neck and shoulder and split him to the breast. 'He cuts like lard, the wretch has no
bones,' he hollered.

Bea went swiftly to Joe and took him in her arms. A faint moan
carried on his failing breath.

'You've killed him,' said Sparrow.

'What we do not need, Alvin!' roared Peskett.

The dog had gone to Bea and stood close at her side as she laid Joe
on his back and set his pillow neat beneath his head, the bed soaked
in blood.

She pressed on his shoulders, trying to halt the coming away. Then
she heard the breath go out of him and she felt the stillness, and the
coldness, of his flesh.

Redenbach stepped away. He sat himself at the table, holding a
bloodied rag to his chin. He took a long draught and wiped his mouth
with his sleeve.

'Damn you for more trouble than we need,' said Peskett.

Bea rested her head on Joe's chest and the tears ran from her
cheeks onto his nightshirt. Her mind swept across her brief time on
the Branch with Joe and Freddie. As if it had never rained, she could
only think of sunny days, of good hard sweaty work and kind words,

of reading to Joe by lamplight, Bunyan, the *Gazette*. Of a time like no other in the entirety of her life, a time when she was not put upon. *What now?*

Joe's skin had already lost its colour. His corpse was pale as tripe. His entire frame was cold and she could not warm him, as she once had.

She heard Peskett growling at his subordinate. 'That puncture might well shut you up.'

Sparrow's eyes locked on Redenbach's bloodied chin.

The soldier took the flagon by the wicker handle and lifted it and tipped back his head and Sparrow saw the bayonet wound, bloodied and raw.

Redenbach spat blood into the rag and folded the cloth in his fist. 'Damned ol' squaddie,' he said. He dabbed at the runnage of blood and bang-head on his neck.

'You killed him,' said Sparrow.

'You just work that out?'

Freddie was back with the cookpot. He stared at Redenbach's bloodied neck and shirt. 'Who did that?' he said. He looked to Sparrow with some degree of puzzlement.

'Never you mind,' said Peskett.

Freddie watched as Redenbach took another swig from the flagon and he saw the running wound in the soldier's chin. 'Balm's no good for that, you need a stitch or two in that. That or a plug.' Then he remembered the bayonet.

In the darkness of the recess he saw Joe, lifeless and horribly bloodied. He shuffled his way to the recess. He sat by Bea, took Joe's hand, and let out a terrible wail.

Peskett took hold of Redenbach's head and probed at the chin wound and Sparrow watched. He reckoned the soldiers quite vulnerable, busied there. He had never been quite the same since he cleaved that axe into Griffin Pinney's head. He surmised he was a better man for it. No longer helpless, weightless, like ash on the wind. He reckoned he might yet get away, him and Amicus. And now Joe was dead. That could be quite helpful: Bea might come too. But it was hard to think past the moment, for Freddie was wailing, a desolate, wretched sound, and Bea's anguish was hidden yet plain, her face in her hands.

53

Neither tide nor wind favoured the deputy constables. They were compelled to lay over on a nameless stretch of the river and thereafter to lay over again, to mend a broken tiller. The loss of time was such that Cuff and Sprodd did not reach Joe's patch until late the following day. There they found the soldiers were gone, having left at dawn, Sparrow and the dog with them. They found Joe, dead, and Freddie at the foot of his bed in a miserable state of confusion.

Bea Faa had stopped up Joe's rear with a wad of linen and tied an old bit of harness tight about his shoulders to hold him together. Then she draped him in his greatcoat and laid him out on the bed, his hands by his side. 'He near cut Joe in two,' she told them.

Cuff lifted the lapel on the coat and saw the nightshirt soaked in blood. He stood there, quiet, head bowed. 'Redenbach you say?'

'Yes.'

'Well, there's a lot of secrets in them woods and one more won't do harm to man nor dog,' said Cuff as he sat himself at the table.

'What secret?' said Sprodd.

'I aim to kill that weasel, drop him down a hole all the way to hell.'

'I'll sit with him for a while more,' said Bea.

'You do that.'

'What am I going to do, Thaddeus?' said Freddie.

'You'll do what we all do my friend: we just keep goin'. That's all we can ever do.'

'I'll try I will, but I . . .'

'We'll see to a decent burial tomorrow, early.'

'Seems burying's all we do, these days,' said Sprodd.

'I would like to stay on, here.' Freddie seemed to be in a daze.

'It's your patch Freddie.'

'It is?'

'You were here, Joe came along.'

'Good pals ever since.'

'Don't you forget that. You and this patch, you were Joe's salvation.'

'I s'pose we was, yes.'

Cuff beckoned the girl. 'Come and sit, we'll talk,' he said. He could see the sadness in her eyes and he wished he had something in the way of comfort to say to her. Instead he was the bringer of bad news. He patted her hand. 'I have no desire to add to your troubles missy but trouble is comin'.' He took the warrant from his haversack. 'I know you can read.'

The dark was fast closing. She lit the candle on the table and the dim residue of the day was charged with a russet glow.

She read the warrant.

Sprodd was by the foot of the bed. 'My Lord, old Joe,' he said.

'They didn't quite spell your name right but I'd say that's you,' said Cuff, poking at the paper.

'That is me.'

'The thing is, if you stay here the military will come for you, once they know.'

She nodded. 'A close call then.'

Cuff chuckled. 'Yes.' He took the warrant from her hand and turned it about and scanned it for the line he wanted. 'Tell me about this Boston negro.'

'His name was Jessop. He was one of five stranded on a sealery in the lower forties, no sign of the mothership. They thought themselves forsaken. Their little settlement was naught but mean huts lined with pelts.'

'Desperate.'

'They had succumbed to a terrible melancholy, and variously suffered the scurvy, their teeth coming away and their gums bleeding and their skin all dappled.'

'You found them somewhat . . . needy?'

'We did. And we found bales of raw pelts. But there was a small batch, finished, the coarse long hairs entirely gone and the hide and the fur none the worse for the treatment.'

'I've seen one of them pelts.'

'Then you know they are flawless, finished to perfection.'

'That warrant says they were butchered in their sleep.'

'Jonas gave them biscuits and grog forthwith, and he promised them carriage off the island on one condition.'

'They trade the cure for their salvation.'

'Yes.'

'Doubtless they surrendered their secret.'

'They did, the makings and the measures, every detail, and for that they got a meal of cheese and salted beef and grog.'

'And what of this Jessop?'

'A bull seal had bit his arm and tore away the flesh and the wound was full of rot and stink and he was much diminished.'

'And the others slept a deep sleep on promises and grog I suppose?'

'They were fell upon, their throats cut, and come the dawn we departed.'

'And Jessop?'

'Wick left him, supposedly to suffer death alone, in that stinking hut.'

'Pure villainy.'

'That's Jonas Wick.'

'You know he had an accident?'

'He did?'

'He got no satisfaction from Alister so he took the ketch to Sydney and got drunk and fell overboard in the dark of night.'

'He doesn't take liquor.'

Cuff did not hesitate. 'Well then, there's your answer. The man's relapsed, his guts are in revolt and he's heaving over the taffrail, his mind swimming, his balance awry, and the boat kicks and tips and over he goes. That's it, mystery solved.'

The girl smiled. 'I will make cocoa,' she said.

'And cocoa will restore our faith in humanity!' Cuff clucked his tongue and smiled that mischievous smile and that made Bea smile, faintly.

They sipped on the cocoa and nibbled on Freddie's hearth cakes and Cuff lit his pipe and they sat quietly with their memories of Joe.

After a while Cuff's pipe began to fade and with that his mind turned to hard matters, matters of pressing consequence. He tapped a finger on the warrant. 'This paper obliges me to deliver you up to the senior magistrate in Parramatta, the Reverend Abbott no less.'

'I have been bought and sold and passed around. I have been used hard. I have served Joe well.'

'The warrant is a mockery to natural justice, I'll say that much.'

'And you would deliver me up?'

'I want the truth as to the fate of the boy Jug, Jason. I believe our Mr Sparrow has spun a yarn to get himself off the hook, and seize his chance up the Branch.'

She paused. She did not look away for she knew Cuff would read meaning into any form of evasion. 'The boy is in a cave on the Branch, dead. A spider bit him.'

'A funnel-web spider?' Cuff leant back and folded his arms, studying the girl.

'Yes,' she said. The warrant had changed everything, even more so than Joe's death. She was at one of those junctions where her own words might save her or condemn her to some horrid besetment –

or the gibbet. She knew with this lie she might seize her own chance, perhaps with Sparrow and the pup for company. With this lie they might make for the other side, or a sanctuary deep in the wilderness.

Cuff seemed to divine her thoughts. 'I believe Mr Sparrow will bolt for the other side if he can.'

The girl nodded.

'And you will tell me Griffin Pinney just disappeared, that too. That right?'

'He just went off. I don't know where.'

'Never came back?'

'Never.'

Cuff picked up a fugitive stick of kindling and tossed it into the fireplace. He was not inclined to deliver the girl into the hands of Abbott. 'I doubt our chief constable wants his past resurrected before the magistrate at Parramatta, I know Abbott would delight in such an opportunity – put a fire beneath a pot of rumours and have them bubble to the top.'

'What rumours?'

'Rumour is Alister and your mother go back a long way. Rumour is he shares you with old Joe in flagrant defiance of a certain Biblical stricture; I know it's not true, Alister's about as carnal as a stick o' wood, and poorly into the bargain.'

'I have no wish to embarrass Mr Mackie.'

'He's got commerce on a pedestal, up there with his filial loyalty to the government.'

'He got me free of Gudgeon.'

'Free of Gudgeon but not exactly free.'

'I'll never be free.'

'You believe this nonsense about the other side?'

'I can hope. There's no hope this side of the mountains, not now.'

'You can find this cave? You know where it is?'

'Yes.'

'You can show me, me and Dan?'

She paused, pondering the question. 'Yes,' she said.

'Alright then.'

Next morning before the sun was up Freddie and Sprodd dug a grave by the peach orchard and they shrouded Joe in a wrap of tattered wagon sheet that once was a makeshift tent. They set him in the grave as the sun inched above the tree line to the east. Freddie tried to say something but he could not get beyond a few words. Bea Faa was intent upon silent contemplation and Sprodd could but shake his head and repeat the only words he seemed to know for the time being: 'Poor old Joe,' he said, over and over.

Under the circumstances, Cuff took it upon himself to eulogise the departed. He took off his hat and stared into the bowl like he was trying to read meaning in the sweat stains. 'As to the solemnities, I'll say just this,' he said. 'Lord, we have sent thy way a good soul. Joe was a straight-goer, never known to practise the petty arts or the slippery ways. He made no parade of his virtues. He was untouched by the prejudice of rank and station. He was a kindly man, neither nitpicker nor stickler, and we'll *all* miss his kindness. As to his affliction, he endured that like an ancient stoic and might have prevailed but for the craven behaviour that took his life. We here are plainly the worse for his loss. Amen.'

There followed a silence that was quite awkward and even Cuff was lost for words until he found some more. 'We trust that God in his wisdom is well disposed to this fine old man and in the meantime we move on, we get on with our business, that's all we can do, all anyone can do, we just . . . move on.'

Bea turned away and wiped tears from her eyes and they left Freddie to fashion a hardwood cross and finish the grave and they headed up the Branch in the company of their silent thoughts.

The track shadowed the serpentine river into the stone country. They followed the course in the cover of grey gums and she-oaks dripping with dew, finches flitting from the brush, a kingfisher perched on high and ducks scattering on lustrous wings to settle once again upon the waters upstream as if drawing them on.

They reached the fish traps and pressed on to the tidal limit and further along the ceremonial ground, where they sat down in the company of the weathered carvings incised upon the fringing trees.

Cuff rested the Kunkle musket on his shoulder. 'You know what's up ahead, the horrible enormities?'

'Yes, I've seen them,' she said.

54

The soldiers and Sparrow had followed a beaten track through the timber for most of the day when Peskett led them up a rocky spur to a vantage where they saw the river ahead of them, a long stretch punctuated by shallow cascades, the banks thick with calved-off stone and spindly river gums aslant over the shallows. In the middle distance they spied a rock wallaby at the water's edge, small birds swooping in its vicinity, darting after dragonflies.

Peskett spoke softly. 'You muzzle that dog and sit quiet,' he said to Sparrow. He primed the gun, hardly a sound. He set off, going carefully down the spur.

Sparrow and Redenbach settled in a copse of fern and woody pear. The soldier forever mopping at the wound in his chin. The dog sat, as directed, untroubled by the big collar that Peskett had fitted, indifferent to the drama at hand.

It was almost dark when they heard the report of Peskett's musket. Parrots scattered, screeching, and then the bush all about them fell silent. Redenbach chuckled. He bunched his bloody sweat rag into his fist. 'Come on,' he said.

They made their way to the river's edge. They tramped upstream, sand and shallows. Threads and filaments of the fresh kill carried on the flow, the guts brightly coloured, the dog snapping up what he could as they moved on, the river water spilling from his jowls. Redenbach chuckled some more. 'Reuben don't miss, I'll say that much for the beggar.'

They found Peskett squatting in the shallows, washing the sand off the butchered hindquarters, freshly skinned, the rest of the carcass red and raw on the sand and the bloodied axe tossed clear.

They built a fire on the sand and set the hindquarters in the coals and breathed in the fragrant smell of the charred flesh, turning the meat as required. Sparrow held Amicus tight, the dog whimpering with delight as the darkness closed on them. 'You make him wait for the bone,' said Peskett. 'That or lose him to dissolution, like some people I know.'

Sparrow held tight to the collar. Peskett was not finished. 'I will return this dog much improved, that or the devil can have him. You understand me, Sparrow?'

Sparrow nodded. A chill cut through him. He was reminded that he and Amicus Amico were soon to be parted, one way or another. He resolved, yet again, to seize his chance when he could. It occurred to Sparrow that all his life he had been afraid – and he was still afraid – but no longer was he caught full in the spell of fear. No longer its boneless object. The thought of Bea lifted his spirits. The plight of the dog put iron in his blood.

They cut strips off the cooked meat and ate them piping hot. Before long they had devoured the better parts of a hindquarter and they finished, picking at the charred coating on the remains, like bears on the near side of winter.

———

A black snake had supped on the juices of the bloody wallaby carcass and dallied there, snug in the early morning light, when Peskett brought down the butt end of the small axe on its head. A cloud of flies rose up. The tail thrashed fitfully and the body with it. Peskett smacked at the flies about his face.

The activity stirred Redenbach and Sparrow. Amicus Amico circled, his instincts tempered by his wariness of Peskett, who took out his knife and speared the blade through the reptile at the nape. He lifted the snake, still thrashing, and held it high for the benefit of the lookers on. 'That's how I like 'em, hooked and kickin'.'

The comment was not lost on Sparrow.

Peskett dropped his catch on the sand and put his boot on the snake's head and he wiped the blade on his britches and holstered it. One swift motion. He picked up the snake and cast it into the scrub on the fringe of the levee and it landed with its fore half in the scrub and the aft half on the sand.

Sparrow went close, watched the snake twitching, the tail thrashing, half dead. In the grass he found an odd bit of flood-wrack, the leg off a rudely fashioned chair, the wood a pale, milky colour from long immersion in the river and the finished edges much battered and the square-cut tongue at one end much splintered and frayed.

He looked upstream; saw an eagle glide over the river, the sun bright on the tipping wing, its shadow on the water, that mighty span. He saw a beaky nosed wading bird stepping in the shallows. He wondered where the chair might be, where the leg had begun its journey. The find gave him hope, but he was not sure there was good sense in that hope. He tossed the leg into the scrub.

The dog was at his heel, sniffing at his boots. He put his hand to the raggedy coat, working his fingers into the nape. He felt his spirits lift by a measurable margin.

Redenbach pushed a drawstring sack into Sparrow's hands. 'That's the meat, don't lose it,' he said. They ate biscuit, drank from the river, and moved off, wading along the sandy stretch, the valley narrower now, the cliffs ever more sheer as their course shifted northward.

That day and the next they trekked deep into the gorge. They kept to the sand levees and the shallows where they could, otherwise weaving and scrambling along the boulder strewn banks or clawing their way through dense scrub thick with mouldering flood-wrack.

Late in the afternoon the play of colour on the cliffs began to fade. A mist settled in the timber ahead of them, tendrils curling like smoke to the failing light on the rim.

They sat clear of the flow on a long, handsome stretch of sand that banked steep at the far end of the reach.

They watched long-legged birds in the shallows and saw faintly the rippling circle of a duckbill. The creature gulped for air and disappeared in a muddied cloud of its own making, the ripples pulsing to the river's edge.

'Strangest thing,' said Redenbach.

'You seen one, head to tail?' said Sparrow.

'I seen one dead on a hook.'

The shaded sand was wet with dew. Redenbach stood and brushed off his arse and turned about and scanned the timbered escarpment, his eyes searching for the mouth of a cave sufficient to shelter them warm and dry.

They heard the savage shouts before they saw a soul, voices from somewhere, the sound ringing about the gorge. 'Look alert,' said Peskett. He took swiftly to priming his musket. Sparrow set his haversack on the sand. He seized Amicus by the collar, drew him close.

At the far end of the reach a tall young savage stood motionless, near naked, spears in hand, his words entirely foreign to them.

'That's Caleb jabberin' at us,' said Redenbach.

Peskett ceased his preparation and stared. 'It ain't us he's jabberin' at.' He snapped the frizzen into place and cocked the hammer.

'He's Hardwick's foundling,' said Redenbach.

'Not out here he's not,' said Peskett.

Sparrow saw a glint of hope notwithstanding he knew hope could sometimes prolong a man's torments. 'He says grace at the table, Dr Woody's table. He's beholdable.'

'*What!*' said Peskett.

'He knows about goodwill,' said Sparrow.

'We can talk to him,' said Redenbach.

'You talk to him,' said Peskett.

Sparrow was wondering why Caleb was just standing there, still as a pond. He recalled what Griffin Pinney had said about old Wolgan's mob: *Trade fair, them savages are true to their word.* He also said Caleb was *honourable*; said he was *a formidable interlocutor.*

He saw Peskett's small axe in the sand. He pondered the abrupt silence. He pondered that word, goodwill. He wondered if there was much of it about. The creature sounds had ceased, a singular peace, the faint gurgle of the cascade upstream, naught but the sound of the river, the endless flow, ever to the sea.

'He's just standin' there,' said Peskett.

'He's givin' me the gallops,' said Redenbach.

They did not see the spear that flew, hurled from the dense cover on the scarp above. Sparrow and Peskett heard the hiss and thud. They saw Redenbach sink to his knees, the spear planted obliquely at the juncture of the soldier's neck and shoulder. The tip sliced through to the flesh of his breast.

Somewhere above them they heard a fierce howl. Redenbach looked up. He could not speak. He raised a hand to the shaft of the spear, still quivering, and took hold of it. Then he fell forward, his face in the sand.

Peskett trained the gun on the scrub at the top of the scarp but he saw no foe. He saw Caleb closing on him, slowly, that familiar limp. He took aim at Caleb and fired. The musket exploded. A piece of the stock sliced off the sergeant's thumb and shrapnel tore into the palm of his hand.

He dropped the gun. He went down on one knee, clutching at the wounds.

Sparrow rose up, nimble as one of them. He took up Peskett's small axe and stepped up to the bloodied sergeant and, two-handed, he brought the axe down on the back of his head, the blade cleaving the skull in two. His one thought: *I'll trust to the goodwill.*

Peskett crumpled to the ground and rolled, the heavens mirrored in his eyes. His false teeth dislodged and caught on his lower lip, the metal band half in his mouth and half out. Sparrow knelt beside him, close to his work. 'You will never have my Amicus,' he said. But it was too late for words, for Peskett was stone dead and his soul winged away to the mansions of light where judgement awaited.

Sparrow was shaking. He felt faint, felt the tremor in his hand as he held tight to the axe. Atop the scarp he saw the shadowed form of the savage in the grey frockcoat, the one they called Napoleon, and on the sand he saw Caleb coming his way.

Sparrow did not know whether to hold on to the axe or to drop it. In that regard he was in a quandary. He called the dog. 'Down,' he said and the dog obeyed, but he could not stay down. He rose up and stood, watchful.

As to the axe, Sparrow decided to offer the weapon to Caleb, helve first, and to offer up Redenbach's axe as well. He wondered what else he might give in lieu of Amicus Amico.

As Caleb approached the bloodied sands, Sparrow sensed Napoleon behind him.

The warriors moved about, scouting the scene, talking to one another as if Sparrow was not there. Sparrow offered up the axe and

Caleb took the axe and there was a brief exchange in that strange tongue, after which the grey coat bent low over Peskett, pushed and poked at the sergeant's false teeth and finally took them from his mouth.

He held them in the palm of his hand, studied them, turned them over, examined the tiny rivets that joined metal to bone, showed them to Caleb, and then he pocketed the strange booty in his coat.

Caleb squatted down in front of Amicus Amico. He prodded the tip of a barbed spear into the animal's brisket and the dog bristled and snarled and edged away, his flanks heaving in time with his quickened breath.

'You can have all their stuff, if you want,' said Sparrow. He did not know what he would do if they stole Amicus. 'I hear the doctor fixed your wound, I truly hope the discomfort is long gone.'

'It is gone.'

'I hear you got to say grace, at the doctor's table, that too.'

'You are the yellowy man.'

'Yes, more's the pity. My jaundice takes a toll in the misery department. It can lay me awful low.'

In the corner of his eye, Sparrow spied Napoleon helping himself to Redenbach's axe. 'Guess you got a hidey-hole somewhere, full o' axes,' he said. He was hoping Caleb might smile at his little joke, but Caleb did not smile.

'Do you wish to meet with Mr Craggs?' he said.

Sparrow was briefly lost for words. 'He's here . . . Mort?'

'Here,' said Caleb. He waved his arm in a lazy arc across the northward scene.

'I would most assuredly like to meet with him, yes.'

Sparrow was not certain that he was most assuredly of this persuasion. He was, on the other hand, most assuredly certain he could not decline to see Mort, not under the circumstances. Mort could help in various ways. If Mort was fraternising with the savages he might put in a word for Amicus Amico, should a word be required. Sparrow could hardly believe the turn in his fortunes. He was free of Reuben Peskett, and Redenbach, and good riddance.

And soon he would see Mort again and Mort, at least, was a white man to whom he could recite his most urgent needs.

55

They heard the first shot somewhere ahead and next day they heard a second shot, which confirmed, as had the first, that Peskett and company were following the line of the river as expected. They slogged on, Cuff and Sprodd and the girl, the going more difficult as the river narrowed and the country about them cut more steep and inhospitable by the mile.

The terrain went hardest on Sprodd, who frequently had to rest his cramping legs. On one of these occasions they took their rest by the pillar of stone where Cuff had formerly seen Moowut'tin snare the eagle. There was not a breath of wind and a faint, feather-touch rain was falling upon them. Cuff chose to say nothing of the mastery he and Mackie had witnessed that day, and they moved on.

They rounded a sharp turn in the river and made for a thumbnail of sand further along the reach where, once again, they might rest.

Midway there they heard a babble and thought fearfully of the savages but, as they neared the beach, they could make out a word here and there, a familiar tongue. Then the tongue fell silent and they halted, the current curling on their shins as they listened for more.

They moved slowly upriver, single file, Cuff in the lead, his musket primed.

They passed beneath a sandstone shelf fringed with rotting logs and frigid, copper coloured pools in the scalloped recessions in the stone, the fry darting for cover. Cuff raised his hand and they paused once more. Not a sound, save the murmur of the waters. Then they heard the voice again, from atop the shelf. 'Oh thy kindly breasts . . . oh Mrs Wise, let me rest my head.'

They were, all three, plainly astonished at the clarity of both diction and meaning in this otherwise alien place.

'That's no savage,' said Sprodd.

'Thank you, Dan,' said Cuff.

'That's the north-west,' said Sprodd.

'That's Manchester,' said Cuff.

'That's Mr Catley,' said Bea Faa.

Cuff considered the prospect. He recalled, immediately, the gossip at the ridge upon the estrangement of Catley and the widow Wise. The rumour was that Catley was most distressed, having been turned away for making of her a mere convenience between his sorties into the fastness. The widow's charge could hardly be denied.

He recalled, too, a certain amount of supplementary information supplied to him by none other than Betty Pepper. That was some time ago, when Thelma Rowntree was still there, before Griffin Pinney whisked her away. Catley had turned to Thelma for comfort, thinking her a most ample substitute for Mrs Wise. He came to her night after night, dipped his wick and then visited all his sadness upon her, and sometimes he paid for an extra session, just talk. And then he was gone, restored, set for yet another heroic assault on the wilderness, in the name of science, England, the empire, the Royal Society, and Sir Joseph Banks.

The voice from atop the rock shelving was now somewhat more feeble. 'Fool that I am . . .'

'That's Catley alright,' said Cuff as he picked his way up the slope at the near end of the shelf.

On the shelf, he saw a hollow at the base of the sandstone scarp. Catley's haversack was there and his prone boots were plainly visible and they were plainly inhabited by Catley's feet, for they were moving in a most agitated fashion. Then they ceased to move, whereupon their owner withdrew them, very slowly, into the darkness of the hollow.

Cuff squatted down, steadying himself with the stock of the musket planted upon the stone and a firm grip on the barrel. 'Good day to you sir,' he said. He could hardly make out the upper half of Mr Catley until the specimen hunter raised himself and the light, such as it was, played upon his features.

Catley stared at Cuff and a look of immense disappointment set upon his countenance. 'I was hoping you might be Mrs Wise,' he said, his voice a mere whisper.

'No no, she ain't here. Now what's the matter Mr Catley, what ails you?'

'You must *never ever* take a good woman for granted.'

'Don't I know it. What ails you Mr Catley?'

Catley continued to stare. 'I have hardly the sense God gave a chicken and a dead arm to prove my own miserable adjudication on the matter.'

Cuff worried that the man may have sunk into lunacy. 'A dead arm you say?'

'Yes sir, a dead arm, much disfigured, poisoned and paralysed.'

'You best come out of there. You know me sir, Cuff, I am with the constabulary, with Mr Mackie.' Catley did not answer for some time. He was pondering Cuff's introduction.

'A most severe fellow, your principal,' he said at last. He could see Cuff and the anonymous boots of another man. For a moment he forgot the information he had just acquired. He felt somewhat fearful, friendless, cast into the hands of unknown strangers. 'I doubt I can move, overwhelmed as I am with regret.'

Cuff thought it might be helpful if he were to respond on the subject of regret. 'It's a torment I know, several fine women having quite sensibly dispensed with me over the years . . . reckoned I was a hard dog to keep on the porch.'

Catley made no reply.

Cuff could see the sleeve torn away on the botanist's left arm, the forearm much swollen, the hairs thick upon the fevered red of Catley's flesh. He beckoned Bea Faa and the girl squatted on her haunches. 'Hello Mr Catley,' she said. 'I do most vividly recall your kindness to myself and Mr Sparrow.'

Catley lit up. The awful sadness visited upon him by the hallucinatory form of those kindly breasts deserted him entirely. He felt a rush of blood, a pulse of exhilaration throughout the entirety of his sentient being, except for his left arm which was numb as a plank.

He inched out of the hollow with the bad arm in his lap. He sat up, squinting, shielding his eyes from the light. He was entirely pre-occupied by the presence of the girl. 'Good women brook no misuse, *per definitionem,*' he said.

'Yes,' said Bea, figuring the Latin was mere repetition.

'You agree?' said Catley, beads of sweat on his forehead.

'I do, yes,' she said.

'I felt from the first we were . . . in tune, you and I.'

'Mr Sparrow and I were most grateful for your kindness.'

'Ah yes, Mr Sparrow, and that dog,' said Catley. 'How fares the dog?'

'The dog is well and Mr Sparrow too.'

'He surprised me, Sparrow,' said Catley, his eyes wandering from Cuff to Sprodd and back to Bea.

'He did?'

'You wouldn't think he'd kill a fly, let alone Griffin Pinney.'

Cuff on his haunches almost fell backwards, such was his surprise. 'Sparrow killed Griffin Pinney?' he said, looking to Bea.

Bea saw no point in denial, not now. 'Yes,' she said.

'I don't believe it,' said Sprodd.

'He rescued me, from that vile man.'

'He did?'

'Pinney took me for his pleasure in the most peculiar circumstance, and Martin split his skull with the small axe.'

Cuff could not repress a chuckle. 'Marty Sparrow brained Griffin Pinney in the act?'

'Yes.'

'Well, that villain got his climax, I'll say that much,' said Cuff, his hat in his hand, two fingers scratching at the back of his head. He brought a sharp halt to his chuckling for he realised it might be indelicate in the presence of the girl.

'Lord,' said Sprodd.

'*In flagrante delicto*, a most honourable intervention,' said Catley.

'I have clearly underestimated Mr Sparrow's capacities and perhaps too his ambition,' said Cuff. He had concluded, quietly, that naught but the allure of Bea Faa could prompt a midge like Sparrow to interpose himself in such a manner.

'Yes,' said Catley. 'The horror of that bull shark, the loss of the boy and so on, I am most sympathetic to the poor man's travails.'

Cuff studied the pitted sandstone between his boots. He cast a glance in the direction of Bea Faa. 'A bull shark killed that boy?' he said.

'I've not surrendered a confidence, have I?' said Catley.

'I was not there,' said Bea.

'But your understanding . . .?' asked Cuff.

'I believe the bull shark story is true.'

'And this cave upriver, this cave's a lie?'

'A good lie,' said Sprodd. 'Got Sparrow off the hook.'

'I believe it did,' said Bea.

Cuff scratched some more at the back of his head and then he rested his chin in the palm of his hand, his fingertips drumming on his cheek. 'Droves of us up the creek on a wild-goose chase,' he said.

Fish were jumping in the quiet flow behind them, dragonflies darting about. Sprodd looked over his shoulder. 'Them perch just beggin',' he said.

A water dragon topped the rock shelf and stood stock-still, watching them, his little legs speckled in white, his head and shoulders dressed in streaks of black and splashes of yellow as if for a carnival or a masked ball.

'Dear me, better the foot slip than the tongue, ever my conviction, yet look what I've done,' said Catley.

He was upset, not so much at the slip as the possibility that he may have alienated Bea Faa. Even in extremis he found his mind, of its own accord, contemplating how a specimen collector in the wilderness, a man of advanced ripeness, might win the heart of a comely girl from Yetholm.

'No harm done,' said Bea, but she was not sure that was true. She felt sorry for the man. He'd been nothing but good to her, and to Sparrow, whose dog he had named, in Latin. He had saved them, quite possibly, from an awful death in the stone country to the west. His reverie combined with delirium no doubt fogged his mind and ushered out the secrets he had so solemnly agreed to keep.

Cuff had cupped Catley's inflamed forearm in the palm of his hand and he was ever so gently pressing on the swollen flesh with the tips of his fingers. 'Am I hurting you sir?'

'I have a stabbing pain, though nothing like the first few hours when I hopped and danced and rolled about in paroxysms of agony.'

'The arm still pains you?'

'It is for the most part numb and useless which I much prefer to the torments of the initial phase.'

'A snake?'

'Nooo, the duckbill.'

'The duckbill?' Cuff was surprised. The little fellows looked so frolicsome and harmless on the rare occasions he had seen one in its natural habitation.

'I located myself as advised by Moowut'tin. I watched and waited and that very afternoon a duckbill surfaced and I hurled my net and the creature in its panic flipped and tipped and spun itself into a complete besetment.'

'You got one, alive?' said Bea.

'I was sure at that point of said duckbill's affiliation with a certain burrow close by. I hauled in my catch and set about releasing those little paddly feet from the netting, but I got stung, small spur on the hind legs. I had no idea of the ruinous venom they carry.'

'Stung by the duckbill!' said Cuff.

'I have been an invalid the days hence, how many days I cannot say. I can report the most terrible stabbing pains, a heat in the arm like fire, swelling and disfigurement as you can see and my rational faculties periodically succumbing to a delirium and thereafter the retrieval of some clarity, as I do hope I am exhibiting, now.'

Cuff turned to Sprodd. 'There's every chance they've walked right by, right under this shelf.'

'Who?' said Catley.

'The military, with your Mr Sparrow in tow.'

'And the young dog!'

'Him too.'

'And me, dead to the world.'

'Yes.'

'The river's a veritable boulevard,' said Catley. 'I'm sorry I missed Mr Sparrow, I did take a shine to that pup.'

'It ain't a *cul-de-sac*, I know that much,' said Sprodd.

'My mule's gone too, I fear now he's meat to the savages,' said Catley.

'That's a shame if you've lost your mule,' said Cuff.

The girl set about making a fire on the rock shelf and Sprodd made a fishing rod from an infant sapling. He took a hook and a horsehair line from his pouch and went in search of grubs for bait.

'Moowut'tin tells me there's heavy rain over the headwaters,' said Catley.

Cuff sniffed the air. 'Well, he'd know I reckon,' he said.

That evening, deep in the gorge, they dined on perch. Catley ate ferociously, spitting the bones into his lap, and then he caught his breath and ate some more. He drank his fill and fell back on the shelf with a heavy sigh that may have signalled a revisitation of the regret he'd felt throughout the day. He dozed, restless. He was periodically given to bursts of rambling patter though nothing further was uttered on the subject of the widow Wise. They helped him back to the hollow and put a blanket on him and adjusted various items in his haversack and made a pillow of their work.

They sat about the fire. They spoke softly, hoping not to disturb the invalid. 'Where's that Daniel when the man needs him, what kind o' man Friday we got here?' said Sprodd.

'I imagine his primary loyalty rests elsewhere,' said Cuff.

'You know him?' said Bea.

Cuff pondered whether or not to tell the eagle story. It was cold now. The cold seemed to drop into the canyon with the heaviness of solid matter. He was intent upon catching some sleep. He untied his bundle and rolled out his blanket. He thought he might crawl in next to Catley, keep the frost off. 'I know him, I've seen him at work,' he said.

Part 12

Mortimer Craggs

56

At the far end of the reach the river was flanked by masses of stone, boulders of monumental proportions, some of them big as a byre.

Mort Craggs was seated, cross-legged, on one such boulder, hands upon his knees. Like a potentate awaiting emissaries, a man of considerable mass with a crop of black curls upon his head and upon his shoulders a mantle of layered pelts and upon his feet a pair of pelt moccasins that looked like dirty rags.

'Had I known you had the mettle, I might have took you instead of Shug,' said Mort, talking like some queer monument come alive in a dream. 'I did not believe you had the mettle Marty, I took you for a biddable cog fixed in the wheels of despotism. I see now my error in that regard.'

'They hung Shug,' said Sparrow, from below. He could see the stumps of Mort's cropped ears, the ridging of proud flesh.

There was a pistol holstered on Mort's hip. 'I wondered if they'd found him,' he said.

'Well they did.'

'Handsome dog.'

'His name is Amicus Amico. He's my dog.'

Mort smiled, cast a glance in the direction of Caleb and Napoleon. 'I don't want your dog, but I cannot speak for my sable friends.'

Caleb and Napoleon had gathered eggs of some description. They were sat in the shade, cracking the eggs and gulping down the contents one after another. Amicus was at their feet, busily licking out the eggshells.

Sparrow called the dog away. 'They got two axes, that's enough,' he said.

'And you got a dog with a peculiar name.'

'It means friend to a friend.'

'That's nice.'

Mort dragged his arse along the top of the tumbledown stone and half disappeared as he made his way down a flight of lesser stone onto the sand and there he stood as if alone, entirely alone, and he studied the golden shallows just inches from his feet, the waters rippling over the corrugated sands, a big, gutted bass in his fist. He tossed the fish onto the sand.

Napoleon had retrieved Peskett's false teeth from his pocket. He and Caleb studied the teeth and then Caleb surrendered them to Mort who took custody of the trophy with some evident pleasure. 'What a bonny day it is, for now,' he said. He saw Sparrow watching. 'Reuben Peskett nailed my ears to the pillory, Marty, as directed by that pig magistrate Abbott, that great gawking tub o' lard.'

'I know,' said Sparrow. He recalled, most vividly, the event in question, the punishment for Mort's heinous behaviour, to wit, the ravishing of a woman in a manner too shocking to relate.

'Next day he cropped 'em, severely. Beyond the lawful limits,' said Mort.

'He did, yes,' said Sparrow.

'I still suffer in my mind the torments and the humiliation of that occasion, but I am avenged,' said Mort, joggling the false teeth in his hand.

'You are?'

'I am now. They skewer 'em, did they, good and proper?'

'Yes.' Sparrow chose, at that moment in time, to venture no further into the particulars.

'Then here I am, at rest in this place, this . . . exquisite fastness.' He pocketed the teeth. He picked up his catch, bent low and washed off the sand.

'Exquisite?'

'It is your salvation and mine, Marty. Don't you forget that if you plan to be free.'

'I do, I plan to be free.'

'You couldn't plan a fit in a madhouse.'

'I plan to be free, I know that much.'

'Remind me, what's that dog's name?'

'Amicus Amico.'

'Alright.'

'What of the village?'

'What village?'

'The village embosomed at the foot of the mountains, on the other side?'

'I don't care for such a village.'

Sparrow was surprised to hear this. 'Griffin said —'

'Griffin! Griffin will tell you what you want to hear to get what he wants to have, lure you into his lair. What he want this time?'

'He wanted his copper worm but that was locked in the gaol, and he wanted a dog to trade, with them,' said Sparrow, gesturing in the direction of Caleb and Napoleon.

Mort cocked his head to one side and caressed what was left of his earlobe twixt thumb and forefinger. 'Griffin's old dog was a ruin, that much I know. I would surmise he wanted that young dog o' yours for himself. I'm surprised you still got him. I'm surprised you're still in one piece. That Griffin plays a wicked game.'

'There's no village, no river of the first magnitude?'

'Marty, there's just mountains, and here we are. I have my own firm conviction based on my own considerable cogitations as to what is beyond.'

'What then?'

'Would you like a cup of tea?'

'Real tea?'

'Bush tea.'

'Oh yes, any tea.'

'In that case we better go and make some tea.'

Mort led the way through the timber to a foot track that ran almost the length of the reach before it met with a gully, deep in shade. They paused there as Mort and Caleb surveyed the river upstream, the sun long gone, the colours fading from the rim rock, the sands calving into the shallows, their form undone by the quickening flow.

'That's the storm in the west,' said Mort.

'It is?'

'Let's us hasten to that cup o' tea.'

They took to the gully, the savages tailing Sparrow and the dog.

Mort seemed to know his apish waddle was under some scrutiny from behind. 'Knees are gone, bone on bone, gait like an old dog,' he said as he shuffled up the gully to a clearing in a copse of cabbage trees and coachwoods, a campsite cosseted and cool. Further up where the creek disappeared in thick scrub there was a cave and at the mouth of the cave a coil of rope, a grappling hook and a blanket tossed across a yielding bough.

Caleb set the fire and Mort threw the fish onto the flames and they sat about, the four of them, peeling the cooked flesh off the bones, morsels, Amicus poised for the leavings.

When they finished, Caleb spat out a piece of gristle, wiped his lips and addressed Sparrow directly. 'We savages dwell here, cast out from the sight of God.'

'Who says that?' said Sparrow.

'That ol' bugger Hardwick.'

'I don't think that's hardly right, or fair.'

'He says my people are lost to the sun of God's warmth.'

'That's not right.'

'Sunk in the ways of ignorance and filth.'

'Nooooo.'

'Doomed to the misery of Hell, eternal fire.'

'I'd say that's not very Christian to say that.'

'Do you love us, then, as Jesus says you must love us?'

'I do, yes, I love you as a brother.' That was a lie.

'A brother?'

'Yes, a brother.'

'Your love for us is deep then, deeper than the love of women?'

'I s'pose, yes.'

Mort was chuckling, watching the exchange. 'They don't reckon we're the Christians, Marty,' he said.

'No?'

'Course not. We're the Romans. We march in, seize the land, crucify them, string 'em up in trees, mutilate their parts. Pickin' the Romans ain't difficult.'

'I ain't no Roman,' said Sparrow.

'Well, that's good to know, 'cause if you was a Roman we'd have to get one o' them long spears and stick it in yer gizzard,' said Mort, still chuckling.

'Who's the Christians then?'

Mort chuckled yet again. 'That's hard to know.'

———

The fire was naught but wisps of smoke. Mort took a long stick and poked about in the live coals, pushing them together. He threw some dry twigs on the coals and they phoomphed into flame. He took a water bladder and topped up the quart pot for the tea and set it on the fire, cocked his head to one side. 'Can you hear it?'

'What?'

'Rain, west o' here.'

Sparrow listened hard, but all he could hear was the crackle of the fire. He licked his greasy fingers. His mind cast back to the poultry-bone leavings on the greasy plates at Peachey's Tap, those final days on his patch, his miserable time at Bet Pepper's, the toing and froing, Hat Thistlewaite's awful smile. The rectal pear. 'They hung Shug with the pony's head strung on his neck,' he said.

Mort paused, took in the news. 'That pony was useless. Mule's what you need, that or an awful big goat.'

They sat in silence until Mort felt the urge to say one more thing on the matter of Shug: 'I hope he died brave; hope he cursed 'em all to rot in hell.'

When the water boiled, Mort took the pot off the flame. He took hold of his haversack and set it between his feet and searched the innards and from the haversack he withdrew a teapot and he set this most unlikely amenity on the fire stones. He grinned at Sparrow. The dark was setting in as he took Peskett's false teeth from his pocket and placed them, ceremonially, on the hot stones beside the teapot. 'Special occasion.'

He removed the tin lid and dropped his tea leaves into the pot, and he set a tin mug on the other side of the ox-bone teeth on the metal rim. 'Why don't you be mother,' he said.

Sparrow watched as Caleb and Napoleon departed in the direction of the river. 'They're going,' he said.

'Theirs is a sylvan liberty. Who am I to bid them stay?' He stood and stretched.

'Did you trade, pay a tithe?'

Mort had to think. 'I gave them Gordy's girl, when I was done with her.'

'Where is she now?'

'I suppose she's where they put her.' There was a small axe and a wad of sackcloth rag by the fire stones and Sparrow wrapped the sackcloth around his hand and he felt the steam on his fingers as he took the quart pot by the handle and poured the hot water into the teapot.

He was relieved the savages were gone. He was puzzled too. Mort seemed awfully settled, here on the Branch. 'Is there no village?' he said.

Mort plonked down on a length of old log by the campfire, his legs spread wide and his frame bent over like he might vomit, but he didn't. He was thinking deeply. He was weighing the question of whether or not to extend to Marty Sparrow the benefit of his considerable cogitations on the matter of the village beyond the mountains.

After a while he spoke. 'I too had this unquenchable desire for deliverance in the far beyond.'

'You did?'

'It was not my conviction that wavered, but my knees. For a time I cursed them, my knees, but then I woke to my true situation, to a life of plenty on the far flung Branch, and I was reconciled.'

'You don't know?'

'Oh I know alright.'

'Tell me then.'

'Marty, I cannot just tell you, not in a word. There's no simple answer here, there is only a line of reasoning through which we must navigate according to reason's compass in order to arrive at the truth, y'foller me?'

'Yes,' said Sparrow, for he was, indeed, ready to follow Mort's line of reasoning as best he could, most particularly if it led to the truth.

57

Cuff led the way onto a stretch of sand that banked steep at the far end of the reach, where the canyon narrowed and the waters hurried down rapids feeding into the long, stirring stretch of river. He watched a wading bird stalking in the shallows. Then he saw the bodies of Peskett and Redenbach, the far-shadowing spear stuck hard in Redenbach's frame.

Crows took flight, fled the remains of the dead soldiers.

'My Lord,' said Sprodd.

Bea Faa went to Redenbach. She pulled hard at the spear but it would not come free. She put her boot down hard on the dead man's shoulder and heaved on the shaft and the spear came away, barbs and all, and she threw it aside. Cuff looked on, as did Sprodd. She rolled the corpse with deceptive ease, saw that wound, the bayonet wound, in the man's chin.

'He's deader'n a dead dog's bone,' said Sprodd.

'And I will see him dead, face up,' she said.

Cuff was standing over Peskett. 'I'd say Reuben never knew what hit him.'

'They're awful good at sneakin' up on us, the very thought gives me the drizzles,' said Sprodd. He was staring down at Peskett. 'Them false teeth are gone,' he said, 'might be he swallowed 'em.'

Cuff studied the soldiers' wounds and he studied their boots and then he set to scrutinising the footprints of two adult savages and the smaller boot prints that he took to be Sparrow and everywhere the imprints of the young game dog's paws.

He could make no sense of the signs. What had happened to Sparrow was a mystery. He could imagine the savages taking the dog but he could not imagine them wanting Sparrow for company, not them not anyone.

'If they wanted Sparrow dead he'd be dead, right here,' he said.

He bent low and studied the wrecked musket, and the bull ants busy on Peskett's ruined hand.

They moved away from the dead soldiers and kept moving, aiming for a thicket of she-oaks that fringed the rapids at the far end of the reach. They sat for a while, watched the river swell, the headwaters flushing out. 'Lucky Redenbach was dead,' said Cuff. 'Someone I know might've finished him off.'

'The faintest flicker, I would snuff it out,' said Bea.

'I believe you would.' Cuff had no objection to the girl's resolute intent. He admired her for the loyalty of her attachments and the strength of her conviction. He now knew enough about Bea Faa to know she'd suffered much and her one chance, much deserved, had slipped away with the death of Joe. As to the warrant, that meant she was not safe on Joe's patch, not now, for sooner or later the word would carry upriver to the garrison at Prominence and the soldiers would come and snatch her away. The one thing that Cuff thought certain – there was no going back for Bea Faa.

Cuff wondered if, perchance, Mr Catley might take her. Even in his addled moments back on the rock shelf it was hard not to notice Catley's eyes feasting on the girl, but she did not reciprocate in any way. She gave no sign of an interest in the specimen collector. The only option for companionship seemed to be Marty Sparrow who, like Bea, had good reason never to go back lest they hang him for the death of Jug Woody or the scuttling of Jug's boat, or both. Cuff was certain he now knew the true story regarding the fate of poor Jug, but a full panel of magistrates would in all likelihood find the bull shark story all too convenient, the work of a midge, a loafer and a slippery deceiver.

Cuff no longer thought of Marty Sparrow in that way, for he had killed Griffin Pinney with an axe and he'd done this deed in defence of Bea Faa who was, by any measure, under siege at the time. He had done a noble thing, even if he'd done it when the advantage was entirely his own, that is to say, when Griffin had his britches down and his member all aquiver. For Cuff this piece of intelligence meant that Sparrow just might be the companion that Bea Faa required if she was to make for the other side. 'What say we set after Mr Sparrow, see if we can find him?' he said.

'Martin and the dog, yes,' she said.

Bea was also pondering her situation. Her options were now somewhat limited. She had warmed to Martin Sparrow and to his dog long before the killing of Griffin Pinney. She reckoned Sparrow would be a loyal friend if ever they could find him. Sparrow was perhaps the only man in the world who might be her friend and not trouble her with doings she much preferred to avoid. The only man who would be loyal, like the dog, and hopefully extend to her a dispensation in the matter of her affections, and were he to be selfless and sacrificial in that way then she might consider a modest rationing in his favour, now and then.

The westering sun had departed the gorge and the last of its colours faded from the forest and the cliff top far above, the coming night turning their minds to shelter.

They hurried forth, scrambling over talus and driftwood on the fringe of the rapids and they followed the quickening river, taking the turn onto the next reach. Way above they could see in dark relief a ponderous forehead of stone, what appeared to be a cave.

Cuff led the way. They scrambled up a slope, skirting the rubble, the rotting timber, angling ever upwards for the overhang that would surely give them shelter for the night.

They were much slowed by the poor light, stepping carefully as they went higher, finally scrambling onto the lip of the cave.

What they found was a spacious accommodation, a sandy floor, bone dry, the remnants of a cookfire, some dry wood, a gathering of shredded bark and here and there the parched white coils of animal droppings.

Cuff set the Kunkle musket against the decorated wall and he studied the painted images: fish, wallaby, man, woman; a shark, little fish inside; stencilled hands, the outlines milky white. He dropped his haversack and worked his fingers on an aching knee. Bea Faa turned her back on the cave and stared into the depths of the gorge and her eye followed it northward, to sandstone cliffs that rose sheer above a forest of ghostly white gums at the end of the reach.

Sprodd dropped down and made a pillow of his haversack, readying for the night. 'Sleep dry, the gilt on the gingerbread I reckon,' he said. They checked themselves for leeches and ticks, searched the nooks and crannies. They scratched for a bit, their lower parts. They rested a while, hardly a word. They shared some dry rations. They talked briefly, and they slept.

58

Mort sat up straight, cleared his throat. He pressed his palms into the log and took his weight on his arms and shifted his arse about, searching for comfortable repose. 'First point,' he said. 'The government back there, they know nothing of the woods; nor of what lies beyond. They tell us nothing but a bird would ever get across. They say the very notion of a village on the other side is absurd, but let me tell you: this vested counsel has no foundation in practical knowledge, or common sense.'

Sparrow had heard this speech before, or something like it, but he daren't interrupt. He thought best to listen quietly, sipping at his tea.

'They would have us succumb to their wicked deception, have us despair of all hope, the better to conform with their need of us. But we got no need o' them and we can be free if we wanna be free.'

Mort's reasoning took hold of Sparrow. He could see the good, straight, common sense of that reasoning with great clarity. 'It's like a dream come true,' he said. He was feeling uncommonly poetic while Mort was feeling pleasurably fluent.

'A dream indeed, Marty boy, for with the dream you seize control and once again the world is yours for the taking. You have to dream, y'foller me?'

'Yes.'

'That's good.'

The trill of the cicadas was ringing in their ears, the insects all about them, like some cruel, midget orchestra hidden in the under shrubbery.

'One thing more,' said Mort.

'What?'

'Old Wolgan, he says I'm his long-dead uncle, says I'm a ghost returned from the other side. Supposedly I bear a striking resemblance to the man, a ghostly likeness, and I am in no way inclined to disabuse this tenacious remnant of their outlandish notions.'

'I imagine a family connection might be quite helpful.'

'It don't hurt.'

Sparrow thought hard on the connection. 'That makes you a great uncle to Caleb.'

'I suppose it does,' said Mort. 'In a spooky sort o' way.'

Sparrow wondered if Mort knew about the murdered blacks, strung up, mutilated and riddled with shot. He thought perhaps he should tell Mort, in case Mort didn't know. 'The soldiers chased down three of them, and killed them,' he said.

'How do you know that?'

'We seen them on the way. Reuben Peskett was most pleased to revisit his work.'

Mort stared straight ahead. Sparrow could see the bafflement upon his countenance. 'Did Caleb not say?'

'They keep a most cautious counsel. I hardly blame them for that.' Mort was poking the fire somewhat vigorously with his long stick.

'Don't he trust you?'

'Oh he trusts me alright, he seen me in the pillory. He knows I ain't no Roman.'

'They hung them from a single bough, and shot them full of holes, and a woman they left dead on the ground, shot through.'

Mort blew on his tea and sipped at it cautiously. 'Got to let it draw a while, this bush brew.' He put a hand to his chest, scratched at his breastbone. He continued with his reasoning, as if the subject of murder had never been raised. 'Even a man of most modest comprehension, like myself, finds it impossible to conceive that a continent so large as this could be devoid of a river, a river of the first magnitude, like the Nile, where they found the baby Jesus in the bulrushes. A river that might upon discovery be navigated to its distant outfall on the far coast. Why, only a lunatic would deny such a likelihood.'

Mort put down his mug and set his palms upon the log once again, his arms rigid like spars. He arched his back. He spoke softly. 'My Caleb confirms precisely what Mr Flinders reported to the governor.'

'What's that?'

'A copper-coloured people.'

'I do recall you mentioned the copper-coloured people.'

'I did, yes. Their beginning in some intrepid Malay vessel that may have been lost, or foundered there, and the crew, finding themselves on a well-watered and fertile savannah, they established themselves there, see, in some harmony with the native inhabitants, making use of the women and so forth, and their issue the foundation of a new race. Thus a village, a vigorous new people, is not only likely but, I have to say, Marty, most probable.'

Sparrow had to ask. 'Why don't you go?'

'Because the search for happiness can be like the search for your spectacles when they're sittin' on your nose.'

Mort could see that Sparrow was slow to fathom his little homily. 'Why might I not go?' he said.

'Bad knees, bone on bone?'

'Well yes, but apart from that? Look about. I got fish, I got meat on the hoof, I got . . . edible greens, I got fruit, wild honey . . . I got medicine too, these woods full o' natural potions. Might help you, that buttery look you got, tells me you need a tonic.'

'I know.'

'It's a hard road Marty, the perils countless. Why would I risk that, whether good knees or bad knees? Why should you? You got your dog, you got me for company, what more you want?'

The question prompted Sparrow to think of Bea Faa but he would not mention Bea Faa to Mort Craggs, not ever. Mort had stolen Gordy's girl, he'd used her, and now it transpired he'd given her up to the savages. He was infamously hard on women. At The Dirty Sack back in Blackley, he'd kept a cane rod pickled in brine and Sparrow could recall several occasions when Mort had thrashed Misty with the rod all about her legs and buttocks, and another time when Misty told him, in confidence, she was going to fix Mort in his sleep, fix him good and proper, but she never did.

The only wise course was to keep the conversation well away from Bea. 'Is it truly a river of the first magnitude?' he said.

Mort was sniffing at his bush tea with his eyes closed, the steam curling about his nostrils. 'I've thought about that Marty.'

'You have?'

'Being of the first magnitude we can but assume this river possesses the usual sinuosities of all great rivers, thus its course cannot be less than two, three thousand miles, perhaps more, and the magnitude of such a flow at the confluence with the ocean so great the only possible host for such an outflow, as yet undiscovered, can be the north-west coast of which, as Mr Flinders himself concedes, we know so little. So, yes, that's where it is, the outflow.'

Mort beckoned Sparrow's dog, clicking his fingers, and Amicus came to him and sat by his knee.

He ran his hand along the dog's lithe frame, the shaggy coat gritty to the touch. 'They're the best friend a man has in this world, you know that.'

'*Amicus?*'

'Consider this: the world may turn against a man, his family may prove ungrateful, our nearest and dearest may betray us and don't I know it. Our reputation may be lost, we may fall foul of our creditors and our betters and find ourselves hounded, punished or outcast, and our friends drift away or spurn us even unto our faces. Yet there is one friend who will never desert us, never prove ungrateful, ever by our side.'

'Our dog?'

'*Our* dog, yes,' said Mort. 'When all is lost, when misfortune drives his master exiled into the world, friendless, homeless, he remains. *He* is steadfast; *he* is constant in his love, not like some woman. *He* is a perpetual balm to our miseries . . . We rise each day and each day he comes to us, as the sun in the east, as the light to our lives, loaded up with a warmth and a fealty that carries to our very heart, warms the very cockles, *ad infinitim.* I got a bit o' Latin too.'

Sparrow wished now that he hadn't said that word *our*. There was no *our* about the situation. He was not going to share Amicus Amico with anybody, least of all Mort Craggs, for to share his dog with Mort would be to give him up entirely.

Mort's attachment to Amicus was troubling. Now he was scratching the dog behind the ears and talking to him like he was a little child. 'You like it here, you want to stay with ol' Mort you can stay with ol' Mort.'

'We have to go, tomorrow,' said Sparrow. The words just tumbled out, caught his good sense napping.

Mort straightened up. 'You just got here,' he said. He pulled the dog close to him, working his fingers in the fur.

'I know.'

'I was thinking we might partner up, you and me.'

'Oh.'

'You never shopped me, Marty, I don't forget that.'

'Thank you.'

'You ever think about Misty?'

'Dancing?'

'No, dead in the dock.'

'I have to go back, help my friend . . . Joe.'

'Joe who?'

'Joe Franks.'

'Why's he need help?'

'He's sick.'

'I heard he was up to his ears in some dusky maiden's muff. I heard he bought her. I heard he shares her with that po-faced straightener Mackie.'

'Mackie helped Joe win the auction, that's all. He helped Joe buy her, instead of Griffin.'

'What's he want, huh? I'll tell you what he wants.' Mort summoned up some gob and spat into the flames. 'Anyway, Joe Franks is dead.'

Sparrow was silent, his thoughts tumbling about, trying to settle on what best to say, mystified as to how such intelligence might come to Mort.

'Cat got your tongue Marty?'

'No.'

'I think you goin' back for the cunny, I think you goin' back for that girl.'

'Nooo.'

'On that subject I can tell you something else.'

'What?'

'That girl's on the Branch. She's comin' up the river.'

'She is?'

'Hmmm. Caleb says she don't look happy I'll give her happy she goes sour on me.'

'I hope you won't do that.' Sparrow's mind was casting back to terrible moments in The Dirty Sack. The only wise course was to keep the conversation well away from Bea, but Mort would not be diverted from his instruction. 'You beat them not to hurt them but to correct them, otherwise there's no peace in the household, y'foller me?' Mort scratched at his chest yet again, looked up to the sky. 'Hard to believe rain's comin'.'

'It is?'

'I'm assured it is yes, storm in the west, comin' this way.'

Sparrow was not concerned about rain. He could not think why Bea was coming upriver unless she was looking for him, but he was not inclined to believe such good fortune would ever come his way. 'Why she comin'?'

'She ain't comin' alone. She's got them ancient constables with her, Cuff and Sprodd.'

'Why?'

'*What why who when* – I ain't the Delphic oracle why don't you go ask him?'

'I don't know him.'

'One thing more.'

'What?'

'Stop saying what and answer my question.'

'*What question?*'

'You lie to me again, Marty, I'll crack your skull and tan a hide with your brains. Now: why you in such a hurry?'

Sparrow knew he had to come up with something good, a good lie in place of a bad lie, lest he lose Mort's trust altogether, for if he did that, if he lost Mort's trust altogether he'd be in terrible trouble. 'I have to fix something, something terrible I did,' he said.

'Fix? Fix what?'

'I took, that is Peachey and me, we took Jug's little boat, Dr Woody's boy, and mid-stream he went in, the boy, he went in after

Amicus and a bull shark took him and what was left of him we sunk, tied to a stone in the middle of the river. It was the most terrible thing and I have to tell the doctor what happened.'

Mort began to laugh, more a chuckle at first but then he slapped his thigh and leaned back and laughed loud, smacking his hands together and stamping his feet. The dog shied away but Mort grabbed him and held him close. 'That's a hell of a story.'

'It's not a story – it's true.'

Mort settled. 'You would surrender yourself and confess all to the doctor, is that it?'

'Yes.'

'You tryin' to be honourable?'

'Yes.'

'Honourable get you pilloried, or hung.'

'It might.'

'I don't believe you're that honourable, Marty, I just don't believe it.' Once again Mort made that terrible, sucking sound and summoned up some gob and spat into the fire. The motion reminded Sparrow of Griffin Pinney looping a great gob into the mud on South Creek and saying something about a rat.

'I'm a better man than I was, I know that much.'

'Be that as it may, you go you go alone, I keep the game dog. You stay we can share him, you and me. I concede I'm no substitute for the cunny but I'll let you into a secret.'

'What's that?'

'Gordy's girl ain't beyond reach if we want her, you and me.' Mort had an awful smirk on his face. He winked at Sparrow.

Sparrow found that thought most distasteful. 'Alright,' he said. But that was a lie. It was not alright. It was not alright that Mort had designs on Amicus Amico. It was not alright that Mort would blackmail him into palling up. It was not alright that Gordy's girl was a captive somewhere in the woods, caught in the most terrible kind of peonage, a drudge and a slave to the passions of savages, one savage in particular, Mort Craggs, him who now seemed intent upon running his greedy eyes over Bea Faa. And it was not alright that Mort would crack his skull and tan a hide with his brains if ever he caught him telling another lie, whether big or small, who would know.

Sparrow cast a furtive glance at the small axe by the firestones. The small axe had a solid and serviceable look about it, a nicely finished helve, the head good and heavy, butt and blade.

That night, beneath a leaden sky, not a single star, Sparrow killed Mort Craggs with the small axe. His tried and true method was slightly modified as Mort was sleeping soundly on his back. Sparrow waited hours for Mort to roll over but Mort did not roll over. He lay there like he was pinioned to the earth, like he was staked out, snoring like an old hog. Sparrow waited and waited, finally concluding that Mort was not going to roll over. It took Sparrow some time to reconcile with the modification required. He would have to stand astride Mort and brain the man, head on, face to face.

He worried that Mort might open his eyes just in time to parry the blow. If that happened, Mort would surely tear him limb from limb or take to him with the axe the way he took to Gordy. The thought weakened Sparrow's resolve. But then he thought of the morrow should he do nothing, the morrow when Mort would surely seize Amicus for his own and perhaps summon up his sable friends and go hunting for Bea Faa.

The dog at that moment was curled up next to Sparrow, sound asleep. Everything Mort had said about dogs was true, the more fool him, trumpeting his opinion. Sparrow felt the resolve come back to his marrow. He put his hand upon Amicus as he raised himself up. He stroked the dog softly, short slow strokes in the neighbourhood of the kidneys. He picked up the axe and the sackcloth rag and straddled

Mort, and paused but not for long because he was awfully fearful Mort might open his eyes.

He put the blade square into Mort's forehead and split his face in two. The skull parted from the crown to the bridge of the nose and cracked into the socket of the left eye.

When the blade came away Sparrow nearly fell over, such was his giddiness in that moment. But he righted himself and held the pose, triumphant, sucking for air in fear he might faint. He felt Mort's hand take hold of his ankle, but there was no strength in that hand and it slipped into the waiting dust, the palm upturned, the fingers twitching.

Amicus was hurrying on the scent to the puddling blood on the downside of Mort's skull. Sparrow threw a blanket over the man's upper half, covering the skull entirely, and he shooed the dog away. 'Get away, go'n sit down,' he said, softly.

Sparrow wondered why he was whispering. He looked about. He feared Caleb might appear at any moment. Caleb had a knack of turning up when least expected, as savages do. If that happened that would be most unfortunate, especially if Mort really was old Wolgan's dead uncle, thus family to Caleb.

He wanted to flee, to get clear of his horrible enormity. He knew he did not have the wherewithal nor the fortitude to head west on his own. He felt himself obliged to pursue the one option that seemed to be available: work his way downriver and hope to find Bea Faa, though how he might extract her from the clutches of the two constables was, at that moment, beyond his reckoning.

Yet, he was able to reckon about some things. He sat himself down in the dirt, a comfortable distance from Mort's corpse. The constables might be coming upriver in pursuit of Redenbach, as Bea Faa would surely have told them about Joe's murder. So long as they stuck to the Branch they would find his body, and Peskett's body too, and they would surely conclude that the carnage on the river sands was the work of the savages, revenge for the killings near the ceremonial ground. And then perhaps – a further reckoning on Sparrow's part – then they would head back to Joe's and after that, with any luck, Cuff and Sprodd would depart for the ridge, leaving Bea to farm with Freddie for the foreseeable future, keeping in mind we can always hope for the future but we never know if there is one.

All of that Sparrow was able to reckon, remarkably, given his distressing situation. In his mind's eye, most pictorially, he could see the constables scratching around the bodies of Peskett and Redenbach, trying to make sense of the slaughter, Bea Faa seated in the shade of a big old rusty gum, watching on, not a word. Peskett, gap-toothed, the blank eyes skyward. The ruined hand. The skull split open from behind. Might she guess?

He imagined he might follow them, discreetly, back to Joe's farm and there secret himself in some obscure vantage like a sooty owl on a bough, patience personified, there to await the departure of the constables, their duty done, whereupon he would make his presence known to Bea and they would sit down at Joe's table and discuss their future over a meal of cooked meat, corn and peach cyder and whatever else might be at hand; perhaps some wheaten bread made from Mackie's flour. He marvelled at just how little his innards had troubled him on the Branch. The Branch might be a tonic in itself. There were sounds coming back to him. Now he could hear the river, flushing out of the headwaters to the west.

He was awfully tired.

59

Sparrow woke in the first light of the morning, the sky above the gully thick with shifting cloud, the roar of the river sounding in his ears. He sat up shivering and hitched the blanket around his shoulders and pulled it across his chest. He watched a magpie picking for grubs on the fringe of the camp. 'You don't care,' he said.

He poked up the fire, dressed the tiny flame with twigs and then moved to the far side of the campsite and he sat in the dirt with Amicus and stared at Mort's carcass, beneath the bloodied blanket. He was not hungry but he thought himself ready and able to drink some of Mort's brew. He topped up the dregs. He drained Mort's water bladder into the quart pot, perched the pot on the edge of the coals, the flames licking up the side. Amicus leaned over the fire stones and sniffed at the pot and backed away and sat himself and watched Sparrow with a most deliberate attention.

Sparrow rifled through Mort's haversack. He found a powder pouch and a handful of shot, a wrap of ship's biscuits and a pair of plain leather shoes with a flap and a buckle. They were threadbare and way too small for Mort and even too small for Sparrow.

He slung the powder pouch on his shoulder, with the costrel, and the biscuits he secured in his haversack.

A lone wood duck winged out of the west. He heard the call of a crow and somewhere nearby the song of a bellbird filled the air, like a dawn chime in the mansions of heaven.

He took the small axe and cleaned the head in the dirt and then he fixed the weapon to his belt. He lifted the blanket on the corpse, one last look, a good long look. The wilderness required the hardness to stomach such bloody doings. He took Mort's pistol from its holster and stuck the long muzzle in his belt but it felt most uncomfortable and he reckoned he might lose it, so he put the pistol in his haversack.

In a drawstring pouch in Mort's pocket he found tea leaves and a flint. He made some fresh tea and sat and drank. Then he emptied the teapot on the fire and he put the prize in the haversack. Sat there, Amicus close.

He considered the item a most important acquisition for it reminded him of Mr Catley's cave house, the old teapot on the window sill, all the comforts of a home signified therein. The teapot fired his hope, his dream of a cave house in a beautiful valley somewhere in the far beyond. If ever his hope flagged he would stop and make a cup of tea and think about the cave house he would have. The teapot would surely spur on the most perfect ambition he had ever known. *With the dream you seize control and once again the world is yours for the taking.* Mort said that, so Sparrow had to acknowledge that Mort was no fool. He was a bad man but he was no fool.

Sparrow flattened the fire with his boot and doused the stubborn flames with cold ash. He shouldered the haversack. Amicus Amico was at his heel, happy as a pig in slop, and Sparrow spoke to the dog and heard his own voice as if for the first time. 'Let's go find Bea,' he said.

He scanned the scene, one more time, and spied the rope and the grappling hook a short way up the gully, useful, might save a great deal of clambering in a fix.

Sparrow headed up the gully, fastened the rope and the hook to his haversack and once again shouldered his belongings. He was about to step away when he heard the sound, a faint whimper from the cave.

For a moment he could not move. His first thought was *run*. But he did not run and he hardly knew why, save that faint sound seized upon his heart. He listened some more, saw Amicus, ears cocked, stalking into the forecourt of the cave.

He slipped the haversack off his shoulder and set it down, softly. He moved closer and listened, heard the sound of a girl, whimpering. He knew now, in all likelihood, that Mort had told him another lie, for he had not dispensed with Gordy's girl, Dot, nor had he passed her off to the savages.

Sparrow wished he had not come up the gully, feeling himself to be, at that moment, awfully burdened. Where such a burden might lead he could not imagine. The worry put his guts in a churn, that churn not helped by the weather as a pall of grey cloud from the west filled the sky above.

The gully was sufficiently shaded and the cave sufficiently cavernous to resist all daylight beyond the forecourt. Sparrow edged in. He felt the cool, damp air on his skin. Leaning forward, he stared into the dark. He took another step. He smelt the rank odour of stale piss. He saw movement. 'It's alright,' he said.

She was sat in the grit, clothed in naught but a cotton shift and her legs drawn tight to her frame like a trussed fowl. There was a tin mug close to her knees. She had a fist closed tight on a crumpled blanket. She dragged herself away from him and the blanket with her.

He bent low, his hands on his knees. 'Mort's gone,' he said. Amicus was at his side.

Sparrow got down on his haunches and waited there, quietly, hoping the girl's fear might settle. He felt the butt end of the axe helve press into the dirt. His eyes were correcting for the dark. He could see her better now in the gloom, the sharp angles of her cheekbones narrowing to that tiny mouth and jaw, the straight hair cut short, it seemed, with some saw-toothed blunt old thing. 'Mort's gone, he cannot hurt you now,' he said.

60

First light was probing the cave when Cuff woke to the call of his bladder. He rose with some difficulty, the blood slow to get moving, his senses awry. He steadied himself, his own right hand upon the stenciled palm on the wall. He trod the sandy floor to the lip of the cave, saw thick grey cloud shifting over the gorge, the river below, forcing to the sea, thrashing at the banks and the fringing trees.

He followed a slender game track northward, watching the spectacle upriver, the spray like low cloud in a copse of ghostly white gums at the far end of the reach.

Cuff knew, as he slipped and fell, that he should have watched his footing instead of the wild waters on the bend.

He freefell some thirty feet and crashed arse first onto solid stone and from there tumbled onto the talus below, whereupon his helpless frame slid down a sharply angled declivity and clattered into the base of a coachwood tree and there came to rest on the leaf rot, sloughed in a heap, his body curled somewhat fetally around the trunk.

He tried to move his legs but the movement visited great pain on his lower back. 'Here I am.' He tried to raise himself but the pain was unbearable. He lay still, heaving for breath, blood dripping from a gash on his forehead.

When they found him they tried to move him, Bea and Sprodd, but he yelped with pain and told them no.

'We gotta get you up,' said Sprodd.

'Not yet,' said Cuff. He looked about. 'Would you kindly retrieve my hat,' he said to Sprodd.

They waited while Cuff examined his hat and then they set to roll him onto his back but the slightest movement was too much pain and they relented.

Sprodd poked about Cuff's parts until he found the centre of the pain, low down. 'That's your tailbone, you've broke your tailbone.'

'Of all the damn places to break my tailbone.'

'Only place I know is down there near your arse.'

The limits of Sprodd's comprehension never failed to entertain Cuff even in extremis. 'I mean here, in the damn wilderness.'

'One way or another you gotta walk out o' here.'

'If it's your tailbone it will mend,' said Bea.

'Can you walk?' said Sprodd.

'I got no choice.' Cuff pressed his lips together and clenched his teeth and smothered the mighty yelp that rose up from deep within as they got him upright, his legs like mush and his back in sharp spasm. 'Sweet Jesus,' he said, and he sucked for air for the air seemed thin and poor and he could not get enough of it.

They flanked him and he put his arms about them and they took his weight on their shoulders and held him there.

'You're up, that's good,' said Sprodd.

'Cut me a stick.'

'Alright.'

The stick was more a staff, taller than Cuff, and there was a knobble about shoulder height that permitted the invalid to get a purchase whether with one hand or two.

Cuff took the staff in two hands, his grip firm on the knobble, and Bea Faa moved away and watched as he shuffled forward, just a few steps, the pain etched on his face. He glanced in the direction of the cave, his possessions up there, haversack, blanket, Thyne Kunkle's Swedish musket. 'I doubt I can walk out o' here,' he said.

'You got to, Thaddeus, you must.'

Cuff chuckled. 'I been dodgin' the musts all my life and look now.'

'Well, this must is the must of all musts and there's no dodgin' it.'

'I gotta sit down, take the weight off.'

They helped Cuff sit, taking some of the weight as he lowered himself ever so gingerly. He was puffing like he'd run a mile. Dan and Bea sat, flanking the invalid, watching the wild river. 'You won't see that in town,' said Sprodd.

A blanket of black cloud shifted low over the gorge.

They looked skyward and saw the colours fade from the rim rock as the gloom set in and the rain harried into the canopy above them. Cuff studied the scene upriver, the floodwaters banking on the turn, the battered rocks like polished stone.

He pressed his fingers into his tailbone. 'Feels like I'm knifed,' he said.

'That's a blessing, you can feel it,' said Bea.

'A blessing in the guise of sweet agony'.

'Yes.'

'Air's so thin I can hardly . . . get enough.'

Sprodd got up and turned about, searching the escarpment, trying to sight the cave through the timber and the rain.

Cuff knew what was in Sprodd's mind. 'Dan, if wishes were horses, beggars would ride.'

'What?'

'You get your wishes in fairy tales Dan, that's all.'

'Well I wish I was in one now.'

'Give a man his wish you take away his dreams.'

'What's that mean?'

'Mean's if we didn't have wishes we'd have nothin' come true.'

'I wish you didn't talk in riddles, that's what I wish.'

They sat watching the river, Cuff probing the cut on his forehead, close to the rim of his rescued hat.

The rapids upstream had thickened to a white froth forcing through the narrows, the sound echoing about the gorge, the river swelling as if some denizen yeast was fermenting in the ooze.

They sat in a line like gargoyles cut from the stone, hooded in their coats, the rain spilling off their hats.

They watched wreckage coursing downstream, flood-wrack, scrub and slender saplings, tubers and orchids torn from rock footings, tangles of waterweed and rushes and all manner of dead and rootless understory and, far above, where the cliff tops touched the heavens, the felled rain spewed from cracks and clefts like pours of molten silver in that strange grey light. And the river boomed like cannon.

'There's a wall o' water comin',' said Sprodd.

Bea Faa looked upriver and tried to imagine what that meant.

Sprodd was searching the escarpment for a way to the cave. 'We got to move.'

They got Cuff onto his feet, his exhalations fierce out his nose. They let him take the weight on his back and his legs and he did so with all the stoicism he could muster.

Sprodd handed him the staff and he took hold of it with two hands, his face drained and pale beneath the broad brim of his hat.

The hammering rain kept on, the river swelling like a reptile engorged.

Sprodd led the way, Cuff inching along the makeshift path, Bea Faa close behind.

'What I need's a palanquin,' said Cuff, loud.

'What's that?'

'Never mind, Dan, we ain't got one.'

Cuff leant against a tree and lowered himself down sucking and hissing. 'That's it, no more,' he said. The rain battered the canopy and mud and leaf litter ran freely about their boots.

They sat beside him. 'Air's so thin,' he said, again.

'Anything else?' said Sprodd.

'Yes.'

'What?'

'I'm wetter'n a fish.'

The rapids now were lost in the depths and the river came down, that cascade shimmering like a molten flow, the glassy form shattering along the banks, the current tearing at the timber, lashing the stone, the water gums bent low, quivering, the eddies piled up with froth and wreckage.

They got Cuff to his feet and they stood there, Bea and Sprodd, treading the slush beneath their boots, their fingers working the cold from their shoulders.

Cuff pivoted his upper half with some care. Studied the traverse.

Sprodd proffered an opinion. 'We best get a fire, get you warm.'

Cuff's one thought was if he didn't move now he might never move. He gripped the staff and his arms took some of the weight and he began to tread the ground, hardly lifting his feet, the pain knifing through his flesh.

They shuffled and scrambled up the slope, helping Cuff as best they could, hardly resting lest the venture stall for good.

In the cave they made a fire and Sprodd cooked up some real tea, *Hai Seng*, and they shifted their mugs from hand to hand, warming the free hand on the curvature of the vessel and sipping at the lip as the tea cooled.

Sprodd gathered some long sticks from the firewood stacked at the rear of the cave and he made a tripod frame and set it close to the fire and he draped their sodden coats upon the frame and periodically he turned the frame so as to favour one coat after another with the heat of the raw flame.

They ate the last of the hard biscuits and set themselves to wait out the rain, thinking the wait could be long. But late in the day the weather broke. The rain paused and the sun shot shafts of the purest light through cracks in the black sky.

'Need some meat,' said Sprodd.

'Take Thyne's gun,' said Cuff.

The prospect of using the Swedish flintlock brightened Dan Sprodd considerably. He had wondered if ever he might get to trial that gun for himself. He went to the gun and felt it in his hands and put the stock to his shoulder and sighted a run of sap on a gnarled old bloodwood beyond the cave.

He primed the gun, readied for the hunt, and he set it back where he'd found it. Then he sat with them again and finished his tea. 'A duck,' he said.

'A pheasant would be nice,' said Bea.

Their eyes were bloodshot from the smoke. They sat with their eyes shut and listened to the river rushing on, the sound pulsing into the cave like a surge.

Sprodd brought an armful of firewood from the rear of the cave and dropped it close to hand for Bea to manage. He put on his hat and his coat and picked up his own musket. 'I reckon I'll take the gun I know,' he said.

He primed the weapon and headed out, northward, taking care not to slip as Cuff had done. The sound of the river filled his head.

The mist thickened as he made his way towards the ghost gum forest on the turn, drenched in spray, the floodwaters hurtling through timber and stone, the ground a peril of mud and gravel. He walked on.

Had they been watching from the cave they might have seen Dan Sprodd disappear in the mist well before he took the turn. But they were not watching. The girl was on her knees at the fire, taking in the warmth. Cuff had propped himself up, resting on his elbows, his palms in the grit. He was hungry and cold and he was worried too, not so much about the pain at the point of his tailbone but more the numbness that visited his lower half with all too much frequency.

They waited, all through the day.

When Sprodd failed to return Cuff did not know what to do. Darkness was fast coming. If Sprodd did not return he would have to rely on Bea Faa, somehow, to get him home, or at least to fend for him until he could walk. He had no idea how long it took a tailbone to mend. He knew enough about her past to know she was resolute and strong but he worried that hunger might cause her to fit again. In that regard, and all others, she was entirely uncomplaining, but in that regard she was a doubtful quantum too.

He wished Sprodd would get back with a fat duck or a big goanna, a possum perhaps, or meat of some kind, any kind, so they might sleep dry on a full stomach. 'Let's hope he's not slipped and broke his tailbone,' he said.

Bea Faa had not thought much about Sprodd's failure to return but now, as the twilight began to fade, she worried. She went to the mouth of the cave and stood scanning the timbered slopes to the north.

Cuff put more wood on the fire.

The smoke swirled about them and burned their eyes as it rose to the ceiling and plumed before it fled the cave.

61

The girl was in no way restrained or shackled. Sparrow put out his hand. She recoiled.

'I will not hurt you,' he said.

She did not reply.

'I will make you some tea.' He pointed to the mouth of the cave. 'I will set the fire and make you some tea, warm you up.'

She looked at the mug.

'We have a teapot,' he said. 'Way out here, yes, a teapot!'

Sparrow reckoned the mention of a teapot might make her think about nice things, homely things, for a teapot was an object of cordiality and perhaps even trust. Then he wondered if perhaps she'd know it was Mort's teapot. If she knew it was Mort's teapot the effect might not register as he had hoped. He hurried to shift the conversation from the means to the end. 'I'll make some tea, just for you,' he said.

Her eyes were fixed on him, like those of some creature caught in a trap.

Sparrow heard the soft pads of Amicus approaching with some caution. He came abreast of Sparrow and stood there, watching the girl.

Sparrow took the dog by the collar. 'Don't be frightened.'

The girl was wide-eyed, her gaze fixed on the animal.

'He's got a Latin name. His name is Amicus Amico, that means friend to a friend. You just call him Amicus and he'll come.'

The girl did not call the dog.

'Go on,' he said and he tapped the dog on his rear and the dog went to the girl and sniffed at her knees and licked the back of her hand.

She did not recoil. She closed her eyes. She stretched out her fingers and Amicus licked her fingers too and in between her fingers, his tongue slurping up the webbing. A tear rolled down her cheek.

'There,' said Sparrow. He got off his haunches but he kept low, not inclined to tower over the girl. 'He'll sit with you, you see?'

Sparrow backed away. 'I'll make some tea then.' He picked up the trailing corner of the blanket and folded the corner at her feet. 'You wrap that around, catch your death otherwise,' he said as he left the cave.

He got a fire underway and some water warming in the quart pot and soon enough he had water on the boil and the tea pot at the ready.

He was calmer now, his mind set upon a bright prospect. If he was to recue the girl then Cuff might look more kindly upon him, and upon his needs, most particularly the biggest need of all – to never go back to Prominence, that gaol, never to risk the loss of Amicus, or the gibbet.

His most recent ruminations on the matter of capital punishment had been decidedly glum. There was every chance he would hang for the destruction of Jug's boat, if not for the death of Jug. The more he thought about his predicament the more he was certain he was a dead duck if he went back. There was the theft of the game dog too and there were hidden crimes, the killing of Pinney and Peskett, and Mort, doings in the wilderness that likewise weighed heavy in the fear and trepidation department. He saw Amicus at his side and when he swivelled about the girl was there, barefooted, wrapped in her blanket, the tin mug hung on her forefinger.

She appeared to sway. She did not seem to be a stable entity.

She could see the corpse across the way, Mort's feet, those dirty old moccasins plainly in view.

'That's Mort, and he's good and dead. I killed him.'

He took the mug from her finger and he poured the tea and passed her the mug and she took it and stepped away.

She sat herself down, the blanket pulled tight on her shoulders, a clump of it bunched in her fist.

Amicus sat close to her. She sipped at the tea and Sparrow watched, hoping for some sign that she liked it. What he noticed was the tremor in her hand.

She dropped her head onto her chest and her wrist went limp and the tea ran onto the ground and soaked into the dust and she did not seem to notice, or care. Amicus sniffed at the wet ground and licked at a scab on her knee.

Sparrow glanced at the darkening sky. He listened to the river. 'We have to go, soon as we can.'

The girl stared long and hard at the shrouded corpse. Sparrow was certain she would ask him how it was that Mort came to be dead, but she did not.

'They shouldn't have took me,' she said.

'I know.' He thought best not to encourage this particular line of thought, bad memories. 'We have to get you back.'

'Who are you?'

'I am Marty Sparrow. I seen you once at the muster, with Gordy. I got a patch on the bottoms.' Sparrow realised now the strangeness of his presence, so deep in the fastness. 'I never did take much to farming,' he said, and with that he thought best to say no more.

'Gordy's dead,' she said.

'Yes. Mort killed him . . . you probably know that.'

He thought then of what she didn't know. 'Shug they caught, and they hung him summarily, at Prominence,' he said. She did not respond. He said nothing of the pony's head, nor of Shug's leap into eternity, not least because he didn't see that leap for himself and he did not want to be the purveyor of outlandish gossip.

The girl leant forward and put her cheek to the dog's muzzle and Amicus licked her cheek and when he stopped she put her cheek to his soft ear, the shaggy hair, and held it there.

'There is a constable on the Branch called Mr Cuff, do you know Mr Cuff?'

The girl nodded. 'Everybody knows Mr Cuff.'

'Do you like him?'

'I suppose.'

'Well, there you are then, we'll find Mr Cuff.'

'Why are you here?'

'I don't know yet.'

In the light of day, gloomy though it was, Sparrow could plainly see the girl's gaunt condition. 'You have to eat something,' he said. The only ration he had was the hard biscuits he'd found in Mort's pocket. He took the biscuits from his haversack. 'You can dip these, soften them up.'

He made some more tea and he half filled the girl's mug, just half, recalling the tremor in her hand for she was ruined enough without burns on her skin.

She took the mug of tea and dipped one of the biscuits and held it there in the hot brew, Amicus watching her with some intent. Then she blew on the biscuit till it cooled a little and she put the soaked half in her mouth, closed her eyes, until it crumbled on her tongue. She chewed the crumble ever so slowly and then she washed it down with some tea and she repeated the manoeuvre with the remainder of the biscuit and then she consumed a second biscuit in much the same way.

Sparrow and Amicus watched on, Sparrow with some relief and Amicus with some interest in the biscuit. 'You best have that last one,' he said.

Her hand seemed a little steadier. She shook her head.

Sparrow thought best to leave her there for a minute or two, with the third biscuit, in case she changed her mind.

He retrieved the pair of shoes from Mort's haversack. He put them by her feet. 'I believe these are yours.'

She nodded. She took the shoes. 'I'll go wherever you want,' she said.

'We'll find Mr Cuff, downriver,' he said. *Surely some gain in that. The girl saved, delivered up to the constabulary, credit where credit is due.*

Sparrow dearly hoped the savages had no part in the girl. He hoped, too, their companionship with Mort was, as it seemed, occasional at best.

'Are you familiar with Caleb and Napoleon?' he said.

'Yes.'

'They know you was in that cave?'

'Yes.'

He put his boot down hard on the fire and kicked up the fringe ash onto the hot core. He drained the teapot and the mugs and he put them inside his haversack and then he secured the grappling hook and he shouldered the burden and set the rope across his chest as he had done before and once again he patted the axe on his hip for there was comfort in the feel of that axe, secure upon his person.

She had some difficulty pulling on the shoes.

'Time to go,' he said.

Sparrow started down the gully, slowly, and the girl followed. Short, careful steps.

'What is your name?' he said, though he knew it already.

'I'm Dot.'

———

He led the way onto the Branch, well clear of the spray, the levees gone, the banks swamped, water gums bowing to the force of the current. He weighed his prospects as he searched out a line through scrub and stone. He could only hope that Cuff would not insist upon delivering him up to Dr Woody. The memory of his time in the gaol was still most bright. So too the picture of Peskett, flat out on the sand, his skull a bloody ruin. The very same man who would have dismembered him without a scrap of pity, who might well have inserted the rectal pear in his arse had it been required – that man was now dead and good riddance.

Sparrow felt no pity. He had a powerful sense that natural justice had been served. He took the view, the only possible view, that Peskett might have killed him had he not told his big lie and so created the necessity to head up the Branch. In that gaol he was entirely at Peskett's mercy, or lack thereof – it was the big lie or rectal ruin, simple as that.

Subsequent events had proved the telling of the big lie was the right thing to do. He was free and soon enough, most likely, they would sight the little party coming upriver. Soon enough he would be reunited with Bea, though he had to concede the presence of the constables was a substantial obstacle to his ambition.

They walked on, the black sky thickening by the hour.

They took a rest among the trees, midway on a long reach where the river ran deep. Dot picked a swollen leech from her ankle, plumb coloured, shiny as polished leather and fat as a frog. Then she took off her shoes and probed at the back of her heels where the flesh was worn away and together they examined the red raw patches atop the joints on several toes. 'A marine gave me these shoes.'

'On the transport?'

'Yes.'

'Did he favour you?'

'I thought so.'

'What about Gordy?'

She paused. 'He was alright.'

'Can you walk some more?'

'Yes.'

There was scree rattling down from the slope above. They looked up to where the slope was almost sheer, where the coachwoods and the turpentines were ramrod straight and seemed to hug the cliff face as if possessed with some deep understanding of perpendicularity.

Sparrow saw movement there and he could hardly believe the sight that now took shape. It was Mr Catley's mule, unmistakably Catley's, for it bore the man's pack saddle and harness replete with wicker baskets and leather panniers.

The mule was indifferent to their presence, nibbling at young green shoots in the under shrubbery. Sparrow searched the slopes, looking for Mr Catley, but saw no sign of the duckbill hunter, nor of Moowut'tin. 'What's happened, I wonder?' he said.

He told the girl to hold Amicus and he started up the slope, some of the way on all fours, pausing to catch his breath. The mule watched him. The animal stepped down the slope with a sure-footedness that entirely belied its mass, the wicker panniers rattling like a tinker's dray. It came to Sparrow and nuzzled at his hand and Sparrow called up the girl.

They set about searching the panniers. 'Don't get behind him, not close,' he said.

They found a few handfuls of corn at the bottom of a small sack, a one-pound cut of salt beef, a small quantity of sugar and a bag full of sweaty onions.

Sparrow poured the sugar into his hand and they each took a few pinches and put it on their tongue and savoured the treat. He fed one of the onions to the mule thinking to strike a bond with the animal as quickly as possible. 'Have to hope he don't kiss me,' he said.

They sat for a while, watching the river as they peeled strips of beef off the cut until half of it was gone, whereupon they dipped into the corn and ate it raw.

Rain began to fall, heavy, heavier by the minute.

They found shelter in a cavity beneath a mass of chock-stone. Water was streaming through the shelter but the silt on either side was banked high and they squatted there with the mule, untroubled by the runnage and the rain.

In one of the baskets there was a wrap of tent canvas. They doubled the canvas over and dragged it under their bottoms for a groundsheet and they sat there, listening to the rain on the stone above and watching the transitory stream follow its course to the river.

Sparrow fed another onion to the mule and he got the beef and the bagged corn and they feasted some more, a little feast.

Amicus sat to attention, watching them eat. Sparrow fed him the last shreds of meat, leaving nothing for the morning to come.

'I wish we had some tea,' said Dot. She was shivering.

'We got no touchwood, nothin' dry out there.'

'I hope Mr Cuff's got food.'

'I expect he'll have something to spare. We'll find him tomorrow.'

Sparrow had no idea if that would prove to be true or not. He hoped to find Cuff as swiftly as he could.

Late in the day the rain stopped but its load carried on, gushing from fractures below the rim and dripping from the trees, glistening, as shafts of the westering sun broke through the cloud and the spray rose wild from the savaged banks and showered down in specks of silver.

Sparrow led the way and they pressed on, cautiously, their progress slowed by sodden ground and thick scrub.

They walked for an hour or so, picking their way and pausing now and then to view the river. On one occasion they studied a mess of debris wedged in a chute and they saw the shape of a man all but engulfed in the white churn. They came down the slope and looked again and saw it was the old constable, Dan Sprodd, the waters pounding his frame, the foreplate of his skull smashed in.

Sparrow was so shocked he had to sit down, which he did, in the wet. Dot stood beside him and for a while they just stared.

He was not about to put a toe into that churn, but he figured there was some chance of retrieving Dan Sprodd's body with the rope and the grappling hook. 'Let's try,' he said.

He fed out several lengths and hurled the hook underarm but it fell way short.

He tried again. This time the hook landed on Sprodd's shoulder and dropped down his back.

Sparrow reeled in the slack, pulling the hook from the churn until the hilt slid onto Sprodd's shoulder. He jerked it hard and a barb bit into the flesh beneath the shoulderblade and held. Sparrow heaved again and the hook bit deeper and Sprodd slumped forward but the current pummeled him back into the wedge.

Dot brought the mule down the slope and Sparrow tied the rope to the pommel and backed up the mule until the slack was gone. He gripped on the rope and began to haul. The body came out of the wedge and rolled around the stone, the dog barking at the catch in motion, and Sparrow had not the power to fight the water, but the mule did.

The mule felt the pull of the load and leant back, his hind hooves deep in the mud and his rump almost set down on the slope. The animal held steady, the rope held tight and Sprodd's carcass twisted and turned on the hook.

They took hold of the rope once more and began to pull and the two of them dragged the catch sideways into the shallows and from there onto the sodden bank where the body lay facedown in the mud.

They rolled him onto his back, shooed off the dog. The hook had taken up under the shoulderblade and the barb was jammed there by the force of the runnage and the heaving that followed. The barb had surfaced below the clavicle and the skin had slid down the point and sat like a ragged frill on the poor man's frame.

'Did you know him?' Sparrow studied the wreckage of the old constable's forehead.

'I seen him at the muster, that's all.'

They lay Sprodd's body across the mule, fixed him at the withers, lashed his legs and arms to the girth on either side and they rested for a while, Sparrow pondering the measure of credit due for rescuing the remains of Cuff's old friend.

He led the way and Dot followed with the mule, Amicus threading the undergrowth, shifting higher as they filed through a copse at the end of the reach, the boles ghostly white, the waters pounding the stone on the turn.

They walked on, anxious now to find cover for the dark of night was not far off. They weaved their way through straight, tall trees, the light fading, the gorge a thicket of shadows.

It was Dot who saw first the flicker of flame in the cave.

They watched the dance of fire shadow in the blackness of the shelter, hoping to see one of their own. They moved closer, higher.

They saw Cuff shuffle into view, leaning heavily on a staff, then Bea at his side. The dog ran to greet Bea and hurried about the cave, nose to the ground, as Sparrow tethered the mule without a word, the body of Dan Sprodd in full view.

With Bea's help, Cuff shuffled down the slope. He put a hand on the animal's wither, felt the creature shudder at the touch. He bent low, studied the damage to Sprodd's skull.

'Hello Martin,' said Bea.

'Hello, Bea.'

'Them black beggars kill Dan?' said Cuff.

'I think the river killed him. We pulled him out of the river,' said Sparrow.

Cuff rested his head upon Dan's frame, a hand set on the harness, like he was saying a silent prayer. 'I'd like a moment with my friend,' he said. 'You all go on to the fire.'

Sparrow and Dot scrambled up to the cave and Bea followed them with Amicus at her heel.

Cuff put a hand on Dan's back and patted him, gently. He could not say he'd ever had a good conversation with the man, but he was the steadiest of companions, ever ready to help, never known to say a bad word. A good soul, not a skerrick of malice in the man. And now he was dead. 'My fault Dan, never should have let you go, not in this weather,' he said. He wiped his wet eyes on his sleeve, first one then the other.

He looked about, the darkness closing, the scene wild, a chill setting in. 'I wish we had a churchyard,' he said. He patted Dan one last time and shuffled back to the cave, his lower back racked with spasm, the pain etched on his face.

'What have you done to yourself, Mr Cuff?' said Sparrow.

'Broke my tailbone. My good friend is dead and, as you can see, Mr Sparrow, my predicament is severe.'

'This is Dot, Gordy's girl what Mort took, Mort and Shug,' said Sparrow.

'I know Dot,' said Cuff. 'She's a good girl and don't deserve any of this. None of us do. Where's Mort?'

'He's dead.'

'You kill him too? Come on now Martin, we know you killed Griffin Pinney.'

Sparrow was shocked to hear this. He could hardly believe that Bea would tell.

Cuff broke the silence. 'We know you did a honourable thing Marty, 'cause Mr Catley told us. Most chivalrous in the circumstances.' He gestured a hand in the direction of Bea. 'No one here's gunna point the finger, *understand*? Good riddance and all that.'

'Thank you.'

'Well, these days it seems all the wilderness does is abet a multitude of crimes and occasionally a smidgeon of restitution. We ought be grateful for that smidgeon I suppose. Small mercies.'

Cuff turned about with some difficulty and shuffled forward and stood, staring at the dark form of his old friend slumped across the mule. 'Why I let him go in this weather I'll never know.'

'You do have a predicament,' said Sparrow.

'I do, yes. My locomotion is severely curtailed.'

'You can have the mule if you want.' He had, in effect, begun to bargain.

'If I can sit him, that mule might just save my hide.'

'It's Mr Catley's mule.'

'Catley's in a fix, I'm in a fix. The Branch is just one pickle after another.'

Sparrow didn't much care about Catley's troubles, he was just pleased to know it was Catley who blabbed, not Bea.

'What happened to Peskett and Redenbach, you see them go down?' said Cuff.

'I did.'

'Well?'

'That was Caleb, and that other one, Napoleon.'

'I guessed as much, for they will have their revenge. Not a notion I care to contemplate right now.'

Sparrow thought best to change the subject. 'I'm sorry about your friend,' he said.

Cuff stared at the fire. 'He was a man of few words but never a bad word for anyone. It's a virtue few of us can match.'

'You want us to bring him in, out o' the weather, lay him out?'

'Yes.'

They took Sprodd from the mule and carried him into the cave and wrapped him in the cut of tent canvas, the dog sniffing about.

Cuff reckoned the river probably did kill Sprodd, but how he came to be in the river was, in all likelihood, more complicated. He might have slipped. Then again, there were savages on the river, killing white men. 'Might be he flung himself into the flow, or got thrown, the river swift enough to bear him away . . . and brutal enough to finish him,' he said.

'We found him stuck in a block-up, that's all we know,' said Sparrow.

'We can bury him in the morning,' said Bea.

'If you would do him the courtesy I would be most grateful,' said Cuff.

62

They woke early, hungry, the stink of smoke in everything. They studied the outline of Dan Sprodd in that dirty canvas shroud.

Bea set to sparking the fire. Dot snapped twigs and laid them, in crosshatch fashion, neat on the little flame. Cuff watched, silent, working his toes, as Sparrow shuffled to the lip of the cave to see what he could see.

The grey dawn gave form to the violence of the river. 'I could take the gun,' he said.

'Forget it, Marty, there'll be no meat on parade till this weather settles,' said Cuff. He could not imagine that Sparrow had much in the way of finesse when it came to hunting.

'I might get a pheasant.'

'You might but I doubt it.'

'What then?'

'You can go forage, that would be helpful.'

'Alright.'

Cuff was anxious to sort a plan for they had to move, as swiftly as the weather would allow. He beckoned Bea Faa and she came to him and he bade her sit down. He signalled Sparrow, and Dot too. 'Martin, you won't know Bea's in trouble but you need to know. She's implicated in some awful doings on the sealeries, to wit the flagrant enormities of her companions.'

Sparrow had to wonder about these enormities. He had to assume they were bloody and cruel, knowing what he did of the sealeries, what he'd heard.

'I cannot go back,' said Bea. Amicus settled close by her side.

'Me neither, they'd hang me for sure,' said Sparrow. He wanted to impress on the present company just how assured that outcome would be. 'Whether for Jug who I did not kill or the boat I never sunk or the dog I just . . . found. Whether for one or all three for good measure.'

'He's probably right. I do believe a panel would hang him,' said Cuff.

Cuff had made up his mind to see Sparrow and Bea Faa safe on a westerly path to the headwaters of the Branch. Beyond that, their fortune was in the lap of the gods, or the divine judgement of heaven. His main concern was the girl, Mackie's girl, but the dice had rolled in such a way that he now had some respect for Sparrow too. The better Sparrow might prove to be a good companion for Bea Faa. The better Sparrow was another variety of Sparrow altogether. The wilderness had fired him up, made him useful.

Sparrow was tempted to ask Bea what happened on the sealeries but he thought that unwise and, anyway, he didn't care. Whatever happened on the sealeries had delivered the outcome he wanted. Best for Bea to tell him in her own good time.

Cuff felt obliged to make clear to Sparrow the full import of his situation. 'You understand, if you don't come back with me, you will be outlawed?'

'Outlawed?'

'You have two capital matters unresolved. You don't come back, the governor will declare you an outlaw as he did Shug and as he did Mort.'

'Me!' said Sparrow.

'It means they catch you they can shoot you dead, on the spot, or hang you, summarily, as they did Shug. It means if you go you go for real, way out of reach, the other side, the far beyond, if there is one.'

'I never thought I'd be an outlaw.'

'And I never thought I'd hear you killed the likes of Griffin Pinney.'

'He killed Mort too,' said Dot, nodding her approval.

'You do continue to wrong-foot my wildest expectations,' said Cuff.

Sparrow thought best not to mention that Mort was asleep at the time. 'He stole Dot and he misused her, most horribly.'

'That's true,' said Dot.

'I won't stand for that, I just won't,' said Sparrow.

'By God, a resolute man. The wilderness has worked its magic,' said Cuff.

'Not the wilderness,' said Sparrow.

Amicus nuzzled at his hand and dropped down beside him, soft and warm.

He was tempted to tell them he had killed Peskett too and thus secured his young dog once and for all. The confession was on the tip of his tongue, but Sparrow said nothing further for there was already enough in the public realm, enough in the way of his known enormities, enough to hang him two or three times over.

'I don't know what you'll find on the other side but here's hoping some of the talk is true,' said Cuff. His mind turned to practical matters. 'If I could walk I'd recommend you take the mule.'

'We don't need the mule,' said Bea.

'No we do not.' Sparrow was westward bound with Bea Faa and Amicus Amico. He wanted nothing more.

'Well, there's some things you can take. You can take poor old Dan's fishing kit, the hooks, the line, take the pouch too. We can split the Chinese tea.'

'There's a river on the other side, I just know it,' said Sparrow.

'You find it you'll be alright.'

'We'll find it.' Sparrow was thinking of Mort Craggs' cogitations on the matter.

'You seem awful sure o' yourself, Marty. That's good.'

Sparrow was not so sure but he wanted to be sure, he wanted to talk up the likelihood as described by Mort. 'Mr Flinders says there's a river over there, a river of the first magnitude, a river with sinuosities three thousand miles long, I reckon he should know.'

'Well, there's a lot of preposterous reckoning about the other side but I have to say Mr Flinders is a most credible reckoner.'

'Mr Flinders says it defies nature not to have a big river, like the Nile, land as big as this, bigger'n Egypt, I think.'

'I grant the reasoning is sound but whether nature conforms to that reasoning in all times and all places, who knows.'

'I reckon we'll find a river.'

'I reckon you will.'

In Cuff's opinion, there was nothing further to be gained by musing on the properties of the other side, nor on such fickle considerations as the savages known to inhabit the mountains to the west, Nabbinum's mob.

'A word to the wise,' he said. 'This river drops as fast as it comes up. When it drops the reaches settle and the levees come again into full view and they dry quick in the heat, good purchase underfoot. You keep to the shallows and the levees you can save yourself a lot of hard work and some peril. My advice is we live rough out of this here cave for a day or two and we'll find the Branch way more placid and hospitable, upriver and down.'

'We gotta eat,' said Sparrow.

'You can forage, can't ya?'

'Yes we can,' said Bea.

Cuff was thinking further on the division of the meagre materials they had at hand. He was thinking of Dan's boots. He did not want to see Dan interred without his boots but he knew that to be a sentiment the living could do without. 'You best take his boots if they fit, boots awful scarce out here,' he said.

'Alright,' said Sparrow.

'One more thing.'

'What?'

'I'm advised, finally, the bull shark did kill that boy, is that right?'

'Yes.'

'I'll take your word on that, on one condition.'

'Tell me.'

'You sign over your patch to Dr Woody. It's hardly compensation for his loss, but it's something.'

'That patch is deep in hock to Mr Mackie.'

'It's my expectation Mr Mackie would waive that debt in favour of Dr Woody, under the circumstances.'

'I'll do it then, I'll sign.'

'Good.'

Cuff took the warrant for Bea's arrest from his haversack and the pen-cil from his vest pocket. On the back of the warrant he wrote the words whereby Sparrow ceded his thirty-acre patch, prime river bottoms, to the doctor and his family.

Sparrow studied the pen-cil as Cuff wrote. Then he took the strange implement and he scratched his signature alongside his printed name and Cuff signed at the bottom of the page as witness. 'You've done the right thing, Marty,' he said.

Sparrow felt no loss, for the patch was long gone from his life, and he was glad to leave it behind. Only the memory of the hens, just the hens, made him sad, for he had let them down. He had failed them and they had never failed him. The very thought stirred some strange instinct, some dormant resolve in his fibre – never to fail like that again, not Amicus, not Bea.

He watched as Cuff slipped the document into the bosom of his shirt and the implement into the vest pocket. 'What is that, that stick?'

'Why that's a pen-cil,' said Cuff.

'Save on ink?'

'Nothing is fixed in this world, Marty, not even the quill, and that's been round since . . . since birds.'

Later that morning Sparrow and Bea loaded Dan back onto the mule and went searching for a patch of ground wherein to place his mortal remains. Downstream they found a cavity at the base of a sheer stone scarp, deep enough to accommodate Dan's body.

They pushed him deep into the cavity, his remains wedged in the tapering stone.

'You better take his boots,' said Bea. She had put aside his hat.

Sparrow took the boots. He did not want to try them on, he just wanted to get done and go. They gathered rubble from roundabout and walled up the crypt with some care as to the fit of the stone. The exercise made Sparrow think fondly of the dry-stone wall at the front of the cave house. 'Mr Catley's habitation set a standard,' he said.

'Yes.'

'Did he blab on me, just like that?'

'Yes, but he was ill, somewhat addled, not quite himself.'

'I don't care anyway. I'm not goin' back.'

'Nor I.'

The weather was clearing, the air heavy with damp, and they were sweating when the work was done.

The mule was nibbling at Sparrow's heels, the dog sniffing at the assembled stone. They stood and paused, watching the wild river, a spectacle by any measure. 'I'm no good at prayers,' said Sparrow.

Bea Faa recalled a line from Cuff's speech when they buried Joe. The words seemed entirely right: 'Mr Sprodd was a straight-goer, never known to practise the petty arts or the slippery ways.'

'Straight, yes, straight as a rush, and never a bad word for anyone.'

'He was good at fishing too. He'd say, *them perch just beggin'.*'

'He would?

'Yes.'

They threaded through the scrub, through bottlebrush and fern and a few dwarf myrtles, back to the cave.

They stayed three days in that cave, surviving on bush currants and milk caps, a few tubers and once on a big feed of *cah-bro*, a hatful that Bea dug out of a rotten log, but otherwise no meat.

The river dropped as Cuff said it would, though not as swiftly as it had risen, and not enough to trek the floor. So they stayed two days more and on that final day, the sky clear, the sun angling into the gorge, the air sticky as sap, on that day they conferenced, and agreed to go their separate ways.

They helped Cuff onto the mule, Dot with a good firm grip on the halter.

Sparrow was most relieved to see Cuff sit the mule with enough ease to suggest the plan might work. 'Dot's a good handler, she knows the mule,' he said.

Cuff grimaced as he shifed his weight. He gestured south. 'I'm in Dot's hands, from one good woman to another. Guess I'm just blessed.'

'Thank you, Mr Cuff,' said Sparrow. He was patting the mule high on the shoulder. Cuff lifted his hat to Sparrow and waved it about in something of a flourish.

'Freddie will see you safe, when you get to Joe's,' said Bea.

'I'm sure he will,' said Cuff. 'He's like poor old Dan, constant in all weathers.' He smiled at Bea and clucked his tongue. 'Girl, you do wonders for that hat.'

'I hope you make it,' said Sparrow.

'I'll make it.' Cuff untied the costrel, loosed it from the pack saddle and handed it to Sparrow. 'You will need this more than me.'

'Why?'

'We got the river, me and Dot.'

'We got the river too.'

'Not all the way you don't, not beyond the headwaters.'

Sparrow was reminded he had no idea what lay beyond the headwaters of the Branch.

'I wish you both luck,' said Cuff. 'I hope it's entirely pleasant over there. I hope they do a nice high tea.'

63

Sparrow and Bea watched as Dot led the freighted mule southwards through the trees. It occurred to Sparrow that prior to the flood both Peskett and Redenbach lay dead upon the sand not far downstream but now they would be gone, gathered to the deep or mere rubbish on the torrent. Dot and Cuff might find them, smashed up like Dan Sprodd. Or they might not find them at all and instead find Dan's musket wedged in a tree, draped in the deathly grey of flood-borne shrubbery, the floodwaters a master of random arrangement.

They went back to the cave, packed the haversack and headed north along the slender path that had proved the undoing of Thaddeus Cuff.

On the next reach they dropped down to the river, for the river had truly settled to its quiet ways, the braided waters murmuring their way about wrack-strewn levees and long thin islands of sand, the crust baked dry in the sun.

At Mort's gully they forded the tributary creek. Sparrow paused. 'Mort's up there,' he said, but he was in no way inclined to go up that gully and survey his work. They walked on.

'Do you ever dream of that bloody deed, that or the other?' Bea asked.

'Only when I'm awake,' he said.

Further along the river parted ways on a mountainous spur, one way running straight on, the other hard to port, westward. They waded onto the westward course, sure in themselves that this was the Branch, for Mr Catley had confirmed the Branch ran through his valley and Mr Catley's valley was westward, of that they had no doubt. *A rose by any other name,* he'd said.

For some days more they made their way west, their progress favoured by the firm sand on the shoulders of the long levees, their stomachs reconciled to a few foraged tubers, the ones Joe called bush parsnips, and now and then a feed of *cah-bro.*

They crossed ephemeral streams running from countless gullies, dark sanctuaries of coachwood and turpentine, anchor vine and fern. Where the banks were a tangle of ruin and altogether impassable they trekked knee-deep in the flow. In the heat of the day, the sun at its full height, they sat themselves in the shallows and they lay facedown in the cool runnage and drank in the water as it came to them. Amicus did much the same, occasionally rolling in the sand and then gambolling back to the shallows to snap at dragonflies and gallop after birds and rear and lunge at finches and miners as they swooped and skimmed.

On their fifth day they followed a beaten path at the foot of the flanking cliffs on the northern side of the river. They walked, enveloped in the deep shade, the far side of the river bathed in the low-angled rays of the sun, the valley basking in a luminous dusk, like the glow from a furnace. They did not see the lithe black figures watching them from cover.

They sat for a while. They walked on in the fading light, hoping to find a shelter for the night. They found not so much a cave as a shallow recess beneath an overhang where the sandstone wall was scalloped out, honeycombed by wind and seepage, the ceiling busy with nests and the air rich with the smell of feathers and bird dung. They sat, chins on knees, staring south across the valley, a faint hammock of moon, the dark closing in.

The next morning they waded across the river and came upon a yam patch on the southern bank. They picked some yams and crossed the valley floor and made their way up the timbered slope until they saw the cave house, cosseted in the trees below the cliff line, the setting deserted save for a wallaby that took flight and then stopped and turned and watched them with an admirable degree of coolness.

Sparrow saw Peskett's tent, still there, much as it formerly was, a catch of rotting leaves and bat droppings in the torn and sagging canvas.

Amicus hurried to and fro, nose to the ground.

Bea pushed open the cave house door. She went in and looked around, the cool air gathered about. The arrangement of furnishings and oddments seemed unchanged, the wild figs and tubers hung like chimes, the swing lamp and the specimens all about, the funnel-web spider skewered on that long black pin, the pelt rug piled up in the snug niche at the rear, the old teapot on the windowsill.

Beneath the windowsill she found a heavy crock, the receptacle packed tight with square cuts of wild meat. She dipped her finger in the liquid, tasted a thick, pickled brine.

The upturned lid served as a plate for the square cuts she took to the fire, Sparrow stoking, the kindling taking the flame. He sniffed at the meat, nodding his approval.

'There's more,' she said. 'We can take some with us.'

She swivelled on her haunches and pondered the rude hut where Moowut'tin slept when he was working with Catley. She wondered why he came and went as he did, and why he was not with Catley on the Branch when the poor man fell victim to the duckbill.

Sparrow noted her gaze, her contemplative mood. 'If ever we see them mountain blacks I do sincerely hope Moowut'tin is with them,' he said.

They prepared a little feast to be followed by a cup of Dan Sprodd's tea.

'It is unseasonally warm,' said Sparrow as they fed on the meat, side by side.

'Not so much as to keep me outdoors.'

'Me neither.'

'You can have his bed,' she said as she sat herself alongside him. 'I'll have the pelt rug.'

'Alright.' Sparrow said alright but he didn't really mean alright. He'd have much preferred to share that bed with Bea. He called Amicus and the dog came swiftly and sat close, planting his rear end snug on Sparrow's foot.

He thought of the men who would take the dog from him: Pinney, Peskett, Mort Craggs, and Henry Kettle, who was still alive. He glanced in the direction of Peskett's ragged tent. He took hold of the dog at the scruff. 'I'll not share you with anyone,' he said softly.

Bea put her arm around Sparrow. 'Not even with me?'

'Oh I'll share him with you.'

'We shall make of ourselves a formidable little party, the three of us.'

'I think so, yes.' Sparrow didn't know what to think but he would hardly disagree. He could feel her arm around him, her fingers pressing on his shoulder. He wished they could sit like this forever, that and one or two other variations in the way of closeness.

In the morning they woke to a discord of creature sounds, frogs and cullawines and kookaburras, and yellow-tailed cockatoos in full flight. They set the fire and cooked a few more pieces of the pickled meat and they plucked baked yams from the coals and they made a pot of weak tea, rationing the meagre supply.

Sunlight filled the valley, the cliff line to the north a shimmer of ancient sediment massed in ripples of red and gold. They watched a mob of kangaroos bound westward along the river, the creatures swift and agile in country pocked with fallen timber and wombat holes.

A flock of small birds winged the valley, numberless in their mass. They sat stock still as a big goanna stalked the camp, and Sparrow held tight to Amicus as the creature went about his business.

Neither Sparrow nor Bea wanted to leave. Already they could feel the warmth in the air, another hot day. It was easy enough to succumb to a certain lethargy and a measure of comfort in the shaded surrounds of the cave house, but neither Bea nor Sparrow was really clear as to why they lingered. They spoke of Catley.

'He is sweet on you,' said Sparrow. He wanted to know what Bea would say in reply.

'He is married to that Sir Joseph fellow.'

Sparrow laughed at the thought. 'He looks at *you* all the time.'

'He is a most oniony man.'

Sparrow chuckled. He was pleased to have no connection at all with onions. 'He will not betray us, nothwithstanding his lapse. I do believe that,' he said.

'I feel the more safe with you.'

That made Sparrow happy, though little pinpricks of doubt made him wonder if it could be true.

Bea had thought about her unlikely connection with Martin Sparrow for some time. She had weighed him up, so to speak. He was not pretty, nor strong, but his fortitude had surprised her and one thing she knew for a certainty: Sparrow had struck up a remarkable association with the small axe and he would defend her as best he could, just as he would defend Amicus Amico. His attachment to them had raised him up, made him better than he really was, or had been; made him resolute, made him anew. And one thing more – she did not fear him. That counted for something. That was a blessing.

They left Catley's patch at dawn the following day. They kept to the sand as best they could, now and then the meander presenting them with a view of the sheer cliffs that flanked the northern side of the river, the sun playing on raw patches of freshly calved stone, their progress scrutinised by reptiles in the scrub, wading birds in the shallows and raptors in the sky.

They walked all day.

Late in the day they startled a wedge-tailed eagle feeding on a freshwater turtle. They watched the eagle soar into the air and circle high above, watching them in turn.

Bea killed the meat with Dan Sprodd's fish knife. She cut away the shell and threw it clear and she fed the tiny head and the feet to the dog and the dog dropped down, gnawing at the leftovers, while Sparrow set a fire so they might cook their small meal on the coals.

They ate slowly, watching the eagle pick at the fleshy remains on the upturned shell. 'I could shoot him,' said Sparrow. But he did not want to ruin the quiet, nor the contentment he felt at that moment. He took Mort's pistol from the haversack and studied its particularities.

Bea got to her feet and looked upriver and down. The eagle took wing. 'I won't be long,' she said and she walked off, downriver.

After a while Sparrow began to worry. Bea had never before taken this long to see to the necessaries. He readied the pistol and set off. He followed her footsteps in the sand. Rounding a turn he caught a glimpse of her downstream. She was bathing in water to her thighs, unclothed, her hair loosed, thick and black.

Sparrow stepped from the sand into the brush and secreted himself as best he could. He watched her bathe.

She laved water onto her body and followed each time with the scrubbing motion of palms on skin. She bent over and washed her face and flicked her hair forward into the water and worked it between her fingers. She tossed her head and her hair flicked left and right and then settled in the middle of her back, errant strands on her shoulder and her cheek. She ran the palm of her hand across the water and looked about. Sparrow shrank back into the brush. He could feel the pulse in his neck, his heart resounding in his chest.

She set her face to the sun and seemed for a time to be locked there by the warmth on her skin. Sparrow wanted to stay, but he thought best to depart while he could, unseen.

He snuck off, hurried back to the fire. The dog was still gnawing at the gristly remains of the turtle, the eagle long gone.

When she returned her hair was secured in the big knot, the wooden pin in place. 'You should bathe too,' was all she said. Sparrow did not know what to make of that.

They walked on, westward.

At dusk they found an embankment where the scrub thinned out and they made their way without much effort to the forest on the northern escarpment. The sun had slipped from view. The sky to the west was a band of blue beneath a vast stretch of fire-orange cloud, the wisps like flames licking up to the immeasurable heavens. 'I didn't know the sky could do that,' said Sparrow.

'Nor I,' she said.

They pressed on.

Amicus had picked up a scent and he hurried ahead, nose to the ground. They followed him up the escarpment, where they found cover for the night, a shelter scalloped out by ancient floods.

A possum scampered along a ledge at the rear of the shelter and leapt to the ground and scuttled away and Amicus took chase.

When he came back, his coat was flecked with bark and char grit, a cut below his eye, his flanks heaving. Sparrow dropped to one knee and brushed him off.

They ate the pickled meat cold, made no fire. The shelter was open to the breeze and the night air was gentle and warm, the weather a mystery. They sat listening to the creature sounds. They watched the night shadows, ever shifting, bats coasting into the canopy.

64

Much to Cuff's surprise the spasms in his back eased with the days and with that easing the bouts of numbness in his lower parts diminished in duration such that, by the time they reached Freddie's patch, he could walk without help, though not without pain.

He recalled Woody's peroration on the remedial motion of a ship upon the lungs and the belly and he wondered, by way of analogy, if perchance the motion of the mule had somehow unfixed the seizure in his tailbone region. Whatever the remedy, he could now shuffle about with an ease he could not have imagined upriver, days back, when the two parties had gone their separate ways.

Freddie was overjoyed to see them, but somewhat puzzled as well. 'You ain't Bea,' he said, staring at Dot.

'No she ain't,' said Cuff. 'This is Dot what Mort and Shug stole off Gordy.' He dismounted with great care, coming to ground as lightly as he could, his fists locked on the pack leathers.

'Where's Bea then?' said Freddie.

Cuff shook his head as if he could hardly believe his own words. 'She's bound for the other side, with Marty Sparrow.' He threw his arms in the air. 'One o' them turns in the road you never see comin'.'

'Oh there's a lot o' them round here, lately.'

Cuff stepped somewhat painfully away from the mule, his fingers pressed in the small of his back. 'You got some meat we can sup on? We ain't seen much in the way o' meat for quite a while.'

'I got fish in a bucket,' said Freddie.

They killed the fish, perch, and cooked them up, devoured every morsel with hardly a pause for breath. They slept a profound sleep in Joe's cabin, Cuff and Dot sharing the bed in the recess as Freddie went about his chores, his mind full of questions he wished he'd put to Cuff, about Bea and Sparrow and the wilderness and the far beyond, and about poor old Sprodd whose death was another one of them turns in the road, a big shock, very sad news indeed, not as sad as Joe but almost.

The next morning, early, Cuff and Dot readied to go. The dawn was just a faint grey on the forested rim to the east, the Branch still as a pond, the slack water before the flood tide.

They took Joe's boat and provisions enough, bread and corn and some peach cyder, and they coursed down the Branch into the mid-river depths of the Hawkesbury, setting the sail for a faint nor'-easter.

The cramped confines did not help Cuff, nor did the flukey breezes help their progress. Twice in three days they laid over and not until late on the third day did they reach Prominence.

The little boat skimmed into the shallows at the foot of the switchback path.

Dot helped Cuff up the path, past Bet Pepper's, no sign of Bet, and they made their way to The Convivial Hive. Fish met them on the porch. 'I'm glad you're back,' he said to Cuff. 'I missed hearin' you talk.'

'Plenty o' time for that, Fish. Now, where's Dr Woody?'

'He's gone home in the gig.'

'Can you go get him for me?'

'I can, yes. Bad news?'

'Nothin' you can put a shine on.'

In the tavern Cuff passed Dot into Sam's care and Sam took her to the kitchen for a feed and he stayed there with her, while Atilio warmed a broth, hoping to learn all he could about what had happened in the woods, what happened to the boy Jug and what happened to Dan. 'Where's Dan?'

'He got drowned in the flood, he's dead,' said Dot.

Upstairs Cuff found Mackie in bed. 'You don't look to me to be . . . resurgent,' he said.

'What do I look to you to be then?'

'You look like a sucked peach. You might have to take to the ocean, like Woody says.'

'That will not happen.'

Cuff pulled up a chair and sat at the bedside, saw the man's scrofulous neck and cheeks, swollen and scabbed, smelt the rot on his breath, heard the rattle in his chest.

Mackie had a tin mug in hand, blood pooled in the base.

'You bring that up in one go?'

'Yes. Did you find the boy?'

'Why don't I just report, in full.'

'Do, please.'

Cuff was about to report in full but Mackie appeared to be so diminished he thought better of it. He saw no reason to report on Griffin Pinney's demise, nor Mort Craggs' for that matter. And the soldiers dead on the river sands, that was hardly urgent. Best for now to keep to matters that were close to home, and the heart. 'A bull shark killed the boy, of that I'm certain. But that's not the end of it. I'm sorry to report, Alister, Joe's dead and so is Dan.'

'Dan?'

'Yes.' Cuff hunched over, hugging his middle, staring at his boots. 'It breaks my heart, that good man.'

'How did he die?' Mackie's voice had faded to a faint whisper.

'He drowned, far as we could tell.'

Mackie covered his face with his hands, his fingers pressing hard on his forehead. 'I never heard him say a bad word about anyone.'

'That's Dan, cheerful in all weathers.'

'And Joe?'

'Joe died in his own bed and we buried him, proper.' Cuff was not inclined to say more, for that would lead to a complicated story best left for another day.

'What of the girl?'

'She's with Sparrow, bound for the other side . . . I had to see that girl safe on her way, in company with someone.'

'If it's Sparrow for company it's a poor bargain.'

'Not as poor as you might think. Affection for a fellow creature can fix a man, make him resolute, worthwhile.'

'Sparrow is a midge, a wretch beyond salvation.'

'Sparrow was a rudderless heart, that's all.'

'Not now?'

'I'd say his better self has triumphed and he's done some good and he might do some more.'

'Wonders never cease.'

'Some of us have the pliability.'

'And some of us don't?'

'That's right.'

They sat quietly, not a word.

'Your report.'

'Yes?'

'There's not much to leaven the misery.'

'I don't fix the path, I just walk it, hopin' there's more when I turn the corner.'

'As do we all.'

Mackie set the mug on the bedside stool, on a copy of the *Sydney Gazette*.

'What news?' said Cuff.

The chief constable considered the question with some care, sifting the options for his reply. 'The *William Pitt* has docked in Sydney, a hundred and seventeen females on board.'

'That's good, we're short on women. What else?'

'The Cape's back in British hands, the fighting done in half a day.'

'That's the Dutch for you, all pomp and no punch, nothin' but a bunch o' two-legged cheese worms.'

'I'm drowning, Thaddeus, in my own fetid muck.'

'I know.'

'My lungs are a swamp, worse by the day.'

'What you need's one o' them sulphurous baths, take the waters like the Romans.'

'We're a bit short on Romans in this neighbourhood.'

'Bit short o' the waters too, that kind.'

'I'm very tired.'

'I'll go.'

'Nothing more?'

There was plenty more, but that was for another day. 'One thing. We found Dot, she come back with me.'

Mackie took some time to consider the news of Dot's return. 'Tell her she can work here, in the kitchen, if she wants. I'll see to the formalities, if that's to her liking.'

Cuff saw this generosity for what it was, but he made no comment. 'I'll tell her,' he said.

Sam pushed open the door. 'You want I light the lamps?' he said.

'No,' said Mackie.

Part V

The Uplands

65

Next morning Sparrow and Bea resumed their course. They walked
for some hours, the river tapering, the brush shouldering in as they
went higher, stepping up faint cascades, the waters fanning out, thin-
ning, until the ground went to slush beneath a carpet of fern and a
scatter of tumbledown stone. They pressed on to the headwall and
then to the rim where they took in the view, the far-flung wilderness
in the heat of the day.

'That's not the other side,' said Sparrow.

'No it's not,' said Bea. The deep green of the forest canopy filled
a valley to the west, here and there the completeness of the cover
relieved by a column of brutally scoured stone, pillars like totem ruins
from some lost world, the far side bounded by a sheer cliff line that
ran raggedly north until it disappeared in shadow folds and haze, and
south until it did the same.

The one break in the ridgeline was to the north-west, a mile away
by foot, perhaps two, a defile where the forest ran upwards to the

cliff top like a smear of thick green paint. The vastness of the pano-
rama frightened Sparrow – a dismembered plateau cut by deep rifts,
a sparse upland consorting with thickly wooded valleys; a geography
that seemed to have no pattern and no end.

They crossed the valley and worked their way north, following
the cliff line through a forest of tall bloodwoods and mountain ash,
past the stone towers they had seen from the headwall, the weathered sandstone filigreed and fretted with bands of ironstone like awry
shelving, set at intervals such that a possum might climb those towers,
but not a man.

They searched several gullies and each time found themselves
with no means of passage, arrested in deep shadowed spaces where
the *gymee* stood like armed sentinels, their flower spikes twenty feet
high, and moss and lichen glowed bright in what might have been
some otherworldly minster or playhouse, or some refuge of purpose
unknown, walled in by the blackened face of the forbidding cliff.

Further along they tried a slot gully hardly wider than the span of
their arms, the lower parts covered in moss and the long, thick leaves
of dormant orchids, the most delicate of fern fronds and maidenhair
sprouting from fissures shoulder high, the walls sheer to a ribbon of
clear blue sky and the heat on the tableland above.

The passageway ended at a jam of fallen stone that angled up to
a cave high in the cliff wall, the cave backlit by a golden glow from a
shaft at the rear.

Sparrow hefted Amicus onto a narrow ledge above their heads and
from there the dog bounded his way to the cave and they followed.
They climbed the jam, lumps of ironstone making for footholds and
handholds, and then made a short scramble on a more hospitable
gradient.

In the cave their eyes were drawn to the the shaft of light at the
rear. They shuffled through bat droppings and bone-dry entrails and
the satin green feathers of some bird. They went on hands and knees

into the shaft and followed its upward turn and found themselves in a sink on the plateau.

Rock wallabies fled a wallow as Sparrow and Bea climbed from the shaft and Amicus took chase and did not return for some time.

The heat on the plateau was fierce, an upland of stunted heath and stone. They took to the shade of the wallow. Sparrow weighed the costrel in his hand, felt the damp, the leakage. They each took a sip, just a sip.

They followed the footprints of a heath lizard on a drift of ash and sand through brushwood punctuated by bursts of waxflowers and coral heath, their line more or less westward, the sun angling low onto their foreparts. Not a breath of air. Not a bird.

They lay facedown in a patch of shade. Amicus lapped the muddied dregs from a puddle in the warm stone. All about them the heath was parched and still, hazed in the afternoon light.

Further on, a startling scene: a weathered-away place where the sandstone had entirely given up its gathered form and lay as grains, drifts, thick upon the earth and naught but contorted gatherings of ironstone prevailed, defying the elements. They found themselves walking amidst outlandish forms perched on squat footings or slim stems, as if mounted upon armatures for exhibit, some of the shapes resembling things they could name – a gigantic mushroom, the ribbing of a mule, a goat's head, a chimney, a sea horse, a boot, the splayed tail feathers of a bird – and other shapes, unearthly forms that defied recognition, all the more strange with their silvery filaments sparkling in the light of the sun.

They walked in this aimlessly sculpted country until the sun was almost gone. They could see no rift that might lead them to shelter and water.

They made a small fire beneath the sparkling ironstone wing of a great bird and set the quart pot on the flames and set to boiling the last of their water. Sparrow retrieved his teapot and dropped near to the last of the good tea into the pot. He searched for his tin mug but it was not in the haversack. He searched again to no avail. Bea said, 'No harm, we can share mine.'

'Thank you.'

She had decided they would share not just the mug but the future, come what may: Sparrow wasn't much but he was something, and he was way better than ever she'd have guessed at the outset. He appeared to be a timid soul and yet he'd rescued her from Griffin Pinney and he'd rescued Dot too, from the man called Mort Craggs, and seen her safe as best he could. Somehow, he had transcended himself.

Sparrow was pleased they would share the tin mug. He wanted to share everything with Bea Faa. He contemplated the long day just gone and the days before that. He felt hope in his heart, hope on several fronts. The memory of her bathing came to him, most pictorially. The world would never be the same.

He unwrapped the last of the pickled meat and set the square-cut pieces on the glowing coals.

Bea sipped on her tea and then set her mug on the sand by Sparrow's knee.

It was dark now and the heat had dropped away as swiftly as the sun and a chill set in about them. A quarter-moon sat squat in the sky.

Sparrow fossicked about and gathered some dry brush. He squatted down and loaded the brush, piecemeal, onto the fire and the flames took quickly and reared up, the wing of the great stone bird sparkling as if one with the heavens.

They skewered the meat and blew on the crust, charred in ash and pickling. They peeled away small strips and ate them slowly.

Bea watched the play of the firelight on Sparrow's face, how the light betrayed the faded pockmarks on his brow and his cheeks and chin. 'Did you once have the small pox?' she said.

'No.'

'What then?'

Sparrow put a hand to his cheek and felt the scarring. 'My father did that.'

She waited, wanting more.

'When the sheriff came for me, my father took me by the hair and forced me to my knees. He sunk my head in a tub of hungry eels and held me there for some time, an eternity.'

'That's awful.'

'I thought they would eat my face right off. I thought I would drown, in that bucket.'

'But you didn't.'

'I had a awful scabby face for a long time.'

'It's hard to see now.'

'Small mercies.'

'Yes.'

'Just one thing can shape your whole life.'

The fire faded as swiftly as it had flared and Sparrow went for more dry wood and they built the fire once again and all about them the ironstone gleamed like the stars above. They slept that night beneath the wing, close to the fire and close to one another, with Amicus curled up at their feet, his back warmed by the bed of hot coals.

Sparrow dreamt he heard the howl of wild dogs. He looked out upon an unfamiliar heathland and saw the dogs, hot in pursuit of a boar; they set upon the boar and tore shreds of black hide from the animal, laying bare great patches of bleeding flesh and Sparrow watched this rending until he sensed his own mortal peril, for savages had gathered around him, their eyes glowing red like hot coals and these savages, they beat him with their waddies and left him bloodied and prone and they departed as swiftly as they'd come and he found himself yet alive, desperately thirsty but alive, and alone, for they had taken his Amicus. Amicus was gone.

He woke with a start. His mouth was dry, the cracks in his lips scabbed over. He felt the stillness of the vast expanse around him.

Sat up. Studied the covered form of Bea Faa, saw faint wisps of smoke rising up from the coals, ghost grey tendrils wasting to nothingness. He saw Amicus, splayed out in the sand, watching him.

He felt the chill air on his skin.

The dog stood, arched his back and stretched his long legs and let out a contented groan.

Sparrow lay down again and tried to sleep. His thoughts were of water – where they might find water, come the morning.

They woke hungry and parched. A scrub fowl of some description skittered away, disappeared into the prickly heath, and a flock of black cockatoos burst skyward as tiny birds flitted about the cover of the brush. Pea flowers there, bright yellow, like butterflies.

'I wonder, are we near the other side,' he said. He sensed they were closer to the known water behind them than they were to whatever water they might find to the west. But he did not want to turn back, not for anything, not even for water.

A wattlebird flew at a honeyeater and the small bird tumbled in the air, twisted and turned and fled into a thicket. They packed up and departed. They stepped down the sand drift onto the heathland and set about crossing to the ridge in the distance, the going much slowed by the tangle of the heath.

To the west the country was all sand and scrub save for the scattering of twisted trees on the horizon. They might squat and hide in this expanse but they would find no place shy of the sun.

They had no course except with the sun square on their backs. In that way they went on through the long morning, forcing a path through the brush, searching the understory for any bright green leafage that might tell of a soak, labouring beneath the sun until it hovered above them, burning into the crowns of their hats.

Sparrow was ruminating upon all the ways he might die in this country when he saw the savages. He had turned about and there they were, far off, three in a line among the ironstone contortions, watching, motionless, like stick figures planted in the ground, fixed in their world, abiding, steadfast, sovereign in their domain.

Perhaps they had picked this time to be seen, as the heat took its toll. Or was it pure happenstance, their presence discovered by chance, exposed on the heath, nowhere to hide, a simple misfortune, like so much else in life?

He knew the answer.

There were native dogs with them, restless things, prowling about, sniffing out the fire place and its surrounds, sucking in the scent of the strangers.

Sparrow squatted down. He primed the pistol, he hardly knew why. He thought the very notion of resistance quite futile.

'Four,' said Bea.

There were four now, in a line, the fourth one squat and stout.

'What are they doing?'

'They're watching us watching them,' said Bea.

The squat one pointed across the heath. He pointed north-west and they heard not words but just the faint tendrils of alien sounds that failed to carry, save for the sharpness. An urging across the waste.

'What to make o' that,' said Sparrow.

'We must give them something,' she said.

'The axe?'

'I hope that will do.'

'Hope is the poor man's bread.'

'I know.'

Sparrow weighed the possibilities. 'I will not give them Amicus,' he said. He gripped firm upon the weapon in his hand.

Amicus was sprawled in the shade beneath the brush, his hairy pizzle sack in full view. Even thus he was way more handsome in

Sparrow's eyes than those scrawny native dogs, the way they loped about the campsite, like pack wolves.

They stood together, he and Bea, stock-still, watching the hunters and their dogs, the sun beating upon them, the heat coming off the ash-ridden sand.

'They might have water,' she said.

'We ought just walk on, see what happens.' He could think of nothing else. There was nothing else.

'Let's walk then.'

'Come what may, I don't care,' he said. That was a lie.

He felt breathless. He felt cheated, bitterly so, but there was still hope in his heart. He hoped they might walk and the savages watch them walk and after a time tire of this and turn away and go back from whence they came, but from whence they came he did not know.

They walked on, Amicus ahead of them, until they were on the rise, picking their way through a gathering of scrub wattle and tea-tree set sparse on the higher ground. They turned once more and shaded their eyes and searched the distance.

They saw them coming. The savages dropped down into the drift, high stepping through the sand and thereafter ambling through the heath, following much the same line as their quarry. Here and there the dogs were seen to hurtle the low shrubbery like fish breaching.

Hour upon hour the hunters tailed along. They kept pace with the trespassers, neither closing on them nor dropping off. When Sparrow and Bea paused, their pursuers paused, like it was some strange game.

Sparrow thought one of these could be Moowut'tin, the savage who had once smiled at him, made jokes about *cah-bro* and marriage and reported on the lethal faculty of the funnel-web spider. Mr Catley's man. They were too far off for Sparrow to confirm or confound his hope but he could see a likeness in the stature and the movement and the feathered braids. He wondered if his eyes might deceive him for, whether poor man's bread or not, hope in extremis was a known deceiver.

The savages dogged their steps all the day long. They were naked but for their loincloths and the ornamentation in their hair and they were unshod and untroubled by the elements. They seemed to move without effort, to shimmer and swim in the haze, to pause and survey and then continue upon their unhurried attendance, like languorous herdsmen upon the heels of livestock driven.

Both Sparrow and Bea were parched, their lips blistered and cracked, their skin coated in a paste of sweat and dust. Their faces now were grimaced, fixed in a squint like a mask stuck to sinew and bone.

'Can you feel your heart,' he said.

'Yes, and I can hear it too.'

The empty costrel bobbing on his hip did not succour anything in the way of good feeling in Sparrow's heart, let alone his thirsty innards. It bobbed there, empty, deficient, a harsh reminder of ill-planning. His mouth was lined with grit and he had not the spittle to eject it. He chose to say nothing of these troubles for he knew they were suffering together and Bea was stoic and silent on the matter of her own distress. He did not wish to be the first to complain.

They walked until the sun was sinking in the west, the heat coming at them head-on, their long shadows dragging behind. They topped a rise and saw before them more of the same: dense, battered heath, rifts, sparsely wooded hills far off, and one startling variation – a big, wide, spreading tree in a hollow, a pale grey trunk and a dense green canopy.

They hurried on. Nearer now, they could see the hollow, set in a creek bed that ran north to south across the plateau.

Amicus was cantering ahead.

Sandflies began to swarm, hungry for blood. Sparrow and Bea made whisks from stems torn off the scrub wattle and fanned their upper parts as they walked on, drawn to the lone tree. They heard the shouts of the savages who stood far off. They hurried on. Sparrow was fingering the blisters on his lower lip. He knew they would have to stop, if only for relief from the sun. Beyond that he could not think.

They trudged into the shade and saw the water, pooled there in the hollow. Amicus was lapping it up, his paws sunk in the mud. They dropped onto their knees beside the dog and they bent low and sucked up the slurry and spat the grit and wiped their lips on the back of their hands. After a bit Sparrow paused and paddled at the dead midges on the surface and cupped water in his hand and sucked it from his palm. Bea did much the same.

For a moment they had forgotten about the blacks but they could hear them now, the jabber, closing. On the rim of the soak they saw footprints and handprints not their own, set like moulds in the drying mud.

Naught to do but wait. They were captives in the sight of these hunters, these herdsmen, and there was no escaping them unless they chose to relent and turn away.

Sparrow and Bea got out of the mud. They stepped around the soak and stood in the deep shade, their muddy hands wiped half-clean on their britches.

Their breath came back to them. They stood, watching the hunters coming at a trot, saw the motion of their long hair, laid like rope, the native dogs ahead of them, the pack in full flight, small birds scattering like shot from the brush, parrots screeching as they took wing, the heathland fused in a pale-yellow light.

Amicus stirred, his hackles spiked up. Sparrow seized hold of him and felt the dog tense beneath his hand, quivering fibre, like rigging in a storm. He tried to hold him but his grip failed as the first of the pack breached the fringing heath at a gallop and Amicus lunged and they locked together and tumbled into the mud in a welter of legs and teeth, Amicus down, the native dog at him, at his throat, his legs flailing as the pack swooped upon him.

Sparrow stepped into the melee and fired the pistol into the heart of the dog at Amicus Amico's throat. The dog dropped dead, his jaws slipping off the sodden brisket. The pack scattered from sight, into the heath, all but one. One that turned and locked eyes with Sparrow from the cover of the scrub, legs splayed, slaver drivelling off its gums.

Amicus scrambled up, his punctured forepart running with blood. His flanks were bloody and a flap of torn skin hung off the damaged bone on his near hind leg.

'They're coming,' said Bea.

They stood together, watching them come, awaiting the custodians of the water.

The savages stepped from the heath. They stood shaded in the dusty fringe, clear of the mud, the sweat upon their skin, glistening as if lately bathed. They were much scarred and their hair was gummed and feathered and dressed with tooth and claw. Sparrow's heart sank, for Moowut'tin was not there.

The squat one was older than his companions, older by many years. He picked up the shot dog by the hind legs and flung it clear of the soak. He gestured at the water and made some indecipherable comment. He pointed north-west and spoke again. He squatted down and spooned his hand through the water and drank from his palm, his gut pressed on his thighs, his steady gaze set upon the captives.

He stepped clear of the mud and came to Sparrow and Bea in an arc about the soak. He stared at the pistol in Sparrow's belt and poked at the costrel on his hip, cupped it in his hands.

Next he squatted down beside Amicus. He took hold of the dog as Amicus shrunk away, not quickly enough. He poked about the dog's flank, shifting the slavered hair off the bloody fang-holes. He spoke again, once again gesturing at the water.

Sparrow and Bea made a show of studying the water. The midges were back, hovering, settling upon the surface, the faintest ripples, the canopy mirrored there, shimmering in the twilight.

The native dogs were inching from the brush. Amicus bristled, held firm in the grip of the squat elder. His companions kicked at the dogs, warned them off. Amicus began to whine.

'His leg's broke, he's no good to you,' said Sparrow.

The elder shifted on his haunches and moved his examination to the leg of the dog. He held the head clear, his fist jammed tight on the collar, and the dog suffered the handling of the wounded limb, snapping and squirming, whimpering at the pain.

Sparrow wished the gun primed and ready and still in his hand. He leant forward. 'You cannot have Amicus,' he said, so softly that Bea hardly heard. He could not think of a time, not in his whole life, where the pain in his heart was as sharp as now, except perhaps when his head was in that bucket of eels.

He knew his words were entirely unserviceable. Perhaps 'no' might be universally understood so he spoke the word. 'No, no, no,' he said. Bea put her hand on his shoulder. There was talk now, they were talking about Amicus. The native dogs crept closer, emboldened.

Sparrow bent low, close to the squat elder. 'You can have the axe,' he said. He was fumbling for the axe, snared in his belt, felt Bea trying to pull him away. He took the axe in hand. The native dogs were stalking, bristling. Amicus was held firm, squirming about. One of the blacks shouted an angry word. He leapt the soak and smashed the bulbous head of a wooden club into the side of Sparrow's face.

Sparrow dropped the axe and sunk to his knees. He fell aslant into the mud, his bloodied skull in the shallow water. He felt himself leaching into the ooze, heard voices crackling as if from throats on fire, the growl of some primeval beast, the flap of wings, sounds, fading to black depths.

66

Dr Woody stepped onto the Hive porch. He was finished for the day, save for unforeseen eventualities, the curse of the apothecary, and the matter of Alister Mackie. The sun was gone and the warmth of the day had not lingered.

He crossed the threshold, saw Sam half asleep at the counter, the trade minimal. Cuff came down the stairs, one arm on the banister, taking his weight. 'I'm here,' he said.

'Walk with me, if you can,' said Woody.

'I can.' Cuff rapped his walking stick on the floor.

They walked to the doctor's cottage at the top of the switchback path, sat on the porch in the gathering dark, a grey smudge on the mountains, the faint remains of the day.

Cuff was anxious to give Woody the finality he craved. He rested his stick on the porch boards. 'Sparrow had reason to want that little boat, but Thomas, he had no reason to hurt your boy. He told Catley about the bull shark, he told me, and Bea Faa, and I believe him.'

'The bull shark.'

'I think so Thomas, I really do.'

They watched the last of the day's light slip from the mountain rim into the world beyond and they sat in the dark, Cuff recounting the expedition up the Branch, the various episodes along the way, the fatalities, the last he saw of Bea and Sparrow, the hardihood of the girl

Dot, and Sparrow's benefaction, his penance, his patch signed over to the doctor.

'Well, he got what he wanted, he's out there now.'

Woody lit an oil lamp, set it on the stump stool between the chairs. He took the paper from Cuff and read the words on the back, Sparrow's signature scratched at the bottom. 'I'll put his brother on that patch, do him good.'

'And Alister will forgive the debt, he's in a forgiving space,' said Cuff.

'He is, yes.'

'He's wasting away, by the look of him.'

'It's a wasting disease, Thaddeus. I've seen lungs like his before. The lining riddled with ulcers, the sinks freighted with pus and blood, thick and fatty, suet-like. And that stench.'

'The stench of death.'

'Yes.'

'How long has he got?'

'His lamp keeps burning but it gutters to a flicker with increasing regularity.'

'Not a good way to go.'

'He's ready to go. Have you seen his will? He's left his acreage to the governor.'

Cuff laughed. 'By God, the man'll be dead and he'll still be craving favour from his betters.'

'Faithful servant of the Crown. That's how it works, the whole empire, like Rome, generous to the faithful servants of Caesar, pitiless to enemies.'

The blackness far off to the west was not without variance, for a crescent moon figured in the distant sky. Cuff could make out the black mountains, like the backbone of some vast creature in repose. He pointed west. 'There's enemies out there yet, your Caleb included.'

'As yet they are sovereign in their retreats,' said Woody.

'Not for long.'

'No?'

'It might be the bolters have the ripest imaginations but sooner or later an official party will get across them mountains and find useful country, and the folk and the flag will follow, that's the way of the world. It's a creeping floodtide and there's no ebb and there's no stopping it. No amount of . . . *goodwill*.'

'Goodwill just gets in the way, is that it?'

'That's it.'

'A sovereignty yet intact but perilously close to extinction.'

'An awful moment, if you think about it.'

'Most don't.'

'And closer yet when the hunting party goes out, set upon vengeance for Peskett and Redenbach.'

'Will you go?'

'I'll let the military avenge their own.'

'And that floodtide will do the rest?'

'It will, yes.'

Woody took off his glasses, worked finger and thumb into the bridge of his nose. 'Why does it have to be thus?' he said.

'Because all life turns on a pitiless wheel, that's why. Because they know their place and we'll never know ours. In that regard we're no higher up the chain than a snake.'

'You really believe that?'

'Some days I do, dark days.'

'What I've seen of that floodtide, I wonder I resist the hard truth,' said Woody.

'That's 'cause you're a nice person. You wish with all your heart it was otherwise, and you try to make it otherwise, even though you know it.'

'Know what?'

'What I said, the hard truth. We're no better'n the snakes.'

'What of the other days, the not so dark days?'

'Them days I remember the likes of Joe Franks and I know we ain't stuck in brutishness. We got a choice, every damn one of us.'

67

When Sparrow woke it was dark and he was wet and cold and tangled in the heath, well clear of the soak. He raised himself up, water trickling down the muddied side of his face. He felt the cut high on his cheekbone, probed at the hurt, palmed the grit away, gently, and wiped his wet hands on his britches.

The night sky was clear, the full span of the starlit heavens. The heathland was perfectly still, a sea of brush, that vast entanglement bathed in a blue-grey light, like an ocean becalmed.

His head was throbbing, the pain travelling in pulses, thudding on bone. His heart began to pound.

Bea was gone and Amicus Amico was gone, like in the dream, and he was alone in that ocean, beneath a lone tree, a big old spreading crooked tree.

He felt himself quite unable to walk. He felt the damp on his skin all down one side. He recalled taking the axe from his belt. The axe was gone. He felt for the costrel. The costrel was gone and the shot dog was gone.

The haversack was there, the leather flap configured about the teapot. They had missed the flint and they had not taken the teapot. But they had taken Bea, and Amicus, and the axe and the costrel, and the shot dog. They might as well have taken everything, the teapot and all. But he had to wonder: *what would they do with a teapot?*

He pulled the haversack close, squeezed at the lumpy contents. The quart pot was gone. The pistol was gone too, but the mug was there. *Strange.*

He sat cross-legged, staring at the dirt, feeling at the cut on his head. Ran his tongue across his bottom lip. The blisters had scabbed over and the lip felt like rough bark. The long cut on his forearm had shed its scab, the fading mark of the flood. So long ago, the coop, the coffin, the crows, the shark, the hook.

An age, a lifetime. Another life altogether.

The stillness out there did not sit well with the churn in his gut, nor with the ache in his heart. He got to his feet. He walked to and fro, loosening his joints.

A crescent moon ascended, lit the heathland, a blanket of shapes and shadow folds. Bats flew north-east, swift and low, into the blackness beyond the far ridge. The land was silent and all was still save a restless soul, alone, pacing the warm earth beneath the big old twisted tree in the vastness of the upland.

Sparrow felt entirely helpless for he knew he could never find Bea or Amicus, not in this inviolate waste. They were gone and there was no finding them and he had not even the rope to hang himself. He looked up. He had the bough, perfectly situated, sturdy. But he did not have the rope.

He dearly wanted to banish such thoughts, rise above them, but he was entirely alone, and he did not know what to do and his mind would not obey his want.

He was searching for a thread of hope in a moment of wretched gloom, but his hope was frayed as old plait and, anyway, hope was not his to summon or abandon. Hope was a mischievous thing, a cruel sprite that might visit or depart on a whim. *They've took her.* Why would they ever bring her back, such a prize. Sparrow knew if he was the squat elder, or one of those virile young men, he'd never let her go, not Bea Faa. As for Amicus, what they might do with him, injured as he was, did not bear contemplation.

He could not go on alone, he knew that. No axe, no meat, no costrel, no companion. Nothing but a teapot, and what use a teapot without a companion?

Sparrow reckoned he might find his way back, across the heath, through the shaft into that cave and on to the high waters of the Branch. Once on the Branch he reckoned he could find Mr Catley's patch, save an ill-starred encounter with the mountain blacks, or with Caleb. Caleb set upon vengeance for Mort.

He recalled Mr Catley's cave house with a fondness no words could express, except perhaps for the word *delight*. But Peskett's torn old tent was also there, the mark of the soldiers. Even there he would not be safe.

Better there than here.

That was probably true. Here he was alone, alone beneath a lone tree in this unplumbed immensity. He saw himself as if from a great height, dead upon the baking heath, some creature, some reptilian thing tearing the meat off his bones. He did not want to die alone in this country, his remains blanketed by flies and feasted upon by crows.

He made a fire from a wizened scrub wattle, long dead. He uprooted the thing and dragged it whole into the clearing and fed the roots and bole into the flames once the twigs had taken and the fire was licking up.

He skimmed water into the mug, the mug that he and Bea agreed they would share, and he poured the water into the teapot, along with the last of Dan Sprodd's tea. He set the teapot on the flame, the black creeping up the metal.

Bull ants fled a hollow in the scrub wattle and he took the tin mug and a stick and set about flicking a procession of them into the mug. *It's all meat.*

He waited for the tea to boil and when it was ready he wrapped the handle in his sweat rag and poured, filling the mug almost to the brim. He put the mug at a tilt near the firelight and watched as the bull ants came to the surface and swirled, a swirl of fire colours, as if beribboned round a maypole, a maypole for the midges. He stirred some more and blew on the tea till it cooled and then he drank it down, all of it, for he did not know when next he would eat.

Sparrow could not help but think of Bea. He tried not to contemplate her circumstances but he found that impossible. His pictorial mind served up some loathsome doings, the likes of which prompted thoughts of Griffin Pinney rutting on her in that cave.

He began to cherish the night hours, wishing for night eternal, for come the day he would have to rise and step from the shade and leave the soak and trek, with neither water nor rations, in one direction or another. He would have to be resolute, alone.

But he was not alone. He heard the rustle of the underwood, the crack of brittle scrub. He looked out upon the heath, a dappling of night shadow, a thousand shapes out there. He watched the brush on the far side of the soak.

Such were the shadow shapes upon the animal and about the animal, the inseparable melt of the elements, that it took Sparrow quite some time to identify the living form within the brush.

It gave him quite a fright but as soon as the animal moved, limped forward, he knew it was Amicus. The dog was hop-hobbling on three legs, the wounded leg angled clear of the ground, entirely unnatural.

'Where have you been,' he said.

Sparrow swivelled onto his knees as Amicus limped into his arms, his tail wagging with the pleasure of the reunion. He could feel the dog's heart, beating like a wedding drum. His own heart was beating in time.

The dog pulled away and hobbled to the water and drank and hobbled back to Sparrow, his whiskers dripping wet. With some difficulty he dropped down, his bodyweight firm against Sparrow's thigh, his head resting there, his scraggy tail brooming the dirt.

Sparrow took the injured leg in his hand. The leg below the hock was soaked in saliva, the skin torn off the cracked bone, a soggy flap.

The dog squirmed and pulled away.

It occurred to Sparrow that if the leg was no good it might have to come off. 'I don't reckon I could do that,' he said, out loud. He reckoned Bea could do it, reckoned she might know how to do it properly.

His worst enemy was fear, that he knew. Fear that sinks into the skin and slithers along one's inner byways and coils about the vitals and squeezes till a man can hardly breathe, that man rendered putty in the devil's sculpting hands, rendered ignoble, unmanned, good for nothing but to run, to flee, or to go down with black, uncomprehending eyes, and wait to be robbed or killed. Or eaten. Fear was a man's worst enemy. Fear was hope's undoing.

He stroked the dog's forehead recalling how Amicus had fought with a fury when the pack had besieged him, fought them all. He would surely have fought to the death. If that dog knew fear, and who could know what he knew, it surely did not paralyse him. It did not rot the rigour in his fibre nor reduce him to a puddle of quiver, as fear can sometimes do.

That was a most sobering reflection. Sparrow took great pleasure in the vivid recall of his own part in that savagery of tooth and claw. How he stepped into the melee without hesitation and shot dead the native dog and scattered the pack asunder and saved Amicus. He resolved never again to allow fear to rot the rigour in his fibre and shrink him to a puddle.

He could hardly believe that Bea was gone. That was the hardest thing. That pained him to his core and the pain threatened to squeeze his vitals and undo him, but now he understood fear and that was half the battle. He vowed he would not be undone by fear.

The dawn light was coming, working new patterns on the heath. The dull ache within his skull had eased. Amicus was twitching and whimpering in some sort of dream. Sparrow lay down in the dirt.

He lay on his side, curled about the dog like a shell around its soft parts. He heard the cawing of a crow, the beating of wings; he felt the pain within him disperse and he with it, a weightless drift on the heath.

The sun came up and the country all about began to warm swiftly, and the sandflies came in, nipping at his forearms and his ankles, searching for veins in his neck and for a time diverting him as he swatted at them, smacking at his uncovered parts.

The sharp movement stirred the pain in his skull.

He dragged himself to the edge of the soak and drank the warm sludge from the cup of his hand, Amicus watching from the fringe of the shade, not caring to move, flies humming about the bloody flap on his wounded leg.

Sparrow dozed some more. His only want was rest but in his rest there was no repose. The bloodied ghost of Griffin Pinney leered at him; the savages came for Amicus and trussed his legs and took him for meat. He saw the bull shark take the boy. He saw eels thrashing in a mess of gut in the keel wash, supping on the viscera. The eels jolted him from sleep.

The dog came to him and they sat, watching the midges buzz about the soak.

He buckled up the haversack and one last time he drank from the soak and they departed, heading north-west across the heath. Now and then Sparrow looked back, trying to guess the north-west line the squat elder had signalled. He angled for a point of convergence with that line. He wondered if that made any sense at all.

They walked on, man and dog, on through the day, the sun beating down. They came upon the putrefied and much diminished carcass of an old wallaby, half devoured, crawling with flies. Amicus took to the carcass, tearing at what was left, shreds of gut, tattered green meat on the bone.

Sparrow squatted in the shade of some charred brush, watching the feast. After a while the dog slowed. Then he hop-hobbled away and vomited in a patch of shaggy pea. Leaves like holly.

They went on.

Midafternoon they reached the far side of the heath and took to the shade of a sparse woodland. He wiped the sweat off his forehead with the back of his hand and he licked the sweat off his skin, the veins there like thick blue cord.

He felt beads of sweat dripping inside his shirt. The heat was much as it had been for days and the wasted leaves hung lank on the trees, thin as the meanest lips, their colour drab and drained. He squatted down in the speckled shade, Amicus by his side.

The dog showed no signs of distress. He licked carefully at the wound, the bared bone on his hind leg. He seemed entirely at home.

Sparrow wished he could feel like that. Even the flies did not seem to bother the dog. He'd just shake his head, yet again, like it was a good thing to be busy, as if the excesses of nature were there to help him pass the day and, in that languid way, endeavour to persevere.

Atop the slope, Sparrow saw clear blue sky to the west. He wondered what was there. He feared more of the same. He could see no sign of cover for the night. There was no going back. Drawn by the vast emptiness of the blue sky through the trees, he walked up the slope. He stopped short when he saw the far cliffs and a void to the fore. He called the dog away from the edge and the dog turned awkwardly and came to him and hobbled at Sparrow's heel as they moved forward, together.

They stood atop a cliff wall that ran north to the dense green line that marked the horizon, above a point where the valley was lost in the braided folds of mountain spurs and patches of stone and a wash of the darkest forest green.

The void was a half mile across, more or less. The far cliffs were fractured by heavily forested gullies and slot canyons carved deep through stone. To the north he could see open patches of grassland on the valley floor, the lumpy shapes of marsupials grazing and smaller things foraging, clustered together, wood ducks, and a flock of black cockatoos in full flight following the line of the far wall, the stone there fissured and scarred like the hide of a dragon.

Sparrow felt the glare of the sinking sun upon his foreparts, the palpable heat off the wall of stone below. He stepped back lest a gust blow him away. He sensed the bond between his own flesh and the dirt and the ash about his feet, as if a mere ribbon of bark or a mean, thin leaf might have more substance.

He retreated a little further and turned about and sat on the slope, looking out upon the scene from whence he'd come. Surely he would find cover if he could find a way into that valley. A cave, some water. He was thirsty. He guessed the dog was thirsty too. 'They should've left me the costrel,' he said. Far off the heathland was shimmering in the heat haze, and in that haze he saw them, two figures.

He saw them threading the heath.

Sparrow could hardly move. He thought his senses might be playing a trick on him. He feared these figures might dissolve into nothing. But they did not dissolve. They came on. They came out of the haze. They took shape, firm and mortal.

She might have been one of them on first sighting, for she was tall and willowy and dark enough to sway the mind, the scene, such as it was. It took but a moment for Sparrow to know it was Moowut'tin and Bea, the savage to the fore, a long spear angled on his shoulder, the girl a few steps behind. The mongrel dog too, ahead of them, here and there leaping the heath.

Sparrow came down the slope yowling and when they saw him he yowled some more and waved his arms in the air. He hoped that Bea would wave back, but she did not. Moowut'tin made no sign but walked on, threading a course to the north of Sparrow's position.

Sparrow hurried along the slope, northwards, the blue sky coming at him through the twisted trees. He felt shaky all over. He quickened his pace and stumbled and nearly fell, his heart pounding his chest. Amicus hurried ahead, Sparrow no match for the young dog's hobbledy quickness.

Moowut'tin's course was entirely mysterious to Sparrow but there was comfort in the prospect they would come together some way ahead. He hurried on for it seemed they were covering ground with a swiftness he could not match.

They met near the headwall of a narrow gully chocked with boulders and rotting wood and shrouded in darkness further down, where a dense canopy of tall trees defied the light above.

The dogs were circling each other, sniffing, renewing their acquaintance.

Sparrow could not help but look at Bea. She seemed much the same as before, if hatless and somewhat weary. 'Here you are,' he said.

'Yes.'

He did not know what to make of her voice, whether sadness or weariness, he could not pick the meaning that carried on that one word.

He saw Moowut'tin had the costrel slung on his shoulder, the defective rim coated with some sort of orange gum. 'You mended it,' he said.

'Yes,' said Moowut'tin. Moowut'tin handed the costrel to Sparrow and he felt the weight of the water within. He ran his fingers along the formerly defective stitching and felt the gum and the leather perfectly dry. 'Thank you.'

Bea reached for the costrel, took it from Sparrow. He thought she might drink, but she did not. She ran a finger along the orange gum, examined the mend with some care. Her hand appeared unsteady.

'Are you well enough?' he said.

'I was attended with some care by the women, then Moowut'tin appeared, much to my delight.'

'What of Mr Catley?'

'What of Mr Catley?'

'Would you not go with him?'

'I would go with you, and Amicus.'

Sparrow felt a joy in his heart such as he had never known. He studied the gully, the way west.

'You must go now,' said Moowut'tin.

Sparrow and Bea picked their careful way into the gully, around masses of stone and rotting boles and branches, into a forest of coach-wood and ribbon gums, cedar wattle and *gymee*, Amicus ahead of them, searching out the ground.

Further down the way was sheer and they made their way past caves and overhangs with the help of anchor vines and handholds in the stone. Nooks and niches resplendent with bright-coloured mosses and lichen that glowed in the gloom, here and there the brows of gar-gantuan boulders dressed in splendid staghorns and bird's nest fern about the footings. On several occasions Amicus had to find his own way, and he did so, disappearing for a time and rejoining them further down, hop-hobbling along.

Near the bottom the grade eased somewhat and they followed a well-worn track through dense fern and grass trees onto the valley floor. From there they followed the cliff line north. They walked side by side where they could, talking about the night and day just gone, Amicus scouting ahead, limping along, now and then pivoting about to stare at them as if he, like Sparrow, could hardly believe it.

They drank sparingly from the costrel. They set out across the valley as the sun in the west seemed to flatten and flare along the stone horizon like a blood orange slick, and clouds like flames licked into the heavens. The parched grassland washed to and fro, a bloody wash on a flaxen sea, and whorls of heat, like tendrils, came off that wash as they walked on, swatting at the last of the flies, the dust and sweat a paste upon their skin.

Sparrow was happy. He was flush with relief, his hope restored, a singing in his heart. Words came to him, from where he could not recall: *in gallant trim the gilded vessel goes, youth on the prow and pleasure at the helm.*

They walked on.

68

Moowut'tin followed the line of the cliff top north, picking his way, looking out across the valley, the mongrel dog at his heel. After a while he stopped. He stepped close to the edge. He squatted on his haunches, squinting into the glare, his free hand shadowing his eyes.

He watched them walk from the cover of the trees onto the grassland, far off figures shimmering in the haze, their substance seemingly devoid of rigour. Trembling, rootless things, misshapen in his eyes, as they walked on, in that red-tinged sea of flaxen grass.

He watched until the sun sank from sight and the colours dimmed and the sojourners were but fading specks in the greyness, departing his country, lost to all definition.

Of his people he knew that once, not long ago, there was only themselves and others like them, and the edged world was theirs alone. They were one and indivisible with their beginnings, with then and now, with earth and stone and tree and all living things, and with the dead and the roots affixed to their bones, and with their spirits, abiding.

He stood and turned about and walked away, ahead of the darkness fast coming. He took to the familiar heath, the ancient track, swift now, the fading light slipping from his heels.

AFTERWORD

The Making of Martin Sparrow is a work of fiction in which the documented past provides points of departure into an imagined world. To paraphrase Henry James, what the historian wants is more documents than he or she can use, but what the novelist wants is more liberties than he or she can take.

Still, these points of departure may be of interest to readers so I will list a selection of them here:

The setting for much of this story is the 'wilderness' west of the Hawkesbury River, notably the 'Branch country'. The Branch was a contemporary name for what we now call the Colo River. The triggering event for the tale is the great flood of March 1806. Reports of the flood appeared in the colony's newspaper, *The Sydney Gazette and New South Wales Advertiser* of 23 March and 30 March 1806. The devastation visited upon the crops caused great alarm in Sydney Town, as the Hawkesbury River flats ('the bottoms') were the breadbasket of the colony.

On the subject of agriculture and farming, I single out one documentary treasure in particular, a booklet called *The New South Wales Pocket Almanack and Colonial Remembrancer 1806*, compiled and published by George Howe, the editor of the *Sydney Gazette*. The *Pocket Almanack* includes a great deal of seasonal information on subsistence and market gardening, grain growing and livestock breeding.

The *Almanack* also includes a record called 'The Chronological Cycles', a table of 'high water' at Sydney for 'every day of the moon's age', with an estimate of the time lag for the high water on the Parramatta River and the upper reaches of the Hawkesbury, where we find the garrison-cum-village that I have called Prominence. There is also a 'Table of Months', which includes the time of the sun's rising and setting on the first day of each month, and the phases of the moon for each day of the month.

Other contemporary sources indicate how the winds and the tides regulated movement on the river. Like the seasons, they had their own incessant rhythms governing everyday life. And like leeches and ticks, they are prerequisites for a credible river setting.

In addition to weather, winds and tides, the economic life of the convict colony was notably shaped by the absence of a sterling paper currency. A barter economy filled the void, with various commodities operating as a medium of exchange – wheat and spirits, corn and swine flesh, American dollars, IOUs or notes issued with a scrawl of a quill and accepted at considerable discount to sterling.

Illicit distilling figured mightily in this chaotic scene because imported spirits – bought by the barrel and sold by the bottle – retailed at exorbitant prices. This was because labour, which was in short supply, demanded payment or part payment in grog. So 'bang-head' made in the bush was the best return available on grain at hand – the most reward for the least work. Just how illicit spirits figured as both a medium of exchange and a profitable sideline in this economy summons a work that predates the concerns of history in more recent times, for even the best recent accounts seem to miss the presence of the economic in the social. For the barter economy and the pre-eminence of wheat and grog as currency and commodity in the convict colony, see D.R. Hainsworth, *The Sydney Traders: Simeon Lord and his contemporaries, 1788–1821* (Cassell Australia, Melbourne, 1972). Hainsworth should be read in tandem with R.H. Parker,

'Bookkeeping Barter and Current Cash Equivalents in Early New South Wales' (*ABACUS*, volume 18, number 2, 1982, pp. 139–151).

Women, too, were commodities, and the occasional sale of a wife was not always controversial because the transaction was a pre-industrial custom from Britain that had been carried to the colonies, though not without some change and contest. A wife sale at the Hawkesbury River settlement in 1811 was well documented because the local magistrates intervened, incensed at the violation of 'all laws human and divine', a case of new middle-class values pressed upon the common folk. On that occasion, a woman was led by her husband into the streets of Windsor with a rope around her neck, publicly exposed for sale and duly sold for £16 and several yards of cloth. Both the divesting husband and the wife were punished quite severely. The sale is reported in a supplement of the *Sydney Gazette* of 14 September 1811, and there is a fascinating essay on this subject, written by Erin Ihde: '"So gross a violation of decency": A note on wife sales in colonial Australia' in the *Journal of the Royal Australian Historical Society* (volume 84, number 1, June 1998, pp. 26–37). For the background, the custom in Britain, readers may wish to consult a long essay by E.P. Thompson in his *Customs in Common* (Merlin Press, London, 1991, pp. 404–466).

A related theme – the *femes soles* – is briefly discussed in a social history of the early Hawkesbury community, Jan Barkley-Jack's *Hawkesbury Settlement Revealed, 1793–1802* (Rosenburg Publishing, Kenthurst, 2009).

It is Thompson, by the way, who confirms the prevalence of wife selling among certain occupational groups, such as bargees and tinkers or travellers, soldiers, sailors and sealers, occupations marked by a high degree of mobility.

The sealers who figure here are privy to a method of curing the fur seal of its hard, coarse hair without damaging the soft fur, thus finishing the product in a matchless state for sale in Europe. The historical discovery of that curing process is attributed to Thomas Chapman of 'the Borough, Southwark' whose patent was breached, sometime after 1798, by 'large manufacturing interests who combined to entice away his workmen'. One may assume the details of this supposedly profitable cure might well have spread further – one of those liberties welcomed by Henry James. Chapman's sad case is summarised in John Alexander Ferguson, *Bibliography of Australia, Volume 1, 1784–1830* (Angus & Robertson, Sydney, 1941, p. 279).

As we now know, the Hawkesbury River and its tributaries were contested terrain. The fraught relations between the first generation of colonists and the Indigenous people are well known, albeit the record covers but a tiny fraction of the horrors. The *Sydney Gazette* reported frequently on the 'barbarities' committed by the 'Branch blacks', but was less forthcoming on the punitive responses, though not entirely silent. The struggle for the rich country on the flanks of the Hawkesbury, and for the river itself, went on for many years, culminating in 1805 when the warrior the settlers called 'Branch Jack', the chief aggressor according to the *Gazette*, was finally shot and killed in the course of an attack on a grain boat. The best, brief account of the dynamics of the warfare along the river is to be found in Grace Karskens' splendid volume *The Colony: A history of early Sydney* (Allen & Unwin, Sydney, 2009, pp. 460–74, 481–491). For a case study of one murderous encounter, readers may refer to Lyn Stewart, *Blood Revenge: Murder on the Hawkesbury, 1799* (Rosenberg Publishing, Kenthurst, 2015).

The governor's concession, 'no more settlements on the lower Hawkesbury', was Philip Gidley King's promise to the 'natives from that part of the river', a promise made in June 1804, to no avail. King refers to his concession in a letter home to Lord Hobart, Secretary of State for War and the Colonies, dated 20 December 1804. The letter can be found in *Historical Records of Australia* (ed. Frederick Watson, series I, volume V [1804–6], pp.166–67).

Governor King's feeble gesture was never enforced with any conviction that I know of. But it was a gesture nonetheless, a vice-regal gesture, and it probably generated heated discussion among the settlers around the question of what choices were available to them to mitigate the brutality of wholesale dispossession. Historians have differed sharply about how this brutality should be judged. They differ on the proper relation between history and morality. The best way into this debate in my view is Inga Clendinen's riposte to John Hirst in 'The History Question: Who owns the past?' (*Quarterly Essay*, number 23, Black Inc., Melbourne, 2006). 'It is only by establishing the span of choices open to these men that we can hope to understand why individuals made the choices they did,' she wrote. The point is, there were people, settlers, men and women, who tried to have amicable relations with the true proprietors of the soil. They should be remembered, this precious few, for facing up to their part in a gross transgression and celebrated for having the humility to know they could learn something from Aboriginal people – something of their practical knowledge or their spirituality, or both.

Freemasonry has a presence here for precisely this reason. It's a presence which is greater than its cameo moment in the novel might at first suggest. Masonry figured as part of the radical Enlightenment and its ethics were something of a challenge to the established order, in both the metropolitan centres of Europe and occasionally in the colonies. Its notions of a 'brotherhood of man' and a 'new conviviality' unaffected by class or even colour were disturbing to say the least, even if they were more honoured in the breach than the observance. For further reading on this subject see Margaret C. Jacob, *Living the Enlightenment: Freemasonry and politics in eighteenth-century Europe* (Oxford University Press, New York, 1991).

The tales of an inland haven, a sanctuary from the military despotism of the colony or the rigours of pioneering, were part of convict folklore. But what these tales can tell us is disputed among historians. One sceptical view can be found in Paul Carter's *The Road to Botany Bay* (Faber, London, 1987). Carter argues that the escape myths about an inland sanctuary were a rhetorical ploy to throw the authorities off the scent. That they concealed rather than revealed a plot to travel, since the real plot was escape along the coast, by means of a boat. That, or a life of bushranging on the remote fringes of the colony. The whole thing a pea and thimble deception.

David Levell's *Tour to Hell: Convict Australia's great escape myths* (University of Queensland Press, 2008) is another reading. Levell has mustered more than enough evidence to show that the stories of a haven inspired some men, and perhaps some women, to head inland, aiming not for the fringes of settlement but for the far beyond. The fable gave hope and purpose to their flight into unknown country, and it posed a serious problem for the authorities – the military, the constabulary and the vice-regal establishment.

The mountainous country west of the Hawkesbury was all but unknown to the acquisitive invaders – and much of it is still largely unknown to non-Indigenous Australians today – being sufficiently harsh and inaccessible to defy the designs of commercial tourism. My understanding of this hinterland – the mountain fastness to the north-west of Sydney – is grounded in a reading of historical and geographical sources as well as my own treks into that country, camping on the river sands and sleeping in the caves. Broadly, it is the magnificent country now encompassed in the Wollemi National Park and the Gardens of Stone National Park, a combined landscape of nearly 5200 square kilometres.

The gorge that figures so prominently in the narrative is, indeed, the Colo Gorge, a spectacular formation flanked by huge sandstone cliffs and forested by fiercely clinging eucalypts, and other trees such as coachwoods and turpentines. From the grandeur of the topography to the shelter of the sandstone caves and the strangeness of the creature sounds at night, these elements and more are vital to what someone usefully called 'the hallucination of presence'.

One final word, an observation on an Old English word. Too often these days we misuse the term 'wilderness' as it was misused back then, as a first cousin to *Terra nullius*, not stopping to consider how the mountainous hinterland west of Sydney was not a wilderness but, on the contrary, a peopled landscape, a much revered and well-worked terrain, where practical knowledge was based on generations of close observation and deep respect for the spirit of the country. The people of that hinterland were, in 1806, still sovereign in their retreats, unmet, as yet, by the creeping floodtide of white settlement.

Looking back, we might see the outcome clearly, but then as now the future was hidden in a fog.

ACKNOWLEDGEMENTS

Writing a work of fiction is a solitary and mysterious business and I am grateful to dear friends and colleagues who were ever so patient and supportive all the way.

Special thanks are due to my literary agent, Mary Cunnane, for her vital interventions, her sage advice and friendship throughout the course of this venture.

I also want to thank David McKnight, with whom I trekked and camped in the gorge country that figures so prominently in this story.

Gathering atmosphere on the water was important too. In that regard I would like to thank Grant Williams for the opportunity to sail with him on the Hawkesbury River and to follow the historic coastal route to Sydney Harbour in a 25–30 knot breeze and a sizeable swell, under full sail. The historic sense of the journey was much enhanced by our vessel – a nineteen-foot couta boat, solid timber, gaff-rigged, built in 1935.

My thanks must also go to Meredith Rose, for her vital counsel during the project's early days. My editor, Johannes Jakob, has been a brilliant adviser and I greatly appreciate both his knowledge and his dedication to the task. I must also thank Ben Ball, whose faith in the project has been sustaining from the outset.

Finally, to Suzanne Rickard, my beloved companion in literature and life, my heartfelt thanks.